FUM D'ESTAMPA PRESS

ANDREA VÍCTRIX

LLORENÇ VILLALONGA

TRANSLATED BY P. LOUISE JOHNSON

LLORENÇ VILLALONGA (Palma de Mallorca, 1897-1980) was an important exponent of Majorcan narrative in the 20th century. Coming from a family of rural landowners, he studied medicine and began to publish articles in 1924. His first novel, *Mort de dama* (1931), courted controversy, though *Bearn o la sala de les nines* (1956 Spanish, 1961 Catalan) is perhaps his best-known work. *Andrea Víctrix* is considered to be his most ambitious novel. He died at home after a long illness.

P. LOUISE JOHNSON (Matlock, 1970) has been at the University of Sheffield since 1996. She discovered Llorenç Villalonga while an undergraduate at St John's College, Oxford, and subsequently wrote her doctorate on his work. In 2002 her monograph *La tafanera posteritat: assaigs sobre Llorenç Villalonga* was awarded the first Premi Casa Museu-Llorenç Villalonga. Louise has published widely on Villalonga, and taught *Andrea Víctrix* (1974) to a generation of students who have been variably receptive to this camp, dystopian vision of Mallorca, and satire on mid-twentieth-century politics and social mores. She has often thought that *Andrea Víctrix* belongs on the musical stage.

'This is, until someone proves otherwise, the best dystopian literature ever written in Catalan. And I say this not because of Llorenç Villalonga's singular narrative talent, but rather because of his exceptional development of a series of ideas that provide Andrea Víctrix with a speculative solidity that is difficult to find anywhere else.'
—Ramon Mas, *Les Males Herbes*

'With the novel Andrea Víctrix, Llorenç Villalonga's amalgamation is a spasmotic, incredible story, accumulative and grotesque, truly original, unique and highly relevant in its own literary context.'
—Andrea Navarra, *The Barcelona Review*

'A truly great novel, beautiful and terrfying in equal parts, tender and groundbreaking, and one that should be read for many years to come. A warning from history.'
—Jordi Llavina, *El 3 de Vuit*

FUM D'ESTAMPA PRESS LTD.
LONDON – BARCELONA
WWW.FUMDESTAMPA.COM

This translation has been published in Great Britain
by Fum d'Estampa Press Limited 2021

001

The moral right of the author and translator has been asserted
Set in Minion Pro

Printed and bound by TJ Books Ltd, Padstow, Cornwall
A CIP catalogue record for this book is available from the British Library

ISBN: 978-1-9162939-4-6

Series design by 'el mestre' Rai Benach

This book has been published with the support of

G CONSELLERIA
O PRESIDÈNCIA,
I CULTURA I
B IGUALTAT

 institut d'estudis
baleàrics

FUM D'ESTAMPA PRESS

ANDREA VÍCTRIX

PROGRESS CANNOT BE STOPPED

Mechanization and cybernetics are the religion of all éclairés *who don't believe in God.*
—Dr Nicola

Many utopias have been written since Plato's Republic, Wells and Huxley. Because – paradoxically – the future also has its traditions.
—Agustín de Foxà (*ABC*, 11 March, 1954)

—All footnotes are the author's own.

CHAPTER I

THE CRIMINAL

'Watch out!'

'*Non abbi paura.*'

We were going at almost a hundred. The street was so long it disappeared into the distance; the buildings so tall we couldn't see the sky. It was a true commercial boulevard, like New York's famous 42nd Street of yesteryear where daylight scarcely penetrated and the eternal neon glared. Adverts for dentists and interplanetary journeys stood out amongst the countless billboards and we were periodically blinded by a slogan in huge glaring golden letters: PROGRESS CANNOT BE STOPPED. Though it was fifty metres across, the avenue felt like a narrow corridor and it reminded me of a boarding house I'd lived in as a student when King Alfonso XIII was on the throne. The proportions must have been similar and the light identical: subdued and artificial. The smell was different, though. The house at times smelled of not always unpleasant cooking and at others, when the El Dorado performers lodged there, of a perfumery. The smell of the avenue was impossible to pin down though it was, without doubt, an inhuman stench of heavy oils and humidity. A stench equivalent to a dull, indistinct cacophony formed of hundreds of different noises, of engines, music, news headlines, warnings, and advertising slogans. Mashed and blended into a purée.

The friend I'd made five minutes earlier – forehead adorned with golden hair, denim jeans – smiled.

'Too bad,' they said. 'Better luck next time.'

I found the joke strange. We'd almost collided with someone.

'The vehicle won't overturn,' continued my friend, 'it's a Rolls, the latest model. We could drive over an elephant and while the car might jump, it would quickly stabilise. And because you can get fined for reckless imprudence, we'd earn ourselves a bag of francs.'

'We would?' I asked, confused.

'Of course. If a pedestrian crosses where it's forbidden, they're the one committing the offence. Some people make a living from hunting these offenders. Do you like hunting?' my friend asked. 'It doesn't happen so much these days.'

So it wasn't a joke after all. I looked at my interlocutor, trying to figure out what the words meant. His – or her – expression was joyous, ingenuous like an infant's, and it unsettled me. I noticed their physical, asexual beauty for the first time. Were they a young woman, or an effeminate man? If the latter, I should note that his effeminacy wasn't what some are accustomed to view as imposture, while if the former, her decisiveness and insensitivity were by no means defects.

'Are you serious?' I said.

My friend shrugged.

'I'm serious. That's the law.' There was a pause. 'Know what? I'm hungry. You?'

'Yes,' I replied.

'Reach into my pocket, you'll find a little gold box. *Ho molta fame.* Put a pill in my mouth, and take one yourself.'

I did as I was told. The effect was lightning quick and Andrea – I didn't yet know if this was their first or second name – laughed, let one hand off the steering wheel and ruffled my hair.

'*Ah, que je suis bien!*' they exclaimed in a measured tone, like a well-educated young lady.

I took my pill (*Aldous Huxley-Brand Soma* was printed on the box) and experienced the same sensations of intense, one might say almost agitated joy, as Andrea. My hunger disappeared instantly.

'Naturally,' Andrea said, smiling. 'Where have you appeared from then, hun?'

I should add that as I'm writing in an archaic language, I have no choice but to attribute a gender to people but as I understood later, everything was neuter for Andrea. Andrea spoke a hybrid of Romance languages which I wasn't always able to decipher. Everything in that new language (and it's important that the reader bear this in mind if they want to understand this) such as articles, nouns, and adjectives, was without gender. My friend had said 'hun' without any intention of addressing me as a male, nor obviously as a female, but had expressed a sympathy or courtesy lacking any kind of allusion to gender.

I was an anachronism. On the 14th of May 1965, tired and feeling my age at sixty-odd, I began a cryo-cure from which I'd awaken in 2050. The doctor had told me that when I came round I'd be '30 years younger'.

Anaesthetized, I was placed in a plastic casket and taken to the basement of a clinic to be kept at 40 degrees below zero with another half-dozen patients including Mr Churchill, Mme. Vorey and Marlene Dietrich. Almost all of them died in the process. The only ones to come though were a diabetic full of sugar, and myself, a reactionary full of angst. It was only a few hours ago that I'd emerged from my casket like a butterfly from its silk cocoon, and I was flitting about the streets of the capital of Mallorca, the name of which was not now Palma, but Tourist Club of the Mediterranean (Turclub for short or, as the snobs pronounced it, *Turcloef*) finding it alien and unpleasant.

Whilst unpleasant, it was an admittedly opulent, surprisingly well-planned city with modern streets and the occasional newly built ancient monument. People's manners had improved, too. Contrary to expectations, loutish behaviour was almost a thing of the past, and no-one remembered Madrid *tremendismo* or Italian neorealism. Everyone was flawless, in both their dress and language. There'd been a return, perhaps, to eighteenth-century courtesy and affability. Why had that stranger, *garçon* or *fille*, with such a nonchalant smile, invited me to get in their car with them?

'*Vuol venire con me?*'

I was just an old man, homeless and penniless, and this curious adolescent seemed to be something of a personage. People stopped in front of the red Rolls and smiled. Some quietly saluted my companion saying, '*Addio, Andrea Víctrix*' and raising their hand like Caesar's soldiers saluting the goddess of love at the battle of Pharsalus.

No, it wasn't altogether unpleasant. In a way it was beautiful, if disconcerting. Now that world, the bastard offspring of the most dreadful catastrophe the centuries have ever witnessed, has disappeared and I can look at it from the perspective of events gone by, dead in reality and transfigured in memory, I recognize that Turclub was, for a time, an earthly paradise. Of course, it's only now that I fully understand some of its values as the only true paradises are those that are now lost. The reader will understand this as they grow to know the greatness and desolation of Andrea which left such a profound imprint on me. Feeling humiliated and helpless in the presence of that child of light, that goddess, that Apollo, I saw my face in the car's rear-view mirror and didn't recognize myself. My complexes had been scattered like a flock of pigeons. I was a young man of no more than thirty with a splendid mane of curly black hair. Even so, I couldn't shake the sensation of strangeness my surroundings produced.

'People are pretty alert round here,' said Andrea, accelerating towards a couple who leaped agilely out of the way. 'Are you a foreigner?'

'Yes,' I said, not knowing what to say. 'I've just arrived.'

'This is the commercial quarter. Do you like it?'

'It's very busy,' I said. 'Why are there so many dentists?'

'It's normal,' said Andrea. 'Everyone here has false teeth.'

It didn't seem normal to me.

'The displays are impressive,' I said, searching for something to say.

'That's because people must buy more, and they're too cautious at the moment... Jupiter only knows what'll happen if we have a sales crisis.'

I thought for a second I glimpsed a superfluous frown, but Andrea neutralized it with a cheerful, kind smile.

'Let's head to the residential district now. Maybe we'll get lucky there.'

We turned right and cruised down Pleasure, a dazzling avenue shaded by hundred-year-old trees, classical colonnades, luxury cafés, and terraces of hydrangea. For just a moment it reminded me of Paris in the Roaring Twenties. The terraces gave off a surprisingly intense perfume, which was strange because the hydrangeas of my day had no scent. Folk strolled, unhurried. Most wore Roman dress: older people sported ankle-length togas while youngsters wore short tunics. Some wore elegant capes draped across their shoulders and a minority favoured jeans like Andrea. The detail I struggled to resolve was whether they were men or women.

'Why do you want to know?' asked my friend, in a puritanical tone tinged with disappointment.

'Aren't you interested?' I asked.

'No,' Andrea replied.

She (or he) paused and asked casually, 'And so what are you?'

I felt my cheeks burning. 'What kind of question–,' I started.

Andrea stifled a laugh before becoming more serious when he (or she) saw my reaction.

'I don't understand,' she said. 'I don't know why you're so annoyed.'

'Because I'm embarrassed,' I said.

My new friend – perhaps male, perhaps female – blushed slightly and smiled enigmatically.

'So where've you come from, hun?'

I need to remind the reader again that they'll have to make an effort to strip my language of all allusion to grammatical gender. I explained my story very briefly to Andrea's rapt attention.

'You knew the old world?' she said. 'From before the constitution of the United States of Europe?'

'I was born in 1898,' I said.

'You got to see horse-drawn carriages and wheat fields?'

'Certainly.'

Andrea kissed me inappropriately, and with no care for anyone who might see.

'Next time you'll have to tell me about these things in more detail. You're marvellous.'

Andrea looked up and the breeze played with his golden hair as she stared ahead. Thirty metres ahead of us a couple were about to cross the road. Andrea accelerated and the two slim figures were thrown into the air. The car came to a halt and a police officer approached.

'They're dead, Andrea Víctrix,' he said, holding out a slip of paper. 'Is this your first time, Your Excellency?'

'No, that's nine.'

The officer stood to attention and saluted.

'You're eligible for a special award. Allow me to kiss you in the name of the Law, ahead of the formal recognition that will follow from our superiors.'

Andrea, with a courteous indifference, leant forward and allowed himself to be kissed before taking a look at the paper slip. It was a cheque.

'Ten thousand francs,' said the officer. 'Congratulations, Your Excellency.'

Andrea gave him back the cheque.

'Please cash this yourself.'

'If your Graciousness desires,' replied the officer.

I was stunned. We'd set off quickly and were touching a hundred again.

'That was appalling,' I yelled. 'Stop the car! You monster!'

Andrea slowed down.

'What's the matter?'

'You just murdered two people!'

The car stopped.

'Why are you shouting?' she asked.

I'd launched into a moralising rant and Andrea was again looking at me the same way the Mona Lisa might have done. That enigmatic expression, however, suddenly changed and the person I saw before me was now a man. An ugly, angry man.

'Get out,' he ordered. I was so surprised I was lost for words.

'Get out and be thankful I don't denounce you for blasphemy!'

'I've blasphemed?'

'Against the Law. Against the State. Get out.'

He swallowed some soma, took a deep breath, and took hold of my arm in a vice-like grip. He was strong, as well as a murderer. I got out of the car. As I walked away, he uttered something that disturbed me:

'You've displeased me.'

Publicity from a travel agent blared out: SPEND YOUR WEEKEND ON THE MOON.

CHAPTER II

After eighty-five years of 'repose', I'd come back to life with just a few banknotes in my wallet which were almost worthless against the strong franc. My house was long gone. In its place was an imposing skyscraper dedicated to a Private Waiters' Club. My friends were dead, I had no family, and I badly needed work. I went to a Job Centre. The employee there looked me up and down and forced a smile.

'Acrobat?' said the employee.

'No, goodness no,' I said.

'Dancer? You're young, handsome.'

'No. Look, I used to be a professional writer.'

I didn't think it appropriate to mention that I'd also been a first-rate footballer, because even though I'd been restored to youth, I couldn't very well turn the clock back and my sporting heyday had been a long time ago.

The employee scrutinized me.

'You were a writer, you say?'

'I am, I mean.'

'What did you write?'

'Literature, essays…'

'Literature about cheese, physics, anti-depressants…?'

'No, sir.'

'So?' He gave me the usual plastic service smile. 'You said essays,' he insisted. 'About what?'

'I don't know, philosophical matters.'

'Philosophical about what?'

'General ideas…'

He opened an encyclopaedia.

'Philosopher,' he read. 'A lover of knowledge. Quite so. But if you'll forgive me, knowledge of what?'

'We're not going to understand each other,' I replied, now bored. 'Please understand that my situation is urgent. I need to earn a living.'

'Who's threatening you?' he asked.

'No-one. But–'

I have no idea what he must have thought. Maybe that I was putting on a grand heroic act to conceal a complex of some sort. In his eyes I was just a rootless neurotic amongst the many thousands of rootless neurotics in the big city.

'If you feel like taking on something more adrenaline-fuelled, perhaps you could try lion tamer, or trapeze artist in the circus.'

'I don't know anything about taming lions. I just really need to earn some money. I'm not rich, and I obviously have to eat–'

'Eat? But the city's full of restaurants.'

'What, and they'll let me eat for free?'

'Naturally. Except the superlux venues.'

'That's fine, somewhere normal,' I said.

'Then there's no problem.'

I just had to get hold of a 'jobless' card or, better yet, a medical certificate stating that I suffered from an 'idle constitution' and with these papers the State would issue me with the corresponding vouchers. I did notice, however, that the certificate prevented me from engaging in any paid work.

'I'm not ill and I'm not idle. I just need a job,' I said.

'Very well, so you'll need to apply for your 'jobless' card which will buy you a few months. But that'll mean you can't be involved in any kind of work. Don't expect to get rich.'

The idle could live comfortably, but not accumulate wealth or fall into expensive habits. On the advice of good psychologists, the State had realised that humans are inherently envious and so wisely cultivated a spirit of emulation, that Faustian will that compels us to possess what we don't need. Everything was perfectly organized in the opulent city. Better even than in the Sweden of my childhood, a country that in modern history represented one of the pinnacles of that socialist, machine-dominated civilization which so enthused Teilhard de Chardin and Queen Marie-José.

That said, at a time when the poor's problems were solved and everyone could be satisfied, the rich constituted an extraordinarily privileged class in the United States of Europe, and especially in Turclub, where people spoke of their wealth in terms of millions. No-one remembered the old aristocracies of the Crusades anymore, or the silver-screen princesses of 1965, or the Soviet patriciate that was so important the year I underwent my cure. But once those archaic aristocracies had been eliminated and the old Establishment had lost its corrosive power, others had arisen. Of course, the poor still existed, yet while they had food and medical assistance, they still felt as 'humiliated and offended' as they did in Dostoyevsky's time (though perhaps as life wasn't sufficiently stimulating, they could allow themselves the luxury of comparison and dissent). The whole of so-called socialist Europe was, for some reason or another, divided and subdivided into castes: scientific, technical, artistic, moral, and economic. Amongst the most important were the all-powerful, quite brutal industrialists, forever speculating or occupied with problems of mechanization, and the more refined caste of *maîtres d'hôtel* and waiters.

The latter were still governed by the old rules of courtesy and traditional etiquette. I won't go so far as to say that those dehumanized, money-hungry hearts were 'tender', but they conserved a veneer which made them pleasant enough provided one did not scratch too deeply. Courtesy had become decoupled from the kindness that had originally created it. In the eighteenth century, courtesy and kindness were one and the same thing, and so it is that in *Manon* we see the narrator approach a stranger, the Chevalier des Grieux, and delicately help him, touched by the grace of the young gentleman and his unfortunate lover, who is deported. People were still refined and sincere in the time of Louis XV and only at Court, where conspiracy and ambition were rife, was such amiability becoming skin-deep.

Below and dependent on the Waiters' Guild was the Classical University, staffed by professors who specialised in ornamental history. Young people no longer had time to learn about the past; such studies would have been considered immoral and hostile under the new regime. Nevertheless, in pre-revolution Paris, elegance and good manners were never considered surplus to requirement. And so they had reached a compromise. With the exception of the aforementioned professors, who had no other use, no-one dedicated themselves to Romance literatures or the mythological sculptures of Versailles, but the Classical University advised the *maîtres d'hôtel* and the big industrialists in matters of good comportment. These forms, or formulae, would be taught 'quickly and without fuss' as per Espriu's fable. So the University was a kind of *Reader's Digest* for those who might like to drop Greek statuary or the affairs of the Madame de Montespan into conversation while taking tea. Its professors filled the grounds with ephebes and Roman colonnades which jarred somewhat amid the confused cacophony of skyscrapers. The institution was, of course, subject to the supremacy of industry and the whims of the Guild: thus when the University decided that plastic fabric was not admissible in a minuet, it was obliged to publish a retraction and declare that nylon was more elegant than Lyon silk. On questions of lesser note, however, they were given some autonomy. Nobody questioned their decision that spoons should be used with forks and that eating wearing gloves was considered refinement. Madame de la Tour du Pin recounts that Marie Antoinette did just that, although she is careful to add, '*en quoi elle avait grand tort*'. But neophytes are more papist than the Pope.

Public employees in receipt of official honours were not as powerful as the multimillionaire industrialists, nor as distinguished as the waiters. The waiters were the *crème de la crème* of high society and, like Proust's duchesses, their vocation was to please. Knowledgeable about wine, cheese and matters of precedence, they were hugely influential in the ministries and embassies, and were the only people permitted to wear tails, although only those older than fifty dared to avail themselves of the privilege.

Without quite knowing why, I didn't feel at home on my island, this despite the evident progress and economic success. Moral solitude and the absence of an occupation contributed to my low mood. Though by now I was no longer desperate to earn money, I would have liked to have started writing again, but I was unable to find publishers for my work which, so they said, wasn't actually about anything. On one occasion, leaving more abstract subjects aside, I tried to address more concrete matters with an essay on Philip II, and they took me for some kind of con artist.

'That topic's already been done, sir,' they said.

'Well, yes–'

'And? Were you acquainted with Philip II?'

'No, of course not. But I've tried to come up with a personal assessment through the lens of History.'

'Personal? Then there's only you who'll read it. We're only interested in the notion of the collective, and we're already familiar with it. Look.' he said, pointing at a shelf laden with books.

'I see that you don't allow the point of view of individuals, and the lyric isn't permitted,' I ventured.

The publisher responded haughtily.

'Exactly, sir. We don't publish pornography.'

Social and moral values were all inverted. In a bath house the day before I had witnessed a truly disturbing scene. The employee – male or female, I couldn't tell – asked me if I wanted him, or her, to wash me and what kind of corporeal treatments I was interested in. I answered 'none' and locked myself in my cabin which was separated from the others by a panel that stopped short of both the floor and ceiling. Through the glass door I could see other clients in the corridor, which I thought was inappropriate. I quickly undressed and got into the bath. A youngster wearing a Greek-style chlamys entered the cubicle from the left, followed by a masseur who looked like an Olympic athlete. While he undressed, they talked about sport.

'Your job really builds muscle,' said the younger of the two. 'You're in good shape.'

'I'm a boxer-masseur,' replied the employee. 'Kisses or punches?' he added sharply. 'The price is the same.'

'Punches, although–,' replied the youth.

'Would you like me to knock you out?'

'I've never tried it. Yes, if it's not too dangerous.'

'We offer compensation in case of accident,' said the athlete.

The young man seemed nervous.

'Will you insult me?'

'It's not included in the price, but I guarantee to make you light-headed. If you want an insult specialist, we've got an old Sephardi–'

'No need. Hit me. I'm sure I'll enjoy it, from you… I don't think I know what I'm doing.'

The masseur laughed.

'If you let fear take over, you won't get the full pleasure. You have to be up for it. If you'd rather I arouse you with caresses–'

'No, no. I'm fed up with stupid kisses. Hit me hard but build up slowly.'

'I'll work your face a bit, then some body shots… It's better if you try to hit me too. You'll feel your heart racing and you'll hurt, but you can take it. And when you're almost out on your feet I'll punch you hard to the stomach–'

'Is there a doctor, and first aid?'

'Naturally. Are you ready?'

'Hit me.'

The scene was over quickly. The sound of blows mingled with the voice of the boxer-masseur as he goaded the client. The youngster punched weakly, imploring mercy. Perhaps he hoped to be insulted and humiliated, but there were no free samples. Only when the masochist begged with tears in his voice 'darling, don't hurt me' did the masseur laugh out loud, provoking the client to despairing sobs. I heard him collapse suddenly to the floor and they carried him out, unconscious. His face was bloodied, and he looked to be smiling. The masseur followed, wiping away his sweat with an air of indifference.

After this scene, a publisher had blushed with shame when I pronounced the word 'lyric' and accused me of being a degenerate. I left the building utterly confused.

Having secured the 'jobless' card which guaranteed me a decorous if not opulent existence, I set about exploring the city. Convinced that there was no point trying to write, the only thing I seemed to be able to do was enjoy myself and, as I was about thirty, that of course meant love. I was attracted by many faces and many young bodies, though more than ever I had no idea whether they were men or women. When I'd come out of the cryo chamber, my first contact with a human being had been disconcerting and I'd felt embarrassed that Andrea had kissed me in public, although no-one seemed to have noticed. I hadn't seen Andrea since, and I had been left with a profound sense of longing.

It's sad to be lonely in a strange city. Before being frozen I had experienced solitude and had sought refuge in cabarets with their exuberant tango dancers, but that hadn't lasted long and in my fifties I'd become more serious, as corresponds to a man at that stage of his life. At that time I was living with an unmarried sister who was a stickler for tradition and very protective of our family line, which was considered both distinguished and disagreeable. We were more or less 'in society', although society's customs were beginning to resemble those of Turclub and were rarely agreeable.

I remember the last time I felt I should attend the opening of a night club. In 1965 those venues had nothing in common with the ever-entertaining clubs of the *belle époque*, and 'modern' music was nowhere near close to the delicate grace of Offenbach. There had been a pianist and a trumpeter on a very modest stage while numerous couples occupied a tiny dance floor. The pianist was wearing a pair of convict's pyjamas and played the same few notes over and over, accompanied by the trumpet which sounded like a furious cockerel. Amid the cacophony, conversation was impossible and we'd closed our eyes – at least the space was very nearly dark – and resigned ourselves to waiting a quarter of an hour before we could decently make our apologies and depart.

Asking myself why people went to places like that, two lovers who were making out gave me their answer.

'To drink, kiss…,' they said. 'Just foreplay… Nothing much.'

As we emerged onto the street, I commented to my sister that I'd much rather escort her to the Seu for the Rosary.

'At least there's the Tantum ergo,' I said.

'There's no comparison,' she replied half asleep, and we got in the car.

Tedious distractions such as popular music, alcohol, and sex would have been archaic in the era of soma and love that was by now so free it had almost evaporated. But cruelty, in its double forms of sadism and masochism, was on the increase as the only means of experiencing tenderness: this was the realm of hysteria. Dancing, even relatively frenetic forms like the twist, no longer held any interest. The travel agents packaged interplanetary excursions with air and atmospheric pressure adjustment, but only the multimillionaires could afford to pay.

The entertainment halls hosted fantastic spectacles, exciting ballets, and acrobatic displays generally featuring young children. The latter in particular were incredibly dangerous. I was petrified watching two pelotaris hurl heroic little seven-year-olds from one end of the court to the other, risking breaking their necks if they did not catch them in their long, curved baskets. Occasionally disaster struck, but few people concerned themselves with the fate of those who, in circus argot, were known as 'ballistic kids'. One evening a child fell dead at my feet and hardly anyone blinked except for the two photographers who threw themselves at the body to take pictures.

'The promoter won't lose out,' said someone sitting close by. 'The kid was very good but he was insured for a fortune.'

I was informed that the majority of children would fly through the air curled into a ball, heads tucked into their arms, whereas the child who had died held himself rigid, arms pinned to his side, and the pelota players hurled him, first head- and then feet-first, between them.

'They're bred for it,' I was told when I tried to protest. 'The State protects childhood. Only 0.01 percent end up in the Games.'

It was certainly the case that children, even those destined to die in the quest for *le petit frisson*, were reared like livestock. In such a rationalist age, their ingenuousness and purity interested the public for the same reasons purity always has: because there is pleasure to be derived from its vertiginous loss. Those little libidinous, blasphemous angels, bred for titillation. It is said that the renowned female libertine Sophie Arnould attempted to divert a philosopher as cynical as Voltaire by having young children throw their arms around his neck and kiss him as he entered her salon. *'Vous voulez m'embrasser,'* Voltaire had said, overcome, *'et je n'ai plus de visage.'*

Irony, like shame, was a quality now lost. One day, in a café, I was remarking on the difficulty of ascertaining the gender of passers-by when it occurred to me to recount an anecdote from the French Fourth Republic. A recruit had presented himself in the offices of the military dressed as an elegant woman in mink. The horrified orderly alerted the sergeant, but the sergeant didn't know what to do either and so informed his immediate superior. The recruit was passed up the ranks until he reached the colonel, who instead of reacting angrily, offered him a glass of wine. 'Well,' he said, 'you'll know that we've just lost Indochina; I wonder if with you as reinforcement…' My interlocutors were barely listening. In the end all they could say was that the colonel seemed like a nice man.

One of the things that surprised me was that cafés and bars didn't serve food. All food and beverage consumables were liquid: synthetic and medicinal juices. 'Liquid menus' were also common in restaurants, and people's dental health was deteriorating as a result, thus explaining the proliferation of dentists that I had noticed on my first tour of the city.

The C.O. (Collective Orgy) establishments, funded by the State and designed to instil 'natural morality' in behaviour, made me nauseous. Some were extremely luxurious and equipped with every mod con, but few people could bear the extremes of the heating and cooling systems which suffocated clients in winter and froze them in summer: such was the Dantesque punishment that God visited on the snobs of Earth, inverting and exaggerating the seasons they strove to suppress, after first inverting sex and synderesis. Moreover, neither the pristine appearance nor sumptuousness of the facilities succeeded in altering the impression that I found myself in a pigpen. Anyone who did not visit these establishments was regarded with suspicion; even so, I only went twice and that was quite enough. Personally, I would rather not talk of such filth, unlike the *tremendista* writers of old.

Football had disappeared. In my time it had already begun to be less a sport of the young and more a sedentary spectacle for bureaucrats. I think it was the fans who caused me to fall out of love with football and drove me to retire when I was at the peak of my game. I adored the sport too much to witness its commercial and chrematistic degeneration: twenty-two sportsmen before fifty thousand rheumatic spectators who'd only turned up for the sake of their pools entries. However, they very quickly realised that if you wanted to get rich from the football pools, it was better not to have a clue what was going on, since if they bet on the best team, the prize would be tiny because it'd be shared between a large number of people who of course would have selected the same team. It is not wisdom, but the absurd, that makes us millionaires overnight. Eventually, those old rheumatic fans stopped going to games and contented themselves with laying bets from behind their desks, the players became more and more indifferent and the directors busied themselves with signings, publicity, and Machiavellian numbers and combinations which no-one believed in anymore. After inflating the price of the physical betting slips, they even simulated games in far off cities and on lost Pacific islands, games that only existed on paper in offices, and in scenes on TV. Nothing, in the end, resisted the slough of corruption and decay.

One of my favourite pastimes was to take a ride in a helicopter and completely lose sight of the city and its inhabitants. I found those dawn excursions purifying. When I recall them today, I recognize that if just ten righteous people might have saved Sodom, then ten ought to have been enough to reconcile me with the Machine Age that, as a nonconformist and romantic, I loathed and wanted to annihilate. Even then, the sky seemed limpid, secluded, and majestic. The clouds below us formed a layer of cotton wool that cut us off from the world and the miseries to which the 'high standard of living' promised by cybernetics had reduced us. I was overcome by the urge to jump out of the chopper and pose on those meringue-like clouds like a cake-top angel; I'm sure they'd have taken my weight.

'But,' objected Andrea later, 'that marvellous spectacle is possible precisely because of the progress that you so detest.'

Andrea was right, and it made me furious.

'Wait and see,' I retorted. 'When the sky is as littered with helicopters as the earth is with automobiles, this won't be so marvellous.'

It was true that the number of helicopters was increasing every day. You could hire them, and so simple were they to fly that the pilots tended to be young boys, generally from Ibiza. They usually went naked in the summer, albeit with a diminutive brief concealing their genitals, a paradox in a country so unconstrained in erotic affairs yet compelled to hide genitals as though they were sinful. Deeply tanned, they often resembled terracotta Phoenicians. In winter they wore soft kid leather and had bundles of uncomplicated charm. They were agile and lively as sparks and so acclimatized to the dangers that more than once mid caper they had hurled themselves from the aircraft. Those daring young creatures had very little respect for life and they really loved money. One of them plunged sixty metres into the sea, obliterating himself, in order to please a wealthy man who had promised him twenty-thousand strong francs. The man, a foreign millionaire and member of the 'Forex' class, was reported to the police, but the matter was resolved with a donation to the hospital, an outcome that seemed both natural and equitable.

Since my incomprehension and discomfort were getting steadily worse, I decided to consult Dr Orlando, a psychiatrist whom everyone spoke about, by some as an undesirable, and by others as a genius. He was an old doctor of the Viennese School, and a devotee of the talking cure. Gaining access was not easy: he had his obsessions and was suspicious of those he did not know, but I succeeded via a young waiter of the highest aristocratic precedence who was enough of a snob to be admiring of everything iconoclastic, as well as being an expert in cheeses, honours, and distinctions.

Dr Orlando must have been more than one hundred and twenty years old. A disciple of Freud, he had the same spirit as the Viennese Jew, the last great Romantic of my time and someone who had resisted the sacrifice of individual rights to those of the collective. He was viewed as a dissident by the Regime and so the formalities and protocol required ahead of my consultation with the oracle were by no means mere window-dressing.

I will begin by saying that Medicine, as it was still understood in the first half of the twentieth century, was not much in use in Turclub due to the depersonalization occasioned by insurance policies. People no longer believed in the prestige of the medical practitioner, an office that had degenerated from all-powerful wizard to State servant. This lack of belief was compensated by faith in medication, which people abused massively and self-administered following recommendations via radio advertising and the publicity of the manufacturers of branded medicines, themselves advised by anonymous scientists who had never seen an ill person in their lives but were very familiar with analyses, cardiograms and scans. The same was happening to clothing as independent tailors had vanished, to be replaced by grandiose stores full of off-the-peg fashion.

As always, however, a minority resisted, and it was they who filled the psychiatrist's consulting room. Since 'alienated' just means strange or different to others, the aforementioned minority must have been truly mad. Though from my own perspective, and because I was one of them, they did not seem at all mad to me: it was the others who were mad. But those of us who think this way are designated 'paranoiacs', which refers to twisted thinking in the eyes of those who don't believe they think that way.

Educated in the different schools of psychoanalysis, Dr Orlando did not believe in the omnipotence of vaccines (tonsillitis he would affirm, is not caused by streptococcus, which is also found on the tonsils of healthy people, but by a moral trauma which upsets the normally beneficial symbiosis) and had his doubts about vitamins and abominated tranquillizers.

'Half an hour's conversation,' he would say, 'can produce more euphoria than any sedative, and a single word can excite more efficiently than a few milligrams of cocaine.'

In these scandalous speeches, he maintained that all tranquillizers were stimulants in the reactive phase, and vice versa. As such, he was seen as a rebel where science was concerned or, in other words, as an atheist. In theory, such unorthodoxy ought to have been somewhat prejudicial to him, since he exercised a people-facing profession which required faith rather than critique. But the opposite had happened; though they remained hidden, the inevitable discontents existed, and threw in their lot with him.

After a week of tests, scans, oscillometry and goodness knows what else, they gave me a certificate of 'perfect physical health', without which no mentally unwell person could be admitted to the office of the oracle. The doctor, small in stature and lean and wearing a kind of black cassock, held out a skeletal hand and had me sit in an armchair. He looked at me with a curiosity that verged on impertinence.

'You underwent the cryo-cure–' he started.

'I slept for eighty-five years in a body freezer,' I said. 'How did you guess?'

'And so are you another one who believes I'm capable of divination and can make people foam at the mouth?' he replied, irritated. 'According to your file, you were born in 1898 and yet you don't look more than thirty.'

'Of course,' I said, slightly disillusioned, because given my nervous state I really would have preferred the doctor to have possessed supernatural insight. 'I keep forgetting that I'm a young man of twenty-eight and a half years old. According to the Salky charts, for every twelve months asleep, I'm supposed to rejuvenate by four, but I don't know how accurate the calculations are.'

'They're approximate,' he replied, 'and they only refer to the somatic dimension. Psychologically I'm sure you don't feel that young.'

'You're right, and I admire your perspicacity. Doctor, I feel old. That's the reason for my visit.'

He looked at me half mockingly.

'Dissatisfaction with life, lethargy, lack of motivation, etc.?'

'Exactly,' I said.

'And there's no object to Creation, being born to die is nonsense, Pangloss was stupid, love is artifice?' he continued.

'Just so.'

The old doctor smiled.

'You feel old because you are old. I've always been opposed to the cryo-cure, and I'm familiar with its effects. I too could have been rejuvenated but I opted for a natural old age rather than spending years as a lump of frozen flesh. You'll gradually start noticing, if you don't get killed by an automobile first, that more than half the population is mad. You have an excellent physical constitution, you're only twenty-nine, but they're twenty-nine years of a 1965 vintage. In our terms, you're getting on.'

'I don't understand,' I said. 'If I'm young then I must be young, if you'll forgive the truism.'

'You're the son of a mother and father.'

'Of course,' I exclaimed, not understanding what he was getting at.

'"Of course" for you and for those of us who came into life that way, but not for others,' he said.

'Which others?'

'Everyone else,' he said, laughing as though slightly deranged.

'All the eighty-year-old youngsters, as the French would say. You're an old man, my friend. A lot has happened since 1965.'

'So rather than me who's got old, it's the era?'

'It doesn't matter,' he replied. 'Your era has become old.'

'No, forgive me,' I insisted. 'It's the here and now that's old.'

I fell silent, realising the absurdity of it all. How can the present be old? I could tell that the doctor agreed, but he was wary of insisting.

'We're getting into metaphysics and you're aware that those in power would rather metaphysics didn't exist,' he replied, smiling.

'No,' I said, standing up. 'I understand that Turclub isn't set up for metaphysics. It's all radios broadcasting slogans, as far as I can see. But doctor, in this office I'm sure all your patients crave a more spiritual life. If they didn't, they wouldn't come.'

'They do indeed. They're tired of living. And not just my clients... In 1985 the United States of Europe were definitively constituted. The President governs from the Élysée Palace in Paris after the revolution that marked the end of the Agricultural Era and the beginning of the Industrial Era. From that point on, many of the problems that once tormented humanity have been resolved. Social organization is incredibly advanced and the State, advised by big business, thinks for us all. Even love... Have you met Andrea Víctrix yet?'

My heart leapt.

'Drives a red Rolls Royce?'

The doctor let slip a laugh and slapped my knee.

'Magnificent! You remembered the Rolls before the person.'

It wasn't true. I'd mentioned the Rolls precisely to be sure who it was the doctor was referring to, but I decided to keep up the pretence.

'Strange creature,' I said. 'I know her a bit.'

I waited, silent, expectant, scarcely breathing, for my interlocutor to say more. Surely he'd reveal some great secret that would poison me. He had alluded to Andrea while we were talking about spiritual craving.

But all the doctor said was, 'Have you seen the Palazzo Víctrix? Have you been lovers?'

I blushed.

'What a question, doctor...'

The doctor was slightly deaf, short-sighted, and did not notice my indignation, continuing softly:

'So, as I was telling you, most of our problems, all of them, perhaps, have been solved. If you don't have work, or are feeling idle, the State will support you for half a year, or more if you have influence high up. But don't repeat that. Now that poverty has disappeared, our quality of life has improved. The aspiration of ancient Rome, *panem et circenses*, has been achieved. Back in your time, the *Reader's Digest* declared that happiness could be measured in metres of piping and numbers of white goods. Now every apartment in Turclub is overflowing with electric, or rather atomic, appliances. Thanks to Huxley's discovery of soma, pain no longer exists. Everyone is young until, suddenly, they become old. At that point, if they haven't already died of natural causes, by which I mean in an automobile accident, they're injected with Parquidine. And you know the result of all this? I'll tell you in figures: the rate of suicide is now higher than in Sweden, which until a couple of decades ago was the highest in the world.'

'In my time,' I replied, 'Sweden had the highest living standards and the highest percentage of deaths by suicide.'

'Quite. Then came Denmark, the Federal Republic of Germany, the USA and England. De Gaulle's France wasn't badly off. In Italy and Romania there were fewer suicides and in Spain, well... we've always been quite poor.'

'How do you explain that, doctor?' I asked. 'It's certainly the case that those with the least don't generally kill themselves. Why is it that so many of the apparently happiest people die by their own hand?'

Dr Orlando, quite the antique, older even than Hitler's Third

Reich, was a comedian.

'Perhaps,' he said, 'they die of pleasure.'

The image of a boxer-masseur bent over an unconscious young man came into my head.

'And do consider,' the psychiatrist went on, 'that the statistics only count voluntary cases as suicides, and they're not the most common.'

'Is there such a thing as an involuntary suicide?' I exclaimed, surprised.

The old man smiled.

'If you think that's an exaggerated way of putting it, let's say "unthinking" instead. The proliferation of automobiles, for example, answers to a desire to end it quickly.'

It seems I was a comedian too. After all, we'd both come into being at the same historical moment. Moreover, I'd taken a soma pill and was high.

'To conquer the distance,' I said.

'Just so. To shorten the distance between the point of departure and arrival.'

'To shorten History!' I exclaimed.

'To simplify it,' corrected the doctor, using an ironic euphemism.

I laughed, but the soma was wearing off so I took a second dose.

'Save that for the acrobatic displays,' he said, referring to the soma. 'You don't need to be out of your head to talk to me.'

Feeling myself again, I replied, 'It'd certainly be great in the cabarets, but I don't go to them.'

'Why not, my dear?' said the doctor. 'You're young. Love...'

I could feel myself getting impatient.

'What have you got against love, at thirty years old?' continued the doctor.

'What kind of love are you talking about?'

'Physical, of course. What other kind is there?'

'There must be others, doctor,' I said. 'The ready availability of sex must necessarily draw us towards a new mysticism, in reaction.'

'But in the meantime...,' he said. 'You're young.' His voice unbearably teasing, he made to play with my curly hair.

'Doctor, please,' I said. 'I'm ancient. Older even than you!'

He smiled, pleased by my fury.

'Not so old.'

'Laugh and I'll flatten you!' I replied.

How on earth was I capable of uttering those completely inappropriate words? The doctor's voice sounded distant, tinkling and silvery, like a bell offering jovial, absurd things, cheeriness and nonsense.

'Go on, go and have a good time in the cabarets, learn figure skating, kill a child. It'd be tedious if we came to blows now...'

Enough was enough.

'Forgive me,' I said. 'I'll take my leave... I'm upset. Another day I'll tell you all about why women unsettle me.'

'Oh, there's no need...,' his far-off voice still sounding like a silvery bell. 'The trees and flowers on Pleasure are made of plastic. Did you know that? You, sir, are asking too much. In order to love, you demand security... you 1965 romantic!'

'Exactly,' I said. 'Security!' I made my escape, pursued down the stairs by the doctor's silvered laughter as he shouted after me.

'Dearest sir, do come again! Come back another day... I know you will!'

The night after my appointment with Dr Orlando, I went to dine at *Le Gaulois*, a restaurant on Pleasure. I chose it because it was red-carpeted, perfumed and adorned with hydrangeas: it reminded me of my era. A *maître d'hôtel* wearing tails bowed deeply, welcoming customers with a stereotypically condescending smile. The rest of the staff, polished and pleasant, were dressed in long, romanesque robes with the exception of the lady in charge of front of house, who wore a black silk dress and a necklace of cultured pearls. Though quite a luxurious restaurant, the cuisine was not of the same standard and the quality of the moderate portions was poor, if not completely awful. They served food that had been chilled or preserved in jars, and nothing seemed to possess its natural flavour. I later discovered that it wasn't worth looking elsewhere because everywhere was the same. In general, customers didn't eat, instead ordering fortified juices which saved time and were apparently healthier.

While I dined, I thought about my visit to the crackpot doctor. Why had he asked me such uncomfortable questions about my relationship with Andrea? What did he think of that disconcerting figure, and what did he think of me? I regretted now not having asked him to explain himself. Andrea must be some kind of celebrity. Why had the psychiatrist associated Andrea's name with love, smiling at the idea I might have remembered the Rolls before the person?

As I waited for dessert, I flicked through the *Official News Bulletin*, the country's only events publication, and was struck by an absurd article entitled *Crime Against Nature*, which read as follows:

An individual has been detained for making derogatory comments about Hola-Hola, *the drink that contributes most tax revenue to our industry. When interrogated, he declared cynically that he [sic] lived "with his parents" [sic] who, with a lack of shame reminiscent of primates, confirmed that he was in fact their naturally conceived son, when for many years the human race has ceased to be viviparous. The transgressors will appear in court and the prosecution is seeking five death sentences.*

Having been served a flavourless casserole and a synthetic apple – it was late and the place was almost empty – I showed the strange article to a young member of waiting staff who was attending me, a veritable cake-top angel in a white tunic. I confess I thought them beautiful, and for that reason assumed that she was a girl. A red flush transfigured her features as she scanned the page.

'How disgusting,' she murmured.

'Disgusting?' I said. 'Living with one's parents?'

The waitress altered suddenly, her eyes ablaze. Not now so much angelic figurine but exterminating angel of death.

'Sir,' she said, 'no-one has given you permission to take such liberties with me. I will denounce you to the management.'

'Denounce me to the Pope, if you want,' I said, feeling an urge to hit him or her.

Two tears rolled down her cheeks. She seemed for all the world a demure young girl and, taking her by the waist and checking that no-one was looking, I kissed her. I was expecting her to push me away or slap me, but she smiled.

'Thank you, Sir,' she said. 'You're very kind, but I have principles. Notwithstanding such a delicate gesture, I will be reporting you for your sacrilegious language. Please forgive me.'

'Don't be silly,' I replied softly. 'We could have a good time, the two of us. You're a nice girl.'

She stiffened.

'You have no right to use the feminine or masculine with

decent people.'

'You're crazy!' I replied.

The slap came hard. Her white uniform reminded me that she belonged to the Waiters' Guild, the highest nobility on the island, and her stylized figure made me think of Andrea. Regretting having kissed her, I became agitated as she approached the counter to talk to the person in charge, whom I supposed to be female. A well-perfumed bellboy was sent across to invite me to talk with her. I was a little nervous as I made my way over, scared even.

'Sir,' she said, although not 'Sir' because she used the neutral form of address that is missing from my language, but which was used by everyone in Turclub out of tact and delicacy. 'Sir, a complaint has been made against you. I ask you to remain calm and help me find a solution which will satisfy the Guild in view of the personal offence you have caused the young *camariero*,' she for some reason said in Italian. 'And avoid a far worse outcome. The Law requires that all citizens, including State employees, are respectful of the caste because it is critical to the progress of our tourist and hotel industry. I think if you were to apologise appropriately and pay damages–'

'Madam,' I interrupted, 'I don't understand what's going on. If I pay damages to the waiter, that's an acknowledgement that I've done something wrong.'

She looked at me with a certain condescension.

'Do I take it that you've undergone a cryo-cure?'

Again! I was beginning to see that it was a stigma.

'I have, Madam. Last Friday I was still asleep after almost eighty-five years.'

'Ah,' she smiled. 'I understand. You still don't know that to be born directly from a mother and father is a crime.'

'Seriously?' I said, surprised.

'It's the Original Sin,' she replied. 'The State does not permit any form of procreation other than the one it controls in its incubators. In the Industrial Era, which began definitively in 1985, the human race has ceased to be viviparous. Around that time there was a great revolution–'

'Yes,' I said, recalling my conversation with Dr Orlando. 'I'm aware that the Industrial Era followed the Agricultural Era.'

'Precisely,' she continued. 'At that point it was considered advisable to control natality, condition it to the needs of industry, and most definitely not leave it to individual whim. It's complicated, I'm not sure how to explain it. Do you know Huxley's founding work?'

'I do, Madam,' I replied.

'Well, just like in *Brave New World*. In order to serve the State, it is indispensable that one belongs to the State, and not to what used to be called – please forgive my being crude – the family. And eugenics are key. The majority of parents – and again, please forgive my language – transmitted serious illnesses to their offspring.'

'They also passed on a tradition and beliefs, etc.,' I said.

The lady at the counter smiled.

'And that's what must be avoided. Families represent individuality and anarchy, both of which are incompatible with the industrial, gregarious regime. Today, the fertilization of healthy eggs in the laboratory is a guarantee–'

'Please, you don't need to continue,' I insisted. 'I said I know Huxley's fantasy, except that Huxley situated it six-hundred years in the future. Are we already there, in 2050? Unbelievable!'

She made a gesture of resignation before my viviparous brusqueness, unrefined by the courses of the Classical University and sighed.

'You'll begin to get used to it,' she said. 'Anyway, please present the waiter with twenty-five francs and we'll draw a line under the matter. I'll convince him to accept them. It's not in your interest for this to go any further. Bear in mind that people of impure origin (with apologies) who are still alive are very closely monitored. If I can be of any service, Sir…'

There was a certain maternal tenderness in her words, and perhaps a nostalgia for a now impossible sin she had not even known. I decided that she was undoubtedly a woman. Attractive, gentle, almost beautiful. Poised.

'Yes,' I replied. 'I find myself in a world I don't understand. I detest synthetic fruit and orange juice that's never seen an orange, and I can't tell meat from fish or what sex people are…'

I was thinking about Andrea and, in truth, my thoughts strayed back to her often. The lady at the counter looked cross.

'You're all the same when you wake up from a cryo-cure,' she remarked. 'We've transcended sex, it's an unimportant accident.'

'Unimportant?' I said. 'And love?'

'Love Humanity, love the Party,' she replied.

'That's too abstract. Can I kiss Humanity?'

'Sir, you may kiss whomever you wish. No-one will object. It's an innocent pleasure. You will become accustomed to the new morality. Did you hear that yesterday they imprisoned someone for writing a novel?'

'Why?' I said.

'They were found guilty of lyricism and lies. A completely false narrative, three-hundred pages of falsehoods.'

It is widely believed that humankind has progressed from the Creation onwards, but it's not true. People who declare that progress is indefinite have to recognize that although on balance it may well be going forwards (which is absurd, as a positive balance is unachievable both while humanity exists, and also once it no longer does), there have been many serious steps backwards. When Thespis first performed Greek tragedy, Solon censured him just like the lady in charge of front of house at *Le Gaulois* with her Parisian airs, black silk dress and cultured pearls, had censured a poor novelist like myself in the year 2050.

'A novelist,' I said, 'isn't a liar, and nor was Thespis when he was on stage. Neither pretends that the stories they tell happened in real life. They want to make people think and enjoy themselves, and they're completely open about it. Whatever Solon thought, Thespis the actor was the sincerest of men.'

But the lady at *Le Gaulois* had no idea who Thespis was and but a single professor from the Classical University knew even two words about him (how far we'd come in 2050!). That said, she was seductive and I sensed she had a certain human understanding. She wasn't young, but fifty well-preserved years old or more, and had a pleasant smile. Although she seemed rather old for me (or too young, depending on your point of view), I was beginning to take an interest in her.

'If you like,' I said to her, 'we could go out together sometime and talk about all these things in a more relaxed atmosphere.'

The annoyance I thought I had detected on her face before was now clearly, unmistakeably visible.

'I don't have time, Sir. Find other diversions. You hold such unacceptable prejudices.'

'You are the only female being,' I started. 'I confess I cannot go without certain things... You're French, aren't you?'

She nodded.

'Ah *oui*, Old France. The eternal feminine,' she said in an attempt at irony, before suddenly turning serious. 'Well, since it interests you, I am a man. I affect a slightly feminine demeanour out of respect for the tradition of my country, and the *belle époque*. This is a restaurant of a certain standing, and the owner would like to create an old-fashioned ambience, which is why I'm wearing a necklace and earrings, which in any case men wear as well, when they like. Thank you for your voluntary donation, and please try to afford proper respect to the Guild.'

Her manner was clipped, and for a moment I feared she might have me detained and sent me off to the moon in a parody of those voyages I had heard a PA system advertise on the day of my resurrection. Was she a man? Had she said so merely so I'd leave her alone? I still find myself wondering.

Just a short while after the restaurant episode, I discovered that Russia and the United States of America had disappeared from the map. The relationship between their respective presidents – the last two autocrats of our Era – couldn't have been more cordial, the cause of this cordiality being the panic they inspired in each other. They say that mutually assured destruction prevents war. Which is true, up to a point. That fear had created an intricate atomic attack and defence mechanism so perfect that simply pushing a button set it in motion. So when one of the two presidents – it hasn't been possible to ascertain which – accidentally caught the button while trying to swat a fly in his office, seven bombs fell *incontinenti* onto one of the two empires, while at almost the same time seven more fell on the other, thus wiping the two superpowers out.

As such, the United States of Europe, with its capital in Paris, had been transformed into lords and masters, exterminating on other continents anything or anyone opposed to their industrial interests. In this way they enjoyed a period of economic wellbeing the like of which History had never seen. In the year 2050, every worker lived in more comfort and luxury than a magnate not just of the Middle Ages, but of the Enlightenment itself. Though the dogma was unarguable, the terms *comfort* and *luxury* might be open to discussion by the inevitable sophists. The problem of China no longer existed because there were no Chinese left, those vast deserts waiting to be repopulated when the time was right with new oviparous generations lacking all social and religious prejudices although respectful still of *Hola-Hola*, vitamins, and atomic household appliances, because these needed markets.

The world was promised an Octavian peace. Europe was

victorious and free of nightmares, and was the perfect synthesis of Marxism and capitalism. In Turclub, where tourism was expanding, people lived a luxurious existence under the sign of the ignorant masses and the most ferocious trusts. In fact, it was the latter who governed the masses, convincing them that they needed atomic appliances and making them suggestive to the consumption of *Hola-Hola* in order to raise their standard of living. In this sense the 'emancipated' populace was more tyrannized than ever and, having been fed a repetitive diet of simplistic slogans, they tyrannically refused to accept any idea that wasn't a dogma accepted and assimilated by the *Reader's Digest*. This is why art had become collectivized, and all movies in the cinemas began with a roaring lion and ended with a lingering kiss.

That said, it is well known that the Universe is formed from a harmony of opposites. Love is to fight and to fight leads to the orgasm, with which it overlaps. Who would ever attend monotonous events like wrestling or the *corridas* if they didn't derive some kind of lustful satisfaction from them? The strength of Cleopatra resided in her weakness while the judge, in sentencing the defendant, becomes hangman and commits murder in order to avoid further murders. Though it is dangerous for me to talk about these matters today because religion and metaphysics arouse suspicion, I will simply say that the priests of 1965 who had ceased to look to the Vatican and instead took a leaf out of the central-European book became so popular and complaisant that rather than minister to the people, they allowed themselves to be led by them. Around that time, the Bishop of Pamplona found it necessary to condemn a number of chaplains who proclaimed that they 'did not recite the Rosary so that they would feel closer to their lost brothers and sisters'.

Over time, from that chaos steadily arose an ever more numerous minority who would resuscitate order and faith – attainable only by the most toxic struggle –, returning everything to an ending and a rebirth. For the time being, life seemed relatively stable, although agricultural produce was becoming scarce. Those of us who remained from the viviparous generation as a result of the cryo-cure were perturbed by the fact we could not distinguish meat from fish and were hardly ever able to tell people's gender. Generations of not giving birth meant that women's breasts had become reduced to simple pectorals and the constitution of the young, now released from the demanding physical labour of times past, was increasingly stylised and elegant. Everything contributed to unification but it was perhaps the suppression of grammatical genders that proved decisive in the battle, as it is – or was – known that from the Word came Creation. Those recalcitrants who refused to use the neuter gender were exiled by the authorities to the wastes of Massachusetts and Hollywood, and in the Classical University professors corrected and purged old texts. Achilles was always referred to as Achilles-Pyrrha, acknowledging that while he was a courageous warrior, in many people's eyes he had also been female. In parks, the public gazed on statues of ephebes while Venus and Hercules were considered aberrant exemplars and confined to secret museums, visited only by people of a certain age and culture.

Denim jeans and shorts, increasingly popular amongst females in 1965, were rarely worn any more. They had been replaced by long or short Rome-inspired tunics. Women dressing as men was considered a bourgeois fashion, since rather than signifying indifference towards a person's gender, it meant that one gender was dominant. Moreover, jeans needed to be cut to size, whereas houppelandes could be mass produced, which was of paramount importance in an industrial and machine era. There was probably another reason too: in Turclub, with its four hundred cabarets, three thousand cinemas and millions of transistor radios (two per inhabitant), everyone suffered from anxiety. What's more, aside from the debts occasioned by buying goods in instalments, people had lost their fear of Hell because the Devil had fallen out of fashion, and antibiotics had made them bold to venereal disease. In their place came two other potential catastrophes: a tourism crisis that would be the ruin of all Turclubbers and, due to the fact that atomic secrets were no longer secret but accessible to many, a nuclear war which could annihilate them all in a minute. The Chinese danger had disappeared, but Europe could not, or dared not – which is the same as not being able to – exterminate the rest of the world, meaning that even the Abyssinians one day or another would become a danger. This is why shelters had been built that would allow people to survive for up to a year: many therefore knew that before they died, machine civilization offered them twelve months of immobilization in a hole with vitamin pills for food. This they knew and were resigned to, and if the siren were to sound while they were asleep, they could slip their tunic on while running for the shelter whereas the old clothes, jeans and suchlike, would take a minute or more to put on. When the fateful moment came, every second would count.

At least for those with any kind of thirst for life. But the multimillionaires, obliged by their prestigious status to become alcoholics in the same way that at other times they'd been obliged to wear feathers in their hat, did not have to worry to the same degree about how long it would take to reach the shelters as the partying and quantities of vodka ingested would finish off their livers first. According to Dr Orlando, this was perhaps the reason they pickled themselves instead of eating and took interplanetary trips with no other end, snobbery aside, than ruining their health.

On the subject of what the doctor had called 'collective suicide', I have to remark that while people no longer crashed their motorcycles because motorcycles were prohibited, they crashed their automobiles at such a rate that this had become the most frequent or natural (this is how it was referred to in medical reports) cause of death. By contrast, deaths as a result of surgical procedures or old age, by dint of being less common, were generally referred to as accidental.

The authorities had taken charge of the problem and had felled the trees that lined the roadside. Instead of smashing into trees, vehicles left the road doing a hundred, flipped twice and burst into flames. When a survey was carried out into how people would rather die, the majority, as inconsistent as ever, replied that they would rather not die, and so engineers suggested building a five-metre-wide lane or 'emergency zone' either side of the main carriageway to be used only if there was a danger of crashing into another car. Very soon the emergency zone was as busy as the road itself and so drivers demanded another. And as the same would have happened again and again, it was agreed that the emergency zone would be protected by a metallic netting that was insubstantial enough to give way should a car collide with it. As a result, the netting was permanently on the ground and had to be strengthened with reinforced concrete posts. With the problem now the same as before the tree-felling, some regressive voices talked about planting new ones, but objections were raised that it would take fifty years for them to grow to the same height as the previous ones. Having already been trialled on Pleasure, plastic happily saved the day and afforded work to a number of workers from among the multitudes now jobless because of the proliferation of robots. The plastic trees could be made to look one hundred years old in twenty-four hours, were more beautiful than the organic ones, and automobiles still crashed into them as though they were real because they were stiffened with steel. Given that people were not attracted to the idea of being crushed to death or burned alive, all cars were equipped with bottles of prussic acid which would break on impact and exterminate the occupants instantaneously. It was as a consequence of this fatal provision that death in a road traffic event began to be designated as death by natural causes, because it was inevitable. Of course, it didn't occur to anyone to ban automobiles.

CHAPTER VII

A LESSON IN POLITICAL ECONOMICS AND SEXOLOGY

'Ban automobiles?' exclaimed the old psychiatrist the next time I found myself back in his consulting room. 'Have you thought about the consequences? Companies going bankrupt, workers losing their jobs, a petroleum crisis, etc.'

'Well, I don't know,' I said, 'but perhaps cars are starting to become a hindrance. Don't you think that in the era of helicopters, society could organise itself differently?'

The psychiatrist looked at me piercingly.

'No, because it's perfect,' he continued, mockingly. 'What you're suggesting is a revolution against God and against Industry, the god of our Era.'

'Against the automobile manufacturers' cartel, anyway,' I replied.

'Worse than that,' he retorted. 'We're talking about the most powerful god after *Hola-Hola*. There are millions at stake.'

'How am I supposed to take these gods seriously?' I asked.

He seemed impatient.

'And how do you expect me not to take them seriously? You haven't been out of cryo oblivion for a month and it'll take time for you to open your eyes to reality. The dogmas of today are every bit as terrible as those of the barbaric religions.'

'As I'm beginning to realise,' I said.

'Not in the same way as someone who has experienced them in the flesh,' replied the doctor.

Dr Orlando had been persecuted. Years earlier, having published a study on the effect of certain vitamins and suggested that they might cause cancer, he was expelled from the Official Academy of Medicine under pressure from the Pharmaceutical Production Conglomerate. Orlando had to retract his study but carried on pursuing his research away from public view.

'Tyranny,' he said, lowering his voice and carefully scrutinizing every corner of the office as though paranoid, 'is appalling, and worse still is that no single person is to blame, unlike before. If someone were, then of course we'd kill them.'

I refrained from seeking an explanation of that mysterious 'we', which seemed to hint at conspiracy. He had closed his eyes and I sensed him navigating dark and twisting places.

'The devil today is anonymous, anonymous,' he continued. 'These faceless companies are the very roots of our State, which is anonymous as well. Oh, if we only had a Hitler or a Lenin. Assassinating *Monsieur-Dame*, a mere figurehead, would be stupid.'

'Who is *Monsieur-Dame*?' I asked.

'The symbol of the State,' said the doctor, 'and the perfect androgyne, my ingenuous young friend!'

'So,' I said, imagining him to be delirious and not wishing to press any further, 'we should reject the theories of Henry Ford and rethink industrial economics?'

'Spengler already tried and it served no purpose,' replied Orlando, recovering himself. 'I'm sure you're familiar with the great prophetic tome, *Der Untergang des Abendlandes.*'

'I am, doctor. And I do consider it a prophetic work. When I was young, I used to think it lacked any grounding in reality. Keyserling, even Ortega y Gasset, understood it as pure theory and without life force. We were still living the euphoria of the *belle époque*–'

The doctor interrupted me.

'Spengler advocated cultures that grow organically, with their roots in the ground and methodical like Nature. These were not new ideas; Buffon had voiced them in the *Discours de réception de l'Académie Française* in 1753. The result, as you can see, is staring us in the face: the majority of those who drive around in automobiles drinking *Hola-Hola* on Pleasure are suffering from hunger.'

The psychiatrist was undoubtedly exaggerating, although it

was true that one did not eat well in Turclub. For those of us who had lived in more classical times, the menus of sandwiches and food substitutes were unpleasant and monotonous.

'Where do you eat?' he asked.

'Almost always at *Le Gaulois*.'

'Ah yes, it has a reputation for being an old-style restaurant. Or it's all very red plush anyway.'

'I'd prefer less plush and more authentic victuals,' I said. 'Everything comes out of a tin.'

'You're asking too much,' he replied. 'You're a long way from the reality we're living in. The Industrial Era has replaced the Agricultural Era. Even the trees are made of plastic.'

'And the oranges. The stall-holders claim they taste better than the real ones–'

He interrupted me again.

'How can we oppose industry if it sustains us? The growers would have to industrialize and force their crops with chemical fertilizer… It wouldn't help them. Their oranges wouldn't be able to compete with the price of synthetic, mass-produced fruit, more vitamin-rich and disruptive to cell tropism than natural oranges: the higher vitamin content is a response to the increase in cancer.'

He fell silent and his face bore an expression of anger and sadness, no doubt thinking back to the prosecution he had been subjected to years earlier for making similar assertions.

'There'll be more and more atomic appliances,' he continued, 'more plastic carnations and fewer natural products. We'll end up doing without agriculture altogether and devouring one another. What are you laughing at? The world is far older than the classical authors thought. Humanity has experienced numerous cycles of civilization which have alternated with periods of anthropophagy. I assure you it won't be long before we're eating human flesh again.'

'Not me, doctor,' I said.

'Well, me neither,' he smiled. 'But don't think this is senility talking. Have you visited the Palazzo Mallorquino procreation centre?'

'Not yet. I've been told that it was inspired by Huxley's work.'

'Yes,' he said, 'it's Huxley's fault.'

'But he wrote *Brave New World* to satirize socialism and the excesses of mass production.'

'And the socialists,' the doctor replied, 'read the book literally and took advantage of it. Playing with irony is dangerous in some quarters.'

I asked him how many procreation centres there were in the U.S. of Europe and he told me that there were four: the main one in Paris; others in London and Genoa; and the Mediterranean centre based in Turclub.

'In the whole world right now,' he said, affecting through inertia the formulaic courtesies of the moment in which he didn't believe, 'there are no more than twenty men and seventy-five women – please excuse my use of such vulgar terms – destined to provide sperm and eggs for fertilization in the incubators. The spermatozoa from England give us good metalworkers, while those from Mallorca and Ibiza – with a preference for the latter – tend to be assigned to the Waiters' Guild. The progenitors are the highest quality exemplars; they live amid parkland and spend their time playing sport and breathing the purest air. Did you know that they're stupid? They're so healthy that they turn moronic, and this has long term repercussions for our race. But we're on the point of manufacturing a drug that produces intelligence when injected into the foetus. It's extracted from the brains of geniuses.'

'Do you believe in these things, Doctor?' I asked.

He shot me his customary mocking, unhinged look.

'What does it matter whether I believe in them or not if they're true for the majority?' His eyes glazed over. 'There are injections of cheerfulness, kindness, and beauty, too... Have you ever thought about being a pigeon? Sexual pleasure,' he continued as though giving a lecture, quickly recovering his scholarly gravity, 'is completely dissociated from procreation, which is the responsibility of the atheist State. Love doesn't enter the picture either; this is a purely biological, statistical affair. Moonlight and lyric were simply links between them–'

'Do you believe that lyric is pornography?' I interjected.

'We don't need moonlight,' he said, a flash of crazed joy lighting up his eyes. 'We have a Ministry of Procreation. I repeat: The State is atheist.'

I then explained that a publisher had called me a pornographer because I'd attempted to express a personal opinion.

'Be careful,' he replied. 'Publishers are State servants like everyone else. In fact, much as in the same way that the State is a servant to the big financial conglomerates, lyric and the novel are prohibited as the natural enemies of cybernetics.'

'And we've come to this, doctor?' I said, though I should have said 'this is how far we've regressed', repeating that ancient misunderstanding between Solon and Thespis that I had already recounted to the lady at the front desk.

Regardless, I understood what was happening. If in humanist Greece, where there was freedom to procreate and eat roast meat, they judged fantasy to be dangerous, it was easy to see how the classical novel enthroning love might cause disquiet in the present state of affairs. The U.S. of Europe had more motive than Solon to be intransigent as it had fallen much further. Lyric would represent the dissolution of customs founded on people's faith in the atomic appliances industry and synthetic products, the symbol of which was *Hola-Hola*. It would mean contempt for advertising, without which industrialization is impossible; for open scrutiny, the primacy of criticality, and of depravation, etc. Yes, pornography was the right word.

'But is it possible for a young couple who love each other not to want to?' I asked. 'Can they remain chaste?'

My indignation was so great that I spouted drivel. I knew perfectly well that it was not about chastity. Sexual pleasures were subject to special protection: they were precisely the most efficient way of putting an end to lyric and amorous passions, proscribed from the moment Venus had been substituted by a ministry with accountants and a typing pool.

'Once we renounce the spirit,' I said in a clear, almost whispering voice, 'everything is permitted.'

The old doctor's wit switched once more to insane mode.

'If you want, I'll sell you two boxes of spirituality capsules.'

I pretended not to hear him. It seemed to me that without sentiment, pleasure was so slight that it must necessarily lead to tedium and aberration. I thought about the scene in the bath house with the young masochist and was quickly able to verify that this vice had indeed become common and perhaps constituted the beginning of a suicide complex that, according to the psychiatrist, characterised a society which had no issues with itself. No-one spoke of homosexuality now. Rather the concept had shifted. In Turclub homosexuality designated an individual who was attracted to a single sex, and this was considered sinful particularism whereas heterosexuality meant not making any kind of distinction whatsoever.*

'Surely there's an instinct that impels us toward the opposite sex, even though the State commands otherwise?' I objected.

'No-one's denying it,' insisted Orlando, 'but education corrects instinct. We weren't born to hang upside-down, but in the circus–'

'The circus is a distortion of physical culture,' I interjected.

'Or the perfection of it. But let's not discuss that, dear sir. Our social legislation determines that anyone can do whatever pleases them best with their body, although their spirit belongs to the collective and to business.'

* Twisting the etymology so that *homo*, instead of meaning *same*, meant *homme* [man].

It was an inverted vision of *El alcalde de Zalamea*'s humanism, precursor of the *Rights of Man*, and even of *Port Royal*.

'Doctor,' I said, 'there must be a minority in Turclub who disagree with the status quo.'

'There is,' he said softly, 'and they have a powerful ally. The Tyrant will be fought with the weapon that materialism considers most capital and that the Tyrant himself, in his blindness, foments.'

I looked at him questioningly.

'Hunger,' he said, 'is the curse of the gods, perhaps the original sin of man as he insists on eating instead of buying vacuum cleaners, atomic appliances and robots.'

He stopped talking as though lost, and I knew he would say no more. I suppose he didn't trust me.

In the waiting room a client looked in my direction, unsure whether to say hello or not, and I thought I knew him but couldn't recall who he might be. Out on the street I realised that I hadn't asked the doctor anything about Andrea Víctrix.

Pleasure Avenue traversed the old town, opening up onto the Einstein Arch at the end (ten centimetres higher than the *Arc de Triomphe de l'Étoile* in Paris), and resembled the Champs Élysées. At its opening were two busts on Roman plinths: Caesar to the right and Pompey to the left, finally reconciled.

Shaded by plastic trees and what Rubén Darío might have called 'the glorious flora of impish publicity', it was full of souvenir shops, travel agencies, Collective Orgy salons, cinemas and cafés whose terraces were adorned with statues and perfumed hydrangeas. Just as in the commercial district, on top of many buildings stood the shiny gold slogan that seemed to symbolize Turclub: PROGRESS CANNOT BE STOPPED.

People wore either short or long tunics, or togas of different colours, according to their Estate. A curious thing was that you never saw children younger than ten years old. Up to this age they were secluded in puericulture centres surrounded by gardens and among pedagogues who inculcated the principles of the new society via reiterative, subconscious methods. A few days before, I had accepted an invitation to take a look inside one of these establishments. The infants were singing Einstein's $E=mc^2$ equation by heart and those who couldn't talk yet had it embroidered on their clothing.

It was mid-afternoon and the streets and cafés were overflowing with people. I scanned the multitudes for Andrea. I hadn't seen her since the morning I returned to the living, when he or she had invited me so charmingly to ride in her car with a, '*Vuol venire con me?*' I remembered her golden hair falling in curls over a clear forehead and the pleasant, well-mannered smile of an educated young lady. Was she a she though? What about that harsh frown knitted into her eyebrows and the steely grip of her fingers? The svelte figure was androgynous, but her 'you've displeased me', as we parted was undoubtedly feminine.

Trying to distract myself, I people-watched and was surprised by the studied elegance of some of the restaurant customers. The biggest snobs ate with a spoon and fork according to the fashion decreed by the Classical University, but a huge majority daintily slurped green or pink juices through plastic straws. The chemical perfume of the hydrangeas, intense though it was, could not mask the fumes of the motorised vehicles. The air was thick and benefited the manufacturers of air-conditioning units. Feeling like a revolutionary, I recalled Quevedo's lines:

And the suffering people become wary
Lest the air they breathe also be taxed.

Recordings of melodious sirens were unable to conceal the roar of engines or the loudspeakers blaring out the merits of refrigerators, chicken stock tablets and *Hola-Hola*. Recently word had begun to spread that while such pandemonium is indicative of the potency of a country, it might not be pleasing to the mass of tourists. In Cannes, hotels were already advertising themselves as radio and TV-free zones, the ultimate in high-end luxury. As a consequence, venues equipped with systems that repeated the latest slogan at a higher volume than others began to spring up, and the authorities didn't dare intervene. Apart from the fact that the masses had become accustomed to the racket and their now shredded nerves needed it to calm their anxiety, would the industrialists tolerate the damage to their interests? And if they did, wouldn't huge unemployment and economic collapse be the result? The only practical recourse was to situate oneself beneath pneumatic bells supplied with air conditioning 'Imported from Mont Blanc by Aeroplane', as the headline went.

So, I bought the *Official News Bulletin* and sat myself down beneath my bell to read the in-depth article that every Thursday examines the indisputable progress of *Ciutat*, as we used to call Turclub. It was statistics-heavy and contained almost as many figures as words, this supremacy of numbers characterizing the New Era. Numbers, while exact, are somewhat purile, because they lack intentionality. Words have intention and spirit, but for that very reason they are subject to continuous evolution. Prudence would urge a harmony between the two systems. I fear, however, that it was precisely this harmony that had been lost from the new era.

According to the *Bulletin*, in Turclub there were two transistor radios per head of population, and every inhabitant had 42 metres of piping. The average in Stockholm was 50 metres, and in Paris, 46.07. But in Turclub the average was increasing by 8% annually, compared with only 4.26% in Stockholm, and an almost static 0.95% in Paris. 'Readers should draw their own conclusions,' said the article, knowing full well that only one conclusion could be drawn.

After examining the happiness of Turclub residents calculated in metres, the article moved on to discuss mental illnesses. The number of patients committed to clinics had increased by 25% in comparison with the last three-year period, which indicated the capacity and significance of such establishments, while at the same time this represented a paradoxical decrease in the number of cases of mental alienation since 62.02% more insane individuals were treated than two years ago. These incontrovertible statistics were proof of the obvious progress of psychiatry: if three years ago only 38% of those unwell were diagnosed, the percentage derived not from 38, but from 62.02. Here the author of the article faded into a fog of whereas, wherefores and a deliberation of relatives to conclude his thesis, which was predictably cheery and optimistic.

The essay was crystal clear for anyone with the time and inclination to decipher hieroglyphics, and ended with a eulogy to synthetic fruit, battery-farmed chicken, and lobsters from

Australia which arrive deep-frozen, sterilized, boiled, de-juiced and headless, ready to eat and served in a piquant sauce that prevents anyone from realising that they taste of cardboard.

Ill at ease, I put down the paper and unbuttoned my shirt. I was one of the few who hadn't adopted the classical style of dress. The June sun beat down on my glass bell and someone was looking at me curiously from outside. He was not in the first flush of youth and it seemed to me that I'd seen him somewhere before. Suddenly I recognized him: it was Dr Orlando's client who had hesitated to say hello in the waiting room. My unease increased and I felt dizzy, half-thinking I saw Andrea in the figure of a young female – or possibly male – crossing the street. I couldn't forget the time that she or he had kissed me in public in their Rolls convertible. The heat was suffocating and made me want to escape my isolating bell as rather than isolating me from the heat of the sun, it seemed to intensify it, presumably because of its curved shape. In the dome next to mine, someone fainted. I thought I noticed an expression of complaisance on the face of the person watching me. The heat was continuing to increase, and the Mont Blanc air now entered the bell with a strange taint of iron, oils and acids that made my chest tighten. Two more tourists were unconscious in another bell. The waiting staff, like beautiful archangels supervised by figures in tails jackets with lines of decorations on their chest, rushed to their aid and I emerged from the hushed cabin into noise and chaos. Loudspeakers advertised atomic appliances and medications which would cure everything except death and mechanical birds tweeted frenetically in the trees, some falling mute to the ground as the nuclear batteries that powered them ran out. Powerful atomizers belched out exaggerated aromatic plant scents, while syncopated music competed half-heartedly with propaganda for tranquillizers and sedatives. And above all of this, multilingual speaker systems from venues selling silence deafened the street: RADIO AND TV-FREE ZONES! THE ULTIMATE IN HIGH

END LUXURY!

Sirens calling for silence suddenly rang out – black light and alternating flashes of silver – and the birds, everything, fell quiet as a *maître d'hôtel* from my café readied himself to speak. Fat and dressed in tails adorned with medals, he approached. Two angelic bellboys carried a small platform covered with red velvet and, using them for support, the not insignificant person of the *maître* mounted it with difficulty.

Amid the now perfect silence, he explained that a faulty connection (mentioning in an aside that the establishment possessed 6620 metres of ducts) had caused mephitic air from a factory manufacturing toxic chemical products destined for disposal at sea to be injected into the isolating bells in place of Swiss air and that those affected would be conveyed at once by helicopter to an exclusive clinical facility at the establishment's expense.

After his address, the *maître* very deliberately and, in my view, needlessly, performed two or three ballet poses before descending from the platform with the help of his angels. The helicopter had arrived and was hovering near my bell but I indicated that I was feeling better and didn't need its help. It moved across to the tourists' bell and unfurled a red-silk rope with two hooks. They gave the tourists an unknown injection and, once secured in cellophane wrap, the two were hoisted into the helicopter to the applause of the public below. I found out later that they were already dead.

As I was about to leave, a red automobile drew up in front of me. The person behind the wheel was a picture of elegance in white Roman robes, had golden hair and was smiling at me. I approached, and was presented with a flower.

'It's a real rose,' she said, inviting me to climb in. '*Sente molto bene.*'

It was Andrea. Having thought about her for weeks and on many occasions believed I'd recognized her in different strangers, she had come to me in person, enchantingly, androgynously feminine. In truth, she was delightful, although she grasped my hand with fingers of steel.

'You're not still cross with me, are you?' she said, giving me a chocolate. 'What have you been up to? I was thinking of telephoning–'

'Perhaps it'd be better if you told me whether you're still driving into pedestrians,' I said, feeling resentful and beguiled at the same time.

Andrea (the name seemed female, but wasn't in the slightest. As she told me later, her eyes had first opened beneath the changeable skies of the Piazza Doria Procreation Laboratory in Liguria, and the name alluded to the great Genoese navigator). Andrea, as I was saying, smiled pleasantly.

'I've had no luck since we last saw each other,' Andrea said. What do you think of my new attire? I'm not sure why, but I wasn't keen on giving up the old jeans fashion. There's a new measure on the way, however, that will require (or rather, recommend) that people wear classical dress. It won't affect me, of course, but I feel morally obliged to set an example.'

'Why won't it affect you?' I asked.

'Because of my role,' laughed Andrea. 'Don't you know that I'm an important person? I answer directly to *Monsieur-Dame*.'

'Who is this *Monsieur-Dame*?' I asked. 'I heard mention of them the other day.'

'The President of the U.S. of Europe. The Unguent of the People. That's his title. As the symbol of the neuter state–'

'Why do you keep on with this subject?' I said, blushing.

'Will I be forced to wear Roman dress too? Will I have to be neutered?'

'Not forced, obviously. We'll persuade you. The Classical University has tabled the proposal and *Monsieur-Dame*, the epitome of refinement, will sign the order any day now. It's framed by reasoned arguments and drafted in the courtliest of terms. The Classical University has done a remarkable job. Their professors have in-depth knowledge of Greco-Roman customs and clothing. Only the *maîtres d'hôtel* and the hippies will be exempt. The former will continue in tails and the latter, at least until further instructions, may wear denim jeans.'

'Why the hippies?' I said.

'Oh, they've become part of the folklore and seem to appeal to some of the tourists. Our insistence on Roman fashion is intended to accentuate the elegance of the city, while at the same time it contributes to the erasure of gender difference, but in any event, since the hippies have never had a very clearly defined gender, they're not bothered either way.'

'And if I ignore these orders from *Monsieur-Dame*?'

'As I said, we'll persuade you,' replied Andrea.

'Who will?' I asked.

'Me.'

'I'd rather wear men's clothes,' I said, putting my arm around Andrea's waist. Seeming offended by this gesture, like a well brought-up young girl from before the great revolution of 1985, Andrea assured me that the world was free and that no-one was compelling anyone.

'Free?' I said. 'Your slogans and your brainwashing won't convince me. The atmosphere you live in is asphyxiating. Your freedom is a hypocrisy. In my time–'

'Our methods are to a great extent inspired by those of your time. Routine repetition, the Coué method, it's all very old. North America was a free country, yet it was governed by means of propaganda and slogans. Remember that the last president, and many others besides, triumphed because he had the money to buy himself the best possible *réclame*. On screens and in magazines, his smile appeared twenty times more often than his rival's, and he had better make-up. Make-up decided the election. The newspapers were full of it at the time.'

'Even so, you won't persuade me,' I replied.

'But seriously,' continued Andrea, 'what's the connection between classical dress and gender anyway?'

'You said that it can contribute–,' I started.

'And even if that were the case, who's interested in whether you're a man or a woman?' she replied, reddening slightly. 'This is about comfort and hygiene.'

'Many years ago, in the General's time, they used to say what you're saying now, but the other way around. Comfort and hygiene were invoked as a reason to wear trousers.'

'General Franco?' said Andrea, slowing down the car and glancing across at me. 'But you don't look thirty–'

'You're forgetting that I was frozen in 1965,' I said quickly, because I didn't enjoy talking about such things.

'You're right, hun; I didn't think. That explains a lot. You must have known Mistinguett. Did she really wear pink velvet and feathers in her hair?'

'It was the *belle époque*,' I replied.

'What an immoral era,' said Andrea, looking at me curiously, perhaps embarrassed. 'But it must have been delicious.'

'Immoral?' I replied. Thinking of the scene in the bathhouse, I relayed it to Andrea, exaggerating the masochistic details and my cynicism, because I suspected that she wouldn't be surprised, and indeed she wasn't.

'And what was unusual about that?' she said.

'Isn't this clearly sexual deviation, depravity?'

'But hun,' she replied, 'there is no such thing as sexual deviation. The human species hasn't been viviparous for a long time. No-one other than those chosen for the procreation laboratories is under any obligation to the species. Do you really mean to say that similar things didn't happen before? There've always been masochists–'

'Amongst the wretched and coarse, yes. Not among decent people,' I said.

'Who were the decent?' said Andrea.

'Those who got married, had children, etc.,' I replied.

'Children they recognized, and who called them "Mummy" and "Daddy"?' said Andrea. 'Do you think that we could have established a social state like ours on such a particularistic foundation?'

'What I don't believe is that your regime is as necessary as you seem to think it is,' I replied.

'That's enough,' said Andrea.

'Why?'

'You dare blaspheme against the State?' asked Andrea.

'Why shouldn't I?' I said.

Andrea slammed on the brakes.

'I'm a major figure in the Party,' she said with fear in her eyes.

'The Party?' I exclaimed. 'What kind of "Party" is it if there's no opposition, no critique?' Though I didn't realise it at the time, my words came as a body blow to Andrea.

'You're a sophist,' she said. 'An atheist. You don't believe in anything constructive.'

'And you do?' I replied.

'Yes, I do. The future must be gregarious. We're working towards erasing what humanists call the "personality" of man, moving towards the reign of pure intelligence, which will prepare for the advent of the Collective Being... What Teilhard de Chardin named the Noosphere.'

'I knew Teilhard de Chardin. He was a mad old man.'

'He was a pure socialist, purer even than Karl Marx,' replied Andrea. 'We've come so far, and we can't turn against the State on the basis of individual and family whim. Don't you think?'

'Are you trying to convert me?' I asked.

She nodded, and I was so moved by her sincerity in showing me her intentions with such candour that I felt at that moment the first pangs of possible love for her.

'I'm grateful,' I said, 'but… you have always said to me that we should use our faculty of reason, though I think you too freely admit many articles of faith such as the idea that the only possible civilization must be socialist.'

'We desire the common good,' said Andrea.

'But in exchange for individual discomfort,' I said.

'Discomfort?'

'Lack of freedom,' I continued. 'Although I know that's a meaningless concept for those who haven't known it.'

'And I know that for the romantics of your era, freedom meant libertinism.'

We weren't on the same wavelength. We had no common vocabulary. Andrea expressed herself like a communist and desired the good of the masses like a Russian in the old times of Lenin, but she had forgotten that the communist system had created a new nobility of officials, technocrats, and business leaders who had much in common with the counts of the Middle Ages. At just eighteen years old, and judging by her white robes and magnificent Rolls Royce, she herself was a patrician.

'I'm Director of Pleasure for the Mediterranean Region,' she said, smiling. 'I am in fact noble, but my nobility begins and ends with me. That's the difference. When they honour me with the responsibility of entertaining foreigners, it is because I deserve it, but it would be unfair if the respect I am due having been anointed by popular power were passed to my–'

She fell suddenly silent, and her face coloured.

'You were going to say "to my descendants",' I said, smiling ironically.

'So?' said Andrea, glaring at me aggressively.

'So it has always been considered natural to honour the

descendants of luminaries.'

'Man has his own worth,' replied Andrea.

'And what he has behind him. Would you deny your inheritance? Even in great racehorses they look for the sire and dam. I'm very happy to have ancestors whose bloodline I can trace back to the sixteenth century.'

'Let's not speak of such things, please! They're repugnant,' she exclaimed, horrified. 'Man has his own worth,' she repeated, the repetition making me wonder if she was not wholly convinced. 'The notion of family, their prejudices and particularisms, constitutes a sin. We have to allow the humble to rise, don't you think?'

'The humble?' I replied, surprised.

'Yes, the poor of spirit–'

'But Andrea,' I went on, 'these are precisely the people who will never be able to rise on their own merits. Your system is even crueller than those of the old regimes, and they really were cruel. If the weak have any chance of bettering themselves, it's through inheritance. You yourself are an example: if you weren't young and beautiful, or rather strong and commanding, you wouldn't have got anywhere–'

'I should remind you, hun,' Andrea retorted, 'that by addressing me as female you're breaking the law.'

'It's not deliberate, Andrea,' I assured her, lying, because I particularly enjoyed treating her as though she were a girl. 'In my old-fashioned language, we don't use the neuter to refer to people.'

'I understand,' she said. 'You may address me as you wish but take care that you're not overheard or they'll exile you to the New York wildernesses.'

I was about to say, 'if you're not humiliated by my getting your sex wrong', but she didn't let me finish.

'I'm more intelligent than you suppose,' she smiled, 'and I know what you're thinking. I believe in the law and I respect it. My mission is to entertain those outsiders who come here, and indeed everyone, but it is not to blaspheme. Tell me what you want from me. I gave you a real rose that cost eight-hundred strong francs. Would you like some oranges?'

'I'd like to kiss you,' I said.

Andrea stopped the car.

'So kiss me,' she said.

The street was busy and we were on full display.

'Actually,' I said, suddenly embarrassed, 'keep going.'

'As you wish,' said Andrea. 'You may do anything you like, but do not disrespect the dogmas.'

'And if I enjoy blaspheming?'

Andrea stopped the car again and looked at me with cold blue eyes. At that moment I was thankful that I hadn't kissed her. She was suddenly a man, a terrible man.

'I should have you locked up in an asylum,' she said.

'You?' I said. 'I'd like to see it!'

'I'm noble,' she reacted unexpectedly, 'and I demand that you address me as Your Excellency.'

She had been born in a Genoese hospice, didn't know her parents, her profession was to give herself to anyone, but she considered herself noble. I couldn't help but burst out laughing.

A swift punch landed hard and put an end to my hilarity. I straightened to repel the attack and was hit again with even more force. I fell out of the car and struggled to breathe from the shock. I'm a strong thirty-year-old and in the prime of life. She seemed so delicate and was only eighteen. I could never have imagined being overpowered like that. She demolished me. Two police officers approached with shields and helmets and, catching sight of the eagle on Andrea's cloak, they bowed and kissed her neck.

'Take this foreigner away,' Andrea ordered.

THE STATE OF UNIFIED EUROPE IS THE BEST STATE IN
HISTORY. THE BEST STATE, THE ONLY INDISPUTABLE
STATE. THE STATE OF UNIFIED EUROPE IS...

Yes indeed, 'the best State, the only indisputable State'. As
soon as I had entered the asylum, they had given me an electric shock. Now, as I began to come round, an almost purring
loudspeaker was repeating the slogan of orthodoxy at regular
intervals. Fifty, one-hundred, three-hundred times. I had been
interned accused of blasphemy, of which I was undoubtedly
guilty. They called themselves progressives and yet were trying
to paralyse History. The irony! A young doctor with a pleasant
demeanour came up to me.

'Doctor,' I said, 'I'm not yet as corrupted as your contemporaries. Can't you turn that machine off?'

The doctor turned a key and there was silence.

'Cryo-cure in 1965?' he asked in a friendly tone of voice.
'But that's why you need to be re-educated, to keep you out of
trouble. It's for your own good.'

'These slogans are far too puerile for an old liberal like me,
don't you think?' I replied.

'I'm not familiar with those times, Sir,' he said, seeming to
gently mock me.

'Can I ask what your name is?'

'Dr Nicola,' he said, before kissing me on the forehead and
walking away to attend to other business.

In the grounds of the sanatorium there was a park that
dominated the bay. I Instinctively looked for the old cathedral
begun in Jaume 1's time, but couldn't see it. It had been transformed into a functional, chocolate-coloured block destined for

some utilitarian purpose. The view was brightened by numerous highly coloured plastic flowers that overflowed the borders and pots in veritable cascades. They changed, or were changed, every day. Though artificial, the scent they gave off was pleasant in moments of breeze, but under a heavy sky without wind, it could be suffocating. What's more, the constant, identical and repeated rotation of flowers that had first piqued my interest because of its novelty value had become predictable and even more monotonous than had the flowers not moved at all.

I asked for a book and was given a treatise on aeronautics, from which I learned that air currents, which I had always imagined to be horizontal, are more frequently vertical, and also more powerful. I wasn't interested and requested some poetry, of a type I'd be permitted to read. They handed me a poetry magazine full of propaganda. When I underwent the cryo-cure, the fashion was for social poetry which related sordid scenes and accidents of workers who fell from scaffolding. Now, though congenital stupidity was still with us, the wind had changed and the weathervane was pointing to the interests of the big industrialists. Castilian hendecasyllables, French alexandrines, Tuscan sonnets, all scanning beautifully, sat proudly on the page and sang the excellence of sedatives, refrigerators and *Hola-Hola*. The joke was too much. I lost my temper and hurled the magazine to the floor before an orderly approached and delivered an immense electric shock. When I came to, a sweet, unctuous voice was whispering from beneath my pillow: DISTINGUISHED CLIENTS MADE TO CHOOSE, PREFER MINERVA FOR THEIR SHOES...

I asked them to turn off the loudspeaker, and they did. The next day I had the impression that while I was sleeping, I could hear voices selling electric vacuum cleaners and sedatives. It was difficult to be sure because as I began to wake up and pay attention, the voices fell silent. And then I discovered the trick: the loudspeaker responded to the sound of my breathing and snoring. I tried pretending to be asleep, snoring, and straight away the voices started up again, quietly to begin with and then in crescendo: COFFEE-MAKERS, SCALES, MIXERS, COOKERS, GRINDERS, FREEZERS, REFRIGERATORS, BEER...

They were trying to replicate the commercial, somewhat social literature well-known in my time,* intercalating slogans praising the State between the adverts. As soon as I sat up, the voice stopped and I realised that they were trying to re-educate me by hypnopaedia.

With nothing to interest me in my fellow sanatorium patients, I instead sought refuge in solitary corners of the park, which were attractive in the fashion of a theatrical set. One morning, in a Galant opera-style summer house, I came across Lola, who like me was fleeing the other patients. It was hot and she was reclining on a bench and had undone her blouse. She had breasts and was a real, attractive woman around forty years old. I excused myself and made to leave, but she called me back.

'Yes,' she said, seeing that I was looking at her, 'I'm a woman like women used to be, daughter of a mother and father. I've heard that you, too, are viviparous.'

'Frozen in 1965,' I said.

'We're almost the same age,' she replied (subtracting a couple of years from her calculation). 'Before the Great Revolution, I was a prostitute. I still am, of course, in spite of the ruinous competition. Nowadays, all of us, women and "fairies", as they call them, are doing the same thing, and almost always for free, which is an even greater vice, depending on how you look at it.'

'A sin of intrusion,' I said, laughing.

She was an ordinary woman with a certain rough-around-the-edges look characteristic of low-status professionals, but pleasant enough and I explained that I wasn't mad but had been confined there for blasphemy.

---

* The voices announcing consumer goods are taken from the Balearic Press from 1963 onwards.

'The same happens to all of us, as offspring of parents,' she replied. 'They want to get rid of us. Do you believe in the Messiah?'

'I don't know what you're talking about,' I replied. 'I'm not Jewish.'

'It's nothing to do with being Jewish. There's a psychiatrist who they say is going to bring redemption to us all. But I see you don't know him,' she added, suddenly addressing me more informally. 'I'm Lola by the way.'

'*Us all*, Lola?' I said, 'who exactly is waiting for the Messiah, and who is this redeemer?'

'I like you,' she said, looking at me distrustfully. 'I, well you know, I like almost all men, but I don't try... I'm already under suspicion and I can't afford to get myself into any more fixes. I don't want to be exiled to the Americas.'

She wasn't badly thought of for working as a prostitute, but rather for being disloyal to the philocommunist Regime and for not presenting herself as sufficiently 'undifferentiated'.

'There are almost no men left,' she continued. 'I mean, I can't get on with battery chickens that don't taste of anything, even with saccharine. These are dark days for anyone who's known French cuisine. Ah, my darling, those Marseilles bouillabaisses! And the flowers! Have you noticed that they're the same colour as the refuse containers?'

Lola was right. I hadn't noticed, but once she'd pointed it out, those sulphur yellows and ridiculous pinks of the containers, planters and basins, repeated in identical series, ended up making me hate those flowers. And the kitchen soap had the same scent.

'Believe me,' she said, 'they intend to finish us off. They're after me because my style of dress is too feminine. They say that they want to reform us! Well, we need to be shameless about this. If we don't play their game, they'll ship us off to New York. Don't trust the doctors. They kiss you on the forehead, or on the lips, the dirty beasts, and then they go for you. Talk about taking liberties. I like Dr Nicola but he's the worst of them all, right in *Monsieur-Dame*'s pocket–'

'Does Nicola have much influence around here?'

'Here and in Paris. Apparently, he's a linchpin of the Regime and has ways of getting things done. Be careful around him. Do they talk to you when you're asleep, try to get you to buy atomic appliances? They're all shareholders, you know.'

'I get the propaganda, yes, like everyone, I suppose.'

'Well, I don't want atomic appliances in my house,' said Lola. 'They already duped me into buying a robot on a purchase plan, and I'm still paying the instalments. On the very first day when it finished washing the dishes, it opened the window and threw them out onto the street. Of course, I complained to the shop and told them a few home truths, as you would. They listened and made a note, but from then on they've had me under surveillance as an 'obstructionist'. It's all a big con. The State reduces taxes, but it's in cahoots with the industrialists to suck the blood of those of us who work for a living. People are dying of hunger, surviving on vitamins, just getting by, and yet obsessed with buying appliances. It's as though they're under a spell. And be really careful what you say.'

'Yes, I know,' I said. 'I upset a waiter and–'

She looked at me, horrified.

'You tried it on with a waiter? But they're the highest nobility! And was this waiter from a good restaurant?'

'*Le Gaulois*,' I replied.

'*Le Gaulois*? You're brave! That's a good restaurant, absolutely. I've had dinner there on occasion.'

'Do you know the lady who runs front of house?' I said, suddenly having an idea.

'No, why?'

'If you've eaten there, you'll have seen her. I want to know whether she's a woman or a man.'

'I remember... Dresses in black, pearl necklace?'

'Precisely,' I said.

'I think she's a woman.'

'Well she's a man, or so she says,' I said.

'Maybe. Are you interested?'

'Not really. And a girl, or youth, who drives a red Rolls, have you come across him, or her? He's in charge of the Pleasure Bureau.'

'Andrea Víctrix?' said Lola. 'Everyone knows him. He's the most important person in the Mediterranean. Have you met?'

'Yes,' I said. 'He invited me to ride in his car. But he, she must be female, right?'

Lola didn't hesitate.

'He's male,' she said, quickly.

'Not possible,' I replied, feeling the blood rushing to my cheeks. 'You're talking nonsense.'

'He's a modern boy,' said Lola, 'refined, a sissy.'

'Shut up,' I said, angrily.

She ignored me and smiled.

'And they even say that although he has this incredibly important role, he had parents, like you and I.'

'Are you sure?'

'No,' said Lola, shrugging. 'That's just what they say. But I am sure he's queer.'

She later confessed that she'd said some of those things so that I would hate Andrea.

'I'm sure she's female,' I replied. 'I don't believe you.'

'So ask him.'

'She didn't want to tell me,' I said.

'That's odd,' said Lola, 'because it has so little importance these days...'

I thought the opposite. The directive was that it had no importance, which meant that it was important, and it was logical that it would be. The State and regulated economy were founded on rigorously controlled oviparous procreation: it was intangible, religious dogma, yet in that secular religion from time to time there were heretics. It had not even been two years since a young French woman, Marie Mercier, had been about to cause a schism with a scandalous book about maternal love and simple family pleasures in a Provençal manoir. The work bore an epigraph by Aina Cohen, the delicate Mediterranean poet who had died in Mallorca at the end of the Spanish Second Republic. Mercier had gathered quite a following and, in Avignon, a thousand romantic virgins had protested in front of the Prefecture waving obscene placards which called for 'the right to be mothers and to nourish children with our own milk'. The movement was quashed and nearly four-hundred virgins lost their lives, but it captured the popular imagination. *Senyoreta* Mercier had to make a public retraction before the professors of the Sorbonne, but there remained volatile pockets that posed a threat to a civilization reputed to be the best possible; that's to say, definitive. Some of the women who still had breasts and hips made a public show of their inconvenient femininity and there was no shortage of bohemians to resurrect old Mexican songs, declaring themselves tough guys and rioting, calling for real potatoes and salt cod with rice. Moreover, and even more seriously, some critically minded spirits – damned intellectuals, as always – began to doubt the efficacy of the piles of atomic appliances that couldn't possibly be squeezed into the minuscule apartments. The case of Lola's robot wasn't unusual. Those mechanical servants were so expensive that if you bought one, you'd be paying it off for the rest of your life, and they often played foul tricks. If so much as a screw worked loose in its incredibly complex electronic brain, a catastrophe was inevitable. The most terrible recorded had been at the Hotel Platja, where a robot afflicted by mechanical insanity went on a rampage stabbing guests until its head exploded like a bomb and destroyed the building.

I was walking deep in thought through the sanatorium park when, as I turned a corner, I came across Andrea. Having seen me from a distance, she was waiting for me in the Rolls with the hood down. The breeze ruffled her white garments and played lightly through her golden hair, a spectacle of triumphant youth on that glorious July morning more than justifying the name which had been bestowed on her. Though the battle of Pharsalus was by now far from people's consciousness, and while almost nothing remained of what had been historically prestigious and beautiful, no-one could have been insensible to such a tangible, human beauty.

She lacked – if one ascribes to classical tenets – breasts and hips, and was certainly rather slender, but she had a delicate style and a deliciously feminine – or should I say androgynous – shape, and made a truly elegant model for those robes. She was only eighteen years old and her curves were not yet fully developed. The unification heralded by moralists, founded on sterilization and gymnastics training, was now a reality almost from infancy through to maturity. It was perhaps true that after middle-age women still presented a tendency to become voluptuous, but by that stage they were no longer considered a danger to social stability.

'You should have a spear in your right hand,' I said, forgetting the grievances I bore her.

'Why a spear?' Andrea replied. 'I've come to see you in peace. Are you still angry with me?'

The words brought back my quite justified annoyance and humiliation at the beating that apparently fragile creature had given me. Her ingenuousness had a certain grace all the same and she evidently had friendly intentions, but I wasn't about to let it go so easily.

'You tell me,' I said.

'I had you interned here so that you wouldn't end up in prison,' said Andrea.

'What a kind heart you have, Andrea! You could have avoided that by running me over in your Rolls.'

Her normally bright eyes lost their warmth. She curled her lip in distaste and for the first time I noticed that one of her teeth was imperfect.

'Why do you always censure me for doing my duty and looking after the wellbeing of my people?' she asked, sadly.

She explained that exterminating pedestrians who break the highway code saves both lives and annoyance. She quoted statistics. We could never escape them. Although the number of accidents was rising in absolute terms, indicating clear mechanical progress, in relative terms there was a reduction. The number of vehicles increased every month by a factor of ten, and the number of victims by a factor of eight. The higher the percentage of vehicles, the lower the percentage of accidents. Naturally, and this was basic mathematics, the day we reached an infinite number of vehicles, the percentage of accidents would not only drop to zero but would end up being a negative quantity. Every day it became more difficult to hunt pedestrians, precisely because they were all trying to stay alive.

'But when we run out of victims,' I said to Andrea, 'people will start to take risks and there'll be more victims again.'

'And we'll hunt them again,' she replied.

'So there will always be victims.'

Both Andrea and I were playing at sophistry and she called me out on mine.

'In your time,' she said, 'you used to do the same, but you were more hypocritical about it. Stepping off the pavement on a Paris boulevard carried a death sentence.'

'What rubbish!' I laughed. 'There's never been any such penalty.'

'Because you were more hypocritical. The State turned a blind eye, but the reality is that stepping into the road at many times of day meant instantaneous death. You, hun, are an obstructionist.'

'No doubt,' I said.

'Are you humouring me?' asked Andrea.

'I think you're a benefactor of humanity,' I replied, and she nodded, my irony lost on her. 'And you accept honours for acting as executioner! Doesn't it horrify you knowing that you're making innocent people suffer?'

'But it's for the good of the majority,' said Andrea. 'It's proven that one victim saves 7.08. And they don't suffer. My Rolls is specially equipped. When I drive into someone, they are injected by ten sterilized needles, anaesthetized and killed almost simultaneously.'

'Why sterilized?!' I asked in shock. Andrea looked at me full of pity. She placed one of those fine, elegant, steel-like hands on my forehead and seemed about to kiss me. I pulled away sharply.

'Why are you shouting? You're right,' she continued. 'It's not actually necessary to use sterile needles, but what can I say... It's only polite not to use infected needles. Would it seem okay to spit on a dying person, even if they couldn't be saved? A little respect...'

So she was the one being respectful. Furious, I did what was customary in 1965, the year they put me into stasis: I launched into an eloquent, rhetorical speech, full of pathos and passion.

I realised that my attitude was absurd, Andrea had grown up in a different world from mine. She occupied a privileged position within the country's highest nobility and lived in a huge, Roman-style palazzo, set in a park amid cypresses and avenues lined with statues, and she received the ceremony appropriate to her rank. Even the president of the Waiters' Guild had to defer to her. The Directors of Mediterranean Pleasure were answerable only to the President of the U.S. of Europe,

Monsieur-Dame de Pompignac la Fleur, who threw parties at the Élysée and only occupied the presidency, so it was said, because they were strictly impartial, that's to say, hermaphroditic. Otherwise, *Monsieur-Dame* was utterly inept, but the excellent French administrators and heads of protocol, graduates of the Classical University, resolved many of their difficulties. In fact, real power rested with the big industrial conglomerates for whom *Monsieur-Dame* was careful to reserve his *bon plaisir* because he had no desire to be removed from his position. He was more interested in living at the Élysée and painting his fingernails than in governing. Andrea was loyal to *Monsieur-Dame* not only because she owed him her position, but because of her puritan temperament, which made her incapable of breaking an oath.

My speech would not work on Andrea because in just a few minutes of censure it attempted to unravel a life's worth of rationalist education. A more prudent approach would have been to distance myself from such a dangerous character, thanks to whom I'd been forcibly detained. I was on official record as a mad man suffering 'paranoid schizophrenia'. Such a diagnosis, together with having been born of parents, made it impossible for me to make my way in a world which, like it or not, was now mine, here and now. Viviparous citizens were closely monitored, and although at the beginning I hadn't thought it possible, we still constituted a threat. We couldn't dominate, but we could disrupt. The majority of my generation who had undergone the cryo-cure had not made it out, but some had been saved. My case wasn't unique in this respect. Lola was another, along with the diabetic I had seen at Dr Orlando's consulting room, as well as a good number of others.

There were also those more transgressive sorts who completely disregarded the law and continued to bear children illegally. To try to prevent this, every human being – with the exception of those destined for the four Global Procreation centres – was subject to sterilization by radiation. Some, however, manage to avoid it. And sometimes the sperm donors and surrogate females themselves worked privately, knowing full well that their crime was punishable by death. The U.S. of Europe – of the World, in fact – was clearly not very confident of their security, and this is what fed their intransigence in matters of dogma. Besides, the economic and social situation was not as splendid as the abundance of plastic flowers and verminous automobiles might suggest. Food was incredibly expensive and getting scarcer, and people were relying on extravagantly processed drinks to feed themselves. It was also true, as Dr Orlando had said, that many of those who were out in their cars and frequenting luxury restaurants, were also experiencing hunger.

Andrea got out of her Rolls, which was also her pedestal, and invited me to sit beneath a magnolia. After my great speech, I awaited what I imagined would be disastrous consequences. Our first two conversations had ended badly. Would this end in blows too? It was barely credible that this slim, aristocratic figure had knocked down a strong young man like me, thirty years old and in his prime. I knew Andrea took drugs. A combination of vitamins and sympathin called soma gave extraordinary strength to organisms until, worn out, death came quickly, suddenly and violently, accelerated further by injections of Parquidine. I looked at Andrea and couldn't quite remember how the scene of my defeat had come about. Hitting a woman (and I saw her essentially as a woman, a girl) is repugnant – at least it was in my time. I had probably just covered up, defended myself, and everyone knows that if you don't hit back, you stand no chance. I was overcome with a strange fury, a desire to throw myself at her and punch her until she broke down. A finely muscled thorax was visible through her dress, and I could make out the fragility of her ribs. I think I could have broken them with my fingers alone, and this would have given me a rare pleasure, a sadistic rush mixed with the tenderness that would surely follow as a consequence of such a brutal attack.

'Listen,' she said softly, her delicate yet steely grip on my knee. 'I'd like us to be good friends. We should talk seriously when you're calmer. Are you being treated well here?'

I had to admit that all the staff treated me well, although being taken for an imbecile was quite irritating.

'They're trying to re-educate me by filling my head with nonsense,' I complained. 'How can the current State be perfect if at the same time progress can't be stopped?'

'Hun,' said Andrea, 'it can't be stopped and nor should it be stopped. By order and maxim of *Monsieur-Dame.*'

'But if something is perfect, progress has already stopped,' I insisted.

Andrea looked at me sadly and stroked my hand.

'Is Dr Nicola behaving well towards you?'

'Yes, I have no complaints,' I said.

'I recommended you to him. He seems intelligent and polite, and he's known for his tact.'

He was. However, I found his facial expressions disconcerting. I couldn't untangle the mixture of mockery and sadness with which he sometimes addressed me. He was cordial, but also frank. It wasn't odd, I suppose, that he should be suspicious of a viviparous person.

'You're a difficult case,' said Andrea, 'and you pique my interest – may *Monsieur-Dame* forgive me. You must keep your distance from everyone. Kiss me, and have this magnolia: *Questi fiori sentono molto bene.*'

She tried to hand me one but couldn't detach it from the stem. I smiled. Whether a male or female, she hadn't kissed me. She'd said, 'kiss me' and had made space for masculine initiative, as no doubt she was aware.

'It's plastic,' I had the impertinence to remark.

'Of course it is,' she said. 'What was I thinking... Did you have natural magnolias in your time?'

'Magnolias, oranges, birds...'

'It must have been a real threat to the plastics industry... Was everyone rich?'

'We were all both poorer and richer than we are now, Andrea.'

'Why do you say things that no-one can understand?' she said, stroking my neck with two fingers.

Everything seemed clear enough to me.

'We have to see each other often,' she went on. 'I have to conquer you.'

'You want to convert me to the religion of plastic flowers?'

'I think you're teasing me. Thanks to plastic, the poor can have access to artificial flowers now. That's progress.'

'It's a step backwards,' I insisted. 'Now the rich don't have real flowers. Almost everyone could have them before. They grew all over the countryside–'

'We'll talk about that,' she said, deep in thought. 'These economic issues...'

She was right. Everything, including flowers, was subordinated to the economy, and despite its sheen of luxury, the economy was in trouble. Apart from the shortage of food, or *disette*, to resuscitate an old word from the French Revolution, you had to be the Director of the Bureau of Pleasure, or very nearly, if you wanted to obtain a real rose.

'We can talk about economics or whatever you want,' I said, in the mood for an argument, 'but first I'd like my freedom back.'

'Nothing easier,' came the reply. 'You can come with me now. I'll sign the release.'

'You're a powerful woman.'

'What are you getting at?' she laughed, looking at me apprehensively.

'You remind me of Louis xiv of France,' I said, 'the Sun King: "I am the State".'

She blushed bright red as though I had insulted her and seemed about to lose control. Upset, she apologised, though I thought it foolish because she must have known that she would sooner seduce me through her charms than by being reasonable.

'Those old autocrats were driven by pride,' she said. 'I, of course, have the authority to determine the fate of those whom I like or dislike, because I am Director of Pleasure. In the same way that the engineer builds the bridge according to his engineering knowledge. Modern democracy doesn't exclude technical categories.'

'Of course not,' I replied. 'It imposes them more every day. It was already the case in my time that in the big North-American atomic factories (North America back then being the epitome of democracy), the physicists wore badges indicating their category and were only permitted to speak to those who bore the same insignia.'

Andrea blinked.

'And that surprises you?'

'Not at all!' I exclaimed. 'You've jumped out of the frying pan and into a major conflagration.'

'Anyway, hun, they wouldn't have been able to understand each other. At that level of ultra-specialization, they no longer had a common vocabulary. It's the same with us. Everyone in their rightful place. Technologies demand–'

'That's right,' I interrupted. 'But you won't deny that these closed circles... Today more than ever, what Einstein said rings true: "Those who have the power to make far-reaching decisions, for good or ill, constitute a cryptocracy".'

'Cryptocracy?' said Andrea.

'A sealed clan. Sealed tighter than a Duchess's salon in Marcel Proust.'

'You're quite the original,' she laughed, somewhat unsettled. 'Come with me. Let's have some fun.'

She was due to dine with a dignitary, the director of a plastic carnation factory, and she proposed that we go together.

'But surely he's expecting you to come alone,' I said.

'Yes,' replied Andrea, 'he wants to have fun. He's bored.'

'Then I won't come.'

'Why not?' she said. 'He might like you more than he likes me.'

I thought it unbecoming to show my indignation in response to such an uncomfortable proposition but she wouldn't have understood so I limited myself to saying that I didn't want him to like me and she blinked again in her characteristic manner.

'But he's here to be entertained,' she insisted. '*Monsieur-Dame* has personally recommended him.'

'I don't want to entertain him,' I said, stubbornly. 'And don't talk to me about such people.'

For a moment Andrea's eyes were filled with anger at the cruelty and insolence of a reply that not only went against State policy but also transgressed the eighteenth century-style courtesy which *Monsieur-Dame* de Pompignac la Fleur, in conjunction with the Classical University, was attempting to re-establish while powdering his nose at the Élysée. Andrea's demeanour transformed and she had all the hauteur of the Sun King.

'And you say that to me, knowing that I am the Director of the Bureau of Pleasure?'

It didn't end in blows as on the previous occasion, but it was close.

'You are indeed Director of Pleasure,' I replied, 'and much good may it do you. I, however, am not and I have no intention of entertaining anyone. Goodbye.'

'Don't you want to kiss me?' she said.

'No,' I said. 'Go away.'

She got into her car, dignified and stoical.

'I'll send you some chocolate,' she said, starting the engine.

I had a restless night thinking about Andrea and fearing that the hypnopaedia voices would instil strange beliefs in me. I didn't want them to alter my personality. I wanted to be myself or die; I wanted to love a woman all to myself or not love at all. I was not disposed to entertain a millionaire who produced plastic carnations from the same materials and of the same colours as the waste containers. I'd had enough of synthetic oranges and *Hola-Hola* and I found the perfume emanating from the flowers in the park disagreeable. I could write a book about those aberrations but who would dare publish it? I decided to entrust it to Nicola. He seemed to me to be an intelligent sort of enemy, and anyway, what did I have to lose? Within the limitations of the dogmatic fanaticism that characterized the Regime, he at least lacked the boorish spirit of the majority of his contemporaries. In medical matters, for example, he didn't simply drink in the propaganda, but instead looked for the truth without openly distancing himself from the suffocating atmosphere. He was diplomatic, reserved, and at the moment was the only human being with whom I could talk freely. A few days before he had confessed to me that for some time, the human lifespan had seemed to be shortening, although he was careful to note that little could be concluded from the limited data.

'And we have to take into account,' he added, 'the significant number of car accidents.'

'Don't you think,' I asked him, 'that when socialised medicine becomes depersonalised, it's less effective for the patient?'

'Before I answer,' he said, 'I would have to ask you whether you believe that it'd be possible today to practise medicine tailored to the individual, as before. If we now have a production-line approach, it's because the level of technical complexity would make it terrifically expensive–'

'I understand that you'd rather not respond,' I interrupted. 'I'm talking about medicine, and you're talking about social and economic matters. Moreover, you appear to think that the present state of political and economic affairs is inviolable.'

'Experiences shows us,' said Nicola, 'that progress is difficult to slow down. Louis XVI didn't want his armies to use machine-guns because he considered them too cruel, and Einstein was aghast at the march of atomic progress and died cursing it. Futile. It was too late.'

'You might be right. As the Regime's slogan says, PRO-GRESS CANNOT BE STOPPED, but that doesn't say much in favour of progress. It's not an optimistic perspective: it's machinery escaping the control of those who designed it...'

'Go on,' he said, eyeing me closely.

Was he inviting me to blaspheme? I wasn't sure whether to trust him, but fear didn't hold me back.

'The civilization that you defend, doctor, will end in catastrophe,' I said.

'You believe so?' replied Nicola, smiling inscrutably. He was inviting me to blaspheme, his expression enigmatic. He must be only a few years older than me and it occurred to me that there was something almost Asian about his features. Prudence would have demanded I stay quiet, so I did the opposite: I laid it on.

'Naturally!' I said. 'I'm detained here, a prisoner, I have nothing to lose, and the only thing I can do is protest...'

Though I couldn't even do that, knowing full well that my protest wouldn't make it beyond the walls of the asylum. Nicola must have thought similarly, and he looked at me without saying a word.

'Be that as it may,' I added, 'it's a fact that since doctors have become bureaucrats, no-one believes them anymore. People will end up doing without you.'

'You're right,' said Nicola. 'Dr Orlando has more clients

than many of us, and there's no way around the problem you mention. On the other hand, we can't deny that public health has improved. Plague, typhoid–'

'There are fewer sufferers of typhoid and more people are sectioned,' I retorted, 'fewer consumptives and more cases of lung cancer. Does a change of names constitute progress in the eyes of the Regime?'

'At least we've overcome the great pandemics of former times, haven't we?' said Nicola.

'And replaced them with automobile carnage. You may object that I'm confusing medicine with motoring, but both are products of the era and of the Regime, of technology. The Industrial Era is inhuman.'

'Though you might think you have nothing to lose with such statements,' he said, now serious, 'you're running the risk that this temporary confinement you're subject to will become permanent, or worse. Please give it some thought. Andrea is protecting you very particularly, but even Andrea's influence is limited. Can we speak as friends? If you want to rebel, be a bit more discreet about it and talk in whispers. I say that as a friend.'

Be more discreet. Yes, it had occurred to me. Andrea was protecting me 'very particularly', as Nicola had just said. Perhaps if I were to ally myself with other subversives, I could attempt to start a revolution by betraying Andrea and extracting State secrets and money from her. Of course, I would never do it, even if she did propose monstrous things such as entertaining millionaires who infest the world with plastic carnations.

Thoughts of rebellion made me restless that night and I drifted off to sleep in the early morning. When I awoke, Dr Nicola was by my pillow with a packet of chocolate.

'Andrea Víctrix has just sent this gift,' he said, 'along with an order to release you.'

He was smiling benignly. Where had I seen that smile before, apparently gracious but oscillating between scorn and

ridicule? Ah yes, the Hoggar, in southern Algeria. The lad who accompanied me on excursions had looked up, surprised by the sight of a plane. He had never seen one but hadn't wanted to say so. 'It's an aeroplane,' I'd said to him. That's when I saw that same smile Nicola now bore, and he changed the subject.

I took the chocolate and instinctively searched for a note.

'Hasn't she written to me?' I asked, disappointed.

The doctor shook his head.

'There's a card with the insignia, the eagles of Victory, but of course no written note.'

'Doesn't she know how to write?' I quipped.

'Possibly not. Few people of that age and rank do...'

Nicola seemed to be taunting me, but his words weren't at all unusual. In fact, I could have guessed what he'd say. Radios, television sets, and omnipresent images were squeezing out writing. So the rebel book I had been writing for Andrea – had it been for anyone else I'd have been exiled to the deserts of Massachusetts – wouldn't even be read? Is that what it had come to? I remembered an anecdote concerning an aunt of mine, a grand lady who would now be almost two and a half centuries old, and who had been almost illiterate. The lady had left a holographic last will and testament full of nonsense and orthographic experiments and the lawyer charged with opening it had observed to the heirs that the composition was that of a lady who had never learned to write 'because she had never needed to'.

As I felt myself overcome with sadness and irritation at this state of affairs, Andrea's sweet voice came through by electronic transmission.

'Join me at the Einstein restaurant, my friend, for aperitifs. You're free. Sending you an affectionate kiss.'

And thus, in the *Iliad*, did the gods soothe their favourites with winged words. Andrea's voice produced a great peace in me and, emotional as I was, I took Nicola's hand and he looked at me with melancholic seriousness. The goddess's voice came across the airwaves again.

'My friend,' she said, 'would you like to bathe in warm water and have masseurs anoint your well-formed body with scented oils?'

They were Homer's words again, refined and primitive, and I was stunned.

'I would like to fall asleep always listening to your voice,' I replied.

Dr Nicola leaned over to me and applied gauze to my nostrils.

'Breathe deeply,' he said and I breathed in and drifted off to sleep to the sound of Andrea's voice, not now speaking words, but singing musical notes.

When I came round, I was lying naked on a table, surrounded by masseurs and assistants. Two black children were anointing my body with aromatic oils.

'What's going on?' I asked.

Dr Nicola smiled like the lad in the Hoggar.

'Andrea has ordered that we look after your physique and honour you as a hero.'

'Me, a hero?'

'You,' he replied. '*C'est son bon plaisir.* You've pleased her.'

I couldn't catch his nuance. It occurred to me that decades previously I had met a gentleman whose title was Count of Royal Appreciation. It seems that history has a habit of repeating itself.

A few kilometres away from the halls of the Palazzo Víctrix, the goddess was following and conducting the pagan ceremony via a screen.

'Put pink pomade in his belly button,' she said in a soft, cheerful voice, taking an efficient interest, thrilled at witnessing a job well done. 'Paint his toenails red. And a crown of laurel like Caesar's on his brow. Roman robes...'

I can't deny it: so much flattery won me over. I felt a sense of wellbeing and a kind of exhibitionist pride that from a distance and out of context will seem ridiculous. When I was ready, still half-asleep through hypnotics and perfumes, I looked at myself in the mirror and liked what I saw. My blood raced euphorically. A nurse approached and gave me an injection to wake me up fully. It was as though a bee had stung me and left honey in the wound. Andrea, Director of Pleasure... I gave a splendid tip to the young attendants who had taken care of me, not caring that I was now penniless. The attendants shrieked joyfully and ran off turning somersaults, screaming like swifts. I was alone.

'Andrea,' I said quietly.

From kilometres away, my delightful friend replied.

'I'll send you a helicopter, hun. You'll be in the air and with me in three minutes.'

At that moment Lola walked in, provocative in a Gilda style from c.1950. She could have been a Giorgione. The warmth aroused by the memory and kindness of Andrea experienced something akin to the lash of a whip and detached itself from its creator to settle on the Renaissance paragon in front of my eyes.

'Andrea,' I exclaimed, 'I'm not moving from here unless you allow Lola to accompany me.'

I was expecting an almighty row, but Andrea's measured tones reached me through the clouds.

'That's not a problem, hun. It'd be very *gentile* on your part to invite her to come. Have you kissed her yet?'

'Not yet, goddess,' I replied. 'Do you want me to?'

'Yes, of course. You'll help me set her on the right path. I'm not one of her favourites. She doesn't like me.'

Lola overheard and unleashed a torrent of bad language and I only just had time to turn the dial of the machine so that it wouldn't carry to the Palazzo Víctrix.

'You're damned right I don't like that anaemic fairy, or whatever he is, fish or fowl... What's that about? And if you're not careful, they'll turn you into some kind of... It's already started, you've painted your toenails. Look, I'm no innocent schoolgirl and I've seen a lot in my profession, but there are things I find repugnant. That woman's dress you're wearing–'

'It's Roman costume,' I said, 'and it's the law.'

'And the Romans,' she shot back, 'weren't they all filthy fairies?'

Anger made her eyes beautiful and I looked at her, laughing.

'You know your history,' I said.

'And you have no shame.'

Poor Lola. Though I wasn't yet twenty-nine, I knew how to extinguish that flame, how to calm that troubled psyche. But just I was about to take her in my arms, a helicopter sent by Andrea bearing the imperial eagle insignia arrived. Dr Nicola accompanied us as we ceremoniously embarked.

Andrea was waiting for us on the uppermost terrace of the Einstein restaurant. Standing against a backdrop of cypress trees and jasmines, she was surrounded by two *maîtres d'* and six young Ibizan waiters between about ten and twelve years old, dressed as angels. Andrea's hair was blonde and the midday sun gave a golden glow to her skin. So resplendent was she in her yellow satin tunic that she appeared entirely gilded. Loving and tranquil, she kissed my forehead and inclined her head so that I might kiss her on the neck between the jawbone and clavicle, close to her ear, as ceremony demanded. The mysterious prestige of world dignitaries! Lola flinched. Andrea noticed, and spoke a few insignificant royal words to her designed to ease the conversation, but moments later the prostitute asked to be excused.

'We'll catch up later,' I said to her.

'Poor girl,' murmured Andrea. 'You did the right thing saying that you'd go to see her. We need to bring her over to our side. She still has influence in Turclub. And, you know? She seems to be in love with you.'

'What do you mean by "in love"?' I said.

'Physical love, of course,' replied Andrea.

The little Ibizans, almost black from the sun, served us synthetic fruit from a Moorish plate decorated with shiny metallic flecks. Andrea wanted to know how I'd been treated at the asylum, mentioning that Dr Nicola was wise and very loyal to the State.

'But he's never wanted to amuse himself with me,' continued Andrea. 'Naturally, I can't be attractive to everyone, though I try. Nevertheless, out of courtesy...'

'What more could Nicola possibly want?' I said under my breath, angry to hear her talk like that. 'He behaved kindly towards me. He even attended my bathing and anointing ceremony. But I noticed his expression was a little curious.'

'In what way?' asked Andrea.

'I don't know. Perhaps he's jealous of you spending so much time with me?'

'Jealous? Unthinkable. You yourself have said that he was attentive towards you.'

'But isn't it logical that it'd be you he's interested in?' I suggested. What I'd meant was that if he were friendly, it might well be as a result of Andrea's recommendation, but Andrea interpreted it in a different way altogether, and responded in a most upsetting fashion.

'You're wrong,' she said. 'If he desired me, he need only say the word. Listen, I need to ask your opinion about something: would you say the little waiters look fine as they are, or are they better naked? Not completely naked, of course. We'd need to cover their sex, but I don't know how. A golden clam shell, given that their skin's so dark? Would you like that?'

I told her that no, I wouldn't.

'Nor me. But until the sexes are completely unified, it's preferable that we shield those differences that do still exist from public view.'

'Still exist?' I asked.

'Apparently, in a few years there'll be no differences. They've discovered a hormone that can be injected into the foetus–'

'Look, leave them as they are,' I said, changing the subject. 'They have a certain charm as angels. Besides, they'd catch their death of cold.'

'I said the same, but they're now manufacturing pills that will increase the calories… It's a State secret at the moment. It'd ruin the textile industry if it were leaked. We'd run the risk of everyone going around naked.'

'If we were all naked, what would the ruin of a useless industry matter?' I asked.

'Though an important industry can't be wound up in two days, we know that at some point in the future we won't have a need for fabrics.'

Andrea explained that people would be swathed in vapours of the colour and temperature of their choosing. They'd wear a lighter-like gadget around their necks that would produce a screen to shield them from the cold and people's gazes. At the moment it was a distance away, however. Civilian applications of atomic technology were moving slowly because the military had priority. In any case, time was needed for manufacturers to adapt their processes to new products.

'I don't understand this protectionism,' I replied. 'This progress that you incessantly talk about is an obstacle. In the middle of the twentieth century, Teilhard de Chardin and other "moderns" fought against reactionaries they accused of being "immobilists". I could accuse you of the same. You're not evolving. It's the same story: all revolutionaries become immobilists.'

'How can you say such a thing?' said Andrea.

'Progress terrifies you,' I replied. 'You want to slow it down to protect vested interests. In an era of helicopters and nuclear energy, you persist with automobiles and combustion engines because you're afraid of the big trusts; you reject vapour screens because of the textile manufacturers. Don't you realise that this is the discourse of the *ancien régime*?'

Andrea looked at me; partly surprised, partly consternated. There was a pause before she said, 'That's not fair. How can you say that? Don't you listen to the Saturday economics lectures?'

'No, I don't.'

'You should. Our world rests on a complex economic foundation that takes more than a couple of minutes to explain. Anyway, I'm not an economist, even though my role is partly determined by the economy; wealth means pleasure, after all.'

'Are you certain,' I said, 'or is that just one of the many slogans in circulation?' She looked wary, and it was clear she wasn't sure. 'Given you enjoy quoting statistics so much, it'd be very difficult to make you see that some of the poor are happier than the rich.'

'Don't think me so foolish that I haven't sometimes noticed this,' said Andrea, 'but my duty is to strive for world prosperity. The very privileged position I occupy means that I must take everything into consideration.'

Didn't she really mean that she was obliged to turn a blind eye and carry on regardless? The same thing happened to Napoleon, to Hitler, and to so many men of action. I took my chance and asked her if she could read. She smiled.

'You're right that we're losing the ability to read because we've got radio, TV and, because I'm a believer, I'll never read a novel; but I know how to read. I like economics and moral philosophy. I'm enrolled on a political economy course, but please don't mention it to anyone. It's not considered appropriate for the Director of Pleasure to be concerning herself with such dry matters. These days we're all supposed to be specialists.'

I thought of asking her why was she doing it, but she was as beautiful when she was thoughtful and serene as she was when she laughed, or when, oh heavens!, she flew into one of her goddess rages.

'On the subject of Lola,' she continued, 'you have to help me convert her. We have to win her over to our cause.'

'*Our* cause, Andrea?' I replied.

'I know you're not one of us yet, but we'll convince you. I'll take care of it personally, and you know that they call me Andrea *Víctrix*.'

'And how would you go about achieving that?'

'You'll see in time,' said Andrea. 'At the moment, by making your life agreeable. I have a plan. Attack on three fronts: gifts such as real flowers and chocolate, etc.; rational argument (by which I mean dialectics); and personal seduction (caresses, etc.).'

I took her hand.

'The plan is delicious and childish, but you're forgetting the blows to my midriff. I still can't understand the beating you gave me on Pleasure. Where does your strength come from?'

'I take drugs, obviously,' replied Andrea.

'Isn't that dangerous?'

'No. They speed life up. I'll be old before I'm thirty, but only for a few hours. Death will be almost instantaneous.'

'How can you be sure of that?' I asked, appalled.

'I'd live longer if I didn't take stimulants, but without the strength to do very much. I belong to the Cause.'

To what cause?' I said. 'To a state of affairs that has reduced men to the level of beasts?'

I thought back to a chicken farm from my time. The hens were immobilized in iron cages narrower than Cardinal de la Balue's in the Grévin Museum tableau and fed around the clock: the technicians had decreed that sleep was a luxury, and at night they turned on spotlights to keep the hens awake so that they'd carry on eating. They didn't have wings: they didn't need them, and anyway the wings had barely any meat on them. The hens looked freakish. They laid prodigiously, programmed with fictitious activity, but were unhealthy and had to be killed before they were a year old. This is how poor quality eggs and meat were produced. I wrote an article attacking intensive farming, and they labelled me a reactionary. Now, it seems that absurd system is being applied to people.

'There's more I want to talk to you about,' Andrea continued. 'The carnation millionaire is upset he didn't meet you. He has a thing for men with parents.'

'Is he a philosopher?' I asked.

'Oh no,' laughed Andrea. 'He just makes plastic carnations, tonnes of them. He'd have liked to dance with you, have a little fun...'

'Do you realise what you're saying, Andrea?' I exclaimed. 'And to me of all people!'

She didn't answer. As always when she was thinking, her expression seemed sad.

'It pleases you to displease,' she said. 'So I'll say the same: how dare you refuse to entertain a VIP in front of me, the Director of Pleasure?'

'*Touché*,' I replied. 'Will you waltz? It's from my time.'

It was a Viennese waltz played at a exaggeratedly slow tempo and we danced without saying a word. Before it ended, the machine skipped and above Franz Lehár's music a voice commanded: IF YOU DON'T BUY A SECOND RADIO RECEIVER, YOU'RE SCUM. HAVEN'T YOU BOUGHT THE NEW EXPRESS COOKER? ANYONE WHO DOESN'T SUPPORT OUR INDUSTRIES IS ANTI-PATRIOTIC. THE STATE NEEDS YOU! The hectoring drowned out the waltz and we had to retake our seats.

'I haven't told you,' explained Andrea, 'that panic is spreading. People are afraid of an economic crisis.'

'Yes, I realise,' I said. 'The compliments the radio offered us just now are similar to ones they threw at us back in my time. I must have been about thirty – thirty real years – when American radio suddenly started broadcasting insults because we weren't buying what we didn't need.'

'The public aren't buying enough white goods,' said Andrea.

'Don't you think they already have enough?'

'That's the problem,' she replied. 'They have enough and the companies who produce them need to sell.'

'So produce less,' I suggested.

'You can't say things like that, my friend. That's against the established order. The companies will accuse you of fomenting unemployment and have you tagged as an obstructionist.'

'Oh, would they? And I'd accuse them of deceiving people and forcing them to acquire things they don't need.'

'The crisis will soon pass,' Andrea said. 'The Ministers are raising the daily wages of the workers to increase their disposable income. They're also going to increase unemployment benefit.'

'I'd rather just be employed.'

'So write in support of the unisex,' replied Andrea.

'Never!'

'You can dance. Work as a dancer.'

'Unthinkable.'

'You're young. You could be a prostitute.'

'Andrea!'

How could she utter such an absurdity so serenely? It was frightening, like witnessing some doll or angel placed carefully among arranged drapes or cream cakes suddenly blurt out a profanity.

'See, you're not interested in working!' she exclaimed.

'But don't you realise what you saying?'

She paused in thought, trying to understand.

'I know that in your time one of these professions was not well considered. But in many ways, I'm a prostitute.'

Her lips puckered as she twinged with pain. Perhaps her puritan core, her innate sense of honour, was rebelling against the morality they had inculcated in her from birth. I looked at her quizzically and when I tried to embrace her, she screamed.

'Andrea, what's the matter?'

'Nothing,' she said, forcing a smile. 'I took a blow to the chest last night…'

She adjusted her neckline as though trying to conceal something from me. I didn't dare ask her what had happened. I squeezed her hand, that fleshless, soft, strong hand of a girl or athlete that so disquieted me. Across the pure, blue sky flew white doves, doves that had wings, doves that didn't seem to be made of plastic at all. The sun was setting. One of those tanned little waiters had taken off his tunic and was angling a bow at me, laughing. The arrow struck my shoulder and I felt a surge of pleasure. He'd injected me with two centigrams of soma.

Lola lived on the top floor of an anonymous, aggressive skyscraper, a beehive, on Maritime Boulevard. Hers was a tiny apartment in a permanent state of chaos. The living-dining-room-kitchen resembled a warehouse full of dresses once fashionable in 1965: hats, brassieres from when women had breasts, unwashed hot chocolate bowls, boxes of sweets, bottles, and plates of synthetic fruit. It wasn't wholly unpleasant. Looking out to the sea, it captured the immensity of a sky not yet rendered entirely impure at certain hours of the day by fumes and aeroplanes, albeit polluted by syncopated music and advertising.

Almost all of Turclub's apartments were squalid. With the excuse of making the most of the light high up (but in reality, exploiting space), Turclub had adopted the old system of skyscrapers and the Mediterranean city, so famous for its sun, was becoming as dark as the island of Manhattan had once been, with the difference that Manhattan largely comprised office blocks, while people had to live, flourish, and have fun in Turclub, as mandated by the State.

The system of building on pillars set into reinforced concrete had allowed the thickness of the walls to be gradually reduced to no more than four centimetres and this, together with the narrowness of the internal patios and the hard, bare building materials, had turned the apartments into soundboxes.

The layout of each of these tiny little beehive cell condos was identical: a living-dining-room-kitchen, a bedroom, and a shower. These three spaces totalled twenty-one square metres. Anything bigger than this with an entrance hall, a small living room and a second bedroom, would make the occupant a multimillionaire. The problem of proliferating atomic appliances was becoming alarming. They could no longer fit physically into the twenty-one square metres of each apartment. Refrigerators were often hung from walls, but this meant a ladder was needed, and a ladder also required space. The manufacturers were tireless and the propaganda, directed by practical psychologists, forced people first to acquire ever more voluminous refrigerators to conserve food, and then to buy a gadget to accelerate their decomposition. As such, a chicken slaughtered at eight in the morning would be rested and ready to cook at ten. In reality no-one killed chickens but instead fed themselves on tinned foods or more often, fruit juices, which was why refrigerators were sometimes used to store shoes. *Hola-Hola*, however, had to be drunk chilled and anyway, refusing to use refrigerators would have been improper.

TV had also given rise to conflicts. Opticians opposed to the Regime warned that at less than four metres' distance, TV damaged eyesight, and of course apartments weren't designed with such splendid perspectives. *Monsieur-Dame* had to summon the ophthalmologists to a meeting and 'convince' them that the optimal distance for television viewing was one metre. At the same time, he ordered the manufacturers to reduce screen size.

The dissident opticians started a campaign against government opticians using clandestine channels, but they were discovered and deported to the Mississippi. Using this as a pretext, and in an attempt to pacify souls, the glass cartel – also experiencing a sales crisis – came up with a plan to increase 'visual space' in the beehive-apartments. This forced people to acquire a complicated series of mirrors which allowed viewers to watch television from whichever distance they liked. It was a scandalous business and along with a shortage of potatoes, it contributed to *Monsieur-Dame* losing the little sympathy he still retained among the populace.

Half-naked and arrayed provocatively on a chaise-longue, Lola was reading erotic novels from years ago: *Seven Nights of Juanita*, *The Naughty Friar*, etc. Notwithstanding her choice of literature, she was a believer and staunch traditionalist, and detested atheists as per the old regime. When she saw me come in, she tossed down her book, which struck a bowl of hot chocolate and spilled the contents.

'Don't worry about it,' she said. 'Have you just come from Andrea's? She's nothing to speak of, right? Chest like a board? And when you see her close up her skin's covered with pimples. She does a lot of drugs, you know, and that plays havoc with the complexion. She can't abide me. She'll engineer a falling-out between us, just wait.'

'You're wrong,' I said. 'It was she who told me to come to see you.'

'Don't say "she" because she doesn't have tits,' replied Lola. 'So she isn't jealous of me?'

'And you aren't jealous of Andrea?' I shot back.

'I'm not jealous of anyone. In my profession… We don't need to be formal with each other, you know, even though I don't take drugs and I'm not a filthy…'

It was certainly the case that according to the moral norms of 1965, both of them were similarly employed, but it couldn't be denied that Andrea aspired to more transcendental ideals which seemed noble even if they were misguided. A few hours earlier I had learned that she was prepared to die for those ideals and so I thought it sensible to change tack and tell Lola that I thought her living quarters were pleasant, which wasn't wholly untruthful.

'You know I'm a bohemian,' she replied. 'There's no order to any of this. Today I spent two hours buying a kilo of potatoes. You should have seen the queues–'

'So buy a robot to stand in the queue for you,' I said.

'Don't mention robots!' she shouted. 'I ended up terrified of the only one I ever had. Just seeing it tower above me, weighing a hundred and fifty kilos, in this tiny apartment… It slept standing up, like a horse, and one evening it toppled over, and if I'd been in the way it would have crushed me, just like that. I had to oil it every day and everything used to stink to high hell of diesel. And then it had this moronic habit of throwing the plates out of the window after it had washed them... They said something about the wiring, a bad connection... I was just afraid that the electronics in its head would go off like a bomb. Oh, it's happened, believe me...'

Applying her make-up in a little silver mirror, she had more colours arranged around her than on Titian's palette. She was beautiful, half naked, and scandalously feminine.

'You don't see many like me these days, do you?' she exclaimed, noticing me watching her.

The telephone rang and while she went to answer it, I looked out of the window. At night-time, the overbearing ugliness of the bay with its skyscrapers and Cathedral converted into apartment blocks, automobile repair centre and a service station, was balanced by a dazzling array of lights and colours. Each hotel was a flare and many had a restless spotlight at their apex that seemed to scrutinize the sky and the water as if looking for an enemy to shoot down. The majority of the buildings bore the golden slogan that had become the credo of Turclub and that was repeated, obsessively, everywhere: PROGRESS CANNOT BE STOPPED. Radios broadcast with more intensity than during the day, their volume ramped up but languid in tone, like the Sirens tempting Odysseus. Propaganda in paroxysms at times drowned out the love songs. The pandemonium was nerve-shredding but also seemed to draw in and mesmerise the passengers who, like the sailors accompanying the King of Ithaca, yearned to throw themselves into the sensuous, acoustic maelstrom that would turn them into pigs.

Some people, however, were starting to protest. Taken in on the one hand by a book by Rusiñol from some hundred and fifty years earlier which promised calm, almond blossoms and picture-postcard country girls and by another, not nearly so famous, volume of a similar vintage which talked about

Elizabethan ladies and antiquated palaces, they felt deceived and had begun to work out that there was more tranquillity to be enjoyed in London than in the Mediterranean. Some of the most expensive and technologically advanced hotels exploited the slogan of silence, filling the bay with incredibly powerful, deafening loudspeakers that proclaimed, though did not participate in, the good news: RADIO AND TV-FREE HOTELS: FIRST-CLASS COMFORT.

I closed the window. Still on the telephone, Lola switched on the air conditioning. The machine made a racket, of course, and after a minute we were freezing cold in our summer clothes and unable to cover up because all winter clothing was in storage. There was no room for it in the apartment. We turned the air-con off again and I heard Lola talking about me.

'Oh, I'll tell him... He'll be very happy. Yes, yes, cryo-cure in 1965, we're just like milk siblings. Oh, of course, he'll want to be there... What day? You don't know yet? Sorry? Research? No research, papers, forms, declarations... I've had enough. Ah, it's you who needs to...? Yes, of course, study for the lecture, let's see if we can unmask them. That's what López said, a great philosopher: "Countries must react". Back to the seventeenth century? Look, I don't know anything about how people lived in the seventeenth century. I did hear that they'd discovered ice cream by then. I'm from the era of Alfonso XIII, and we lived very well then. Wasn't La Chelito magnificent? I'd love to go back to my time when a woman was a woman and a man was a real man, you know. You understand what I mean. Yes, yes, you're right... And Pedro Mata was a good writer, wasn't he? Don't you think? You and I are alike. He really understood the human heart. I remember a duchess, a real duchess mind you, who fell in love with a nephew of hers, seventeen years old. She, well, she's a proper lady, but what could she do? She fell in love. And she took him to bed. It's just life, you know. It might seem coarse, but there you are. It's the same old, same old. I have a friend who says "*abreviemos*" and cuts to the chase when she's on the end of flattery and attentions. She's English, and it's the only word she knows in Castilian. Anyway, as I was saying, the duchess... Then come the regrets. I would never have had so many regrets. I don't remember now how the tragedy ends. No, no, the husband doesn't kill her. I don't think she had a husband actually. Maybe she was a widow. It was the young lad who died, poor boy, I think in an accident. Ah yes, that's right, shouted out as he died and the duchess heard him from her balcony. Yes, it's called *Un grito en la noche*. A really good novel, really good. Sorry? Yes, I said he'll come. Understood. You're welcome. Bye now.'

'Who was that?' I asked as she hung up the telephone.

'A friend of yours from the clinic in 1965,' said Lola.

'Diabetic?' I asked.

'Yes, but cured now. Except that he's a conspirator, so he makes out that he's still diabetic so he comes across as inoffensive.'

'What's he planning?'

'He wants to remake the world. Don't you think it needs it? Remould it, like God did with the Great Flood.'

'But he's not going to create a flood,' I said.

'Just a lecture at the moment,' replied Lola. 'I promised him we'd both go. He doesn't know yet when it'll be; he's getting "documented". What an odd expression, don't you think?'

As we chatted, I had taken off my shirt and was looking at my shoulder in the mirror. I told her that when we were on Einstein's terrace, a little black waiter had shot me with a soma-impregnated arrow. Lola laughed.

'The little pimps! Einstein's soma is laced with an aphrodisiac, don't you know? And did you...?'

'Me? Nothing,' I said. 'I came to see you.'

'Of course, I know Andrea wouldn't seduce you. You still have some self-respect, but if you're not careful, you'll lose it.

You've already gone off football, and if don't watch yourself, you'll end up not liking women. Luckily for you, I'm here.'

She looked smug. I didn't want to destroy the illusion of her little feminine victory, nor explain – and she wouldn't have understood anyway – that if I hadn't been with Andrea (young men of my generation were puritans in matters concerning sexual practices), it was because I hadn't dared out of a possible sense of shame.

'Now, sweetheart,' she said, unbuttoning her blouse, 'the pleasure is all Lola's.'

CHAPTER XV
CIVIC BAPTISMS

Andrea wanted me to visit the Mediterranean Procreation Centre, and I was resisting.

'I'm predisposed against such places,' I said. 'You're a fanatic of the Oviparous Era, and I'm Viviparous and proud. So don't insist.'

'You may do what you wish,' she replied, kissing my forehead. 'But I'll try to win you over. One day you'll understand that our age isn't as bad as you judge it to be, and in any case, it can't be any other way.'

'I don't know when that day will come,' I replied.

'Nor do I, hun; perhaps sooner than we think. Right now, when you're in a good mood, you admit that not everything is bad. This Palazzo for example...'

'It's magnificent,' I said. 'But it isn't your creation. It's simply a Roman copy.'

I could see she was thinking.

'Yes,' she said. Architecture has moved on. But the fact that we appreciate the relics of the past...'

'Relics of the past...,' I repeated. 'And yet you convert the Almudaina Palace into a hotel?'

'It had already been renovated,' she said, 'improved beyond recognition.'

'And then you've destroyed the Seu, a thirteenth-century monument. It looks like a bar of chocolate now.'

'Perhaps architecturally it's a pity, though I didn't see the original. The Classical University deplores it. But it was far too dangerous a symbol, representing a religion that could resurface. I suppose in a way we now represent another religion.'

'Don't say "in a way",' I said. 'You're creating a monstrous religion.'

'My dear friend,' she replied, sitting up and kissing my

hands, 'could you not apply a little *rondeur* to your judgements?'

'I'm sorry,' I said, 'but I suspect that you're so taken by the material, so awed by everything metallic, that you rebuilt it to create little cage-like apartments and converted the naves into garages. Don't expect me to tone down my language.'

She smiled.

'Very well,' she said. 'I'll do it for you. The apartments were necessary, and the garages more so, but we reserved a room of thirty-eight square metres for worship above the service station. We're more tolerant than you think. I want you to become a moral human being, useful to yourself and to others. Sometimes you're wonderful, you have a sense of humour, you're loyal, you're not resentful, but this lack of activity is eating you up. You should work.'

'I would love to,' I said, 'if only I could write what I like.'

'You know that's not possible,' she said quite naturally. 'You'd end up either heretical or lyrical.'

I took her hand and began to recite a poem.

'Moonlight,' I purred. 'The lake… *Un soir, t'en souviens-tu? Nous voguions en silence…*'

'Be quiet,' she said, turning pale. 'That's Lamartine. When I was fourteen some criminal read it to me to corrupt me and they sentenced him to death.'

A criminal? Corruptor? Where was the *rondeur* now? Could Andrea and I, so different, want the same things?

'What fanatics you are!' I murmured.

'I try not to be,' she replied. 'Since you can't write, I think you should dance. It's healthy, and it would distract you. And assuming prostitution holds no interest… I could make you into a celebrity. Have you dance for *Monsieur-Dame.*'

'You're raving,' I replied. 'Don't talk nonsense.'

'See? Well, since you won't be persuaded, come with me to the ceremony we're celebrating on the seventh. An extravagant, formal affair: a civic baptism with *Hola-Hola.*'

She slipped a cocaine sweet between my lips and I couldn't help but laugh. Lola had told me about *Hola-Hola* being used in baptisms, but I hadn't taken her seriously.

'Does that really happen?' I asked.

'Why are you laughing?' Andrea replied. 'Yes, it's what happens.'

'You're delicious,' I went on, the cocaine sweet having improved my mood.

'Why am I delicious? Or do you think I'm simple?'

'Simply delicious,' I clarified. 'These baptisms sound... entertaining, yes.'

'Wasn't water from the River Jordan used before?' asked Andrea. 'I think I read it in an encyclopaedia, but an act of such transcendence, marking one's entrance into the world, demands solemnity.'

'Of course it does,' I replied.

I was still laughing and didn't want to argue. *Hola-Hola*, 'cordiality in a can' as the well-known slogan had it, was the holiest of international sacraments. It belonged to the most powerful enterprise in the whole of Unified Europe, was present in every establishment, and was said to have miraculous properties, which in fact it must have done, because the marvel that inspired such veneration and constituted the symbol of an epoch was, in reality, nothing. A clandestine publication entitled *The Veil of Isis* was doing the rounds in which the author lifted the edge of the veil to reveal, before the horrified reader, nothing but a bare wall:

In the eight months I was employed by the company, wrote the degenerate author, *I worked like an admittedly well-paid dog without a clue what I was doing. Such processes are common today. The atomic energy technicians, for example, transport raw minerals, manage equipment, derive cubed roots using electronic machines, and weigh out substances, but they don't know each other and never achieve an overview of their collective labours. Menial operatives don't have the right to address their superiors, and in any event they wouldn't understand each other. They don't even speak the same language. So while I was with the company, we worked in isolation, not only through being shuttered off from one another, but mainly because of the differentiation of our activities and technical vocabularies. The mathematician knew nothing of chemistry, nor did the person who transported the raw materials know anything about what he was transporting. For more than half a year I was a stupid little cog in the most cynical of deceptions. Only in the final few weeks was I able to unearth the devastating truth. In a previous life I'd been a cross-dresser and ventriloquist and it was these skills that gave me the idea of passing myself off as different people so that I could infiltrate different sections of the production plant. Fed up of watching diminutive red bottles file past on their way to being emptied into bigger bottles, I found my way into different process areas and discovered that a number of operatives were introducing a red-coloured granule into each little bottle, and that the bigger bottles contained nothing but water. After watching in disguise and in fear for my life at each of the many workstations, I realised that the red granules were just inactive dye. Beginning to get worried now about what was more than a suspicion, criss-crossing the plant as a chemist, porter, whatever it took, I finally managed to get a complete overview of the production line: Hola-Hola, internationally renowned cordiality in a can, was in fact nothing, which explained why it was always served with slices of lemon, and mixed with gin or rum. The scientists in laboratories weighing milligrams of powder and carefully releasing drops of reagent into test-tubes from pipettes were analysing nothing; the eminent mathematicians and robots solving equations may as well have been ploughing the sea as all it came down to was reddish colouring and tap water. I thought I was going mad. I understood that in our culture, as in Ancient Egypt, there was nothing behind the veil of Isis, but at the same time I told myself that the veil – the millions of theologians and believers – was necessary, and I remembered that whoever tears away the veil has to die.*

And that's precisely what happened. The author of the volume had been incinerated on the top platform of the Eiffel Tower and his ashes dispersed, blown to the four corners of the globe. On the day of his execution, four-hundred and sixty million cans of cordiality were consumed on our continent.

'It's a very glamorous ceremony,' Andrea insisted. '*Monsieur-Dame* will be present via TV. It's important that he sees you at my side, I know that he'll like you. People have a poor opinion of our viviparous citizens and they don't trust you, but I've promised that you'll never be an enemy to him.'

'You shouldn't have done that,' I said. 'How do you know whose side I'll take if the revolution comes?'

'I know that you won't go against me.'

I didn't want to acknowledge it, but she was right.

'On the seventh,' explained Andrea, 'the five-hundred infants who were born in our Centre yesterday will be baptised. The chief executive of *Hola-Hola* will be there with his retinue. If *Monsieur-Dame* had attended in person, as we'd planned, the CEO would not have shown his face: in reality, he's more powerful than *Monsieur-Dame*, but at an official event with the President in attendance, the honours are reserved for *Monsieur-Dame*. Do you understand? The Pope will be there too (at his own request), but incognito.'

'What on earth?' I said, totally confused. 'How is that possible?'

'*Monsieur-Dame* is magnanimous. He's made an exception.'

'But... the Pope in Rome?'

'Yes. The one who lives in the Transforo, I think. There are two, or three... I know of one who lives on the fourth floor of a block on the Via Nomentana. With no elevator, the poor devil.'

In fact, the real Pope had died during the Great Industrial

Revolution, when the hordes burned down the Vatican. He was a diplomatic sort who tried to ingratiate himself with the revolutionaries in the interests of the church, but the conservatives abandoned him and at the moment of truth he found himself on his own. The cardinals were divided and elected two Pontiffs, who were later joined by a third. Such a plurality together with the relaxation of dogma – attempting to appear modern in order to appease their followers – ended up alienating believers.

'These popes, Andrea, are not real popes,' I said.

'Perhaps not. All the same, they have the approval of the *Hola-Hola* CEO and are very amenable. The *Hola-Hola* company too: for events such as this, they produce a special recipe made with water from the Jordan like in the time of John the Baptist. Oh, His Most Illustrious Chief Exective has such delicatesse! And what's more, he's a true hermaphrodite. Look. Moving, don't you think?'

She showed me a photograph of some old queen, past his best, who looked a little like *Monsieur-Dame*. One of the holy fathers of this new state of affairs, he held half plus one of the company's shares, and along with the insipid drink he stood for, his washed-out persona constituted the perfect representation of the neuter gender, which is why the advertisements said, 'Everybody likes them, and they're everybody's favourite,' which was tantamount to saying that no-one liked them. Regardless, people drank nothing but the beverage of neutrality, and mysticism had triumphed. Lola, of course, disagreed with Andrea's assessment of the hermaphroditic CEO.

'He's gross,' she had said. 'In our time we'd have pelted him with tomatoes, but today, as you can see, he's more powerful than the old popes. He even institutes sacraments. He's a complete crook. The refrigerator sector is in crisis because everyone's eating tinned food, but because of *Hola-Hola* he's still managing to create demand while taking his cut, naturally. The stuff's undrinkable unless it's served well chilled with hot pepper.'

I didn't attend the baptism, though it was evidently a flamboyant affair, as the number of automobile accidents demonstrated. The hermaphroditic CEO delivered a great speech and Andrea occupied pride of place, dressed in purple. Since she couldn't kiss all the infants, she kissed and embraced the civil governor. I went to bed early back at my lodgings. Before I said goodbye to Lola, she mentioned that the diabetic's lecture was due to take place the following day at eight in the evening.

There was no-one else there when we arrived except the speaker, a cryo-cure survivor from 1965. Lola introduced me and I recognized him as the man who had seemed unsure whether to greet me in Dr Orlando's waiting room. Probably about my age, he seemed older. I soon understood that being made-up to look older was precisely one of the ruses he'd adopted to conceal his true identity. He'd dyed his hair grey, and to put people further off the scent (thinking he was clever), he pretended to be a bit of a simpleton. The simpleton revealed himself as soon as he opened his mouth, his first words invoking John of Austria. Accordingly, the current circumstances demanded that we 'react', although he didn't explain how this should be achieved. When he tried, he tripped over his words. Alluding to low agricultural productivity, he preached the advantages of natural manure over chemical fertilisers which deplete the soil of nutrients in the long run, and in this he wasn't wrong.

'But who has access to manure?' shouted a voice. 'That was another time. People survive on juices these days.'

Moreover, in Turclub's tiny apartments, any leftovers considered dangerous were incinerated, just as bodies were cremated and sewage ended up in watercourses and in the sea. This absurd situation, explained the speaker, would never have happened in the age of latrines, and that's what we needed to get back to.

There were murmurs of discontent and almost certainly more than one person was thinking that such a solution meant a full-scale return to the plague pandemics of the Middle Ages. There was a risk, of course, but how could agriculture survive if it were deprived of organic nitrogen? The speaker proposed – as though we were deputies rather than persecuted dissidents on the fringes of the law – we confiscate people's garbage and redistribute it to those few farmers still around. At this point a gentleman-farmer (a kind of feudal lord in his village, put into cryo stasis before the Great Revolution) rose to his feet and declared that he'd ordered the purchase of all the manure to be had.

'When I returned to my lands,' he said, 'I was met by a shocking spectacle: piles of bottles, rusty cans, and plastic wrapping. This is the manure the Industrial Era reserves for agriculture.'

The speaker railed against manufacturers of canned foods, losing himself in pointless laments and cursing Denis Papin, Thomas Edison and Henry Ford like some old, enraged priest. He steered clear of *Monsieur-Dame*, presumably thinking him or her either too dangerous or too stupid. It was true that the problems of the Industrial Era had no easy solution, but the cryo survivor made no attempt to explore the psychological, political, or moral causes that had brought us to such a state of affairs. The few people present applauded dutifully and slipped out, giving each other sideways glances, happy and scared to have heard almost an hour of blasphemous censure. They probably feared being deported to the Massachusetts deserts, which judging by the number of people already exiled there, couldn't possibly be as deserted as their Biblical namesakes.

It was said that the exiles were not only intelligent and dangerous, but that they were in touch with savage peoples from any number of Polynesian islands and counted terrible chemists among their number, just as dishevelled as Einstein, who one day might create problems for the U.S. of Europe. Such rumours were almost certainly defeatist gossip, though the people accused the government of negligence and demanded 'light and stenographers', transparency and accountability, as in more liberal times. The Pacific region was a nest of vipers and a complete unknown for the average person, who was misled by official radio stations and their tendentious reporting and by consistently contradictory clandestine channels. The excess of information made it impossible to be reliably informed about anything and every citizen would have required the talents of a Sherlock Holmes to make out the truth from the chaos and misrepresentation on all sides. But by working twelve to sixteen hours a day to buy atomic appliances, the public did not have time to decipher the hieroglyphics. The government must have been aware of the dangers lurking in those latitudes, but *Monsieur-Dame*'s administration, renowned for its blood-lust years earlier, was losing its edge, and no longer dared opt for the most radical course of action.

The industrial crisis hit the United States of Europe with alarming gravity. When I returned to my lodgings that same evening, I was met by a notice informing me that my unemployment payment was going up thirty percent to compensate me for the *diseta* (*disette*, a Gallicism which had become part of our vocabulary, meaning scarcity or, more brutally, famine). In exchange, I was obliged to purchase a middle-of-the-range fridge every four months, a blender for mayonnaise, and was reminded that the oil and eggs should be replaced with cheaper substitutes or replacements which presented no contamination risk and had a higher vitamin content. The only disadvantage was that sometimes these surrogates caused hives, but they were treatable in any event with lemon juice, although this was incredibly expensive because lemons were so rare. Suspecting that this would make Lola lose patience with the regime once and for all, I mentioned it to her. And that's exactly what happened.

'Eels,' she said, which in her slang meant thieves. 'Vile, slimy eels. They convince us that the latest refrigerator models barely consume any electricity and yet it turns out that I have horrendous bills to pay. "They", you can be sure, will be taking their cut at the public's expense.'

Who were 'they'? Lola didn't know, but like everyone she suspected foul play and Machiavellian intrigues targeting her pocket.

'We're always crippled by instalments,' she continued. 'I'm still paying for a revolting, threadbare, old-fashioned overcoat. They convinced me that artificial mink was better than the real thing and it's shed all its fur. D'you know how many monthly instalments I still have to pay? The record player, vacuum cleaner, television set, air-conditioning, etc. And I definitely can't do without that because the air from the street's unbreathable and gives you lung cancer. Well, that's what "they" say, to sell air-conditioning units, but it's true that automobiles are poisoning us. Nowadays breathing is a luxury.'

'I was almost killed off by air from Mont Blanc in one of the isolating bells on Pleasure,' I reminded her.

'I remember that incident. But that was a bad connection, so it doesn't count.'

'I almost get killed and it doesn't count?'

'We know progress isn't risk-free. It's not as though we can live like they did when Maria Castanya was queen.'

'I didn't know Maria Castanya was a queen,' I said, surprised.

'She was,' said Lola, with a certainty that made me doubt myself to such an extent that I wouldn't dare suggest otherwise even now. 'And I bet she wasn't bothered by exorbitant electricity bills.'

'For example?' I interjected, distracted.

'Oh I don't know,' she said, laughing. 'The refrigerator is definitely very modern, all nickle and enamel. I'll show you. You and I would fit inside, and it makes hundreds of little ice cubes I don't know what to do with. It's all about spending for the sake of spending.'

'Unplug it and your money's safe,' I ventured.

'It's not worth it,' she replied, before lowering her voice and whispering. 'Let's face it, this money's all a subsidy.'

Lola, the affirmed atheist was repeating expressions more commonly heard from the Regime faithful: subsidies for an industry that was at the point of collapse.

The obligation to purchase appliances was having an unfortunate effect. The more fractious wondered whether it might be preferable to give up on progress and cultivate the land, which would have been as difficult as turning the clock back to the time of Don John of Austria and likely to unleash mass fanaticism while the masses, in spite of their desperate situation, would not have relinquished the material symbols of progress which by now had attained almost mythical status. Reality was more complex than the defrosted speaker seemed to think.

'That was very eloquent,' I said to him afterwards. 'But I do think you need to explain how we go about returning to the sixteenth century.'

'Well, Pérez Martínez says that–,' he started.

'I'm more interested in your opinion,' I interrupted.

I wasn't really interested, but rather talking for the sake of it. Perhaps it was indeed possible to destroy everything and start again, remould the world as God did after the Flood. But going back just a short way and stopping whimsically in a particular century seemed childish. Material progress had been much more rapid than the moral and legislative mechanisms needed to regulate it, and that speed had weakened the social fabric and threatened to destroy it.

'That's why I say that we should go back to the monarchy of Philip II,' replied the speaker.

'How,' said Lola, in a clumsy attempt at wit, 'if Philip II is dead?'

The lecture was hosted in the basement of Rufo's tavern, a disreputable place frequented by dissidents and revolutionaries, including a few priests and former aristocrats who were now ruined and starving. The event was so discreetly organized that hardly anyone turned up. That's the tragedy of secret societies. Once upon a time, Descartes travelled to Germany to make contact with the Rosenkreuz Order and couldn't find any members. Among those few people who did attend, I thought I recognized the front of house lady from *Le Gaulois*. Regardless, it was clear that the first stone had been cast and that the first ripples of discontent were being felt.

I went home with my head full of contradictory ideas and emotions. What would Andrea say when she discovered I'd attended the meeting? Barely sleeping, I intended to tell her everything and at daybreak I headed to the Palazzo Víctrix. She was taking a walk around the park and we sat down beneath a real holm oak.

'I know,' she said, kissing me on the forehead, 'that last night you went to a clandestine lecture. It's important that you stick with Lola and try to bring her to orthodoxy. I have a lot of time for her. We perform similar professional roles.'

'Don't say that,' I exclaimed, beginning to regret betraying two conflicting causes. 'There's no comparison.'

'How was the speaker?' asked Andrea.

'Poor. I won't lie: I'm closer to the revolutionaries than I am to you and the Regime.'

'I'm aware of that,' said Andrea, 'though I'm confident I'll seduce you. How do you find me this morning?'

'Pale,' I said. 'You've lost weight.'

'My skin's very dry. Wait here a moment. Do you see the two rabbits in that cage? They look mechanical but they're real. You can have one. I'll be back in a second.'

She returned looking elegant, her skin plumper, and she explained that she'd just taken a new medicine that reinforced the effect of soma. It acted on the circulation of blood and the metabolism of water.

'That's why it makes you thirsty,' she said. 'It produces a state we call *morbidezza*.'

'Is it harmful?' I asked.

'In the long term, yes, but I'm destined to die in a few years anyway. In the meantime, it increases my strength and sense of wellbeing.'

'You'll have to let me try it,' I replied.

'Never, hun,' she said quickly. 'Never.'

A *maître* around fifty years old with sideburns, starched collar and tails was walking down the avenue carrying a glass. He was clearly from a significant establishment.

'Drink, Your Excellency,' he said. 'The doctor has ordered that every half hour you must, because…'

She silenced him with a look and drank.

'*Ah, que je suis bien,*' she murmured in French, sounding genuinely happy. Without realising, her neckline had shifted slightly to reveal a fresh bruise above her ribs.

'Andrea,' I started, but she looked up, suddenly annoyed.

'I told you, so why act surprised? I fulfil my duty. There were two of them and I couldn't defend myself. I lost my soma.'

Though mediocre, the lecture had mobilised opinion. People's curiosity had been aroused by a speaker put into cryo in 1965 and the fact that only a few people had attended favoured him. That large numbers hadn't been exposed to his anachronistic dialectics was important, though more so was that for the first time since the Great Revolution of 1985 a clandestine – albeit in a sense public – event had taken place in opposition to the State. The authorities were aware of it all, though for the time being they held back from taking action. Faced with rising prices, *disette*, and the threat of unemployment, they felt insecure and hesitant. In an attempt to ward off the crisis, the government had just implemented the Forcible Purchase Plan, giving the optimists some hope. It was essential that state employees, workers and the passive classes acquired new atomic appliances and destroyed their old ones. 'Obstructionists' would be punished severely. This is why salaries had been increased, and while a rise in inflation would surely follow, this would be cancelled out by the fall in numbers of unemployed, whose eight months or so of benefits were ruinous for the State.

There was also talk of reducing the number of neurotics who, once labelled 'constitutionally idle', earned at least as much as the unemployed without having to demonstrate a willingness to do anything useful in their whole life. This being the case, doctors were requested to issue as few as half the number of 'idleness' certificates as before, and if targets weren't met, a decree would be issued to suppress this highly antisocial neurosis: the Official Academy of Medicine would announce that the idleness neurosis was the creation of a group of reactionaries from whom this self-applied title would be withdrawn, and legal action would be taken against them on the basis of obstructing the Regime and the interests of the country.

Using euphoric public opinion as cover, once the financial situation had stabilised, the conspirators would be exterminated. In the meantime, it made political sense to allow them their freedom so that they'd reveal themselves and could be discreetly monitored.

There was a lot of activity at Dr Orlando's regular gathering. The centenarian doctor was growing increasingly aggressive, but his ever more reckless behaviour probably saved him from prison, since it opened the way for the police to gather intelligence.

'We must unmask the Anonymous, the Collective Being,' he pontificated. 'There is no guilt in the singular. The Anonymous, as you know, Societies and Corporations, etc., knock on their doors... But which door? They will always pass you on to another department, and if you ever get to the non-existent Absolute Superior, this beast will refer the matter again to the subalterns for information. You'll get lost in corridors, elevators, and mountains of paperwork. The Anonymous ignores and despises you. Do you believe that an amalgam of men can incorporate the Spirit, the "Noosphere" which is the Collective Spirit and which according to Teilhard Chardin, is evolving towards God? Heaven converted into a tenement? The Collective Being and *Hola-Hola* are drawing us towards Satan and hell, not to God. Only the Singular can save us. Only he is human, concrete. The Anonymous is an abstraction, a name, a monster. Take a look at his palace. You find yourself before a business leader. He dines on a boiled egg. He's lived the life of a hermit for more than half a century. He throws a party every year. The servants wear livery, champagne flows, but he doesn't budge from his hole. His grandchildren will squander his millions. The champagne is for the others, he drinks only Vichy water. Perhaps he strokes a Siamese cat on his lap? Ah, how tender-hearted the wicked are, seen up close, in concrete form! Such animal lovers! I wonder if perhaps they even love the poor. They fund refuges, and on their own give no cause for complaint. But together, what a monstrous sum they become!'

A young voice, probably a girl, spoke up.

'Doctor,' she asked. 'Can't we make them better?'

'No,' came the reply. 'Because they're perfect.'

'Or they think they are,' corrected someone.

Enraged, Dr Orlando looked about to suffer an attack.

'They are!' he shouted. 'Perfect like the detonators of atomic bombs! Make them better? Young lady,' he continued, 'we will burn you alive, we'll purify you as we'll purify them, in their plural… The anonymous plural! Fire purifies, young lady!'

He fell silent and closed his eyes. We were all quiet, not knowing what to say. When he opened his eyes, he looked distractedly around him.

'I called you young lady,' he said. 'Though I don't know whether you're a boy or a girl.'

'I'm a girl, sir,' she replied, shyly.

'Ah, that's good,' he replied. 'I admire you, young lady, but you too will burn.'

A woman came in, also defrosted from another time, and still good-looking in her figure-hugging feminine outfit. She sat down, relieved. As she'd been flying over an internment camp for 'criminal lost causes', the police had fired on her helicopter.

'They were drawing and quartering a friend,' she said. 'When they saw me watching them, they almost brought me down.'

She explained in tears that the victim had physically shoved a four-year old child who was shouting $E=mc^2$. There was an anxious silence. Neophyte that I was, I didn't understand what was happening and had to ask someone to explain.

'The equation $E=mc^2$ is official dogma and disrespecting it is an unspeakable sin,' came the answer. 'The dogma is inculcated in all infants by continued repetition. The remains of the criminal will be incinerated and released to the wind from the Eiffel Tower.'

That night when I described the scene I'd witnessed to Andrea, she put an arm around me and kissed me.

'Do you think it should be lawful to pervert children?' she asked. 'Our regime is generous and humanitarian but attacking Einstein's formula is unforgiveable. It'd be absurd even to consider regressing to the physics of Newton and Galileo.'

'That's not what I'm saying,' I said. 'I'm perfectly aware of the phrase PROGRESS CANNOT BE STOPPED, but what do infants know about physics? How are they supposed to understand the equation?'

'They can assimilate it without understanding it.'

'Like *Hola-Hola*.'

The colour drained from her face.

'Hun, try not to speak of *Hola-Hola*; it's a sacrament.'

'For you it is.'

'And for you, too. It's important to know when to be humble.'

'And generous,' I said. 'And ripped to pieces if you don't think like us.'

'What other solution do you propose?'

'I don't have one. But you think I'm retrograde because I criticise you and you don't realise that you behave like the Holy Office of the Inquisition who in 1757 had Damiens dismembered. I take it you know who Damiens was?'

'No,' she said. 'I don't.'

'Damiens attacked and wounded Louis xv of France and was hacked apart while still alive, like the lady's friend I told you about. His torture lasted hours. At that time the king's person was sacred and justice hadn't moved on since the Middle Ages. I'm an old liberal and I grew up understanding the horror of Damiens' martyrdom.'

'You're a utopian,' she said, seemingly troubled at what I had said. I was about to respond when she put a strip of chocolate into my mouth. 'I'd be really sorry if some terrible misfortune were to befall you as it befell those poor people you're talking about,' she said. 'You must be careful not to draw attention to yourself. Though the government aren't intervening at the moment, Dr Orlando's meetings aren't safe for you.'

That was obvious. We went along to those gatherings apprehensive and in disguise, just like the police themselves. I can't remember ever having seen so many false beards, so many youths made up to look like old women, and so many old women pretending to be young girls. I was one of the few who made no attempt to hide who I was because if things got dangerous, I could show the police my safe-conduct from Andrea. If the revolutionaries discovered it on me, they'd label me a traitor to the cause and a government spy. How much truth would there have been in such accusations?

Even I couldn't work it out. I conveyed everything that was said at Dr Orlando's meetings to my delightful friend and hid nothing of my discontent at that mystical, industrial civilization. We were loyal adversaries: Andrea wanted to attract me to her side, just as I was trying to bring her over to mine. To do so, we were both open with each other. Were we spies, diplomats or missionaries? Who could dare be sure of anything? Our glory or infamy wasn't going to be determined by what we did, but by the course of events. And events, as we know, are as changeable as Cleopatra.

Andrea was extraordinarily busy. After one of her bacchanalian nights, she would wake up looking almost ugly, desiccated, and jaundiced like an old minister. I would arrive at the Palazzo around nine to tell her what we had spoken about at the doctor's gathering, and she would type it up for the record. She would receive me in the reproduction Roman salon based on the Villa Borghese's great marble hall before the secret police came in pretending to be dance and physical culture instructors so as not to give themselves away to me. After kissing her neck and accepting a chocolate sweet, they would inform her of events in the city and any revolutionary activity, which Andrea would then compare with the details that I had given. At eleven o'clock the doctors, masseurs, and real physical culture instructors arrived and took her to her private rooms, returning her three-quarters of an hour later rejuvenated and as strong and svelte as the May morning I was first invited to ride in her car.

It was cocktail hour and the goddess was out in the Rolls, entertaining the most distinguished tourists personally and checking on those agents whose responsibility it was to be agreeable to the rich and poor – although in truth it was more the rich because, as we all know, gold is sacred. I declined my daily invitation to accompany her and she left shrouded in a certain sadness. She would have loved me to be part of her seduction endeavours, to create a post for me in the Department of Pleasure, and she never managed to understand the reasons behind my refusals.

'Because neither you nor your Department have any idea what love is,' I said.

Andrea had looked at me wide-eyed, astonished.

'Don't you like me?' she asked.

'Yes, very much. You are the most beautiful woman…,' I replied. Noting her irritation at this, I corrected myself. 'The most beautiful *being* I've ever come across. But without intimacy there can be no love, or even pleasure. You're positivists.'

She didn't understand.

'When two people love each other,' she replied, 'they barter sex. That's to say, there's a negotiation which benefits both parties. Do you think it would be acceptable if one were to give everything and the other risked nothing?'

No, we didn't understand each other at all. When Andrea was gone, I discovered that she had ordered the government to continue paying my allowance even when my 'jobless' card ran out. With my head full of romantic notions, I hadn't noticed and she hadn't told me. My scruples over accepting money from her must have seemed ridiculous, but doubtless her generosity of spirit had got the better of her critical sense.

Before getting behind the wheel, she took an extra-strength soma pill to keep her breath fresh, and then shot off like lightning, her glorious smile taking in all of humanity, her golden hair framing her innocent features. Some days I would sit in cafés in the city centre and would see her drive by accompanied by beautiful young people. This was was bad enough, but the time I saw her with a surly-looking giant of a foreigner (a king as I discovered later), I was profoundly upset. The thought that maybe she'd spend the night with him horrified me. Why wouldn't she give up this repugnant profession? Though my jealousy made it difficult to bring up certain subjects, I questioned her about it and she tried to downplay the significance of her sacrifice, like a good soldier avoiding talk about his heroic feats.

'Of course, it can be gruelling,' she replied. '*Monsieur-Dame* would rather I only went with important, elegant dignitaries. There are agents aplenty for normal tourists, good-looking ones too, perhaps more than me. I supervise them.'

'Has there ever been a case of a notable, beautiful character you didn't like?'

'That would be a crime,' replied Andrea. 'Such a person must necessarily be attractive to me.'

'And if you weren't attracted to them?'

'I could pass them on to one of my agents. Provided it wasn't a minister or the Supreme Head of the Waiters' Guild.'

'And if it was an elderly minister or a repugnant waiter?' I asked.

Poor Andrea. I could tell by the sad, serious expression on her face that she'd found herself more than once in similar situations, but she reacted valiantly.

'In really extreme cases there's a triple-strength soma I can take that produces a special sense of euphoria. It's much more potent than cocaine or LSD.'

The Palazzo Víctrix was surrounded by parkland while the 'hall' was a reproduction of the Villa Borghese, decked out in marble and adorned with sculptures of figures from mythology. Given Andrea's eminence and the fact that she was above banal categories such as Good and Evil, the figures were depicted without vine leaves and with their genitalia intact. Men and women appeared as distinct and complementary beings. Andrea expected that I'd understand such matters would not affect her, but the differentiation tolerated by the old regime was immoral for the masses. The art of those times impelled man towards woman – Athletes towards Venus.

'Is that such a bad thing?' I asked. 'Men and women being attracted to one another?'

'Not for you, no,' Andrea said. 'But you, my friend, belong to another era. Our world was founded on the dissolution of the family and so it was essential that love became independent from sex and lost any connection with such an incredibly dangerous concept as intimacy. The State must control procreation; it can't be left to the whim of the individual. You were already talking about these things in your time: "If we don't do this, in fifty years' time there won't be enough food on Earth".'

'But that's because all your energies are channelled into industry,' I replied. 'There's still the sea, which is much bigger than the land mass. If everyone who manufactures atomic appliances and foul-tasting drinks were to go to sea to fish, the problem of feeding people would be more than solved.'

'But that would hurt the interests of industry,' she said, horrified. 'You can't talk like that. Don't speak ill of machines. They represent "increasing rationalisation" and the concretisation of human intelligence. They free us from the slavery of mechanical work.'

'That's not what those who work their whole lives manufacturing machines say,' I retorted.

'Sophistry,' said Andrea. 'Machines are both the product of our spirit, and spirits themselves.'

'Evil spirits,' I said. 'A society that prohibits people from having children is a monstrous society that has turned its back on nature.'

She looked at me, mournfully.

'*Birth-control–.*'

'Even when you say it in English,' I interrupted, 'don't think for a minute that machines create wellbeing or lead us to democracy. They cause war, as we well know. What such a society deserves is Terror. And that's what it will get.'

Thomas Mann's Naphta had already said as much and the lack of differentiation propounded by Andrea exasperated me. Neither of us said anything, and I realised I'd allowed my bad mood to get the better of me.

'Though you're right,' I said. 'In my time we did talk about these things.'

'You're Catholic,' replied Andrea, 'so you'll remember that the Church allowed, or was on the point of allowing, the Ogino method.'

'It's a bit more complicated than you think,' I said. 'It wasn't the Church that induced the State to reduce the number of children, but "progress". In any event the Church simply followed progress, the machine spirit, architects who built "functional" apartments with two bedrooms. Together with the socialist tenancy laws, they created a housing crisis that made family life virtually impossible. Some of the feebler Catholics gave way rather than fight the changes.'

'Weren't they behaving sensibly?' asked Andrea.

'What, by destroying both the home and love?'

'We've discussed this so many times, hun… Exclusive love,

between two people, is a social sin. We must love all Humanity, the Collective Being, like Teilhard de Chardin said. You know that for Teilhard, it's essential that the millions, billions of human beings be assimilated to a Supreme Being which – as he can't call it God – he calls the Omega Point.'

'I'm familiar with all this nonsense,' I said. 'Dr Orlando brought it up recently.'

'It's not nonsense. In the materialist era of your youth, you talked about the Biosphere (animal life in the terrestrial sphere). Now we've entered the spiritual era, we can quite justifiably speak of a Noosphere (life of the spirit). No longer do we have to deify a person and single them out. Instead, we deify the whole of Humanity: our neighbours, as Christians would say. This is why we encourage pleasure and debauchery, but without focussing on a particular person and without making distinctions between the sexes. It is a pleasure shared by all.'

She was alluding to the State-sponsored Collective Orgies. This was probably not what Teilhard de Chardin had proposed, but this is where his theories had brought us and I couldn't bear to listen to such obscenity. Nor did I want to ask what would become of our awareness of shame because Andrea, innocent and puritan that she was, had none. Or at least, it took on a different form. Ugliness, stupidity, injustice, and bad manners all made her suffer; in libidinal matters, however, everything seemed permissible. Even physical pain – short of death, or perhaps not, who knows – was legitimate in her eyes, as it is for the boxer, who considers it part of his sport. She was courageous and not frightened by her clients, even when they were drunk. She had a candid, heroic temperament, like the little Ibizan acrobats or Roman gladiators. She had no respect for life, but was more wary of physical pain (except when it went hand-in-hand with pleasure) and this is why she considered Parquidine to be the doctors' most wonderful invention.

'You mean executioners, not doctors,' I said.

Not picking up on my irony, Andrea didn't reply. Executioners in the U.S. of Europe also used Parquidine because it's one thing to suppress one's enemies and quite another to have them suffer unnecessarily.

The nights she wasn't working – generally Thursdays, which she reserved for her own private business – she received me in the marble hall. I found the vast salon calming and reminiscent of a culture long since disappeared, transporting me to more dignified, human times. It might seem difficult to believe that during all those nights, alone together for hours, nothing had happened between myself and Andrea that couldn't decently be displayed in daylight but, simply put, I didn't dare. And never once did she intimate that we should. She didn't intimate anything to anyone. She was amiability and courtesy personified, considering nobility to be what it has always been, when it has been anything at all: an act of service. From her high status, she shaped herself to the desires of her inferiors.

Andrea inevitably thought me slightly mad, and never quite managed to understand my romanticism. She understood well enough that I liked her, but she saw me vacillating between various incomprehensible, metaphysical states of being and feared doing damage to them. Moreover, the libertine existence she'd been dedicated to since childhood meant that Andrea was indifferent to carnal pleasures, and what she valued more than anything – even as the representative of materialism – was tenderness. She was more romantic than I was. The idea that I wouldn't kiss her or dance with her because I wasn't sure whether she was female or not seemed unhealthy, even monstrous to her.

'Your byzantinisms are absurd,' she said one evening. 'If you like me as I am, you don't need to know what I am, and if you don't like me, the same goes.'

She preferred to avoid the subject for the time being and rather enjoy the sentimental affinity we shared, no doubt planning to win me over to 'normality' one day.

My relationship with Lola didn't annoy Andrea in the slightest. Instead, she considered it – transitory, animalistic, and insubstantial as it was – a kind of hygiene like any other physical exercise recommended to us in the gymnasium. She did think I might profit more from intimacy with someone less differentiated, although she never again asked me to entertain anyone like she had with that carnation manufacturer she'd told me about in the gardens of the sanatorium. While unable to understand my attitude, she respected it.

'Tell me what you've done and where you've been today,' she said, as she often did.

I explained that I'd spent the morning at Quiet Repose Beach.

'Did you enjoy your swim?'

'No,' I said. 'There are too many people, too many chairs, transistor radios, and boats. It's impossible to find a moment's peace there. Turclub is an uninhabitable city. And yet twenty kilometres away, the countryside is emptying out.'

'I know,' said Andrea, 'and I've spoken about it with the governor, even with *Monsieur-Dame*. At the moment there doesn't seem to be an answer.'

'The loungers go right up to the water,' I complained. 'It's as oppressive as being at the cinema. You're surrounded by hawkers and radios. And it's even worse if you dive into the water because the boats don't let you swim.'

'I know. I was there yesterday in disguise. It's distressing.'

In spite of all the advertising offering visitors a tranquil paradise, the penny had now dropped with many that the reality was very different. Andrea had told me that months earlier, a romantic like myself had made two beaches for 'solitude and silence' available on a trial basis. It was difficult to know what to conclude from the trial as no-one went to one of the beaches.

'Isn't that what the romantic wanted?' I asked.

'Well, it was always going to be a relative solitude,' explained Andrea. 'A few, maybe half a dozen, refined types turned up, obviously. Anyway, the shareholders lost their stakes. But they made a lot of money from the other beach, when for some reason it suddenly became fashionable. But solitude and silence went by the wayside. The State could of course subsidise quiet beaches, but spending money so that no-one goes...'

Yes, the problem was insoluble.

'My friend,' I said, 'there is no way out of the situation. You've created an antinatural world.'

'Antinatural? Why? Everything in existence is natural; a radio as much as a pigeon.'

'Yes,' I insisted. 'But you have more radios than pigeons.'

'And what would you do with the pigeons?'

'Eat them,' I said. 'I'm starving. The synthetic steaks they serve in the restaurants are revolting.'

Andrea smiled and ordered lunch served. A *maître* in tails appeared followed by six little Ibizan boys in purple tunics with torches in hand, running and screaming like mad things. The chandeliers dimmed and the boys were picked out in the torchlight turning somersaults in a fantastical ballet. A few dared plant a kiss on my lips and one of them was brazen enough to touch Andrea's face with his hand.

The silence sirens went off – black light alternating with silver flashes – and the boys stood to silent attention. The *maître* at once climbed onto a red footstool, carefully performed two or three ballet poses, and read out the menu in French. The names were pompous, but the dishes were mediocre and in truth, one ate almost as badly at the Palazzo Víctrix as at my second-class restaurant. Andrea asked what I thought of the Academy's recommendation that the *cucchiaio* should be grasped with the *forchetta*.

'It's an affectation,' I replied.

'Why do you get angry so easily?' she said softly, upset by

my categorical response. 'It's an eighteenth-century fashion.'

'The Academy ruled that?' I replied. 'The spoon and fork were never used together in the eighteenth century.'

'Perhaps, but it's baroque.'

'Arch-baroque,' I said, laughing. 'More so than wearing silver ships on one's head, which is what the ladies at the court of Louis XVI did.'

Andrea was distracted. When she was thinking, her clear eyes had a poetry to them.

'What an interesting period,' she said, 'but dangerous... the National Convention did the right thing in guillotining the monarchs. The monarchy was absolutism, don't you think?'

'Are you sure Louis XVI was a dictator?' I replied.

'I don't know,' she replied. 'Perhaps not. But he was foolish.'

'That's another thing entirely.'

The clock struck eleven and the silence siren rang out, with more prolonged black light and silver flashes than had announced the arrival of the *maître* an hour earlier. I thought this time it must be the President of the Guild, the Grand Master Waiter in the service of Democracy, but the image that appeared on the wall to the right was the President of the U.S. of Europe. Later they said that he had decided to say a daily goodnight and send a smile to all his subjects to cheer them up because the general state of unease and discontent was so acute. Twelve older waiters entered and positioned themselves either side of the apparition, the opening bars of a dance melody sounded, and the grotesque features of *Monsieur-Dame* came into view, fifteen times larger than life, with lipsticked lips and the expression of an old procuress.

'*Bonne nuit, mes enfants, je vous envoie un petit baiser...*'

I burst out laughing and Andrea gestured to me in concern, looking over at the waiters so that I'd regain control of myself, but it was too late.

Dr Orlando's daily gatherings were by now very well attended and the old psychiatrist no longer bothered to take precautions. An order had been issued repealing the decree that required state employees and dependents (in effect almost everyone was one thing or the other, except the big industrialists who controlled the State) to acquire a specific number of atomic appliances. 'Order, plus counter-order equals disorder,' said the 1965 diabetic, repeating what someone else had said. An amnesty was also announced for the twenty-two people accused of offences against the noble estate of the Waiters' Guild, a decree which caused scandal because of its revolutionary nature. *Monsieur-Dame* was appalled and appeared on TV three nights in succession kissing the President of the Guild but was reprimanded by the conglomerates for forgetting his place.

This indecisiveness indicated serious dissent within the Party and some apparently well-informed individuals declared that the decree concerning the non-obligatory purchase of domestic appliances was Machiavellian. The word 'obligation' hit the wrong note in a so-called democratic civilization. The Regime's psychological advisors, seeing or perhaps sensing discontent (the weight of propaganda and control of information meant that no-one could possibly know what the people were thinking, if they were thinking anything at all), preached the use of the word 'liberty'. It sounded better but would need require a campaign of civic re-education and re-orientation courses so that confused citizens would know exactly which appliances they needed and desired. Only after attending such courses – the fees were incredibly high, and a percentage went to relieve the refrigerator crisis – would individuals receive a 'Certificate of Free Will to Purchase'. Moreover, it was announced that the thirty percent salary increase was to remain in place.

A few days later the Regime's psychological advisors initiated a new propaganda drive. Bland and camouflaged to begin with, it then became aggressive and, as happened during the 1929 Great Depression, exhorted people to buy at least two radio receivers or be denounced as scum. At the same time, the system of paying by instalment was ramped up with manufacturers offering payment plans, thus increasing the price of goods by twenty-five percent. Indeed, the more brazen of those at Orlando's meetings called them earning plans. The public took the bait, just as they had back when Miller wrote *Death of a Salesman*. History, it seems, is destined to repeat itself.

The manufacturers were safe for a while, but the public quickly realised that while their salaries had gone up, they couldn't eat. Drowning in repayments and excited by the chance to acquire new atomic appliances because diabolic advertising convinced them that they needed the latest model, they were perpetually tormented by debt.

Meanwhile, food was becoming seriously scarce and malcontents had begun to instigate acts of sabotage. There were frequent power cuts and disruptions to transport and planes exploded unexpectedly mid-flight. The press and TV attempted a cover-up and distracted the starving with assurances that their new appliances would improve their already high standard of living. These shiny new nickel and enamel gadgets not only didn't fit in people's apartments, but they started to make many wonder what use a pressure cooker or peeler was if there were no meat or potatoes to be had.

'Man,' said my diabetic companion, 'will never be characterised by logic. I know a middle-grade worker who's bought a safe on credit. There's nothing inside but the instalment receipts.'

In that febrile atmosphere, Dr Orlando announced that a friend of his, a former cryo patient well versed in economic affairs, would give another talk on industrialization and purposeless activity.

When I notified Andrea, she already knew. We were in the Palazzo's marble salon, the regal stable of a bronze horse set on a pedestal. A while before, Andrea had confided in me that by turning the horse's eyes like the dial on a safe and kissing it on the mouth, a secret drawer opened up beneath its abdomen. I'd suggested that she might keep papers in there, but she'd replied that it contained something a lot more powerful. I didn't press, but shortly afterwards and without my asking, she told me that secured within were the detonators to the world's four atomic devices.

'So you can blow up the whole world?' I asked.

'Not on my own, no. My detonators belong with those that *Monsieur-Dame* has at the Élysée Palace. This way we won't have a repeat of the catastrophe that destroyed Russia and North America. It's dangerous for everything to depend on one person. The nuclear devices aren't active without their corresponding detonators.'

'Everything depends on the two of you, then,' I said.

'And now you, as well,' she replied, calmly.

I was horrified. Was Andrea a fool? A purifying angel?

'Why have you confided this to me?' I murmured. 'You know what my beliefs are. What would *Monsieur-Dame* do to you if I said anything?'

'He would certainly kill me,' she answered.

There was a long pause, and then I spoke up.

'I don't understand why you're confiding in me and potentially exposing the Regime you represent.'

'Perhaps,' she replied, 'it's a way of protecting it. Now you know that my life depends on your loyalty, I feel you're closer to me and I've got more of a chance of redeeming your soul.'

'Is this about my soul or the Regime?'

'Who knows, they might depend on each other.'

'I'm not sure how you conceive of the soul. Are you Catholic?'

'Well, what can I say? It's necessary to believe in something.'

'Don't you believe in *Hola-Hola*?' I asked her, surprised.

'Shut up,' she said, with an anguished voice. She'd gone pale. After a moment, she continued. 'I can't explain what I feel, but I'm clear in my own mind.'

'What are you clear about?' I asked her.

'That only love and trust can save us.'

'Can't they also damn us?' I replied.

'Yes,' she said, wavering an instant. 'But since both things are possible, don't you think it better to put your faith in the more noble of the two?'

'Ah, but it takes courage to play that game voluntarily. You're heroic, Andrea.'

'It's necessary to believe,' she repeated. 'The defrosted speaker due to give the lecture tomorrow will say terrible things about us.'

'You should go in disguise,' I suggested. 'I'll come with you if you'd like.'

'I won't go, but the police will record it. I have no time to lose. *Monsieur-Dame* has just named me Economy Minister.'

The news took me by surprise, both the appointment itself and the casual way Andrea had communicated it to me.

'Will you give up your role as Director of Pleasure?' I asked.

She shook her head and this worried me, because that morning when I'd seen her, she'd looked scrawnier and more haggard than ever. For the first time, I had noticed a few small spots around her neckline, just as Lola had indicated.

'Will you be able to manage such an excessive workload?'

'These are difficult times,' she replied. 'It doesn't matter to me if I live a few years less. The government wants it to be Andrea Víctrix who defends our old civilization and makes it agreeable to the people, for whom my beauty is so important.'

'You are an absolutely charming being,' I said, considering her objective ingenuity, her childlike innocence and the extreme elegance of that asexual, stylised body, reminiscent of the best examples of Greek statuary. 'The admiration you awaken reconciles a part of me to this society and this civilization that I so detest. It wouldn't surprise me if they admired Lola, but it does that they appreciate your almost intangible charisma.'

Andrea smiled sadly.

'My friend, you're very kind. I'm not so handsome now. I was, perhaps, some time ago–'

'You're charming,' I interrupted, not wanting to admit that she might be right. 'And I'm not the only one who says so. Everyone–'

'My attractiveness, assuming it still exists, is appreciated only because the publicity has sold it so well. *Questa volta la luna è stata più grande del sole.*'

'Well, I am reconciled to the publicity.'

'Thank you,' she said, stroking my cheek with two skeletal fingers. 'Beauty needs both a mascot and good publicity. Just like *Hola-Hola*, cordiality in a can.'

She suddenly fell silent, and this time I didn't want to interrupt, waiting instead until she chose to speak. But she didn't, and so I had to say something.

'Why are you quiet?' I asked.

'It's my secret,' she said, tears in her eyes. 'A secret more terrible than even the bronze horse. I'm sorry, but I can't confide it to anyone. It's a sin for which there's no absolution.' Andrea had just referred to the salvation of the soul. And now to an unspeakable sin. Would she end up talking about the devil? Was there a mystic behind her supposed positivism?

'Not even to me?' I urged.

'Especially not to you. I need to convert you. It's awful to live without believing in anything.'

'So tell me what it is that you don't believe in,' I said, harbouring an intuition.

She caressed me tenderly and tried to smile through her tears.

'I believe in everything I have to believe in. Forgive me. It was just a bad moment. I'm thirsty.'

I looked at her in silence, before instinctively asking, 'Would you like *Hola-Hola*? It's a sacrament!'

Her face turned ashen and she burst into tears while I held her in my arms, shocked.

'When did you stop believing in *Hola-Hola*?' I asked.

She didn't answer, but just cried, because as she'd quite rightly said, in order to live it's necessary to believe.

'When did you stop believing?' I repeated.

'When *The Veil of Isis* was published,' she confessed.

Andrea admitted that she'd read the work in secret and, realising her atheism, had considered committing suicide. Before being incinerated, the author had written her a dreadful letter yet she hadn't been brave enough to implore *Monsieur-Dame* for a reprieve, fearing, quite rightly, that it would destroy the Regime.

'*Hola-Hola*, our highest sacrament, is a fraud, a deception perpetrated by charlatans who've seized all the gold on earth. Even so,' she said, 'the whole of our industrial mysticism is founded on this sacrilegious baptism.'

I mistakenly thought that my moment had come. I had her in my arms and was whispering in her ear, though I can't repeat everything I said to her. I talked about my time, about the home and children, about Gothic cathedrals, the majesty of the liturgy, beautiful fields of wheat and, transported for a moment to my early youth, I waxed lyrical about the pleasures of football when sport wasn't yet commercialised, about blood circulating normally through veins without the need for stimulants, and restorative sleep without sedatives. I described an Arcadia which combined Virgil's *Eclogues* with the sensibility of Lamartine. When I got to the poem entitled *Le lac*, she shot me a withering look, and I stopped.

'Rise up against *Monsieur-Dame*,' I suggested, changing tack. 'Let's conspire together.'

'I won't betray my own,' she said. 'They honoured me with their trust. *Tropo tardi*.'

'Why too late? You're still young…'

'Hun,' she said softly, 'I may not even live another year. Propaganda needed its mascot. That was me, but it could have been anyone. My new post will of course mean a lot of work, but I'll get through it with the help of triple-strength soma. We've just come up with a new, vitamin-reinforced haemoglobin that counters the anaemia caused by soma and overwork. Anyway,' she said, mustering a cheerful smile, 'I know how to read, and economics are quite familiar to me. I've always been very clear that economics are the basis of our current world and we have them to thank for the high standard of life we enjoy.'

Hadn't she understood me, or was she pretending not to understand because the situation was past saving? The sadness of her expression didn't square with the optimism of her words and things were going badly. The Regime was doubting itself and couldn't find a way out of the labyrinthine mess it found itself in. The nomination of the Head of the Bureau of Pleasure as Economy Minister went against the principle of specialization championed by the State, but the State was attempting to align itself with Andrea's erotic prestige because it understood that it was becoming unpopular. When reason failed, it became necessary to elevate desire in its place and impose a new mysticism. Where physics couldn't reach, metaphysics thrived. The U.S. of Europe's high standard of living could now only be sustained magically by an act of faith.

'We're regressing to the Middle Ages,' said Dr Orlando. 'Science itself is becoming an act of faith. According to Berdyaev...'

Before Hitler, people talked a lot about Berdyaev, but I wasn't sure what to make of him. He looked to me then like a gloomy Nordic prophet, a characteristic that grated with me in my youth. Though subsequent events seem to have proven him right, something of my youthful antipathy towards him remained and the doctor realised.

'His generation was educated in the "advanced" ideas of 1789,' continued Orlando. 'Your friend Gabriel Alomar still lived, metaphorically, in the midst of the French Revolution: democracy, indefinite progress, Estates General, etc. You seem slightly Voltairean to me as well.'

I didn't know whether he was mocking me. And anyway, Voltaire wasn't a democrat.

'I'm not sure whether I am as you describe,' I replied, 'but I was never wholly convinced by Berdyaev. Pascal was a good Catholic.'

The doctor's smile widened, his mockery now clear.

'And in his *Traité du vide* he distinguishes between those disciplines in which authority governs by recourse to faith, like theology, and those subordinated to the senses and reason, in which he states that *l'autorité est inutile*. Pascal, unlike Berdyaev, knew how to distinguish experimental science from religion.'

The doctor smiled diabolically.

'Can you define experimental science, my friend?'

'The dictionaries generally say that it's "the knowledge of phenomena according to their origins and causes",' I replied.

'Exactly,' said the doctor. 'Good boy. So that means that there is zero experimental science. The only science is theological. What we call experimental, observed by the senses, never reaches the originating cause, but sends us in the direction of even more distant causes. The elemental particle of matter used to be the molecule; then it was discovered that the molecule comprises atoms, and these became elemental. Now, each of those elements… just imagine! The primary, ordering cause can only be God, the Principle of Wisdom that derives from the Principle of Authority. Pascal – and you as an opinion writer have an obligation to know this – represented the struggle between the mystic and seventeenth-century man, the experimentalist of the *nuova scienza*. Only the first is great. Today, the other makes us laugh, as Galileo's system does. At that point *scienza* wasn't yet magic, as it is now.'

'You mean, doctor, that it was "already" not magic.'

The oracle was furious. He was given to demented outbursts and owed part of his prestige to these. The blood rushed to his head, making him look like a cockscomb.

'I mean what I say!' he shouted. 'Life is complicated enough without anyone taking it upon themselves to interpret my words. In the seventeenth and eighteenth centuries, science was "still" – I said "still" – a child's game. Forgive me,' he continued, changing his tone, 'for interrupting you when you were speaking about Pascal. Do you really know his works on the *vide*?'

I had to confess that I knew it only through references. But my enraged friend wasn't wrong. Science was relatively simple and accessible to everyone in those days. Madame de Châtelet needed nothing more than a thermometer to study the nature of fire, and physics could be explored in the drawing room or in the kitchen, before both marquesses and cooks. If we wanted to prove a theorem today, we'd have to fill the walls with calculations and no-one would understand them.

'Do you think,' asked the oracle, now calmer, 'that Einstein's devotees understand anything of his research? In his lifetime only half a dozen people had a clue.'

'But today–,' I ventured.

'Physics today is even more complicated,' he replied. 'It's accepted because of appalling realities like the atomic bomb – which you won't deny is a reality –, but we know nothing of the primary causes of this reality or even of its theories, which are changing continually. In my youth they demonstrated that the electron was simultaneously a wave and a particle. That, you would surely agree, is a greater paradox than Zeno of Elea's denial of motion. In trying to explain it, they brought that paradox together with the theory of quanta, according to which quanta or packets of energy give rise to forces. Have you ever understood what this gobbledygook means?'

'No, I haven't,' I replied, 'but others have.'

'And there's the act of faith. It's exactly what they inculcate in children from the cradle: $E=mc^2$, $E=mc^2$, etc. You, my little ones, can't comprehend this mystery, but our holy science has its teachers, and today we have to admit science by faith, just as we accept Greenland exists.'

I was confused, thinking one moment that the doctor was right, and the next that he was wrong. In reality few people could understand science, but few had ever visited Greenland, and I don't believe, or at least I'm not sure to what I extent I believe, that admitting the existence of those glacial zones constitutes an act of faith, because in the end it's perfectly possible to verify the affirmations of those who have visited them. The doctor read my mind.

'It's not always possible to personally verify that Greenland exists, dear sir. Only a very small minority can afford to make such an expedition and, what's more, it's not enough simply to get there and be shown frozen surfaces. That doesn't prove anything. We have to verify that those frozen wastes really are Greenland, and to do that we need instruments that not everyone is able to use, and technical knowledge that almost nobody possesses. It's the problem of Isaac and the angel that Sartre wrestled with. If an angel sent by God commands you to sacrifice your son, you have to obey God's command. But the first, inescapable difficulty is establishing whether the angel is real. So, if it's not always possible to verify that Greenland exists, it's no more possible to prove scientific reasoning. Only a very few experts manage to do so, but this is where a further ineluctable difficulty arises: because the time scientists dedicate to their area of expertise prevents them from dedicating themselves to other specialisms, their position is catastrophic. They end up ignorant of everything that doesn't fall within their circle of expertise.'

I had to admit that Ortega y Gasset had denounced the savagery of specialists a long time ago.

'Yes,' continued the oracle. 'Savage and superstitious, or idiots. The word is offensive, I know, but that's what I think. Anything they don't understand, which is pretty much everything outside of their specialism, should be classed as an article of faith. And there are going to be more classes every day. So Berdyaev was right when he announced a new Middle Age that'd be much darker than the previous one. What do you think? Was he right or not?' asked Orlando, angrily. 'I warn you that I'm not impressed by the force of your twenty-nine years, because I am stronger than you, sir.'

He then showed me a pistol about the size of a cigarette lighter, indicating that he could shoot holes in me if he wished. Just in case, and because he had at least in part convinced me, I acknowledged that Berdyaev could be right.

'Lose the conditional,' he replied. 'There's no 'could' about it. He is.'

I smiled. He'd left me with no choice.

'He's right, doctor.'

He smirked and tossed me a sweet from where he was sitting.

'A lady visited New York shortly before its destruction,' he continued, 'and there she met a certain Professor Philips, an important entomologist – the greatest in the world, they say –

who showed her a recently discovered butterfly which they had called Menelaus. The lady congratulated the entomologist on the witty name – the butterfly had two huge antennae that looked like horns – but the entomologist not only didn't know who Menelaus was, but had no idea about Sparta or the Trojan War. And he was the outstanding global figure in his field! What do you think about that? Are you doubting me?' he asked, falling suddenly quiet and glaring angrily at me.

'No sir,' I replied. 'I'm enjoying listening to you.'

'I thought you were laughing. Philosophy is running away from us and while we can laugh long and hard, we've entered the darkness of Babel. The waiters and the nobility,' he said, laughing more loudly, 'will surely come to our rescue.'

To tell the truth, I didn't feel like laughing. However unbalanced Dr Orlando was, deep down his words resonated with me. The optimist Voltaire, newly married to virginal science, advised us, *voyons tout par nos yeux*. Times had moved on and the virgin had become a cocotte and it now seemed absurd that a doctor might 'understand' a robot or that a mathematician should write essays on sociology. Humanism was dead. No-one could speak more than a single language and if we suggested any different we'd end up knowing but a dozen words in two dozen languages and never be able to understand each other. The analogy of the tower of Babel was accurate. At precisely the moment languages were becoming unified, we were becoming more confused. The chaotic combination of three or four languages would produce a kind of *volapük* of foreignisms and neologisms that no dictionary would collect because the publishing houses were too slow to keep up with the appearance and disappearance of argot. The rapid advance of specialized science and technologies contributed, paradoxical though it might seem, to the same result. With each day that passed, we were all more ignorant while, isolated within their disciplines, scientists used precise language that was unintelligible to the rest of us mortals, misconstruing the meaning of scientific terms before turning them, too, into argot. Thus, in spite of the fact that students worked very hard in the academies, or rather, precisely because they did, they became savages.

The accumulation of experimental data leads to ignorance. Classical reality, seen through human eyes, seemed made to human measure. Yet seen through more and more powerful microscopes, it would seem ever more infinite to us. Moreover, it'd be subjective, because man would select randomly from the vast quantity of data which constitutes Nature, composing a reality to suit his taste. In 1926, two years after Planck had formulated his theory of the quanta, De Broglie took the double nature of light – which sometimes behaves as a wave, and sometimes as a particle – as his starting point and indicated that matter might behave in a similar way, and that electrons, which are particles, might at the same time be waves. In my youth I'd read up on such reflections. Later, Heisenberg and Schrödinger developed the mad fantasy of the French prince creating quantum mechanics, a kind of eclecticism which satanically enthroned contradiction and which in order to create light, plunged us into darkness. That, in addition to the many other absurd and contradictory (yet truthful) doctrines that had surfaced since. They were legion, and their number increased daily.

'Quite so, doctor,' I said. 'You will recall the theory of the quanta...'

But he didn't remember.

'Quanta?' he asked. 'Rings a bell. If you don't mind, can we turn to more practical matters? Did you have plans for dinner tonight, my young friend? Two synthetic oranges? We're starving and you talk to me like a Byzantine about quanta and negatively-charged particles of atoms. And so negatively, dear sir. Go to Rufo's tavern on the 22nd. There you'll hear genuinely interesting things. Take notice of the speaker, who'll be there in disguise, of course. Observe him carefully.'

'Do I know him?'

Doctor Orlando laughed and slapped me affectionately on the back.

'Yes, you do, my defrosted friend. You know him, but I hope you won't recognize him. All will be revealed in a later episode, like in the old serials.'

CHAPTER XXI
PHILOSOPHY WITH LOLA

The door was ajar. Through the gap I could see Lola in a provocative Gilda dress, languidly singing a risqué little number from her own time and painting her nails in front of a small mirror at her dressing table:

Hay más hombres, le dice la gente,
como todas ya lo olvidarás...

I coughed.

'Ah, it's you,' she said, still facing the mirror. 'Come in, darling. I'm getting ready. How do you do?'

'Why are you speaking to me in English?' I asked.

'Because I didn't know who you were, my love.'

'You said it was me.'

'I said "you",' she replied. 'Everyone's *you.*'

I laughed.

'Of course.'

'I don't like the English,' she added, as she positioned a ringlet. 'They used to pay well. Now they're more self-interested and they prefer the Collective Orgies because they're free. You're one of the few decent men still around. You'd be perfect if only you had money.'

'That's a pretty serious crime!'

'Ha!' she laughed. 'I'm a stupid female and I like you as you are, poor. Let the others pay. When you arrived I was thinking of you.'

... pero ella es diferente,
porque quiere al suyo y a nadie más.

'Pretty, don't you think? It's from my time.'

The couplet didn't strike me as being particularly fitting of her profession. Lola moved from poetry to prose.

'D'you know what I heard?' said Lola. 'I heard that Andrea has syphilis.'

'In our time, perhaps, *ma belle*, but syphilis is long gone,' I replied.

'You're wrong, handsome. There's an antibiotic-resistant strain of the clap; it's on all the radio stations. And you know they say she's the daughter of a mother and father and that her mother was a loose woman.'

She chattered her way through contradictory gossip, having on other occasions said that Andrea's parents were unknown. It seemed to be true, however, that antibiotics were beginning to produce different results from those initially observable. There was no shortage of people who attributed polio, viral hepatitis, cancer, and staphylococcal pneumonia to antibiotics. When penicillin and its clones destroyed one microbial equilibrium to treat an infection, they unleashed another. This was known in Fleming's time, and Marañón had urged caution in the use of so-called electro-shock treatment, but doctors were no longer oracles and they were overwhelmed by pharmaceutical products. Just as *Hola-Hola* had replaced God and the Pope, drugs had taken the place of the physician. Even Nicola himself, one of the most illustrious figures in the whole Regime, admitted that doctors under socialism were losing prestige to the extent that their clients, who knew the name of so many medications, no longer knew the name of their doctor. If to that we were to add the economic might of the pharmaceutical industry and their scandalous claims to be able to cure everything, it's understandable that the profession found itself trapped between the ignorance of some and the greed of others.

The statistics still indicated that the average life expectancy was increasing, although the rate had slowed recently. And although civilized man was living longer than in other eras, his strength was declining. The regime of hunger to which almost everyone was subjected favoured the elderly but harmed the young, who were ever more emaciated and neurotic. The system limiting natality also meant that the proportion of older people was growing, but the most significant contributing factor to the ruin of that inhumane civilization was the ballooning number of people physically damaged by the traumas of machine progress. For every one hundred people killed in car accidents, there were another ten thousand injured, many of whom never fully recovered. Illnesses were another obstacle. Not all were fatal but almost all were incurable, caused by atmospheric pollution and the toxins from vehicle emissions. *Monsieur-Dame* was the first to express his horror, to the point that he would no longer breathe even a lungful of European air, not just because of the risk of lung cancer, but because he feared damaging his complexion. However, not everyone could do as he did and send tankers to the Himalayas to procure clean air.

'I've heard,' said Lola, 'that if they were to perform an autopsy on us, they would find our lungs to be as black as the building façades. How idiotic, applying face cream on the one hand, and going around with blackened lungs on the other. And what about the water? Haven't you heard the underground radio? In Germany, the rivers are all poisoned and there are no longer any fish. The same will happen here. The bay is surrounded by hotels using disinfectants that all end up in the sea, and that's the end of fishing. Pretty soon we'll have to explore the depths of the Pacific to find even a single fish.'

'And that's precisely where there are no fish, Lola. Fish don't live at great depths.'

She looked at me warily. Accustomed to the banter and tricks of the brothel, she often thought people were pulling her leg.

'Seriously,' I continued. 'fish spawn in coastal waters.'

'Well, that's even worse,' she said, seemingly reassured,

'because the coastal waters are filthy. And don't even think about swimming because you'll come out in a rash and your eyes will swell up. I've always been a healthy woman and, depending on your perspective, I have wholesome habits. I drink alcohol – a glass or two at most of really good champagne if someone else is paying – and I arise fresh in the morning with no hangover and a clear conscience. No, don't laugh. I have a friend who gets up in a frightful state. She's a pig. She's in with the Collective Orgy crowd. She's mad, like lots of people. Apparently, you have to queue to get into the asylums these days. I've never been with more than one man at a time, honest. You know what? I don't have any time for this "third sex business". What nonsense, don't you think? because there isn't a third sex, and if two men want to do you together, it's because they're into each other, you know? That's why I'm not interested. Is it immoral? Well I know it's not moral by today's standards. *Monsieur-Dame* wants us to enjoy ourselves without any kind of distinctions? Well he can go screw the Collective Being! Oh damn, I've smudged my Rimmel.'

'You can't be philosophising while you're putting your make-up on,' I said.

'No, it's just that the Rimmel's bad. My friend doesn't care, but me–'

'Leave your friend alone. What were you saying about the Collective Being?'

'Dear boy, I don't want to know anything about it, I don't believe it, that everyone comes together to become a single being. You mean that if I wanted to eat a cake, it wouldn't matter if someone else ate it? Or if someone did something disgusting, I'd be the disgusting one? And for a priest to have written that, really!'

'Have you read the theory of the Noosphere?' I asked.

'Why on earth would I do that! I just know that Humanity's headed in a bad direction. Now they're saying that they'll manufacture artificial water and it'll be pure, but more expensive than wine. It's all about profit. Just think, air and water are luxury items… Breathing's getting really expensive. It's a miracle we're alive.'

People were working harder and becoming increasingly agitated. The working day was officially eight hours, but industrial mysticism was so powerful that everyone worked double so that they could afford the appliances their conscience, if not their desire, told them to buy. So primitive man sacrificed to their gods a large part of the sheep whose throats they'd cut. Appliances were taking us back to the caves. Similar things were happening before I underwent my cryo-cure: in 1964, Lévi-Strauss had said that technological progress was beginning to be used above all to compensate for the shortcomings it engendered.

Both Lola and I had witnessed the genesis of what was going on now. She recalled that people from her village had lived a happy and relaxed life until they built a refrigerator manufacturing facility nearby that awoke unexpected appetites. As early as the Second Spanish Republic, enterprising towns were introducing those nickel and white-enamel idols and people had started to worship them. History repeats itself. In exchange for English glass beads, the indigenous peoples of Sri Lanka handed over natural pearls. In order to buy these frigid marvels by instalment, everyone started working longer hours, getting themselves into debt and using drugs. It wasn't enough to ruin oneself financially on the altar of these new idols; they also demanded the sacrifice of people's health and peace of mind.

The blacksmith, Lola explained, had always been high on sympathin, working seventeen hours a day until he was felled by galloping consumption. He couldn't stay still, and in his delirious dying hours he had become determined to shoe the mayor, whom the fever had transformed into a horse. There was such an uproar that the poor mayor had to leave town!

I remembered the case from having read about it in the

press. It was when machine industry was popularising the kind of activity here already common in the Nordic countries. Around 1929, Waldo Frank in his *Re-discovery of America*, extracts of which were published by Revista de Occidente, affirmed that action and activity, considered as intrinsic values, constitute ideas which are completely modern and chaotic within recorded History. The classical tendency of human activity – again, within recorded History – had always been towards unity, to repose in the definitive being, in other words, God. 'Knight-errancy', wrote Frank, 'meant action; but the goal was the Grail, and the Grail meant rest'. The Modern Age, by contrast, enthroned movement for movement's sake.

'It's all down to the experimental sciences,' I said, thinking aloud. 'The senses have been amplified by microscopes and telescopes, and innumerable phenomena are being discovered because Nature contains everything. Since facts are essentially infinite, we choose them at whim without the guiding principles which we used to have, and from just a few facts we construct a subjective truth which is always provisional and variable. Experimental science is not, therefore, objective, because the selection of facts on which it is based is arbitrary. So we're running around without knowing where we're going.'

I don't know what Lola thought of these far too serious reflections, which I should never have shared with her. Her reaction perplexed me, as while I was pondering the teachings of Waldo Frank, Lola was cooking up poison against Andrea.

'It's you who don't know where you're going,' she said. 'A man who's fallen in love with a fairy. I know exactly what I want and where I'm going.'

'Not towards unity, certainly,' I replied harshly.

It occurred to me that she hadn't understood my malevolent allusion to her profession, but she laughed and kissed me on the lips.

'Lend me your white hand, darling, and witness me reduced to "unity". I like you because you know a lot and you're quick. I think you're right when you say that we tell lies without a care. I have a friend–'

'Did I say we tell lies?' I interrupted.

'That we shape the truth to our taste,' continued Lola. 'Like this girlfriend who accused me of corrupting minors... All because I was teaching the alphabet to some children and one of them got ideas. Is teaching them to read corrupting them?'

'Possibly, but let's forget about your friend,' I said. 'I only said that we're not getting anywhere, and Waldo Frank had already said as much. Do you know who he was?'

She hesitated.

'I think I remember him. Some sleaze who cheated me out of four-hundred strong francs. A blond guy, goes to the Einstein a lot?'

'Not him. I mean the essayist who studied contemporary activity and argued against the so-called "professors of energy". Have you heard of Hitler?'

'Someone who divided Germany, a very great nation?'

'I'm not sure that was his aim, but it was certainly the result. Apparently, stimulants contributed to the German defeat. After four days of taking sympathin, the pilots were spent.'

'Ah yes,' said Lola. 'I heard it on the radio the other night. The pilots who bombed London were taking drugs and because they were off their heads they dropped the bombs on Berlin instead.'

'And that's how History is written.'

'Why are you laughing?' Lola interrupted. 'Wasn't it them who destroyed Berlin?'

'Indirectly, yes...,' I replied.

'Does indirectly mean wrong?'

'To a point.'

'What's the matter with you today? What you need is some sympathin to clear your head.'

'Haven't we just said that it wears you out?'

'That's what the radio said.'

'And do you want to wear me out?'

My arguments had lost her, but she was entertaining in an arch-feminine way. I stood up and embraced her. Andrea connected from the Palazzo Víctrix to convey her approval:

'Elle est charmante. Et toi aussi.'

'If only Andrea could see us!' said Lola, smiling in my arms and totally clueless yet again.

The mysterious speaker, apparently a friend of Dr Orlando, was in disguise when he arrived at Rufo's tavern, although as Orlando had intimated, he seemed familiar. He was perhaps a man of around my age and so had logically taken on the appearance of a young spinster, perfumed, made-up, and open to offers. In an age when togas and tunics, vitamin-fortified soma, and sterility were coming together to unify the sexes, in order to pass oneself off as a woman, people found it essential to exaggerate foundation, blushers and Rimmel. The speaker turned up looking like a temptress *à la* Bertini.

He – she – had adopted a somewhat stupid expression. It was no secret that at Rufo's there were police disguised as old ladies or yobs, reluctant to intervene at the moment, but who would sooner or later detain the speaker, assuming they didn't end him with a Parquidine injection first. The speaker was well aware of this, but like a gladiator destined to die in the arena, or a martyr, he attempted not only to conceal his identity, but to mask his words and present himself as a fool in order to delay the inevitable.

The martyr, whom we'll call the Vamp for the time being, climbed onto the stage, pale and swaying like those equivocal, new women of the 1920s. Beneath her tunic she seemed to be sporting two rubber breasts, and this is what confirmed the disguise to me, because for a long time now, real women didn't have breasts. Like a *maître*, she performed two or three ballet poses, an indicator of good manners in Turclub, and announced her subject: *The Global Peril of Industrialization*.

Such blasphemy resulted in a faultless silence, and those present looked sideways in fright at the old ladies and yobs as both groups played their part (the former with a senile expression and the latter snorting and slapping their thighs) by pretending that they hadn't understood a thing. The play-acting was grotesque and demonstrated the extent to which in the year 2050 all sense of irony, so necessary for the regulation and agility of truly civilised relationships, had been lost. The leaders of Turclub were more than a little ingenuous, while the average inhabitant couldn't even aspire to the level of its leaders. It was only us old cryo types, standing there smiling, who thought this all a farce.

The Vamp, slightly breathless at his own daring, begged the forgiveness of those who might not agree with him and asked that they postpone judgment until the end when, frightening himself still more, he declared that he would be even more controversial. His voice was becoming quieter, as though he wanted to erase the impression caused in those first few moments. By my side and scandalously feminine, Lola squeezed my hand and awakened a sensuality in me that, rather than focussing on the living Giorgione who had given me so much pleasure during ardent Turclub nights, projected itself – the folly that is Eros – onto the gaunt image of a being whom I had only ever kissed ceremonially on the neck, between the ear and collarbone.

I distracted myself by thinking about Andrea. I imagined her skinnier than she was, and closing my eyes I could almost count her ribs. She had a purple bruise on her chest near her heart, the brutal gift of some drunken Scandinavian or Nigerian lover. Andrea had ingenuously compared herself to a prostitute, but I pictured her dressed in sackcloth and spiritually possessed among the religious statuary of the Valladolid Museum.

When my attention returned to the Vamp, I was surprised by the retrospective tone of his speech. His sources included a number of philosophers from before Hitler, sociologists from the Spanish post-war, and everything from before the Social Revolution that had given rise to European hegemony following the destruction of the USSR and the USA.

'It's vital,' he said, with both certainty and caution in his voice and gaze, 'that we allow a little history to inform our understanding of the problem, and to demonstrate that there's nothing gratuitous about our motivation in obstructing current politics, well intentioned though they may be.'

While he spoke, he observed the old ladies, who remained impassive. Whistles from the audience convinced him that it was dangerous not to press on to the end. I thought he seemed unsettled for a moment behind that 1920s vampish make-up, but he bit his lip, rearranged the neckline of his dress as though adjusting the lapels of an old-fashioned blazer, and resumed his flow.

'It's clear that the world is experiencing hunger,' he said, heroically grasping the nettle. 'Food stuffs are scarcer, increasingly poor in quality and nutritional value, and are getting more and more expensive. And while the State has increased daily wages to compensate for the rise in prices, it fails to realise that the problem is not so much the lack of money as the lack of food: *disette*.'

The audience interrupted, shouting, as in Louis XVI's time, and excited by the terrible word: *La disette! La disette!*

'I am no economics expert,' continued the Vamp. 'But what's happening has been on the cards since the middle of the nineteenth century and the beginning of the socialist Industrial Era denounced by Schopenhauer, Nietzsche and later by Spengler in *Der Untergang des Abendlandes*. From the 1848 revolutions onwards, the workers' parties, justifiably demanding greater rights, had begun taking over the State and setting quite luxurious salaries that quickly led to improved living standards. In principle, that ought to be welcome, but it's notable – and this is where it all starts to go wrong – that this material wellbeing of the "people" only really had an impact on some of the people, specifically the industrial workers. Agricultural labourers were excluded, as were workers in the colonies and workers of colour, who all earned a tenth of what their European counterparts were paid. Social demands for increased rights were limited to white workers in industry. This is what caused progressive rural depopulation which in turn engendered *disette*, or *diseta*, since we've adopted this archaic term, modernized it and made it our own. Capital lost interest in agriculture more quickly because industrial enterprise was more profitable and the city, with its money and boorish entertainments – Roman *panem et circenses* – was dazzling and attractive to peasants and rural landowners alike, who neglected the upkeep of their estates. That situation favoured the development of industries and produced a temporary sense of economic wellbeing that gave rise to a population explosion in the West. The advent of such prosperity was almost certainly too rapid. That humanity and wealth multiplied in such a way, ignoring Nature and biological laws that move slowly in comparison, wasn't an indication of health: fever is also capable of momentary force and a malign tumour can spread vertiginously.'

Everyone looked at each other. I was keeping an eye on one of the old women, the oldest of all of them, in whom I thought I'd noticed a slight gesture of impatience. She had reached inside her garments with her right hand, and for a moment I thought she was about to take out a pistol and shoot the Vamp. But it didn't happen, and the Vamp went on.

'There wasn't yet any concern about the market for manufactured products. The world was divided into two zones, namely northern Europe and America on the one hand, where tools and machinery were deployed to produce more tools; and the agricultural zone, comprising the rest of the world, which was destined to buy them. Skilful advertising, intelligent if nothing else, which has evolved to occupy the place of the old religions, dazzled the simple farmers, who let their wheat and livestock go in order to purchase mendacious radios and vacuum cleaners for carpets they didn't possess. Things, however, changed a while ago, whether our rulers dare acknowledge the full and implacable reality of what is now going on or not. History, as so-called progressive Marxism would have it, doesn't stop.

Populations beyond Europe and North America woke up to these new possibilities at the beginning of the twentieth century and began to establish industries which produced merchandise at lower prices than white workers could. In 1910, particularly in England, there was growing alarm about the "jobless". Preparations for the war that broke out four years later warded off the threat of the dole, and when the war ended in 1918, the huge reconstruction effort meant that for the time being there was no shortage of work. Ten years later the problem was once again urgent. The Western workers were very productive, but they couldn't find the markets they needed and the high price of their goods made them uncompetitive compared with those produced by workers elsewhere, especially the Japanese. Since at that point no government had yet resolved to pulverize the Asian workers, the situation seemed unsolvable until the advent of the Second World War, which turned out to be much more destructive than the First. As a result of those two catastrophes, Western industries were able to rebuild, taking advantage of markets for products that no-one would have needed had it not been for the massive destruction. The white worker, the true parasite of society, has been able to live off the backs of the workers of the world because of two collective crimes: the great wars.'

The speaker paused a moment to wipe away the sweat which had smeared his make-up and then took a gulp of water. Just as he was about to continue, the suspicious-looking old lady I'd continued watching straightened suddenly and then fell to the ground, crying out. Roused by her convulsions, the audience called out for soma and Parquidine. But the Parquidine wasn't needed. Two ex-cryo doctors examined the body, removing its clothing and uncovering a youngster carrying an atomic-musical pistol* and vials of injectable poison. He had a miniature tape recorder strapped to his midriff.

* The police used a model of pistol that transformed the report into musical notes and a dance rhythm so that they could execute a target in a given venue without anyone but those sitting in the immediate vicinity noticing.

There was huge confusion. The audience threw themselves at the corpse, bent on destroying it. The old ladies exchanged a signal they'd obviously already agreed upon and left the tavern followed quickly by the yobs. Almost immediately six magnificently imposing praetorian guards appeared and their mere presence was enough to re-establish order. The speaker had disappeared and there was no search. They simply spoke to the doctors who certified that the young man disguised as an old woman had died as casually of a rapid wound as others die of pleasure.

The instruction to sweep the matter under the carpet was scrupulously observed. Such tolerance from a regime not averse to bloodletting, shooting the virgins of Avignon and exterminating the Japanese because they were manufacturing affordable transistor radios, raised suspicion. The atmosphere was charged. A kilo of meat cost more than three kilos of automobile and had no taste whatsoever. The hens were going mad and suffering muscular degeneration. Though the advertising claimed that synthetic fruit had more vitamins than real fruit, the synthetic version produced scurvy in small doses and manic outbursts in larger quantities. The shortage of food was supplemented with liver extracts that no longer contained liver but were produced synthetically in labs. As foodstuffs became more expensive, pharmacies became more important and this favoured the low-income classes because Health Insurance provided free access to medicines. Wasn't it absurd, the Regime's doctors declared, to ingest half a kilo of food that is damaging to the stomach simply to derive a few grams of benefit and expel the rest? The *panem et circenses* of decadent Rome had become *medicamenta et circenses* and the money previously destined for the market could now be spent on atomic appliances, which made life easier; or on plastic flowers, which gladdened the heart. What's more, scientifically formulated nutrition eliminated the perils of obesity. 'Today,' proclaimed the glossy magazines, 'we can have the same flat stomach at sixty years of age as we had when we were children,' and some surgeons advocated the removal of metres of intestine because it was about as much use as the tonsils or appendix.

But there remained those of us in the new civilization who were old-fashioned enough to want to eat, obstinate individuals who preferred to be sure that before they danced with a woman, she really was a woman, and would rather a second-rate but real carnation than an artificial, double carnation. Those of us who underwent the cryo-cure before 1985 were obviously the most rebellious and determined. Unfortunately for us, however, our lives are bound in prejudice. Lola had pointed out that the plastic flowers were the same colour and made of the same material as the waste bins and wash bowls, which increased the prestige of the bins and bowls, and diminished that of the flowers.

Andrea was preoccupied. The new role of Economy Minister was all-consuming. She spent her time surrounded by transmitters, attended to the complaints of the malcontents, and made notes about the clandestine lectures and the people who attended them. Only around midday did she take time away from her toils for cocktails on Pleasure and the seduction of those tourists she thought worth her while. The contradictions of her personality were becoming disconcerting, and their consequences, terrifying. She would emerge from the Palazzo resplendent: fresh, cosmetically enhanced, dosed up and smiling; and she'd return ugly and yellow, shutting herself into an office full of transmitters and receivers with her secretaries. At midnight, having taken drugs again, she began her tour of the cabarets and the unspeakable tableaux that she spoke of with such charming innocence. In the early morning she was returned to the Palazzo in an ambulance by the police and accompanied by two doctors, beaten to a pulp.

According to the Regime's records, I was listed as 'State informer', and it was true that I told Andrea everything I heard. At Rufo's tavern however, where everyone knew about my relationship with Lola, they saw me as a friend of the rebellion. I didn't like the ambiguous situation, but I couldn't think of a way out. Andrea seemed a supernatural being to me, a goddess with whom my physical contact was limited to a protocolary kiss on the clavicle. 'If you like me as I am, you don't need to know what I am,' she'd said, tapping into her puritanism. 'It's me you should love, if in fact you do, not your prejudices. Her words revealed an exalted spirituality that I, romantic by definition, didn't feel able to understand. Lola, on the other hand, was vulgar, slightly absurd, but had a certain genuinely feminine appeal. In such a mystified and mystifying country, how could I not make her my lover? Andrea herself was encouraging me so that I could convert her and bring her over to the Regime, but also because as Director of Pleasure, she considered it her duty to procure entertainment for me.

'You're nervous, agitated,' she said, not for the first time. 'I don't understand your repugnance towards the Collective Orgies and it pains me, because if you were able to overcome your prejudices–'

'Never,' I replied.

'Before you entered the cryo chamber, you enjoyed sport. That's what you told me.'

'Yes,' I agreed.

'So? Exercise tones the nerves. Our era is anti-sport, but the Collective Orgies are excellent exercise, their moral and educational value aside. Some people say they wear you down. All exercise consumes the body, but if it's balanced with the right medication, it fortifies the musculature. In many C.O. centres you'll come across all manner of acrobatic exploits, and everyone can satisfy their tendencies, whether masochist or sadist. You'd make a good sadist.'

'Some days I'd pick a fight with a lot of people, true.'

'You see? But punching someone is a crime, unless they're a masochist, and if they are then you're awarded a diploma, not punished. And if you accidently injure or kill your partner, you're covered by the State. Provided, of course, that your sadist licence is up to date.'

'I'd like to punch a waiter,' I said. 'I hit a few when I was young.'

'You're not asking for much,' Andrea said. 'That's a risky thing to say.'

'I'd like to punch the Head of the Guild.'

'Seriously?'

'Or better still, *Monsieur-Dame*.'

'That's enough,' said Andrea, nervously. 'That's a profanity, not a joke.'

'I'll shut up, but don't persist with your absurdities.'

'Very well, hun. I know you're an enemy of our civilization.'

'I am,' I replied. 'It's suffocating.' I'd picked up a curious fifteenth-century jewelled Italian dress dagger and was examining it.

'You can have it, a gift from me,' said Andrea. 'That period must seem better and more human to you than this.'

'Doubtless,' I said. 'Your whole civilization rests on *The Veil of Isis*.'

She wavered, and seemed to be trembling. Her expression told of infinite bitterness and she wiped away a tear.

'You detest our civilization,' she said, 'but what would you substitute it with? You're not the only person to think as you do; it's easier to destroy than it is to build... Machines are necessary. The cybernetics you abhor are indispensable to banks and offices. Without scientific and machine progress ninety percent of humanity would perish. Or at least that's what Zischka claimed many decades ago, citing the Diesel engine as one example among many technologies that were a third more efficient than those that they replaced. Though of course today that engine has been superseded. He also pointed out that the Haber-Bosch process by which atmospheric nitrogen could be fixed from the air had led to prodigious increases in agricultural yields.'

'That must be why there's *disette*,' I replied. 'Be honest, Andrea. Now we don't have colonies or workers overseas to exploit, you're putting your faith in interplanetary conquest to be able to live at the expense of others. The industrial spirit which unleashed the great wars of the twentieth century would not have baulked at a space war, but you've failed there too.'

She flushed and I saw that she was getting angry.

'That's not true,' she replied.

'You tell me what you get out of going to the moon or to hell: to survive there for an even an hour you'd even have to take oxygen with you. You've made it to the moon, and what? Just like if you were to make diamonds in the laboratory; they'd end up being more expensive than natural diamonds.'

'Don't be such a pessimist,' Andrea said. 'There'd be more *disette* without progress.'

'That remains to be seen.'

'Progress cannot be stopped, and the world can't go backwards.'

'Who told you such a fairy tale, Andrea? Even if it can't be stopped, it can explode. More advanced civilizations than this have disappeared.'

'Which ones?' she asked.

'I don't know! In *The Exploration of Time*, Robert Bowen says that the Earth is more than 4,500 million years old, and judging by ancient legends has suffered a multitude of vicissitudes: floods of water, floods of fire, just like the ones you're contriving with your atomic devices.'

We were in the great marble hall of the Palazzo Víctrix and I pointed towards the belly of the bronze horse positioned in the centre.

'In the Bible–'

Andrea looked up.

'Who remembers the Bible?' she said. 'Don't let yourself be taken in by Dr Orlando. He's a fanatic.'

'He's as much a fanatic of obstruction as you all are of action.'

'But we can't live without doing something. I work as much and more than I can.'

I imagined Andrea's bacchanalian nights and felt the blood pulse in my temples.

'Bingeing on soma and filling a Roman palace with atomic detonators is not how to live!' I shouted. 'Are you really suggesting that we couldn't get by without these? We certainly can't with them. You're preparing a catastrophe of Biblical proportions! I'm not censuring you because it's inevitable, but because you can't see it!'

I was about to lose my temper.

'Why are you censuring my blindness if the catastrophe is inevitable?' she said. 'I won't be here to see it, of course, because I'll be dead. Soma is accelerating my ageing.'

I regretted having shouted but was still resentful and the sacrifice of that wonderful being made me even more furious. I couldn't conceive of myself without her and, in my egoism, I saw her as egoistic.

'You think like Louis XV,' I said. *'Après moi, le déluge.'*

My words were offensive and unfair and that's why I'd said them. She looked at me calmly.

'You think that of me?' she said.

Of course I didn't, but I was despairing.

'You're over-excited. Go and find Lola. You like Renaissance women.'

That was almost an affront in the context of the new Regime's morality.

'And what do you like?' I answered.

'How can you ask me that? Everything. Everything that might give pleasure to others.'

'And yet you punched me on Pleasure.'

'Because you'd blasphemed. You forget that I–'

No, I wasn't forgetting that Andrea was a goddess, albeit not born of a swan like Helen, but in an incubator. Some spread the rumour that she was viviparous, but such gossip was designed to topple her from her privileged position. Poor Andrea. While certainly a bacchant, depending on your perspective, she was a nun too. Why bacchant? The idea had come to me straight from an old poem by Madame de Noailles:

I close my eyes and see her in the distance of time, white and angelic, immaculate, circled with a halo and the smile of a child.

This sublime vision suddenly became mired and I imagined her in a brothel, brutalized by a frenzied sailor. The brothel was the Roman circus, the sailor the wild animal, and Andrea represented the martyr who was indispensable in any theology. Even now I know why I always respected her.

Amid increasing dissent, and while officials were planning another reorganization of the economy and a better distribution of foodstuffs, the authorities came up with the idea of organising an homage to Andrea to lift collective spirits.

It was the beginning of May and tourists were arriving to enjoy the sun, tranquillity and entertainment promised by the travel agencies. In reality, our entertainment – based on drunkenness, drugs and popular music – is precisely the opposite of tranquillity, as Pascal had similarly observed. Breezes were warmed by combustion engines and the scent of the sea was impregnated with heavy oils and petrol. But the slogan and the brand worked their magic, as they almost always did.

The week of popular celebrations preceding the event were anything but original (anything popular is never really new) and so there were football matches, dances, car races and jets. Only three motorists were killed, but bad luck resulted in two jets falling on the crowds and this increased the number of victims to 350. (It was pointed out at the time that as the year has 365 days the average number of deaths per day was derisory, since 0.8 victims doesn't even make one and it's not possible to think in terms of fractions of victim). There was folklore too, it having evolved since Aina Cohen's time. Back then, country girls wore embroidered *rebosillos* and danced modest boleros, but since this was too bland for the multitudes of visitors to the island who had no interest in historical customs, the organizers abandoned their integrity and were as likely to pass off a bullfighter for a typical Mallorcan peasant as a nun for an odalisque.

'That,' said Andrea, attempting to justify such aberrations from an economic perspective, 'is because the island itself is poor. It's all about attracting the foreigners who have converted

Turclub into one of the four greatest cities on earth. Foreigners don't really distinguish between nuns and odalisques, and these things amuse them. They like civil guards, gypsies, and pious bullfighters, all of them wearing reliquaries around their neck. It's doubtless immoral, very immoral, but what can we do? Tourism creates wealth and contributes to mutual understanding between nations.'

I think it creates confusion. Believing Turclub (formerly Palma) to be part of the Canary Islands, more than one English woman had asked where Mount Teide was, saying: '*Il volcano, il volcano*, please. You do not understand?' They couldn't even speak the language. Individuals of undefined nationality plied their trade in financial centres in which they made absurd pitches and confused possibility and obligation, *deure* and *haver*. Supersonic travellers visiting the whole world in twenty-four hours asked questions like: 'What's that? Where are we?' incessantly. 'Don't worry,' the guides replied, 'when we reach our destination, the TV will tell you everything you need to know in ten minutes, and so that you can tell your friends in turn, you'll all be given a 560-word account which will outline the history, monuments, folklore and cuisine of the countries you've visited.'

Ah, Berdyaev, how right you were, and how wrong of us to doubt you! We'd returned to the Middle Ages with new acts of faith, though today our prophets and miracle men were tourist information offices explaining the world in 560 words. Yet however debased the masses were, those stupid explanations didn't satisfy everyone. The reappearance of certain illnesses once thought eradicated, such as infectious hepatitis and scurvy, began to encourage heresies. Were we witnessing the failure of sterilization and synthetic vitamins? What about influenza? How had the 'flu not been eliminated given the proliferation of antibiotics? And death? Why did we die when every day more effective medications came on to the market and surgeons could transplant tissues and organs bought from the peoples of

Polynesia? Provided they compensated well, it was perfectly fair for the rich to profit from the poor. They already bought their blood and eyes, though they hadn't yet managed to transplant brains. Pessimists didn't think it would ever happen and judged it immoral, but they were an obstacle to progress and had to become puritans to justify their ill humour. According to them, modern medicine was useless against even the common cold.

Nor did it make sense that the food was so poor in such a rich city with so many distractions and such an abundance of machines and appliances. *Disette will finish us yet* went the refrain of an underground song gaining in popularity. Clandestine editions circulated of Marie Mercier's book in which she sang of 'maternal pleasures and the right to be a mother', and the authorities were fearful lest there be riots like those that had occurred in Avignon. One morning, Lola came to my lodgings to find me.

'I've got two tickets from Rufo for a porno,' she said. 'There's a married mother breastfeeding her child with her husband by her side, a husband just for her... I'm thinking of going disguised as a police officer dressed as an old woman. Marie Mercier's going to be there. Did you know she's in Turclub? She's come for the première. Imagine how much courage that takes. They're saying that *senyoreta* Mercier is a virgin. Like before, you know? Poor thing, she just talks on and on about marriage and she wasn't able to marry. That must be why she writes poetry. She underwent the cryo-cure, too. When she was already getting on, around fifty years old. Well, now she's young, but it makes no difference. She was honourable, still is. Not like me, I'm past caring. I'm as much of a lost cause as Andrea.'

'Don't you dare mention Andrea,' I said.

The venue for the film showing was rammed. As expected, the police were there in disguise alongside many other inhabitants dressed up as police in disguise. I don't understand how the authorities permitted the event to go ahead just one night before the homage to Andrea but perhaps, conscious of the vulgarity of the celebrations to come, they thought the film might contribute added spice. If so, they were right, because in effect the porno constituted the main feature, but all it did was damage the Regime. Opinions were divided by a display of indecency that would have been perfectly moral in my time. Those protesting against *disette* made political capital out of the film and the showing took some of the shine off the homage to Andrea. In my eyes, the film was nothing more than a cheap sentimental flick. Love, moonlight, a babe in arms attached to his mother's breast who stops suckling to gaze at his prize while the faces of his progenitors stream with tears.

'Did you see, Antoni?' said the mother. 'He laughed…'

'I did, Margarida,' replied the father.

'Are you happy?'

'I am, darling wife.'

The film ended brusquely and a voice from off started declaiming emphatically, 'You have just seen, dear viewers, what our system has destroyed, amputating the most noble sentiment in human existence: maternal love.'

I won't deny that I was affected. For some, however, it was indecent in the extreme and they threw up. In front of me, a person of distinction, possible a waiter, hesitated and started talking to himself.

'Give suck to a child?' exclaimed the person. 'That makes a woman no different from a goat! And what about the risk of infection?'

The audience demanded that *senyoreta* Mercier say a few words.

'I'm not a mother,' shrieked the poetess, her eyes welling up, 'but I have the same maternal desires as those four hundred virgins sacrificed ten years ago on the plains of Avignon.'

And then she burst into tears, singing an old lullaby:

What shall we give the mother's child,
What shall will give him that isn't absurd…

The public then took up the catchy refrain and started singing along:

raisins and figs and sugar and olives,
raisins and figs and honey and curds...

I imagine the inexplicable delirium that overcame everyone, including those oviparous products of incubators, was a reaction to that striking display of food products now almost consigned to history:

raisins and figs and sugar and olives,
raisins and figs and honey and curds...

Only a few very privileged individuals allowed themselves to serve real olives with their vermouth aperitif and take sugar in their coffee, and it occurred to a member of the secret police to shout via a speaker concealed under his clothing that saccharine was more potent than sugar. Seeing the attitude of the audience, however, he had to shut it off.

Andrea was following the course of events from the Palazzo Víctrix, while doctors and massage therapists restored her physique for the homage scheduled the following day. There were suggestions that she'd cried, and she confessed to me that she had, but in anger. The situation had shown Turclub's governor to be totally inept. The President of the Waiters' Guild, accompanied by six Ibizan angels, presented themselves at the Palazzo Víctrix to propose they stage a coup d'état, offering Andrea command of the province and leaving *Monsieur-Dame* with no choice. But the doctors' opinion was she was in no state to take on new responsibilities.

I arrived at the Palazzo just as the President of the Guild, sporting a full array of medals, was leaving. Andrea was on the massage table wearing nothing but a plastic vine leaf. Her gauntness was alarming. That slight, nineteen-year-old creature appeared withered and almost yellow. The well-shaped androgynous pecs just about concealed the ribs and there was a purplish bruise on the right thigh. Her eyes were closed and a microphone was reciting slogans and precepts of political economy. This poor body, I thought, has to parade naked tomorrow in front of the public. I couldn't resist the urge to kiss her golden locks. She opened her eyes and smiled.

'Hun…,' she said. I think she was sedated.

A doctor approached with a syringe full of some drug.

'Wait in the room next door,' he said. 'Nothing to worry about. She'll be completely restored tomorrow.'

CHAPTER XXV

The homage was due to take place at midday. Beneath the Triumphal Arch at the end of Pleasure, a throne had been installed that was accessed via sixteen red-carpeted steps. Two golden lions stood guard, mechanical prodigies able to move their head, open their jaws and lift their paw to greet or perhaps take a swipe at those present. No-one knew quite which, according to Lola.

Andrea's condition was worrying and it seemed to me that the monstrous *Monsieur-Dame* was prepared to let Andrea be devoured in order to save himself. The idea of appointing her Economy Minister and finance champion was both absurd and beyond the capabilities of the ailing figurehead, though Humanity is always in need of redeemers and so *Monsieur-Dame* was offering up the goddess as the Israelites had sacrificed Christ. The moment urgently demanded someone who was still capable of electrifying the doubting multitudes. That was the word: electrify, fire up. How History repeats itself, and how old the world is! As I recalled pleasant hours spent reading about eighteenth-century France, it occurred to me that John Law had done exactly the same with those deluded investors who had dreamed of rocks encrusted with diamonds and mountains of gold in the Mississippi Valley at the time of the Company of the West affair. To fund the exploitation of such treasures, Law didn't have silver coins, but questionable banknotes. To whip up investor fervour, 'he took a group of ten savages to Paris, tattooed and wearing feathers, the entourage of a queen of the "Missouri Nation". They hunted deer in the Bois de Boulogne and danced with gay abandon. They were showered with gifts. It was utter folly.' In a pretty tale quite befitting of 1715, the queen of the 'savages' managed to get wed to a talented officer, but the finance collapsed and the Regent expelled Law, who had to seek refuge in Holland.

The night before the homage I retired late, hoping to pick up some gossip about the event and gauge the pulse of public opinion. The city was resplendent with lights and pennants, but although the crowds were numerous, they seemed subdued and there was little talk of Andrea in the bars. Instead, the main topic of conversation seemed to be the crimes of a sadist who had killed thirty-two masochists in a branch of the Collective Orgies. Two professors from the Classical University were discussing the case.

'It was really exciting,' explained a yob. 'He knocked off five guys just like that, yelling insults and blaspheming like a condemned man. At the beginning, the masochists were in their element, but then panic set in and they started shrieking like harpies. This just aroused the sadist more and he began stabbing wildly at people... What a fantastic guy!'

'Are you sure the sadist was blaspheming?' asked one of the professors.

'He even insulted *Monsieur-Dame*,' came the reply.

'What's the penalty for that?' someone asked.

The two professors looked at each other.

'First,' said one, 'we'd have to know if he really was a criminal. Were all the victims masochists? If so, it's not a crime but mutual pleasure, legal entertainment, provided the killer has his sadist's licence, of course.'

'He has,' said the yob. 'He showed it.'

'Then he deserves a medal. He's broken all the records. What's more,' he said, turning to the yob, 'I understand your admiration.'

'But you're forgetting,' the other professor said, 'that he insulted *Monsieur-Dame*.'

'Yes sir, he did!' exclaimed the yob, guffawing. 'When he was stabbing a fat old man who looked like a skinned pig, he yelled in a falsetto "Hey rosy snout, you're as pretty as *Monsieur-Dame*."'

There was silence.

'Does that amount to contempt?' asked someone.

'It could be interpreted as deference,' replied the professors. '*Monsieur-Dame* is in effect as pretty as a rose. If there's ridicule or mockery at all, it's aimed at the old man who was stabbed, and he's a masochist so there's no case to answer.'

Other, more animated, groups were talking about food. Suckling kid meat and real oranges seemed to be of more interest than Andrea.

'Andrea will say what she always says. Oh, except that she'll let us see her naked.'

'As if we haven't seen her naked a thousand times...'

'Apparently, the governor is going to talk about the food crisis.' 'We'll see...'

In a Terreno cabaret I came across Dr Nicola with a youngster who looked to me – I was beginning to get better at this – like a girl from before the Great Revolution. The doctor glanced in my direction, and after saying a few words to his companion, came across on his own to my table.

'Still in love with Andrea Víctrix?' he asked, kissing me formally on the neck. 'I imagine you won't miss her apotheosis tomorrow.'

'Nor, I imagine, will you, dear Doctor,' I replied.

'Of course not. Tomorrow the whole city will be able to contemplate the most beautiful body of our age.'

The Classical University had indeed just conferred this honorific on Andrea, following a suggestion from higher authorities. My friend looked at me with amused curiosity.

'Andrea has a lot of time for you, he said. 'She has a noble heart. Those objections that you might have about the Regime, as a cryo-cure survivor... Did you go to the lecture at Rufo's tavern? What did you think of the speaker?'

'I don't get involved in politics, Doctor,' I said, trying to avoid the question. 'Precisely because I'm an old cryo-cure survivor–'

'I applaud you for it,' he replied. 'Things are getting tense. Half the city is spying on the other half and the government is beginning to attract criticism, but tomorrow's event is expected to shore up its popularity.'

He seemed to be hedging his bets. I could see he was trying to get me to talk, and I took my leave. At the door I bumped into a very excited Lola.

'I was looking for you,' she said, breathlessly. 'Let's spend the night together and tomorrow you can accompany me to the homage. They're saying it's true that he'll parade completely naked.'

'Who?' I said.

'Him. Andrea. You and I can drop the hypocritical neuter gender nonsense.'

'Andrea is a girl,' I replied.

Lola burst out laughing.

'We'll see about that tomorrow. Shall we have a bet on it? I've known for ages that he's a–'

'Oh do be quiet,' I interrupted.

She stopped talking and kissed me on the lips, as she always did when I rebuked her.

A quarter of an hour before midday, Pleasure Avenue looked magnificent. Myrtle, flowers, and flags were everywhere. We were lucky enough to secure two seats on the front row from which to watch the parade. Many crowd members were dressed elegantly in Roman style, the young wearing short tunics and the older spectators wearing togas down to their feet. First to parade past were the obligatory cultural groups: bullfighters from Poble Nou, *majos* from Sencelles and sword dancers from from Sineu. Then came dozens of white angels and heralds. After them, the industrialists, kings of steel, plastic, uranium, and synthetic oranges, all wearing golden crowns, and workers' representatives with placards displaying lions and symbols of atomic power that they ingenuously attributed to their own labours and which instead resided within the crowned heads of those who preceded them. Then came numerous, horrific robots before the nobility, the chic of society passed by: the Guild of Waiters with a vanguard of Ibizan angels.

The procession was spectacular, well-organised, and becoming unbearable. People were impatient, trying to spot Andrea Víctrix's chariot. The Einstein march started up a number of times, dark and triumphal, with a muted theme of liquid notes, only to be drowned out by powerful, insistent Wagnerian trumpets. Lola squeezed my hand.

'Mark my words,' she said. 'This music doesn't bode well.'

The march indicated that the goddess was leaving her Palazzo, and the first setback very quickly occurred when *senyoreta* Mercier fainted and her friends hurled insults at Andrea. I got to my feet. Amid modest cheers, a Roman chariot drawn by four white horses made its way down the avenue. The goddess was standing, wearing nothing but a purple cloak that hung from her shoulders and contrasted with the golden white of her slender body, lauded by the Classical University and displayed generously and chastely for all to see. Her sex, or perhaps absence of sex, was concealed by a tiny silver vine leaf on her lower abdomen. Lola and I exchanged glances as both of us claimed to have won our wager. From a distance it was hard to imagine a more striking scene and the crowds applauded accordingly. Closer up, however, the picture changed: in spite of all her doctors and injections of temporary filler, she was a debilitated, cachectic organism, though her bone structure was still elegant, her neck fine, and her smile perfect. Her seductive features were framed, halo-like, by cascades of golden hair but despite everything, this was no longer a human figure but an outline sketched by an artist of genius, an abstract conception that life had not adorned with flesh. It was doubtless true that cosmetics had worked miracles, but when I saw her up close,

I shut my eyes and had to accept that the triumphant goddess was dead.

The crowd must have felt the same, as the ovations petered out as Andrea came ever closer.

'Isn't she skinny!' shouted a couple of yobs. 'Someone give her some cod-liver oil!'

Lola drew my attention to her right thigh. The make-up hadn't completely covered a purple mark that I'd noticed the previous day, the result of some brothel fight.

'See, she's even more of a tramp than I am,' said Lola, though realising she'd referred to her in the feminine, she added indignantly, 'More of a tramp or more of a fairy, whatever.'

The goddess had reached the triumphal arch and was making her way up the staircase to the throne. Once seated, two Ibizan angels rearranged the cloak hanging from her shoulders so that it fell across part of her bruised thigh, a pair of incredibly slim basketball players presented her with the helmet and spear of the Roman Venus Víctrix who centuries earlier had determined the outcome of the battle of Pharsalus in Caesar's favour, and the crowds applauded with slightly more enthusiasm. There was some confusion as the hired support waited for a signal from the Head of Protocol before breaking into the first shouts of 'Andrea Víctrix' ahead of the expected chorus from the multitudes. The Guild of Waiters seemed to be in discussion with the governor, who was on his seat surrounded by councillors and secretaries. The waiters were pressing for Andrea to speak while the governor, worn out by years of power and adulation, was hesitating over giving the order. Andrea remained silent, smiling stereotypically, beautiful from without and broken within. A dignitary finally gave her the sign, but instead of launching into a rousing speech, Andrea simply waved a laboured greeting side to side with her right hand, like Grace Kelly once did years ago in her role as exquisite princess.

'Hello, hello,' she repeated.

Too cold and too academic, it didn't go down well and the enthusiastic shouts of the claque went unaccompanied. The governor's speech was optimistic on the surface, all smiles and kisses for the onlookers, but desperate and empty in substance, and was lost on a bored audience that was beginning to drift away. The wind was up and the sky had clouded over.

'Thanks to your lover, you're going to catch a chill,' said Lola sarcastically.

The same had occurred to me. I looked at her through my binoculars and saw her shivering on her throne, naked and helpless. As the representative of the highest nobility, the president of the Waiters' Guild offered her his arm and accompanied her to the Roman chariot, which departed post-haste amid the victorious and panicky notes of the Einstein anthem. As she passed in front of us the wind caught her cloak and just above her waist we glimpsed a horrific, still bleeding wound. Morality and psychology had become so intertwined that Andrea's martyrdom could just as easily be considered heroic as abject. The wound provoked insults, principally from veterans of the cryo-cure, but in a process of contamination – blood excites wild beasts – many from the younger generations joined in. Nobody was happy.

Some weeks had passed and the governor was lurching from one miscalculation to another. Surprised by the speed of events, those in power fluctuated between a dictatorial rigour that failed to solve the problem of *disette*, and cowardly concessions that undermined the principle of authority at moments when it was most urgently needed. The failed homage to Andrea had made the situation even worse. *Senyoreta* Mercier continued writing poetry and weaponizing the sacrifice of the four-hundred virgins killed at Avignon, while the song *L'infant de la mare* was becoming ever popular due to the increasing difficulty of obtaining sugar, raisins and figs. In the meantime, the United States' formidable police were aware of everything. They had millions of records in their archives, but when the moment came to take action, a weary Paris recommended diplomatic solutions and coexistence.

When an epidemic of scurvy broke out, the deeply divided Board of Physicians was unable to issue an opinion. Independent doctors, courageous, exasperated and starving, attacked the dogmatic medicine peddled by the Official State Academy, and declared that the reliance on tinned food was responsible for the epidemic. According to them, synthetic vitamins were ineffective. Nicola, meanwhile, believed they worked as well as natural vitamins and so couldn't cause scurvy, although he admitted the possibility that they might produce cancerous degeneration which was easily confused with scurvy.

'Many medical problems,' he told me, 'are problems of nomenclature. In the Middle Ages, everything was plague. At the end of the nineteenth century, everything was influenza. The horrific epidemic of 1918 was identified as 'flu even then, although eminent doctors pointed out coincidences with plague.

Tuberculosis almost vanished from existence halfway through the twentieth century, but lung cancer emerged as a threat. All a bit suspicious, don't you think?'

I preferred not to comment, being naive in such matters and especially regarding questions of nomenclature and lexis. The language of medicine is so inaccessible to the lay person as to close all doors to reasoning. Like almost all subjects, medicine can only be grasped via faith. In fact, I have arrived at the conclusion, although sans serious grounds, that there exists just a single illness which always leads to death, of which all others are mere symptoms. But this is a personal fancy, and I digress.

Industry, like the apoplectic who dies from an 'excess of health', was entering a crisis caused by excess activity, and industrialists had begun to clamour loudly for greater state protection because the general public were no longer exhausting the supply of atomic appliances on the market. The ill intentions of the 'obstructionists' were also a factor: these heretics created the rumour that the vacuum was slower and more complicated than the broom, and doctors opposed to the Official State Academy discovered that many cases of gastritis and hepatitis originated with the use of refrigerators. Then the robots, stronger than bulls, more delicate than butterflies, and controlled by inexpert hands, caused so many accidents that their owners began to be scared of them. Andrea was worried and kept asking me what I thought of the situation.

'I won't hide that many people are unhappy about the food shortages,' I told her.

'Yes, I know,' she replied. 'Things are not how they should be. Tell me: do you think it would be difficult to bribe Dr Orlando, now that his star is rising?'

'Very difficult, I'd say. Popularity, like puritanism, goes straight to the head.'

She seemed to be mulling something over.

'I agree,' she said, finally. 'But do you think that mad old man and *senyoreta* Mercier are more capable than us? Be honest. Your intuition is valuable to me.'

I didn't know. I've never been a true essayist and I lack creative genius, and therefore incline towards negative critique, a quality I tell myself is 'philosophical' when I want to buoy my spirits. Over the years I've become lazy, and we know very well that it's easier to pull down than it is to build up. I did my best to avoid the question.

'First of all,' I said laughing, 'what do you mean by "us"?'

'The Regime… and you,' came the reply.

'But I'm an enemy of the Regime!'

'You, I think, are your own enemy,' said Andrea. 'You enjoy tormenting yourself. You love the Regime because you love me.'

'I love you and I detest the Regime.'

'See? You're a romantic. One day you're going to have to find a synthesis, a way of agreeing with yourself.'

'And that day–.'

'You'll be mine,' she said, without hesitating.

'Maria Mercier was completely ridiculous,' I said, wondering where such faith could come from and changing the subject. 'All that crying and yearning for raisins.'

'I'm worried about famine, hun. I can see that things aren't working, but the answer can't be a return to agriculture as it used to be.'

'So what's the solution?' I asked.

'Almost certainly chemicals,' said Andrea. 'But I've got so much studying to do on the subject. I say chemicals but I know things are already getting out of hand.'

I looked at her, surprised.

'I thought you were a materialist,' I said.

'Oh, *mio caro*,' she murmured. 'All the old values, the old systems (Galileo, Berthelot) are being revised. When the prince de Broglie began to understand Einstein–'

'Do you really think that reading scientific theories will put more bread on our tables?'

'Not more bread,' said Andrea. But that's not what it's about.'

'Or more Corinth raisins?'

'We'd have to do without raisins, of course. Austerity is coming and I don't need you to give me a hard time right now. In a few weeks I'll be more prepared. I'm studying as hard as I can. Yesterday I studied for fifteen hours and didn't go out. Do you think I look frail?'

Frankly, she was ugly, and for the first time she confessed that her health was poor.

'You can't lead this kind of life, Andrea,' I said.

'No.'

'Who on earth's idea was it to appoint the Director of the Bureau of Pleasure as Economy minister?'

'Don't imagine that it's some huge error,' she said. 'Now I'm aware of the detail, I can see that economics isn't exact, or tangible, but is actually an act of faith.'

I thought she was delirious and found it disconcerting for her words to remind me of what Dr Nicola had said on one occasion.

'The people don't understand economics,' she continued, 'and neither do the economists. Ford himself had a go once. Nevertheless, we have to have belief. Every modern, intensely complicated civilization is built on credit. And if credit fails, well... And because I was beautiful the government chose me to convince the masses.'

I played along with the drama.

'Because you *were* beautiful!' I exclaimed. 'In the past tense.'

'Quite: past. You must know that on the day of the homage I heard the things they were saying. Lately the nights of pleasure have weakened me significantly; I don't have the strength to defend myself. Triple-strength soma no longer works for me. I'm old.'

At that point the doctor eavesdropping from the room next

door (everyone was equipped with receivers and transmitters hidden in their clothes) came in and put an end to the conversation.

'The Excellency has a temperature,' he said, his tone bordering on impertinent, 'and needs to rest.'

Staring at him, I said that I'd do the Excellency's bidding and Andrea gestured for the doctor to leave.

'He heard you when you said that you're an enemy of the Regime,' said Andrea. 'Be careful. That doctor is one of *Monsieur-Dame*'s lovers and a particular favourite.'

Though out of character, I swore using a word from one of the excrementitious novels that circulated in my time. Luckily, Andrea didn't understand it.

Amid all the unrest in Turclub, the sudden death of Dr Orlando complicated matters. He was more than one-hundred years old and was going to die at some point. If he'd been killed in an automobile accident, no-one would have thought it worthy of comment, but he was found dead in bed, which aroused suspicion. An investigation was opened in an attempt to head off rumours, but this added fuel to the fire. The public seemed more attuned to melodrama than natural death.

'Natural within the current state of affairs,' screeched a pirate radio station. 'The government thinks it's normal and acceptable to exterminate anyone opposed to their immoral politics, whether by injecting carbon dioxide into the air-conditioning which supplied air to the deceased, or asphyxiating Pitusso, the innocent canary, in the same room. Our listeners will agree that this double death is most suspicious.'

The authorities committed an error that is common when power is waning: they tried to account for the deaths, publishing a statement explaining that the canary had been suffering from cardiac problems and had been treated months earlier in a clinic. A psychiatrist even certified that the bird's collapse had been triggered when it saw its master dead in his bed.

'Far too much information for a canary,' declared the enemies of the Regime.

And so days passed, and Dr Orlando's corpse was removed and stored in a refrigerated unit and subjected to autopsies and analyses, the interpretation of which was always questionable.

Finally, they decided to cremate him and bury – metaphorically speaking – the matter, but the atmosphere was too tense. That delirious old man, an enemy of the Regime, had been a national legend when nations still existed and people were born from a mother and father. His appalling prestige (it was even said that after the 1985 Revolution he'd had two children and written a sonnet) radiated a diabolic glory. People were desperate for affection, and some of the waiters, the highest nobility and marked by snobbery, couldn't accept that the Doctor had disappeared in so banal a manner. He was a symbol of rebellion. Hadn't he dared say that synthetic fruit caused scurvy? Hadn't *senyoreta* Mercier visited him, greeted him as father of the oviparous population, and asked him for three ounces of raisins and a handful of dried figs for her children – or for those she might have in the future, since she was still a virgin? The Doctor wasn't rich, but he sacrificed his only diamond and three silver forks for a packet of Corinth raisins that the sweet poetess ate in tears on the Doctor's balcony, watched by the roused and rebellious multitude that had congregated there. When Lola had seen what was happening, she cried too, but then she cried easily. Even more absurd, however, is that her tears made me cry, though I'm embarrassed to admit it. The ovations from the crowd were frenzied.

They had found Dr Orlando dead the day after the hysterical, historic balcony scene and public opinion initially pointed the finger of blame vaguely at the 'government', but the accusations quickly became more focused, singling out Andrea. According to the conspiracy, it was Andrea who had ordered the now deceased's air-conditioning to be connected to a carbon dioxide supply as revenge for the gift of the raisins to *senyoreta* Mercier. When Andrea heard, she sent a helicopter and two Ibizan cherubs to fetch me straight away. The boys were lively and couldn't have been more than eight years old, but during the brief flight together they seemed frisky as goats and I couldn't get away from their pranks and caresses. One of them aimed an arrow impregnated with aphrodisiac soma at me and shamelessly told me that Andrea was waiting in bed for me, offering to prepare me to behave as required. Andrea later told me that it was their innocence and purity that caused them to treat certain subjects in so playful a manner, though I still wonder.

She was indeed waiting for me in bed, but with a bronchopneumonia that she'd contracted the day of her ill-fated homage, and that was proving resistant to antibiotics. A radio nearby was talking about economics. The room was dark, and the radio wasn't proving any more illuminating.

'Do you really think I could be so envious of a packet of raisins that I'd kill both the Doctor and his poor, innocent canary?' she asked.

'It's nonsense,' I replied. 'Don't worry yourself, it's not worth it.'

But it wasn't nonsense. Some hours later, when police had visited the home of an 'obstructionist' accused of obscenity (he was brazenly refusing to buy refrigerators or vacuum cleaners), a large crowd gathered at the door of his house. The accused had come out onto his balcony and launched into a tirade against atomic appliances and the Collective Orgies, which he denounced as depraved.

'Very soon,' he said adopting a messianic, crowd-pleasing tone, 'we'll see fire fall from the sky. What can we expect of a country that only thinks of money and has a whore who assassinates apostles and canaries as its idol? Isn't it the whore whose behaviour has unleashed hunger amongst us? Wasn't she also about to murder a great poetess, the dainty Maria Mercier, cherished disciple of Aina Cohen, chanteuse of noble love and almond blossoms?'

What happened next was unprecedented and unthinkable: a spontaneous demonstration against the goddess broke out and protesters carrying insulting banners marched towards the Palazzo Víctrix. This time the reaction of the authorities was ruthless, the repression savage and more than eight-hundred people died, *senyoreta* Mercier among them.

The riot had serious repercussions in Paris and the centre of power was alarmed. The *chansonniers* of Montmartre and the crazy ladies of Montparnasse suddenly felt the appeal of romanticism while, paradoxically, chastity became an ally of maternity. Perhaps unwillingly, *senyoreta* Mercier had died a virgin and those fired-up young women desired virginity because it was forever lost to them and never again would they feel that primitive unease – fear and desire – before the male. Those gentle-souled *chansonniers*, ironic and wearied by unfulfilled ambition, would have loved to be austere and independent, fantastic like Dr Orlando, basely assassinated with his canary Pitusso, a true artist of a bird, delicate and helpless. Though the authorities had banned the song *L'infant de la mare*, the eternal Maurice Chevalier from Ménilmontant, ever alert to opportunity, debuted the following day with *Orlando's Canary: What shall we give Orlando's canary...*

Watching the performance on TV from the Élyseé Palace, *Monsieur-Dame* de Pompignac la Fleur fainted while the governor of Turclub was horrified and immediately resigned. Along with the now international figure of *senyoreta* Mercier, the repression had cost eight-hundred victims and unnerved the tourists, many of whom cancelled their hotel bookings. With the murder of the canary Pitusso (whose photo had appeared in clandestine publications and on unlicensed TV stations) as a pretext, some English women brought up the old legend of Balearic cruelty with the most bookish citing the Phoenician invasions. The Waiters' Guild, although mostly siding with the government, nevertheless recognized the threat of a crisis in the hospitality industry, and even though the most senior waiter, bearing the title 'Cousin of *Monsieur-Dame*', made no personal statement, he allowed seven of the Guild's Ibizan cherubs to lay a real carnation on the tomb of the sacrificed canary.

When did the French Revolution truly begin? Some would say with the summoning of the Estates General in 1789, but others date it to the year that the good and humanitarian Louis XVI re-established the parliaments that his grandfather had abolished, and there are even those who see its origin with Louis XIV himself and the Fronde which in effect put an end to the feudal power of the nobility and cleared the way for the bourgeoisie. If we were to try to identify the precise moment the Industrial Era began to fall apart, we'd find ourselves with the same difficulties as historians of the *Ancien Régime*, though at a push we could probably say it was the moment that seven Ibizan waiters made an offering of a real carnation to a canary named Pitusso.

The Society for the Protection of Animals got involved and as the canary, like Orlando, was a victim of political despotism, it amounted to a show of rebellion. When public powers weaken, they tend to become liberal, and it's then they seem most despotic. The authorities were undoubtedly attempting to appear tolerant, and although they couldn't sanction talk of children born of parents because it undermined the dogma of the oviparous generation on which the State was founded, they didn't dare prevent the songs doing the rounds being sung in the cabarets, in spite of their lyrics. Andrea was alarmed.

'We didn't kill the doctor or the canary,' said Andrea. 'Although if we had, it would have been for the common good. When civilization is at stake, one death matters little. Just as your ancestors in the sixteenth century were heroic because of the honour code, so are we heroic because of the imposition of technology. Besides, deaths are inevitable and will only increase if we are to maintain a high standard of living. What do you think? Why are you laughing?'

'Oh,' I said, 'no reason.'

I didn't want to argue in case I got called a sophist again, feeling it pointless calling oneself a revolutionary only to admit to imitating ancestors from the sixteenth century.

You're right,' I said. 'What does one more death matter today?'

'Nobody's considering getting rid of automobiles,' she continued, 'or robots, or soma. Civilization can't be put on hold because of some people's over-sensitivity, which is what being outraged at inevitable death is. As well as stupid. We killed *senyoreta* Mercier and I was the one who made the recommendation to the police because she was publicising obscenities. But the accusation about the canary is false and reveals a deep-held resentment against the State.'

And so it was. The government was more and more unpopular as *disette* became entrenched and the price of groceries soared. Wages were increased to avoid hunger, but this meant that prices had to rise again. People tried to compensate for their hunger with vitamin-enhanced remedies readily provided by Illness Insurance at no cost, but substituting fresh liver with injections of liver extract didn't solve the problem of the lack of liver. I suggested that it would be cheaper to give away steaks for free.

'Not quite,' Andrea pointed out, 'because then everyone would ask for steaks, and injections are only given to the ill.'

But soon everyone was demanding injections because all the available liver had been bought up by the laboratories and there was none in the shops. Andrea resigned as Director of Pleasure so that she could dedicate herself fully to her studies, living surrounded by books, but the President refused to accept her resignation and sent her half a dozen peaches from the Élysée along with twelve practised French prostitutes capable of reciting Racine who were designated to take her place entertaining foreigners. It was high time: she was exhausted.

In the eyes of History, her personal retirement from such entertainments, together with the waiters' homage to Orlando's canary, were some of the first symptoms of the bankrupting of the machine civilization: Pleasure made way for Necessity, just as drug traffickers in Barcelona's Raval at the end of 1936 abandoned cocaine and began selling bread on the black market.

The idea of Andrea giving up debauchery filled me with joy.

'See,' I said to her, 'if you don't take any more soma, you'll be back to normal in no time. You're only nineteen.'

'I'm old,' Andrea replied. 'I've lived at an accelerated rhythm. I don't mind dying if I can strengthen our situation. I'm sure you'll say that in politics, just as in anything, definitive consolidation just isn't possible, because progress brings variation. Even so, some of our victories seemed as important as Archimedes' discoveries.'

She fell quiet, lost in thought, having said 'seemed', not 'seem'.

'And they don't now?' I asked.

'No, I haven't lost my faith,' she replied. 'Famine isn't insurmountable, but we're a long way from success. Two years ago, when they appointed me Director of Pleasure, I thought the problem was almost resolved and that the only befitting thing was to have fun.'

'And that fun has cost you dear,' I said.

'I know, but I wouldn't mind if my endeavours had been of some use.'

I reminded her that there were famines in the Bible and there always seemed to be a way through. I was so emotional that I didn't fully grasp what she said next: something about original sin I think. Her reasoning and supposed materialism had for a while taken on a mystical direction, searching for unattainable truths.

'We'll get through everything, Andrea,' I said.

'I don't know... I'm not just referring to famine. I've witnessed an even more terrible crisis. What I'm experiencing is different to orthodox morality, from what they taught me, and from what I have to believe. I can't explain it, but it seems absolutely transcendent. So much time, so many innovations to pave the way to pleasure, and yet pleasure is further away every day. The last few months have been my martyrdom.'

'You're worn out, but you'll recover,' I said. 'You're young.'

'Chronologically I've just turned nineteen years old, but if you factor in the quantities of soma I've taken, I'm eighty-two.'

I tried to comfort her as she broke down.

'That homage at Einstein's Arch,' she said. 'At the last minute they came up with the idea of the purple cloak to conceal the wound on my back. I was so ashamed when the wind blew it aside... And on Pleasure... So many loudspeakers announcing *Hola-Hola*, the sacred beverage... I read *The Veil of Isis*, hun, it's just too much. I doubted and will be punished. So many automobiles, helicopters, heavy oil engines, artificial birds, billboards, slogans... Pleasure Avenue... Oh that avenue... Dante himself couldn't have made it more hellish... Occasionally, isolating bells for the most privileged, but they don't isolate because the loudspeakers still boom in your head... At the nights in Gomila Square, that oven, breathing in the engine fumes... And love... Oh love, drunk on aphrodisiac-fortified soma... Scandinavians the colour of roast beef eating raw meat... Some of them weigh a hundred kilos, their hands like steel and all as stupid as robots... Soma got me through, until suddenly...'

She had put her arms around my neck and was crying.

'The only thing that grieves me about dying,' she continued, 'is that I'll have to leave you... I realise that I love no-one more than you, and even worse, I know how this all started... It was the second time we saw each other, when you blasphemed against the State, when you insulted us aloud... Your abuse of the Party was like a punch to the solar plexus: "What kind of Party is it if there's no opposition?" you said. And by saying it, you risked death. I almost hit you with a shot of Parquidine; it was my duty, and it still is, but I wouldn't be able to now... Oh hun, you're a hero, and I even think I love you because you're a real man, like in the olden days...'

She pulled away from me, covering her face with the cloak. I grasped her around the waist. She was beside herself. I have never seen such anguish, nor so much elegance or charm in so frail an organism. My resistance was giving way, and I whispered in her ear alluding openly to her gender, embarrassed like a schoolboy by what I had said.

'Listen, Andrea, I know you're a woman, no matter how often Lola might say the opposite. I know, but I need you to...'

She transformed suddenly and was yellow, horrible, with rheumy eyes and wizened skin. The skeletal body in my arms looked for an instant like the young Italian dynamiter who in my youth had thrown a bomb at Milan's La Scala. I remembered him from a poor quality photograph in *Blanco y Negro*. I let go of Andrea.

'I'm going,' I said. 'I'll come back when you're calmer.'

'Come back when we're both purged of bad desires,' she replied, watching me walk out of the room. 'It was monstrous of me to say that you were a man like they used to be, but I will not commit a mortal sin. Whether you come back or not,' she said with seductive, childlike candour, 'I didn't have the canary Pitusso killed.'

The revolutionary speaker who could have been Bertini's double, unironically called 'Vamp' by the public, had announced another appearance in the basement of the Rufo, his confidence boosted by the gradual weakening of Authority.

The matter of how one announces a clandestine conference is more difficult to explain. The Regime was failing, contradicting itself, and the most bloody of revolutions known to humankind that had brought it to power was now a distant memory. Uncertain of wider opinion and yet attuned to it, the Regime imagined all manner of dangers and catastrophes. It would have liked to transition from tyranny to democracy, winning over public opinion once and for all, suspending History, and pleasing everyone. Though the intention was beyond reproach and, for that very reason, preposterous. Having allowed *senyoreta* Mercier to sing *L'infant de la mare*, it gunned her down, killing another eight hundred people in the process and immediately banned the song, but tolerated the popularization of *El canari d'Orlando*, by *chansonniers*. The Regime's information-gathering systems were mathematically precise, but such quantities of data were difficult to synthesize, and faced with the brutal reality of famine and automobile accidents, its leaders were unsure what position to adopt. The immeasurable *Monsieur-Dame*, for example, considered the possibility of becoming proper democrats, therefore shifting all the blame onto the populace, but he also worried the people might turn on him, with fatal consequences. Do we tame the wild animal with whips or caresses? The trick is to be alert to its behaviour at every single moment: get it wrong and it will devour you.

The police had orders to observe but not to intervene. Andrea, meanwhile, having indeed given up her role as Director of

Pleasure, had taken on responsibility for the economy and with the innocence of her nineteen going on eighty-two years, was proposing controversial thinking to shed light on the situation, but *senyor* de Pompignac la Fleur feared it would merely muddy the waters. And so *Monsieur-Dame* would not authorize the Vamp's lecture, but nor would he ban it, and thus the guidance given to Turclub's new governor was perfectly clear (in both senses), and so drove him mad.

I couldn't see Andrea. One of her secretaries had requested that I shouldn't attempt to communicate with her until further notice, and would I kindly accept a hundred grams of chocolate. I was presented with the gift by two little seven-year-old waiters, almost black from the sun and wearing the new summer uniform consisting of a golden clam shell which covered their genitals. They appeared at eight in the morning drunk on soma, jumping on my bed, pulling my hair and proffering vulgarities to wake me up. On this occasion I didn't find them at all amusing and I slapped them away, but they insisted on coming back and I dared not hit them too hard because I knew they were members of the nobility. I called Dr Nicola who said he'd come over straight away with a sedative to calm them, and he advised the utmost care because there was a situation developing high up. He didn't say for whom, but we all knew that any nervousness up there often translated into the persecution of cryo-cure survivors. It took him three minutes to get here. The two little devils in the meantime were working off their excitement in aerial leaps and expletives. When Nicola entered, he found them gripping one another on top of the wardrobe and about to attempt a double somersault. As he tried to get them to come down by threatening to report them, they jumped down head first and broke their necks. One of them had lost his clam shell and I was surprised to see that he had no genitals.

'Andrea's caprices,' said the doctor.

'I don't understand.'

'It's important to suppress all gender difference,' he replied. 'Medicine isn't sufficiently advanced yet, and since a clam shell is easily dislodged, it was thought best…'

'Have these children had surgery?'

'Beautiful surgery, yes,' he said. 'You can't even see the scar.'

My surprise was undimmed.

'Andrea ordered such a monstrosity?'

'It's the new morality,' he said, staring at me impassively. 'They weren't destined to be sperm donors.'

An ambulance arrived and took them off to the crematorium. As they'd died entertaining me, the assistant asked me if I would like their ashes. I shot back a brusque 'no', and he thought I was being ungrateful. People in Turclub really were so very sensitive.

'You've still not been amongst us for long, and you're not used to–,' said Nicola.

'I will never get used to this,' I interrupted. 'I must come across as very odd.'

'Don't you believe it; there are many like you, but they conceal it. You're not so careful, and you do a lot of damage.'

'Why do I?' I said. 'My life's not important.'

The doctor sat down beside me and put his hand on my knee. Seemingly sincere as he spoke, almost confiding, he was doubtless far too aware to open up completely to someone as impulsive as me. He told me that he'd joined the Party when he was very young and enthusiastic and that while time had cooled his ardour somewhat, it had allowed him to understand the dissidents of this machine civilization. He observed, as he had once before, that life is not nothing, and even if it were, one shouldn't surrender it to one's enemies for their own purposes. From what he was saying, I understood that suicide (he used the euphemism 'to go away') was more logical than allowing oneself to be taken. But, in his opinion, dissidents had the chance to rebel.

'That's what I'm doing,' I said.

'No, forgive me,' he replied. 'You say that you'll rise up, but all you're doing is ensuring your enemies are on your tail.'

What was he suggesting?

'Wouldn't it be curious,' I said, 'if you were to explain to me what I have to do to dethrone *Monsieur-Dame*.'

Nicola smiled.

'I am a member of the Regime and I serve it as a scientist,' he said. 'But nowadays I am no more than that: a scientist, or technician, if you prefer. Your case interests me as a psychiatrist, and I feel a real sympathy for you because I can see that you're loyal, and tortured. Loyalty's so rare today, and out of reach for most. For example, I'm not as loyal as you. I find I have to compromise from time to time.'

I laughed.

'Join forces with me,' I said, 'and we'll make revolution together.'

'And Andrea?' he said, looking at me. 'You're in love with Andrea. Truly, she's enchanting.'

There was silence. Nicola's face was impassive. Just for an instant I thought I'd seen something akin to brotherly love in him, a soul capable of opening itself to mine. But the beautiful moment had passed and my distrust returned. He stood up.

'Don't concern yourself about the death of the children. I am a witness to their having died in an act of service. They'll send you part of their ashes and I'll say that you've requested them as a memorial; that'll go down well higher up. It's important to make the right impression. In a way, both of the children were heroes.'

Finally alone, I opened the chocolate. There was a letter inside:

My friend, I really am very busy (you know that I don't lie to you). They've upped my dose of soma and my system can only work now at 200 percent which means that every twenty-four hours, I age forty-eight hours. They tell me that at this rate, I can still live for a few years with a lucid brain, and I'm going to make the most of the time working for the cause. No more sexual acrobatics (pornography, as you used to call it) for me. No-one's even permitted to kiss me. What utter monotony love is, what senseless drain! I admire Lola, my sibling in sex, because she can still look on her profession with fresh eyes. It's true that she doesn't take soma, and although she's older than me, she's also much younger. Love induces a kind of panic in me now. If I'm honest, there were just a few moments when I enjoyed this, and a rose lives for longer: l'espace d'un matin. No-one knows that my life has been a martyrdom. Lola takes pleasure from love because, wilful and atheistic as she is, to a greater or lesser extent she chooses people she likes. Although officially I also had the right to choose, I wasn't able to in reality. My mission was almost the opposite, to go with the brutal and boorish, and try to refine them. Shortly before I met you, one of my lovers broke two of my ribs. I was still young then and I healed quickly. I was very strong until a short time ago. I remember your surprise when I punched you off your feet on Pleasure. You've said as much many times: a girl of eighteen (you've always looked at me as though I were a girl) and a man of thirty! Soma gave me strength that seemed superhuman, but it was all completely natural, because the drug allowed me to expend many months' worth of energy in just a few minutes. Isn't that how nuclear physics works, unleashing and destroying in a second energy that has lain dormant for centuries? In moments of anguish, I've wondered whether I've made a mistake... Having been forced to love Humanity, an idea, I quickly had to detach myself from material beings, whom I tended to see as enemies... I enjoyed killing people with the Rolls. Not only because I was doing traffic and Humanity a favour by teaching people to behave as the Code demanded but, perhaps, for the pleasure of exterminating some freak who desired my body, or perhaps also taking out some poor wretch who would end up dying anyway. I don't know. Everyone frightens me, even the police who kiss me on the *neck according to protocol. Only you, hun, who've never been my lover, would be capable of filling my existence if only you weren't an atheist and a dangerous materialist. I can still hear your sacrilegious words: 'Before I tell you that I love you, I need to know…' With the advent of the oviparous and machine generation, we had suppressed original sin (which our dogmas define as eating as well as being born), and you want to resuscitate it revering sex. If I'd known you a year earlier in the plenitude of my moral beliefs, I'd have taken a drastic decision to save you, but I have nothing left now. Try to understand me: we're trying, and we're almost there, to create a single sex, to destroy marriage and the family, both obstacles to progress and opposition to Teilhard's coveted Noosphere. Robots are starting to do our work for us, and you want man to go back to earning a living through physical labour and sweat, like before. You would dismantle everything, you're destructive. It's true, as my secretaries have doubtless told you, that I'm extremely busy studying so that I can refute the heterodox arguments of our enemies, but you know that this isn't the main reason I don't want to see you. When you are clean, when you learn like the old theologians, that spirit transcends flesh, that flesh is just a very bad joke, then…*

I put the letter down. The drastic decision she referred to that was supposed to 'save' me was surely mutilation, as in the case of the acrobatic waiters. An idea struck me. Might Andrea, in her own fanatical mindset, have mutilated herself? Though I didn't frequent the Collective Orgies and wasn't intimate with anyone but Lola, I had realised that when eroticism diverts from its concrete ends and flows through the muscular and vascular systems, it becomes acrobatic, amorous gymnastics. The young lad who'd had himself beaten up in the bathhouse must be a relatively frequent case. Almost all the erotic diversions in Turclub were tinged with sadism or masochism because danger was so exciting. After a night of intense debauchery, Andrea would often return scratched or hurt. The young lad, shaking with fear, had said to the bathhouse attendant he'd hired to overpower him: 'Punch me hard: I'm fed up of stupid kisses.'

The world is an ever-changing paradox. Doctor Orlando was right in opposing the practice of submitting people to the cryo-cure for years on end and having them wake up in a society that would of course seem strange to them. The homily Andrea had dedicated to me – morality, spirituality, materialism, obscenity, shamelessness – was the same as a man of my generation would have dedicated to her. From different points of view, we were making the same mutual accusations. Was it worth believing in anything at all? It wasn't a novel example. The judge and the accused could always switch roles, although not in so radical or decisive a manner. Were Andrea and I enemies? Were we in love? We were both, and that was the real predicament. 'Only you, hun, who've never been my lover, could fill my existence… if you weren't an atheist and a dangerous materialist.' Would it have excited her, perhaps, to be my lover precisely because my materialist atheism meant that she had not been? This would make atheism the attraction. Was the syllogism correct? I doubt it. I suspect we could draw a completely different, also unorthodox, conclusion by turning it around: virtue would have been the attraction. Different roads can lead to the same destination. And why not, since we know that both the earth and the whole of creation is round?

That letter: ardent, inflexible, mystical, icy, and hopeless by turns, filled me with sadness. There was nothing I could do. When Heisenberg and Schrödinger developed their mechanical model of the atom, they dismissed the principle of contradiction which had guided humans since Aristotle and enthroned the Absurd. Possibly for the first time in recorded History, these devils presented phenomena in the field of physics that can only be interpreted via contradictory theories. No longer is there harmony, logic or fusion; just facts. Contradiction is irreducible and has to be accepted as legal tender. We have to accept struggle, and renounce victory and synthesis, and this can only be possible following total annihilation. But what good would struggle serve then? What kind of hope, what kind of expectation can move those of us in the world who are not blessed with a simple faith?

In order to attain a human, classical universe, we would need to limit it, look at it with our eyes and not through the telescope Galileo used to refute Ptolemaic cosmology, or the prince de Broglie's electron microscope that, along with Einstein, contradicted Galileo's.*

Let us have the courage to declare once and for all that we are anti progress. Rousseau did so in his *Discours sur les sciences et les arts*, and Voltaire, man of the moment and *esprit fort* of the Enlightenment, responded that when he read it he had the urge to walk on all fours. Nevertheless, that same *esprit fort* ended up implicitly agreeing with Jean-Jacques. Four years later, in *Candide*, he wrote that this world is not perfect and, although at the end of the work he advises us to cultivate our garden, it's

* 'Einstein's theory has revealed that Galileo's *nuova sciencia*, the glorious physics of the West, is affected by a keen provincialism.' Ortega y Gasset: *El sentido histórico de la teoría de Einstein*.

not because he aspires to convert us into supermen or robots, but rather into wise gardeners, humble believers – into men of Rousseau.

One would need incredibly well-balanced, almost vegetative nerves to accept existence with the placidness of a sheep. Naturally, vitamins and soma destroyed the conception of a paradise-like world. As a child I was happy in the fullness of nature amid the mountains of Bearn, a place articulated as a perfect symbiosis of landscape and God's creatures. That earthly paradise is poeticised in my memory through the image of Coloma, a young blonde girl with whom I picture myself lying stretched out on a mound of straw near the baroque fountain of a deserted village square at that hour of the afternoon when everyone is sleeping their summer siesta.** We couldn't have been more than ten years old and I suddenly realised that we were as perfectly alone as Adam and Eve. She had closed her eyes, and I had my arm around her shoulders. I think I dared give her a kiss. My heart was beating at the same rate as hers. Time stood still: the tempting serpent created the illusion that we were immortal and without sin, because we didn't know what sin was.

In the year 1965, by then old and fatigued by technological progress that was beginning to make its presence felt in all spheres of life, I had committed the folly of undergoing a cryo-cure in order to wake up eighty-five years later in a world much advanced in angst, a tragic and stupid world in which baptisms were carried out with *Hola-Hola*, and which just wasn't mine. My mistake was wanting to survive my time or overtake it. They say that's what glory – posthumous glory, naturally – is, but if we don't believe in the present, what advantages will an ever more problematic future bring that at the same time is non-existent for someone who no longer exists? Championing ataraxia, I had destroyed my own, just as those who go to the

** See *Les Fures*, a novel by Llorenç Villalonga.

moon do with their tanks of air and vitamins, attempting to show that one can't breathe there.

This doesn't mean that I haven't had some pleasant times in *Monsieur-Dame*'s Turclub, but such moments have simply been repositories of the calm I experienced as a child, and of the capacity which seems lost to people today to contemplate the grotesque with an ironic gaze, just as God must look down from heaven on the vanities of the world and of those we call wise. Perhaps I can't complain about my fate after all: I've lived amongst nightingales, sheep and village chaplains; while in the second stage of my life, I've flown in a helicopter above the clouds, I've felt like an angel surrounded by lascivious waiters, and I've known mystery in the company of the most disconcerting being in Creation: the being who gives their name to this 'novel'.

Others made it no further than the loudspeakers and plastic carnations. Andrea herself, for example, the Incarnation of Victorious Pleasure, never knew the tranquillity of yesteryear and had confessed her life to be a martyrdom. Her organism, burnt out by stimulants, was incapable of savouring calm. Machine industry, aided by soma, was in the process of consuming everything.

In the eyes of such an all-powerful industry which had created its own dogmas and its own morality, canaries and nightingales constituted illicit competition for vinyl record manufacturers and the spectacle of nature lost its audience share to other more profitable entertainments. If the Regime favoured trips, it was to support the bus companies, ensuring that the public were used to movement because tranquillity is never a source of wealth. Nervous equilibrium would also have damaged the labs that manufactured more tonnes of sedatives than the wheat grown in the fields of Castile.

Andrea had been raised from childhood in the cult of restlessness which, considered as an intrinsic value, is according to Waldo Frank the principal characteristic of mechanical civilization. I remember in particular one of the last celebrations she held in my honour in the marble hall. She had already suffered a number of serious depressive crises, knowledge of which was kept as a State secret by her entourage. I was on good form. We had just dined together with the accompanying ceremony of *maîtres d'hôtel* and ballet that befitted the rank of goddess and of one who, like me, was held to be her official lover by the public. In vermilion-coloured Napoleonic dinnerware, a veritable museum collection, we had been served dishes of such poor quality and so badly prepared that we could scarcely taste them, but soma, which I had taken to excess, made me outrageously euphoric. Half intoxicated, I had attempted to explain to Andrea who Xauxa was from a comedy that had been fashionable in my parents' time. It was no masterpiece, though it amused me then, and I had wanted poor Andrea, pale and subdued, to share my childlike joy:

...the dogs
are tied with strings of sausages
and their bellies are so full
and their teeth so restful
they gaze indifferent
at their inciting chains.

Andrea had seemed in a world of her own. 'Do you think their indifference could be happiness?' she'd asked. 'Wouldn't happiness be a creation of their illusion?'

I'm sure there was something in what Andrea had said, and I remember her tone clearly. Reflecting now, I don't know whether happiness is indifference, but it must at least be serenity. The hale and hearty who are unaware of the health of their organs are full of a joy of life that Andrea only ever experienced for a few moments, induced by drugs. 'Regardless, we need to get hold of some food. Don't you think?' I recall laughing, because in reality neither I nor Andrea lacked the basics.

And even when we had food? I'd thought. The hallucinatory effect of the soma had worn off and Andrea's depression was suddenly contagious. The dogs in the old stage play, tied with strings of sausages, seemed more sad than happy. Was indifference actually the path to happiness? Happiness was about illusion, certainly.

My thoughts turned to my youth and I pictured myself as a fourteen-year-old on a tram going to El Terreno. It was a warm July evening. On the right were the Bellver woods, yet to be obscured by skyscrapers, hives of cell-like apartments or German-style steel cages. Below and to the left was the pristine blue sea, populated by nereids and dolphins, and unconstrained by concrete breakwaters and functional hotels. The Machine Era had not yet disfigured the geography of the island, nor had the profusion of motorised vehicles, multiplying like ants, polluted the sky. What an exquisite paradise! What's more, I was fourteen. The heat made my anticipated swim all the more desirable, that immersion in cool water and its mirrored blue sheen. The thought made me laugh. A soldier close by appeared to notice my joy.

'I'm going to dive in and swim for three hours,' he said.

He was a tanned young man, and like me, eager for thrills, but his words were clouded by mood. Three hours? Once in the sea the heat disappeared and swimming lost its attraction, becoming even unpleasant. Why did that idea make me so intensely sad? I was incapable of admitting that human happiness could last three hours. My blood pressure in those days must have been low. It was also true that my yearning for happiness was excessive. The tanned young soldier nearby, rough and strong and perhaps originally a country labourer, must have been more grounded, happily considering life beautiful. Simple faith...

Was simple faith still a reality for some? Years later, shortly before my cryo-cure, I came across someone similar near a spring in the mountains. He was almost ninety years old, so he said, kept sheep and was satisfied with his lot. It became clear that he considered himself the richest man in the world and would exchange places with no-one.

'Not even with a thirty-year old?' I asked

'No,' he'd said. 'I'm perfectly happy as I am. Why would I want to swap?'

I found that orientalist philosophy interesting. I would have liked to talk to him, and I objected that if he had been young, he would have had more years of happiness before him. I didn't tell him that my reflections might dilute the happiness he currently enjoyed, even destroy it, and his guardian angel put an end to the conversation as one of his sheep had gone astray and he politely took his leave.

His faith really was simple. At the time there were probably more than ten such people on my island, and that's why it survived, and the sea was still blue, there were no slicks of oil, and the sky was limpid. Under the mandate of *Monsieur-Dame*, there were no longer ten righteous people in existence, and as I considered this horrific truth I realised that Sodom would not be saved.

There were a number of undercover police in the diverse, packed audience in the basement of the Rufo and the intentionally neutral, semi-Roman dress wasn't always successful in concealing the gender of those present. In some there was a deliberate desire to look like men, while others passed themselves off as women, and it was impossible to untangle the innocent confusion. The speaker was more Vamp, more Bertini, than before, but I was in little doubt that he was a man, and highly intelligent. In an attempt to come across as more Giorgione, Lola had padded out her breasts and hips too much. Such excess came across as suspicious and drew everyone's attention. She could be a male, but only I could testify that she was a woman. People were trying to mask the suspicious, fearful atmosphere with smiles and I could make out traitorous transmitters and receivers everywhere. In the Palazzo Víctrix, Andrea was getting ready to tune in. I glanced instinctively at Lola, who was radiant, beautiful, blooming, without secrets and secure in her sincerity as a wanton woman.

'Darling,' she said. 'I can say with a clear conscience that I have never deceived a man.'

Very true. In my time they used to say that while honourable women don't come with baggage, it's the promiscuous who are drama-free. As such, their comfort would lead others to consider them unimportant. We all came into the world to contribute our ounce of tragedy. Lola wasn't at all foolish, and she knew it.

'Yes, I know you like me, you like me like a good roast, but I also know you don't lie awake at night thinking of me... Just as well, because I don't want to hurt anyone. But if Andrea were to call you...'

She was right, of course. Because we're masochists, as they'd say in Vizcaya.

The speaker had mounted the stage and, in something of a *coup de théâtre*, began his address by blaspheming and repeating the last words of the lecture that the sudden death of the police officer had prevented him from finishing.

'The white worker,' he said, 'the true parasite of society, has been able to exploit the workers of the world through two huge crimes: the world wars.'

Once he had the audience's attention, he moved quickly on to examine the theories of Karl Marx. According to the speaker, Marx, as a good German, had too provincial and localist a concept of History.

'He never saw the whole picture; his spirit was feudal. From 1848, this localism has constituted Marxist orthodoxy. In his eyes, the world is divided, as I said before, into two zones: the "advanced" industrial zone, and the "backward" agricultural zone. But the world was much bigger than that vision. It was, and especially so, more complex, and it wasn't resigned to having to accept exports from Europe and North America in silence. White workers didn't live as the result of free industry, as they proclaimed, but from the monopoly of imposing their products on agriculture-based economies that had no industry. Where necessary, this monopoly was imposed not only through propaganda, but by guns and boots on the ground. The Marxists no longer believed in human fraternity as the progressives of the eighteenth-century had done. Those pleasant and slightly naïve times had passed. As openly stated by Marx himself, "class war" prevailed. The fact that one small part of Europe enslaved the other continents didn't constitute to his mind an attack on the rights of the proletariat; rather, he termed it "colonial politics". North American civilization has never been anything other than a copy of Europe's, and thus neither European nor logically North American trade unions would permit the daily wage to be reduced. As such, the problem of unemployment was born. To mitigate the impact, subsidies were introduced and there was an attempt to make essential provisions more affordable. Thus we see, as Spengler noted, that in England in 1850 import duties on corn were suppressed, sacrificing the interests of English farmers to those of industrial workers. In spite of or rather because of such protectionist measures, the economy suffered. Young agricultural labourers preferred to work in the city factories, but the import of industrial products continued to be difficult until the year 1929 when the US stock market crashed and led to the crisis known as the Great Depression. History records that financial catastrophe, and the literature of the time bears its imprint, too. One of the most important American authors, Arthur Miller, took his inspiration from it for *Death of a Salesman*. The panic was so intense – unemployment, bankruptcies, suicides – that the big industrial companies as well as those in power ended up insulting the public who were incapable of absorbing expensive, abundant and, moreover, unnecessary products. "Call yourself a patriot? Buy two receivers." "Only scum don't buy an electric vacuum cleaner." For the first time, industry was becoming a religion and had its own dogmas.* Let us suggest that the Second World War salvaged the situation, creating an outlet for the products that filled warehouses to the rafters, since the advertising and insults directed at people to incite them to buy more were not enough. When Hitler unleashed war, it was providence for the Americans. I'm talking about previous times. Today's problems aren't the same, but they have the same origin, and it would be unfair not to recognize that England, belatedly deciding to give some degree of protection to her farmers, as well as the U.S. of Europe, have attempted to come up with solutions.'

Just as in the first lecture, the amount of whistling from the audience told the speaker that many of those present weren't interested in considered argument. He soon found his rhythm again.

'They've tried, too late, and without success, to offer palliative solutions to a situation which isn't about to be alleviated.'

* The Vamp's ideas and data are taken from O. Spengler's *Jahre der Entscheidung*.

The resultant ovation was unhindered by the few furious whistles.

'Today,' he went on, 'the struggle between white and coloured workers I talked about in my last lecture is over. Our fumigations have simplified the problem by exterminating the Chinese and Japanese, just as the disappearance of Russia and the USA has simplified issues. The European worker and big industry no longer have enemies: they're almost on their own. Oceania is remote and, if necessary, the factories in Africa could be destroyed rapidly. But...'

The Vamp paused for effect before continuing.

'Our products have virtually no competitors. Very soon, though, they won't have any buyers. The colonies where we could have forcibly placed the goods are gone, and the independent states – Latin America, certain Pacific islands, and a small part of Africa – have become industrialised and can meet their own needs. This was already a phenomenon in 1962: North American markets crashed and, just as in the Great Depression, Kennedy resorted to insults, calling businessmen sons of bitches. At the same time, a number of economics journals started to examine the real root of the problem: the agricultural crisis, the origin of *disette*. A purely economic crisis, confined to the stock market and caused by a lack of credit or inflation such as the one Germany suffered following the Treaty of Versailles always has a solution, even if this means ruining a lot of people. The Deutschmark, then worth almost nothing, was replaced by a new mark. Those who held large quantities of old marks lost out, but the country continued to move forwards. Today things are different. The crisis we are suffering today isn't only economic; it's a problem of mass psychology, of the fight between man and machine, between industrialisation and agriculture. Two contrasting ways of understanding life. Above all, the great danger posed by this struggle isn't the lack of money but the shortage of food, the *disette* we're all experiencing... No, don't applaud yet… Let's keep our heads to better understand the problem. Do you know what Doctor Orlando had to do to buy a box of Corinth raisins for *senyoreta* Mercier? He was forced to sell the silver cutlery he'd inherited…'

He was about to say 'from his parents,' but stopped suddenly. Some of the audience yelled at him to continue.

'Yes!' someone shouted. 'Say it! Inherited from his parents! That's why he was assassinated, like *senyoreta* Mercier! Because he was born of parents! Because he had two natural children! Because he demanded the right, like the virgin of Avignon, to have children and love them! But that's what got him killed, him and the canary!'

These last words lit the fuse. Like a flash of lightning, a crack of thunder, the revolutionary hymn reverberated around the basement:

What shall be give the mother's child,
What shall we give him that tastes good…

I looked over to the police. Obliged by their role to hide their true persona, they were singing too, some with a hostility that seemed directed as much against the government as towards the people in the room. Others put on a more affected expression so as to better conceal their identity, with tears rolling down their cheeks. But who could say whether this was pretence? Perhaps they were carried along by the sentimental, catchy tune. Weren't they starving too? Didn't they all dream of the box of Corinth raisins the virgin of Avignon had eaten before she died?

We'll give him raisins and weighing scales,
We'll give him figs in a little basket…

Figs and raisins and someone shouted, 'Death to Pompignac la Fleur!' I switched on my microtelevision and connected to

Andrea. Surrounded by machines, she was alone in an exquisite, columned room, pale and preoccupied. The Vamp was startled and gestured at them to let him continue. Once he'd managed to calm the tumult, he announced that the lecture was adjourned until the following day, at the same time, 'if we don't all end up sleeping in jail tonight.'

From nowhere the sirens commanding silence screeched out and the figure of Andrea was projected onto the wall of the basement. Not the gaunt Andrea who had just appeared on my screen but the goddess of six months ago in the full splendour of her beauty.

'I have been following the Vamp's fascinating talk,' announced Andrea. 'No-one will be sleeping in prison. This is a critical moment and we have to work together and collaborate if we are to find a way out. When the Vamp has finished setting out his ideas, which I'm sure will also be of interest to *Monsieur-Dame le Président*, I will respond with a series of three lectures that will require a few weeks of preparation, as the Vamp has clearly done his research. *Monsieur-Dame* will decide the date and it will be announced in due course. You are all invited. If you would now like to watch me preparing for bed, it would please me to sleep, purified by your lust.'

Six Praetorian guards and two young Ibizan waiters immediately appeared on the screen and started to undress the goddess. Her delicate ephebe body shone white and while a section of the audience applauded, the rest were silent.

'What a nerve,' murmured a voice next to me. 'That projection's from half a year ago, with the dialogue changed. They're treating us like idiots.'

'I broke off my talk yesterday,' the Vamp began, 'because the mood was getting heated, and we needed to be able to examine the struggle between industrialisation and agriculture serenely. Today we'll be talking about the crux of the problem. I am encouraged to continue by the kindness, even blessing of that divine being who enchants us all and was generous enough to display herself naked to us yesterday, calming troubled minds. The matter requires focused intellectual attention. I was telling you that in spite of everything, the economic situation seems less serious than *disette*, and you might well reply that for the rich there is no *disette*. That's true, but at the expense of the vast majority who remain poor. Food is expensive precisely because it's in short supply, and if we increase the salaries of industrial workers, which seems to be the Élysée's approach, as it was Henry Ford's in 1929, people will have more money but food will be less plentiful due to a greater demand. That's why I said the problem is as much psychological as it is economic, and it comes from our having turned our backs on Nature. If people enjoyed working on the land, they'd flee the big cities, factories would produce fewer dazzling white goods (so dazzling that they blinded even Teilhard de Chardin, who saw them as the salvation of Humanity), the so-called high quality of life would drop and we'd regain the lost equilibrium.'

From amongst the audience, more numerous and colourful than ever, came contradictory exclamations.

'Now we're oviparous!... Artificial insemination!... The new Era!... Silence!'

'Listen,' the Vamp continued. 'It's important we stay calm because I'm going to give you names and facts. In May 1962, the Barcelona review *Cristiandad* published a global panoramic study with data and statistics from the Bank of Bilbao. I want to talk about that study and the work of engineer Lluís Creus Vidal, because it portrays a situation that has only worsened in the years since. Moreover, I'm not in a position to give you remotely accurate figures for the current situation because today in 2050, the government has such a degree of control that all data coming to us are mediated by them, and we know very well that the technicians in Paris crunch their numbers... with a lot of *savoir faire.*'

Though true, it must have been an unpalatable truth to *Monsieur-Dame*, who was listening while admiring the scent of a rose in a golden chamber of the Élysée. The Vamp took a mouthful of some revolting drink and carried on.

'The study I'm referring to said that an industrialisation complex has today spread throughout the world, even within those countries typically considered agricultural. Chile exports machinery, Venezuela and Colombia manufacture steel, Argentina and Brazil automobiles, and what's most curious is that they're all relying on the export market to place their products. But when every country in the world is trying to sell machines, who are they going to sell to? *Cristiandad* published this in 1962, and the sales crisis arrived. The expectation of being able to export "abroad" is an outdated dream. Remember that the author of the article is referring to 1962 and it's been downhill all the way since then. Industrial production increased and has continued to increase in geometric progression. By contrast, agricultural production can only increase at a much slower arithmetical rate because wheat takes eight months to ripen, and calves nine months to mature. The result could only be *disette*. Not a somewhat artificial and localised famine such as that which Paris suffered in the time of Louis XVI, fomented by enemies of the Court, but a real *disette* that affects everyone, except perhaps Paris, where *Monsieur-Dame* resides. Notice that when industry was reaching its apogee and becoming a religion in the second half of the twentieth century, there began to be shortages of wheat in Russia, which had always been an exporter of wheat; and there were shortages of beef in Argentina, which had always been an exporter. Using language common in 1962, it's now possible to state that everything is done to popularize electric refrigerators, but we don't know how to fill them. Had advances in astrophysics and aeronautics permitted, famine would certainly have driven the leaders of industry – whose ambitions were a thousand times more imperialist than those of Charles v – to unleash an interplanetary war, but this imperialist dream has come to nothing. The stars haven't given us a single cabbage or calf. The energy used in rocket propulsion is energy stolen from agriculture and livestock farming. Clearly, the problem isn't quite the same as that denounced by Spengler in *Der Untergang des Abendlandes* and *Jahre der Entscheidung*. It's not about the struggle any more between white workers who want higher wages and workers of other races who become their competitors and corner the international market. There is now no international market and the U.S. of Europe has had to absorb the products it manufactures. The destruction of North America and Russia, together with the great fumigations of China, have suppressed all our competition, but have also destroyed our potential consumers. The millions of vacuum cleaners, freezers, radios and so on have to be purchased in our country, and the market is quickly saturated. As the saying goes, "whoever makes it, pays for it". It became necessary, therefore, to create artificial appetites, and to convince the masses that they need what they don't need: mayonnaise-making machines when no-one has the ingredients to make mayonnaise, vacuum cleaners for apartments that don't have carpets, and refrigerators to preserve food which is so expensive that it can only be acquired in minute quantities. And all this on credit.'

The Vamp paused briefly before going on.

'But I insist: rather than an economic problem, what we're

faced with is a psychological revolution, a deep-rooted disturbance. It clearly cannot be healthy politics to establish organizations on the wasteful practice of consuming goods that aren't
needed while basic necessities can't be provided. The energy
invested in producing noxious beverages and useless mechanical
gadgets, organizing Babel-like tourism and aimless movement,
would be better directed towards more logical, moral ends, capable of satisfying real human yearnings, like religion, art, and the
contemplation of nature. Industrialists wrench us from nature
and art, but not religion, as they create their own mysticism
which allows them to supplant the classic religions. Our Era
is represented by a monstrous man whose role is to enrich the
Trusts. This man finds himself separated from natural, often free
pleasures such as thirst quenching spring water and the song
of the nightingale, and is drawn to more profitable pursuits,
more unsavoury gratifications that provoke disgust and neurosis
and blunt his sensibility. This man is intoxicated by turmoil, he
loathes the countryside and "needs" the syncopated rhythms
and tainted air of the metropolis. According to Lévi-Strauss,
progress in 1964 was in a downwards spiral of evolution, "and
virtually its only use was to make good the shortcomings of
progress itself". The Machine Era, especially after the atomic
bomb, adopted mass destruction as its mode, pulverizing thousands of original, irreplaceable structures while proceeding to
hunt down new imbalances in order to produce energy at the
cost of new destruction.* The housing crisis, for example, was
and is a fact, and while the shortage of apartments grows, the
number of automobiles increases so that people can flee this
progress they can no longer tolerate but that, nonetheless, they
need. We've got everything the wrong way round: a socialist,
gregarious era should prohibit cars, radios and private television
sets, all of which make people anxious. But what happens is
precisely the opposite as it encourages private ownership. A

* See Clausius for the concept of entropy, and the energy loss confirmed by Einstein.

democratic State couldn't condone the different technological "castes"; a progressive society that wants to do away with "slow, antiquated" agriculture and that aspires to travel to the Moon and back ought to have mothballed cars and combustion engines. These paradoxes point to a significant mental confusion and suggest an absence of philosophical and truly humanist vision. It appears difficult to persuade the public that in order to live well they need two radios when they manifestly have no need for them, but at the same time the manufacturer can't survive if he doesn't sell them. But people are credulous and since they stopped going to mass, they've become superstitious. Propaganda and advertising and the art of deceiving the public have risen as the new religion at the service of the plutocracy.'

No longer able to contain themselves, six business leaders disguised as frail old maids sprung quickly to their feet and left the venue.

'Hey, look,' said Lola, 'the little old ladies got young.'

Many in the audience burst out laughing. But not all were revolutionaries.

'Has the government suddenly become reasonable?' asked someone behind us. 'Accused of being tyrannical, even dictatorial, even though it has all the power, it's allowing people to speak out. So liberal…'

'It's this liberalism (born of fear, don't forget),' their companion replied, 'that will lead to accusations of tyranny, and it'll be the government's fault, because they'll let them say it.'

'Advertising,' continued the Vamp, 'is the religion of our times. Before its death, North America infected us with it, a virus much more terrifying than polio. Advertising is the art of presenting things from the perspective of their advantages while silencing their shortcomings, or rather – and let me be very clear about this – advertising is the art of the lie. It takes different forms, though principally it works through the magical repetition of words and routine. People aren't totally rational.

When they have debts, they don't need a safe; but if they are told a thousand times that they needs a safe, they'll end up buying one on credit. What is clear is that the day people begin to think more, they'll finally understand that the majority of their atomic goods are not only useless, but that they clutter up their increasingly tiny apartments. And then the crash will come and the working-class writer–'

'And?' screamed out an anonymous progressive before being silenced. 'Imbecile!'

'And so,' continued the speaker, 'there's no way out. We'll have to carry on giving work to the industrial workers, having them produce goods that we don't need, getting high on music, increasing daily wages and, using slogans and other deceptions, giving with one hand while taking away with the other. Thus *Monsieur-Dame* de Pompignac la Fleur condemns us to hunger, sympathetically parodying Marie Antoinette with his phrase: 'If they don't have bread, let them buy a freezer.'**

That was too much. In Paris, *Monsieur-Dame* must have made some kind of gesture and frowned. And so in the meeting an old lady got to her feet, took off her tunic, and transformed into a resplendent figure before making straight for the speaker.

'Dr Nicola,' said the old lady, 'you're under arrest!'

The Vamp removed his wig and wiped off his make-up, revealing himself to be Dr Nicola. They led him away and I connected with Andrea via my micro-TV set. She was alone in the Roman salon and had covered her face with her cloak, like a character in a neoclassical tragedy.

** 'If the peasants don't have bread, let them eat cake.' The phrase is now considered to be apocryphal.

218

Dr Nicola, Regime insider and head of the Mediterranean's most prestigious psychiatric centre, lost to the Revolution... Such a coup could be serious for *Monsieur-Dame*, lurching from misstep to misstep, because he didn't dare make his enemies disappear, even discreetly, instead letting them speak so that the official savants might refute their arguments later.

Dialectics rarely have an outcome. Paul Valéry said in this respect that there is no idea that does not contain its own refutation within it and the Greek sophists were pleased by the limitless panorama of the intellectual universe they had just discovered. After he had convinced his young disciples of one order of things, Socrates would change his reasoning and convince them of the contrary: gymnastics which strengthen the intellect at the expense of morality, and which condemned him, or perhaps he condemned himself, to death by hemlock.

But this wasn't merely about ideas and noble games; *disette* was much more pressing. 'Fuck famine, damn disette!' chanted the yobs, scandalizing the Classical University. The incontrovertible, existential truth for them was that they needed basic subsistence. Across the abandoned countryside, the stupid proliferation of empty fridges and freezers continued unabated, but while the Regime wavered between economic liberalism and blind state intervention, refrigerators and other household appliances were undergoing a crisis of their own.

The 'fridge trial' serves to illustrate this loss of direction. Since apartments were getting ever smaller and tinned food could be stored at room temperature, a new product designed to buck the market trend was introduced, dedicated exclusively to *Hola-Hola*. It had no motor, made no noise, and didn't malfunction. It was the 'Perpetual Actuality' model. The Cold

Guild condemned the fridge and it was banned. Appliances without faults and an unlimited lifespan, determined the court, were antisocial and must be replaced by others with built-in obsolescence in order to provide manufacturers with guaranteed work. But, as Dr Nicola had said, a civilization based on the absurdity of creating artificial need and fabricating objects which deliberately break and continuously go out of date could not be economically healthy. It brought to mind the chaotic restlessness or action considered as an intrinsic value that Waldo Frank saw as the characteristic and aberration of the Modern Era. The materialists failed to bear in mind that when things don't last long enough to become assimilated, men tend not to value them, and with time this inconsistency extends to friendship, love, and sentiments. Here you have the genesis of a particular type of moral imbecility that affects us these days: tourism.

Food was scarce and of poor quality. Had the government put its trust in studies carried out by technologists who were attempting to make bread from seaweed? The experiment had been piloted with ten Abyssinians and all ten had died, but what else could one expect if fantasy, once the realm of lyric poets, was now the focus of scientists? It was the business of financiers too, as illustrated by the case of Jacques Necker, the great con artist, at the end of the eighteenth century. Necker presented his *Compte rendu* to the French king, but it was dismissed by some even at the time as a work of fantasy.

Having destroyed agriculture, the Minister of Economy and Finance in Turclub proposed the creation of subsidies for food growers, saying, 'If they're abandoning the land because they can earn more and with less effort in the city, we have to raise their wages...' The reasoning was logical, if bordering on sophistry. Industrializing the masses and exciting them with heady, coarse pleasures, the *panem et circenses* of ancient Rome, was easier than turning them on to the rural with Virgil's *Eclogues*. After decades of unproductive restlessness, and with ataraxia a now distant memory, the proletariat was drunk on pandemonium, alcohol and cinema, and detested the countryside. A whole new proletarian sensibility was needed though such a thing had long since been dismissed as antiquated. It was easy enough for a diabetic cryo survivor to devise as he pictured us back in the seventeenth century, just at the time Galileo would have been scrutinizing the sky with his telescope and the mystic Pascal was sacrificing himself to the poison of the experimental sciences.

Moreover, the only practical way to introduce the proposed subsidies was to tax the industrialists who had money and represented not only economic strength, but also a large part of public opinion that was very dangerous to disappoint. A kind of mysticism had grown up around atomic appliances. On the path to perfection, the latest invention always promised to be definitive. This path towards a non-existent goal was called progress, but if we acknowledge that the public might distrust their idols and even end up rejecting them, would industry have been able to tolerate overwhelming burdens such as subsidies in favour of the land? The ruin of industry would be the downfall of machine civilization. Powerful, stupid machines vomited out terrifying quantities of automobiles and fridges that no market could absorb. Surely international or colonial markets didn't exist? According to Creus Vidal's forecasts, even traditionally agricultural countries were producing machinery instead of wheat or livestock. The world was saturated. However much we widened streets and roads, we couldn't contain the mechanical pollution that overflowed them, pouring into the side drains or over the edges. As always, advertising offered eternal glory in the form of the latest domestic appliance (at least until the next appeared) and managed to sell it, but every penultimate appliance was forgotten, and this by increments made life more expensive and filled the beehive cell-apartments and urban wasteland with unwanted steel.

Monsieur-Dame de Pompignac la Fleur, indecisive as ever, put off making a decision about subsidies and counselled moderation, *rondeur et un certain sourire*. Hate mail came flooding in and in a panic he had the television stations multiply his smile on air and turned his gaze to the Palazzo Víctrix as though begging for help. The smiles were sour though, and the Palazzo, surrounded by those insulating avenues of cypress trees and plastic roses, frowned back at them. The fresh-faced and amenable goddess from years gone by was now studying political economics, and we know that if one studies to excess, the human organism loses its equilibrium and becomes all forehead or nose. Did the president still have faith in the popularity of Andrea, in the charm of her boyish lines, in the air of moral purity that surrounded her? Years of excess had eaten away at her physical beauty.

I'm not in a position to speak from personal experience, because I've only ever kissed her neck between the ear and collarbone, as per protocol, but if anyone in this world has ever detested purely carnal pleasures, it's her. The burden of flesh landed on Andrea at seventeen years of age like a block of concrete. And she bore it like the good soldier bears being strafed by a machine gun. If she experienced moments of happiness, they were moral in nature, such as believing that an individual who sold their soul contributed to collective prosperity. Or perhaps she found happiness in the pleasure some ghastly partners derived from contact with her skin, while she suffered.

At that time a group of medical eminences in Turclub, whose self-importance had been inflated by the atmosphere of revolt and the hesitations of the Élysée, published a communiqué demonstrating that the increase in rates of lung cancer was caused by vehicle emissions poisoning the air. Like all controversial studies, it was well documented with figures and statistical data, called for the use of *ancien régime* fossil fuels such as petroleum and diesel to be banned, and for cars to be powered by atomic energy. Otherwise, they said that within just a few years, cases of cancer would have rocketed by fifty per cent.

The communiqué alarmed public opinion and the governor, beside himself with fury, sacked the head of censorship who was a close friend of *Monsieur-Dame*. Five minutes later, *Monsieur-Dame* sacked the governor. The Party was steadily falling apart. The Regime had lost all sense of direction and, torn between conflicting opinions, it ended up adopting meaningless compromises that led nowhere. Nothing was working.

I wanted to call on Dr Nicola. Now though, after the shock of the last lecture, I understood everything: his reticence in the bar that night in El Terreno, the night before the homage to Andrea and, later, the morning the two little waiters killed themselves in my room, high on soma. My own 'fanatical' ideas in favour of the old regime, and the trust I enjoyed at the Palazzo Víctrix, made me an important but dangerous figure whom Nicola both wanted to and was afraid to confide in. My love for Andrea aside, he considered me reckless and impulsive. Nicola, by contrast, was in perfect control of himself. According to the radio, he hadn't been placed in solitary confinement, and was able to receive visitors without a guard present. The government was outdoing itself in trying to establish its liberal credentials, but no-one trusted them. It must be the case that the private room set aside for friends of Nicola was wired with multiple bugs. This was undoubtedly about winning the trust of the Regime's enemies so that they could first be put under surveillance, before being silenced in an instant like a snake swallows a bird. The atmosphere of insecurity seemed worse even than *disette*. There were rumours a machine had been invented that captured brainwaves and could read people's thoughts. If this proved to be true, the State would have power never before seen in history, and the human soul, unique to the individual, would be dead and gone forever. The roll-out of that invention, subject to absolute secrecy, must be incredibly complicated and expensive, but I had my suspicions that they'd probably already wired my room so that they could spy on me.

Given my status as Andrea's first lover – at least that's how everyone saw me – it was impossible to imagine that anyone would have dared bug me without the goddess's permission, but it was also understandable that she should try to discover what I was thinking. She had told me very loyally that she would spare neither effort nor means in bringing me over to the Cause, whatever it took: gifts, dialectic, seduction. I never got to the bottom of this and now, with Andrea's disappearance from the scene, I doubt I ever will. Under that regime, we always ended up at the same point: for better or worse, having lost our slow roasted kid, real oranges and breathable air, the possibility of intimacy was stolen from us. We were turning into ants or caterpillars and according to some this should have created in us a greater sense of fraternal love but as far as I could see, it was more likely to cause us to rip each other's eyes out. More than once while I was alone in bed, I thought about how Andrea in the Palazzo Víctrix responded to my most intimate, almost oneiric thoughts.

'*Amico*,' said Andrea, 'go and visit Nicola. Without fear. Tell the guard that you'd like to see him in the white room. He knows what that means.'

It means, I thought to myself, that in the white room there would be no scrutiny or supervision. I would be the spy, in effect, under cover of friendship, because Andrea knew that I would tell her everything Nicola confided in me. There was a pause, and I froze as Andrea whispered to me, as though responding to my hesitation over the morality of the idea.

'Why do you doubt me? she said. 'There's no ulterior motive...'

Her voice seemed to reach me from a long way away, somewhere in a hidden, serene, loyal world. I was reassured. If Andrea were spying on me, it could never be ill-intentioned.

Many times I have recalled that androgynous, ingenuous, confident voice, incapable of lying to me. I involuntarily associate it with rainy mornings when as a student in Madrid, my blood pumping hard because of the cold, I would call Velasco to see if he wanted to swim in the covered, tepid pool where we'd watch the winter snow through the glass skylights. We'd swim maybe six-hundred metres together, breathing in tandem, and in that moment focus all of our youthful potency, shaped by confused desire, yet channelled towards noble ends by morality and sport. We would swim – according to my friend's happy expression – until we 'sweated under the water.' I was five years older than Velasco and in the penultimate year of my degree. He was in his first. I knew more than he did and was stronger, both of which could be calibrated but he, unlike me, was without measure. My obsession was to imagine him weak, because only that way could I protect him. But in reality he was the more dominant. 'How are you? Did you sleep well?' were always my first words. And the reply, far away on the end of the telephone, was always the same, 'I'm well, thank you. Why?'

He wasn't just being polite, evidently. That distant voice seemed to rise from the darkness of sleep, called forth by a question that was incomprehensible to him. 'Will you come for a swim with me?' There was a touch of snobbery in my words, but only sincerity in his. 'Won't it be cold?' 'No, we'll soon warm up…' 'We can swim till we sweat and then take a cold shower.' 'If that'll feel good…' 'Divine. I want to make an Olympian of you.' I liked that he, specifically Velasco, considered me a god. I wanted to protect him, but it was I who needed him.

It was similar with Andrea. I had come to worship her. I would have kissed her, not on the lips, but on her feet, or robe.

'Dearest Andrea,' I said, half asleep. 'I'd like to see you.'

'Look over at the wall to your right,' she replied.

She was smiling at me, golden and androgynous. She had recovered her *morbidezza* but, alert to the tricks of technology, I wasn't certain whether that beautiful image was live or recorded.

'I won't blaspheme again,' I think I said, 'but allow me to come to see you in person.'

'That's not possible, hun.'

The word horrified me. Not possible, forever? That's how I understood it, and I was right. In the letter delivered to me weeks before by the two little acrobat waiters, there still seemed to be some hope. I knew it by heart and had read it a thousand times: 'When you are pure, when you understand that the spirit transcends the flesh, which is a joke (a very bad one), then…' The 'then' had disappeared. Andrea was ill and was firm in her decision to prevent me from entering the Palazzo. I knew that much intuitively and needed no machine to capture her brainwaves. Earthly Paradise was closed to me forever and from that moment it began to take on its true category of a Paradise Lost. I could have screamed, but I didn't. In my despair, I heard myself pronounce strange words,

'If you insist,' I said, 'I will work for the Cause.'

'I would like nothing better,' she replied, 'but I'm incredibly busy. I'm preparing the refutation of Nicola.'

She probably didn't believe me. And I didn't completely believe her either.

'How's your health?' I asked.

'Good. Bearing in mind my considerable years, I could still live up to six months.'

I was almost sick. This is what I feared. Dead before twenty… Sacrificed to an inhuman civilization fit only for the likes of beasts and the stray dogs that devoured Jezebel… Andrea's voice had become faint. I didn't catch the words that followed but then her voice rang clear as a silver bell again.

'And afterwards the dogs will devour Andrea.'

'Andrea!' I cried.

'What is it, hun?'

'You said something about… dogs?'

'No,' she said.

'Didn't you mention the dogs that devoured Jezebel, mother of Athaliah?'

'I don't know what you're refer–' Her sentence was cut short by two frightful alexandrines:

The dogs in her inhuman blood quenched full,
And the torn members of her hideous corpse.

'Enough, Andrea!' I shouted, now fully awake.

'But I didn't say anything,' came the reply.

There was silence. And then, after an interminable minute or so, I heard her again.

'I'm sorry. There seems to have been a small technical problem. It wasn't I who was talking about dogs. The technicians report that you recited two lines of Racine.'

'It wasn't me, I swear,' I said.

'Or you thought them. From the tragedy *Athalie*.'

'So you are actually capturing what–'

'I'll explain it to you sometime,' interrupted Andrea. 'It's… complicated. But don't say "you". You said you'd work for the Cause. And now, I must leave you…'

'Just a moment, Andrea,' I urged. 'This image of you… is it of you now?'

She hesitated, as though deciding whether to lie.

'It's… from a recent transmission. Not from now.'

'I'd like to see you now,' I said.

'I'm on the massage table, I'm not wearing make-up.'

'I don't care. I want to see how you are now.'

'In just a little while I'll be different,' Andrea replied. 'Better…'

'Artificially?'

'There's nothing artificial about it. Everything that is, is natural,' said Andrea.

'I'm not in the mood for metaphysics.'

'It's not metaphysics… Can you wait half an hour?'

'Not a minute,' I said.

'As you wish.'

She appeared naked on a table, surrounded by doctors and masseurs and was even more emaciated than the last time. There was still a harmony to her lines which revealed the most perfect neck and back you could ever imagine, but her skin was flaccid and yellowish. You could count her ribs. Her eyes were closed, her features motionless. It was the face of a dead person. The magnificent golden locks that fell over her forehead could not brighten the morgue-like aspect of the operating table, circled by busy shadows and muffled voices. Someone gave her an injection. Another listened to her heart.

'We need to fill the wrinkles in her neck,' a voice commanded. 'These two depressions, beneath her shoulders…'

I wanted to cry. Without opening her eyes, Andrea's anaemic lips twitched.

'Are you crying?' she asked quietly.

I didn't visit Nicola. What could he have said to me, even had the white room not been wired with listening devices? If he attacked the Regime, he'd be preaching to the converted. And anyway, I didn't want to betray Andrea, her smile about to work a miracle in the midst of revolt, as now was the moment for me to confess that this cursed civilization had, like everything, its compensations. The monstrous, uncomfortable, New York-style skyscrapers, reminiscent of the cages in which Louis xi confined the traitors of his time, took on a tragic character both late at night and in the captivating light of dawn. One of Louis Bromfield's characters said that New York has a harsh beauty; the same could be said of Turclub at certain times of day. Racing at a hundred and fifty across the sterile plains of Mallorca, trading the ugly for the petrifying, and fleeing beaches that were noisier and more crowded with blaring transistor radios and rude people than those even of Italy was all sometimes a source of pleasure, because when the vehicle crashed, death was instantaneous and the occupants felt nothing as they were overcome by fumes from the bottles of hydrogen cyanide that exploded mechanically on impact. Liberal doses of Parquidine also put an end to pain almost before it began. Philosophers and moralists sang its praises, the former as a system by which suicide could be popularized – 'the only way of exercising free will in modern societies' – and the latter as a solution to human terrestrial congestion, or the parasitic part of it at least.

Helicopter flights across a sky still occasionally pure were both stimulating and calming, with the attraction of the clouds seemingly offering a refuge of cotton wool beneath our feet. Surely the most significant of Turclub's compensations was the magical figure of Andrea, her white skin, golden hair (that some starving poet would doubtless have compared to a sun-drenched omelette), strong hands, and slightly androgynous appearance. You, Andrea, could have saved this mad civilization single-handedly, and you almost did, though at the cost of your life. It's true, however, that *Monsieur-Dame* de Pompignac la Fleur's nauseating smile acted as a repellent. Many of us could no longer stand his physical presence and, oblivious to this, he imposed it upon us every night.

'*Bonne nuit, mes enfants,*' he would say, '*le Président vous envoie un tout petit baiser.*'

And he would then produce a smile of such hypocritical proportions that we were filled with the urge to hurl plastic potatoes at him.

More and more clandestine radio stations were broadcasting every day and the authorities seemed powerless to stop them. While Lola had gone to see the prisoner, I had stayed in the apartment and tuned in to one such channel. They were discussing a subject that the goddess and I had talked about. Humans seemed destined to starve to death because they were increasing in number more rapidly than agriculture could provide for, but food from the sea had been identified as a solution.

'The sea,' explained an anonymous voice on the nameless station, 'covers three-quarters of the Earth's surface: there will always be more fish than men.'

Whatever the demographic growth, there would be more than enough fish...

I knew the argument by heart and turned the radio off. In theory the problem was resolved; the difficulty was that the ocean depths contained far fewer fish than people realised while the young would rather operate coffee machines or manufacture *Hola-Hola* than brave the sea to catch fish. 'Persuading' them to abandon such meaningless activities meant, however, ruining many industries, and the progressives opposed such action, becoming immobilists. Industry was its own dogma, and it underpinned the whole civilization of the United States of Europe. This state of affairs meant that the population of the western nations decreased compared with the number of Pacific islanders.

Dr Orlando had once reminded me that life began in the oceans, that in evolutionary terms, man descends from fish and that fish – especially since the release of enormous amounts of nuclear energy – had experienced mutations that would make them more powerful than humans. While these were clearly the ravings of a lunatic, they were not without some merit. But the idea that fish might emerge from the sea to eat us humans, rather than vice-versa, seemed a grotesque social subversion and I couldn't help but take the hared-brained doctor to task.

'So how is humanity to be saved?' I asked.

'Evidently not by consuming poisons and limiting procreation.'

Lola returned from her visit to Nicola full of enthusiasm. She'd come across a lot of people she knew, some of whom were her clients.

'Men like you and I, viviparous I mean, and a few women, real women, too. Wouldn't life be wonderful if everyone was who they are and behaved decently? I met two women from our time who'd undergone a cryo-cure and they told me that tomorrow they're going to a smart café dressed as women, each carrying a romantic novel. Let's see what happens. I feel like going with them, wearing a revealing neckline and heavy eye make-up. I've got a really tight dress from before, a Gilda. I don't know whether you remember the trend. It's red satin. I used to cause such a scandal when I wore it. Oh, they could see I was a woman then. It makes me more *jogione*, as you say.'

'Giorgione,' I corrected her.

'What does *jogione* mean?' she asked, without rectifying her pronunciation.

'He's an Italian artist who painted women like you.'

'I've never heard of him. Did he know what I'm like?'

'Did he know?' I laughed. 'He knew plenty about women.'

'Why do you say he knew?' asked Lola. 'Is he dead, poor thing?'

'He died centuries ago,' I said.

'Are you teasing me? Wait till you see me in the Gilda dress. You can see my whole bosom. And no, it doesn't make me look anaemic. You'll see…'

I tried to dissuade her, partly out of selfishness – in truth, I needed her – and partly because if she were exiled it would be indelicate of me to ask Andrea for clemency.

'I don't think they'll punish us,' said Lola, 'and if they do, it won't be for long. This regime's on its last legs. I can see myself coming back from the deserts of Massachusetts and appointed Minister of the Interior. I'll appoint you as official poet.'

Her words reminded me uncannily of Andrea's when she advised me to write in support of the government or become a prostitute. Official poet! Was it worth conspiring to overthrow a regime if the new movement ending up dictating poetic subject matter? Composing an epic on the subject of a bearded gentleman or a paean to the beauty spots of a ministerial favourite? No, I'd already seen too much.

'If they make you a minister, Lola, I'll join the opposition.'

She laughed and kissed me on the lips.

'I like decisive men,' she said. 'They're more men, even if they don't know what they're making decisions about.'

She paused, most likely philosophizing on the mystery of more manly men, because then she said quite randomly,

'Nicola doesn't seem like a real man to me, you know? I bet he's Andrea's sort… You like him too.'

'Don't talk about Andrea,' I said.

'Careful! Andrea's like the Greek queen who was born of a swan.'

I laughed. I hadn't thought she was so versed in mythology.

Lola narrowed her eyes.

'Wasn't she born from an egg, like Andrea? Or am I confusing her with Cleopatra?'

'You're not confused,' I replied. 'The swan that gave birth to Helen of Sparta was Jupiter.'

She looked at me in astonishment. The way she fluttered her eyelids was very pretty.

'That's not right,' said Lola.

'It's gospel,' I insisted.

'There's no need for heresies. Mythology is a lie. Jupiter wasn't a bird. Jupiter didn't exist.'

'He wasn't anything if he didn't exist,' I replied. 'But according to mythology, sometimes he would adopt the form of a swan, or a shower of gold coins...'

'You're pulling my leg. You can try that on with Andrea but not with me.'

Every time we argued, she would bring up Andrea and attribute the most contradictory things to her. Sometimes she would assert that Andrea was an effeminate male, and on those occasions when she considered her female, she'd label her a tomboy. To her mind, I was an unstable neurasthenic in denial about my real inclinations.

'Yes, yes...,' said Lola. 'That's right, you can have desires without knowing about them, and that's what Freud says in the story of wretched little Hans, a six-year-old carrying on with his mother. Disgusting, that such things happen in the world...'

One hears all kinds of things in brothels, even psychoanalysis. Films are very educational too, particularly about salmon fishing and Lola had acquired a certain amount of culture in her own, sweet time.

'You're attracted to Andrea because he's a man,' continued Lola, 'but you don't know that's the reason why.'

'I'm sure you're right,' I said, taking what she had said as a joke.

When she saw me so calm, her anger increased and she re-directed the attack with an insult I hadn't heard from her before.

'Actually *he* disgusts you' – she stressed the masculine – , 'but you want him, because he's rich.'

'So tell me why I'm attracted to his wealth.'

'Ah! So you acknowledge he's a man? I never imagined you were such a gold digger, or such a pig.'

She knew perfectly well that I lived off my unemployment allowance, and she'd chastised me plenty of times for not taking full advantage of my connection with the Palazzo. She knew that Andrea had offered me political positions and that I'd refused them. Her ill intention started to annoy me and I was tempted to offend her in turn.

'Darling,' I countered, 'you're just jealous, and that's not going to work out in a profession like yours.'

'Me, jealous?' she said, taking the bait. 'Who do you think you are?! The Maharaja of Kapurthala! You haven't got two pennies to rub together and you lie through your teeth. Get out of here, go tell Andrea that Jupiter was a swan. You're not making a fool out of me.'

'I don't need to tell her,' I replied. 'Because she already knows.'

The jibe hit home.

'Well!' said Lola. 'She must be as wise as the Greek queens.'

'Where did you hear that the Greek queens were wise?' I asked, now also irritated, it showing in the derision written across my face.

'I've always known about the seven queens of Greece,' she said.

'The seven sages, you mean. The seven wise men!'

'The seven queens!' she shouted back.

'In which particular geometry treatise, if you will?'

'I'm not talking to you.'

'So be quiet'.

'No, I don't want to. This is my house.'

'So talk.'

'I won't talk.'

'Don't shout.'

'I'll shout if I want!'

Our voices were getting louder. The apartment walls only had a two-centimetre skim of plaster, a design inspired by the functional and economic theories of Le Corbusier, and the next-door neighbour rebuked us loudly, shouting, 'I'm trying to have my siesta!'

'It's not siesta time, and I'm in my own home,' replied Lola.

'And so am I!' came the neighbour's response.

'Yes, spying on your neighbours!'

'Do you think I find your rows even mildly entertaining? Give me strength!'

'So don't listen.'

'I don't listen!'

'Nor do I. Your words, my dear sir, go in one ear and out of the other.'

'Enough, Lola,' I cut in.

'Oh, so you're taking his side? You're defending that idiot?'

'I said that's enough.'

'This is my house!' she shouted. 'I'll do what I want!'

'I said don't shout!' I shouted.

The door opened and a robot one metre ninety tall stood before me with its arms crossed and a threatening smile on its face. Lola was inconsistency personified. Even though she loathed those devices because they scared her and cluttered her apartment, a sales rep had rhapsodized about the largest model in the series, and Lola had bought it – on credit, of course. She'd forgotten her previous disaster. This was a new design. 'It can pick up and carry a piano,' said the advertising. Neither Lola nor anyone else had a piano, but she bought the robot anyway.

'In your profession,' the rep had hissed, 'you need a brawny servant. I'll calibrate its brain in case anyone oversteps the mark. The robot is strong, but it's also a very sensitive model. Don't imagine you're buying an elephant. It has the latest "psychological" configuration, so if a client raises his voice the robot will be on him like a police dog.'

I won't be able to reconstruct the scene accurately. We were arguing angrily, absurdly, when Lola in a fit of bad manners, called me a 'pervert' because I'd fallen in love with Andrea. Let me remind you that I underwent the cryo-cure in 1965 and Lola's insult was unimaginably offensive to a man of my generation, which was precisely why she'd used it. I reacted instinctively and slapped her. The psychological robot smiled – was still smiling – and took a step towards me. I was suddenly afraid and Lola, poor girl, realising the danger I was in, shrieked. The beast bared its teeth. I grabbed a vacuum cleaner and smashed the steel handle on its head, triggering a malfunction and an epileptic fit that dropped it onto its back. Lola screamed at me to press the immobiliser switch, but it was located above its kidneys and I couldn't reach. The creature was breathing fire through its eyes and from its mouth there vomited a stream of insults that would have shamed even a condemned man.

'The insults key is in its belly-button!' she shouted.

I didn't think we were in danger while the monster was crashed out and I grabbed hold of Lola to drag her from the room. The robot then suddenly jumped up, tore Lola from my arms and threw her out of the window.

Thinking I'd find her dead on the boulevard below, I ran to get the lift – her apartment, as I said, was on the top floor – but before I reached ground level a fearsome explosion shook the whole block. A short-circuit had blown the robot's electronic brain to smithereens and I was blinded by the fireball that engulfed the whole building. I couldn't find Lola. The robot had been so strong and the block so high that she had landed in the sea and it wasn't until the following day that her body appeared floating in the water. After searching fruitlessly, I took a helicopter to the terrace of my lodgings. There awaiting me were a box of chocolates and six real wax candles with a card from Andrea expressing her condolences. Later a *maître d'hôtel* bearing the insignia of the Palazzo Víctrix arrived with more gifts: a box of raisins and three roses. The *maître d'* was young, perhaps twenty-five years old and male, I think, well-groomed and good-looking. He introduced himself attentively, with a French accent, and asked me in Andrea's name what he could do to distract me from the sadness that the death of the 'illustrious prostitute' had caused. He spoke courteously and without affectation.

'I'm a dancer,' he offered, 'and I've danced for *Monsieur-Dame* at the Élysée.'

I declined, telling him bluntly that I wanted to be alone. He kissed me silently, and at the door informed me that while I was in mourning, I would receive a daily visit from *dei bambini* and some other token from the Palazzo.

'Sir needs kindness at this time,' he said.

I learned later that he was a pariah of sorts, believed to be the child of a couple from before the Great Revolution. The fact that an individual of such questionable birth had risen to the rank of *maître d'hôtel* and had performed for *Monsieur-Dame* was a mystery in which some saw Andrea's influence. Starting the following day, three little Ibizan waiters would call by every morning and present me with fruit or real flowers. They arrived before I awoke and waited until I dismissed them. In my semi-dormant state I'd hear their muffled giggles and faint fluttering movement punctuated with bird-like shrieks in the corridor. They couldn't have been more than seven years old and looked like sugar angels. The first few days they addressed me as Your Excellency (a title enjoyed by those of Andrea's friends who were permitted to enter the Roman salon), but they quickly became less respectful, and would throw themselves onto my bed, laughing and tickling me. Destined for the circus and already displaying notable acrobatic skills, they were amusing, but it troubled me that they had to take soma in order to perform their acrobatics. Once the effects of the drug had worn off, they fell to the ground spent, and it was sometimes difficult to bring them round. I informed Andrea of my concerns via short-wave radio, and said I thought it was criminal.

'Why?' she replied, resigned. 'According to the doctors, they'll live to almost eighteen.'

'And you think that's okay?'

'You're difficult to please,' she murmured, sadly. 'You want the impossible. You like children and yet you'd let them get old.'

Her voice became faint and another, stronger voice instructed me curtly not to create difficulties for the Excellency. I asked who was speaking, and the line went dead. The Regime's capacity for courtesy was becoming as rare as potatoes.

Contradictory rumours circulated about Andrea's health. TV propaganda showed her glowing with youth and beauty: Andrea, naked, emerging from the sea, concealed by a scallop shell like in Botticelli's portrait; Andrea seated proudly in the red Rolls Royce, swathed in white Roman robes; Andrea on Pleasure allowing herself to be kissed by a police officer, etc. These were old reports. But for at least a century now Mallorca had seen more movement, more people, and more activity than a souk. Santiago Rusiñol's gently teasing *L'illa de la calma* was still influential in people's minds, as was that other little book that talked about big houses and grand ladies. Where were those mansions now? Converted into hotels. And the canons and cats of the Seu?

The Mallorca of yesteryear, of Llorenç Riber, *donya* Obdúlia, was long gone, and so too was the silence and the clarity of the sky. The tourists who headed to the island to enjoy these attractions were instrumental in their disappearance. Halfway through the twentieth century Mrs Seymour was upset that a motorway had been built to encourage excursions to the Gorg Blau. It was certainly a smoother ride than the old road, but its snaking presence and the traffic it brought completely destroyed the charm of the Gorg. Shortly after, they built a tunnel to facilitate access to the Torrent de Pareis, a solitary spot that thanks to the tunnel, became anything but.

'But what's your point?' Andrea had said, months previously. 'We already talked about this when we were discussing the Quiet Repose beach, the one our enemies call Nightmare. I'm the first to deplore what has happened. Solitude and silence contain their own tragedy, just as virginity once did. Those who value such treasure are the ones who destroy it, and if the treasure were not prized, if no-one knew about it, it wouldn't exist.'

Andrea was right. It was tragic in the Greek sense and, saddened by this, I had attempted to argue my way to an eclectic solution.

'I'm not saying that no-one should go there,' I'd said. 'But these crowds of halfwits…'

'Of course. You were born a "gentleman" and I understand your wanting to reserve certain experiences for the privileged.'

'For those able to appreciate them,' I'd replied. 'It might be that years ago the poor, if they possessed the right sensibility, enjoyed such things more than the rich (perhaps the rich were deterred by the thought of travelling on packhorse trails), but virginity isn't a commercial proposition and today everything is about profit.'

'That profit,' Andrea had said, 'all that money, brought progress to Turclub. Before the hordes of tourists arrived, we were poor.'

I had pointed out that when we were poor, the houses in every rural hamlet had three bedrooms, a large reception room and a yard for animals.

'Nowadays,' I'd argued, 'you'd add bathrooms, give the walls a lick of some awful coloured paint, and turn a single one of those houses into three or four apartments.'

Andrea had seemed pensive.

'What do you think of Le Corbusier?' she'd asked.

'They should have hanged him. You're deceiving yourself, Andrea. We're not rich now that we have money. We were rich when we could eat real potatoes. And these tourists who you're misleading will end up seeing through the deceit. We can't eat here, or breathe, or even sleep, and everyone is bad-tempered.'

The English in particular often suffered from radio complexes, and even the least powerful of sets could trigger a nervous attack. It was around about that time when a well-known British financier stabbed a diner in a restaurant who had a transistor radio on his table. Witnesses stated that the guest hadn't turned on the radio, and the financier acknowledged this to be the case, but the terror he experienced at the thought of it had made him see red. There was always someone in the cafés who couldn't bear radios and tried to have them silenced, and the psychiatrists studied, or rather, gave a name to, because there was no cure, a new psychosis: 'musical allergy'. The music that soothes savage beasts was starting to infuriate men.

One Dane, as mad as Hamlet and seduced by Santiago Rusiñol's work came to the island thinking he could undergo a silence cure and attempted to have all the radios in his spa hotel turned off. When he was unsuccessful, he purchased the most powerful set available, installed it in the foyer and turned the volume right up. When they tried to caution him, he started waving a pistol around. 'This is my right,' he shouted. He defended his right without eating or sleeping for forty-eight hours until they subdued him with chloroform and shut him in an asylum. The matter became more complicated when it transpired that the desperate Dane was as rich as a Rothschild and his lawyers demonstrated that he had, indeed, been exercising his right to play his radio in a country where on average every inhabitant owned two sets, and where the governor was striving to save the struggling radio industry by telling Turclub residents daily that if they didn't buy a third set, they were the dregs of society.

Dissident doctors intervened. Musical allergy was real and they provided statistics to show that there was a clear correlation between the increase in cases of madness in Turclub and the increasing number of radio sets. The graphs were very precise, with abscissas and ordinates of P, and to demonstrate impartiality, the data was taken from both official centres and industries with a vested interest in proving that there was no such thing as an allergy to music.

The Official Academy of Medicine was outraged. There wasn't an increase in madness but rather a rise in diagnosed cases because of scientific progress under the New Regime (that others now considered old). The psychologically disturbed and 'alienated' who had previously wandered the streets were now confined in appropriate establishments. As for the so-called 'musical allergy' psychosis, it was simply the invention of a few snobs and other members of a rabble who were hungry for sensation and bent on obstructing the industries responsible for Turclub's greatness.

Two sides formed and, needless to say, those people already unhappy about *disette* and the death of Pitusso the canary found themselves aligned with the discoverers of music allergy (who responded to the Academy with an exceptionally well researched protocol quoting specific cases and even more statistics). According to the former, the canary had been murdered by manufacturers of radios and mechanical birds who were unable to compete with real canaries. After the canary's death, more deaths had followed, all similarly unexplained. The industrial conglomerates had a particular interest in eliminating the pleasures of Nature because they free people and allow them to spend less money, thereby creating unemployment.* The canary named Pitusso once again occupied the front pages, while in cafés, restaurants and trattorie, customers could be seen wearing a yellow canary on their chest. The new governor was horrified and spoke to *Monsieur-Dame*, who attempted to stall the revolution by installing himself as its leader, that very evening warbling a song in honour of canaries and other small birds. This then drew the wrath of the powerful industrialists, investment bankers and the Waiters' Guild, and *Monsieur-Dame*, carried away in a fit of lyrical enthusiasm, uttered the word 'Nature'. What was the president thinking? Such obscenity! This really was revolution! This was just a step away from sanctifying the memory of *senyoreta* Mercier. Popular agitation was growing and the Regime's discomfort was palpable. It was agreed that Andrea's lectures should be brought forward, while Andrea herself had been cloistered in the Palazzo for a month, refusing visitors and researching intensively.

---

* *Monsieur-Dame* had put Wagner's *Forest Murmurs* on the Index in case the public were tempted to listen to real murmurs in real forests. This however would have benefited the transport sector, and the ban damaged record manufacturers who were already having a hard time.

The lectures were scheduled to begin on 1 June.

A secretary announced that a communiqué from the Official Academy of Medicine would be read out ahead of the goddess's disquisitions to correct certain misinformation relating to public health and the reported increase of non-contributors in all social sectors. The general public were beginning to notice that the deplorable hygiene and trauma of life in the Industrial Era were leading to a rise in numbers of the insane, the incapable and the impoverished. *Monsieur-Dame*, meanwhile, wanted to ensure that opinion was on his side and avoid becoming the subject of accusations. The Academy communiqué thus declared that the Regime was looking after all its citizens and paying particular attention to those most in need.

What it said in substance was that as humans were living longer as a result of advances occasioned by civilization, man would therefore have to confront disabilities and processes of decline derived from ageing, something which had not previously been encountered. While old age was a primary cause of disability, there were other factors such as injuries and illnesses arising as a result of progress (explosions, shocks, fires, poisonous gas leaks, etc.) which was the price everyone had to pay in the form of partial disability or complete invalidity. In earlier times, there was general familiarity with preventive and curative medicine, but it was not until Howard A. Rusk that rehabilitative medicine, now so urgent and important, came to prominence.

And so, according to the Official Academy of Medicine's communiqué, Progress, like a careless god, was trying to rehabilitate those whom it had previously disabled. Next to me, two youths were quietly discussing the same conclusion I had come to, that the communiqué was lost somewhere in its own dense, rhetorical undergrowth: *We have faith in the rehabilitation of the blind, who will come to see, of the deaf, of those who are paralyzed, mentally deficient, who suffer with leukaemia, sclerosis, etc.*

I smiled in the direction of my two neighbours, who returned a complicit glance. After lengthy enumerations designed to invite applause, we were getting to the crux of the matter, to the technical detail of thousands of systems that science draws on to perform its tricks and miracles – medicine, mechanics, psychotherapy, hydrotherapy, vitamins, sedatives, antibiotics, tranquillizers, etc. –, and then to Freud and the Count di Cagliostro. The litany was endless and those interminable remedies and exploratory methods such as clinical and radiological analyses, encephalograms, metabolic measurement, etc. were costly and complicated, required thousands and thousands of specialized professionals, and threatened to transform the world into a vast sanatorium wherein after huge efforts an individual who had lost his hands in a second, might in time and after huge efforts, provided he didn't die first from boredom or some new injury, learn to use his feet instead.

The following day was cloudy. The 1st of June. At eleven in the morning a storm rolled in and swept away the flowers and pennants from Pleasure Avenue and damaged the enormous screen at the Einstein Arch that had been due to show Andrea's enormous image ten times bigger than life-size. It was nothing if not a bad omen. At *Le Gaulois*, the gossip sotto voce had taken an alarming turn: Andrea was dead. When I tried to communicate with her, I managed to speak only to her secretaries, and they refused to pass on my request: the Excellency would see no-one until after the last lecture. She was incredibly busy.

'I'm the first consort,' I said angrily, 'and she sends me chocolate every morning. I'm sure she would be very happy to talk to me.'

'Sir, there are no exceptions,' came the reply, 'but you will be able to see your friend after the third lecture at the public reception in the park at midnight.'

'She said that–' I started. But they didn't listen. The secretaries seemed to be talking amongst themselves.

A more authoritative voice took over.

'Are you the handsome cryo survivor from 1965? The lover who has never slept with the Excellency?'

'I am,' I had to say, feeling both furious and embarrassed.

'I hereby notify you that you've committed a serious offence: you said "she" three times when referring to the Excellency.'

'Would you stop being ridiculous?!' I exclaimed down the phone. The line went dead.

By the afternoon the weather had improved. Three thousand flag-carrying robots made their way to the Triumphal Arch to lay a wreath of flowers before the image of Andrea. Flights of white doves flickered in the uncertain light of the setting sun. The goddess appeared full-length on the screen, smiling in her purple robes. She carried the helmet and spear of the Venus Victrix beloved of Julius Caesar. The Party's bought-in support chanted ceremonially: 'Andrea, Andrea, Andrea! Pharsalus, Pharsalus, Pharsalus!' I heard a voice nearby, possibly a cryo survivor, ask their companion ironically if Pharsalus came from 'farce'.

At the precise moment when the robots were handing the wreath to six Ibizan cherubs who had to place it at the feet of the image of the Venus, the Einstein march started up like a thunderclap, almost masking a muffled, barely perceptible liquid theme which was repeated through the whole composition, growing in intensity when the Wagnerian trumpets tailed off, and disappearing, fearful, when the trumpets returned insolently, only to reappear, faint and insinuating, like the bitterness of a Jewish slave girl kissing out of obligation while holding a dagger behind her back. An anxious theme which entered your head and stayed there even when it couldn't be heard, when the victory trumpets sounded out that the world is beautiful and the hero immortal. Droplets of water that fall one by one and eventually wear through the skull of the prisoner in a mediaeval oubliette. Lola had said that nothing good would come of the march, the genius-inspired work of a Germanic neurotic who killed himself after composing it by throwing himself onto a burning pyre, ensuring his own self-publicising artistic glory alongside that of Wagner and Einstein.

When the six Ibizan cherubs had laid the wreath, they each took a dose of soma and, high as kites, climbed up onto a raised platform where they performed unbelievable feats of acrobatics. Halfway through, the carrier who supported his fellow acrobats wobbled and was given an injection. Happily, the number was completed without further incident, and the acrobats leapt from the platform turning double somersaults to the acclaim of the crowd. Minutes later, the carrier who had received a double dose of soma died suddenly and was disposed of there and then in the latest model of portable furnace. The operation lasted two minutes and almost nobody realised what had happened.

A black light alternatingwith silver lightning bolts heralded the beginning of the lecture and everyone's gaze fixed on the enormous smiling image of the goddess on the screen. Also enlarged and bowing down before her was the president of the Waiters' Guild. There was silence. The president kissed her neck according to protocol, and Andrea spoke.

'Friends,' said Andrea, 'the Senior Waiter has informed me that one of the six Ibizan cherubs has passed away. The cremation has already taken place, and the ashes will be placed on public display. He was a beautiful and courageous seven-year-old. We know that he did not suffer, because a very able and considerate medical practitioner helped him along with an injection of double-strength soma. He could have lived for decades, becoming old and infirm, and instead his light has gone out while he was young, happy, and adored by everyone. Please forgive such an introit to an economics lecture, but I hope that such a gracious gesture as the death of this child will stand out like a real carnation amongst so many plastic flowers, or a real canary among thousands of mechanical canaries.'

I was surprised. From the beginning of the broadcast I'd wondered whether Andrea's voice was that of a double, since voice acting and indeed all acting-related roles had developed something of a tradition since the first talkies. Now I had the feeling that I was listening to a psychological double: the tawdry attempt to curry favour with the enemies of plastic flowers and mechanical birds, symbols that had come almost to represent modern civilization, was more the style of a toadying politician such as *Monsieur-Dame* than a puritan like Andrea. But I thought I recognized the manners of an affectionate and well-educated young lady alongside the stoicism of an adolescent hero. The tenderness combined with the moral fortitude and soma-induced physical strength of the person who accepts reality and death, the ingenuousness evolved through a series of experiences that enriched, rather than destroyed her.

'It's clear,' she said, getting to the point of the matter and taking on a moral tone was very familiar to me, 'that our food supply issues are at crisis point. This is partly because people are deserting the countryside to take up employment in urban industries. But this isn't the core of the problem because, as we will see, agriculture and livestock farming are now incompatible with modern life because they are intrinsically slow. If it really were the case that the Regime favoured the industrial worker over the agricultural labourer, the solution might lie in making subsidies available to those who work the land, and we know that the government is willing to study this option. My personal view is that all of us who love the Regime understand that *disette* won't be resolved with smiles and warm words. Radical, untried measures are required: agriculture is past its sell-by date and chemistry must step in. Let's not flog a dead horse. I've followed recent clandestine lectures with interest. As you know, in order to study and prepare my counter arguments, I stepped down as Director of the Bureau of Pleasure, and I've sacrificed both my beauty and my physical strength. It was these qualities that not even a year ago led some of my innumerable lovers to compare me to a feline. Those days, my friends, are gone forever, and if my research helps to change the way you think, I will not miss them. From a distance you will still be able to look kindly upon me, but no-one will see me up close, or kiss me with lust in their eyes ever again.'

For a second time, I pictured the effigy I'd seen in the Valladolid Museum, a skeletal penitent in sackcloth bearing a cross on her shoulders. When I dismissed the image from my mind, the penitent had materialised before me on screen.

'We accuse industrialization of alienating people from the countryside and from traditional skills, of dehumanizing us and separating us from Nature. If this is how we understand our attempts to control the forces of the cosmos and use them to our advantage, our response would be that man has never done or been able to do anything different, because he needs to survive. Those who censure us today for building robots would also have to castigate our primitive ancestors for inventing the lever and the cartwheel. They accept them, of course, because they're traditional, but they forget that a long time back these were hugely revolutionary.'

This was true, and I was annoyed to have to acknowledge it.

'What does it mean,' continued Andrea, 'to suggest that we're acting "against" Nature? Atomic physics is no less natural than the germination of a grain of wheat' – 'no less natural, certainly, but much more harmful,' I muttered between my teeth – 'and the mechanical bird created by science is also, in the end, natural. The countryside, traditional skills and craftsmanship, the spontaneous elegance of the flower and the hand-turned wooden bow, all belong to the Golden Age. "There was no need to force the land then", said Don Quijote. "The trees generously offered us their fruits". If that happy age truly existed (because the sufferings of our primitive ancestors in times of famine were tragic), it is now gone forever. Can you imagine what would happen if we tried to live off what the land "generously" offers us? To be anti-industry today is blasphemy, pure and simple. Industry is sacred and millionaires are saints. According to Sombart, the great economist, from the beginning of its recorded history in the sixth century until 1800, Europe's population never surpassed one-hundred and eighty million people. By contrast, in a little more than a century (1800-1914), the European population shot up to four-hundred and sixty million.'

Although Andrea's statistics were accurate, they weren't having the desired effect on me. It's hardly ideal that population numbers should 'shoot up', and I recalled what Dr Nicola had said in his first lecture: 'that's how cancers grow'.

'In De Gaulle's time,' Andrea continued, 'A. Zischka claimed that without scientific and technological progress, the human population would shrink to a tenth of its size. We might say that rational man has substituted the old religious precepts for others such as Industry and Propaganda, which are even more rigid than Moses' commandments. Yes, we're dogmatic because progress irremediably pushes us in that direction. Today there are far too many people in the world and not nearly enough coconut palms for us to live off coconuts, and even when humans did live this way, the average lifespan was no more than twenty, whereas today it's more than seventy. Pandemics are disappearing–'

'What about the automobile pandemic!' shouted someone.

In the Palazzo's golden room, Andrea must have heard the interruption and the applause it drew in support, but she carried on regardless.

'Humanity and industry are increasing in geometric progression, while agriculture is only increasing arithmetically. This is true, and we are right to be critical. In recent years governments have not sufficiently controlled the birth-rate. Today, with the authorization of *Monsieur-Dame*, I can announce that we will reduce births state-wide by twenty-two percent. We will pursue those responsible for unauthorised births, blasphemy and pornography, and we will exterminate offspring born illegally with anaesthetic gas just as Hitler once did.'

Minutes before she had presented rocketing European procreation rates as positive progress, and now she was talking about limiting them. At times I thought I recognized Andrea's manner and tone, but someone else's input was discernible in that reasoning too, and I didn't know what to think.

'What I am saying,' interjected Andrea as though reading my mind, 'will ameliorate the situation by eliminating those with healthy teeth, but it will be important not to take suppressive measures to an extreme, since industry requires a workface and, of course, future customers. Let us not forget, as the glorious and blessed Ford himself said, that every child born is a potential customer. We therefore have to look elsewhere for a radical solution to *disette*. The belief that *disette* originates in a shortage of rural labour, as the engineer Creus Vidal stated in 1962, and as the Vamp has since claimed, is false. Today's agricultural machinery requires very few operatives, proof of this being that in many areas those who refuse to move away from casual farm labour for a living spend weeks and often months without work. This is one of the reasons why I oppose raising the wage of day labourers, as were we to make life pleasant in the countryside, unemployment in the agricultural sector would become more serious. The problem isn't the shortage of casual labourers, because there is no shortage. It would be more logical to reduce the workforce and increase the use of machinery, as we have been doing thus far, because the agricultural labourer is heading for extinction. But this is not the solution, and the issue goes deeper. My friends, as I said, agriculture and livestock farming obey a much slower rhythm than industry. One hundred years ago, a machine might have produced fifty pairs of shoes a day. Now it will produce three thousand. By contrast, the Vamp in his last talk, a talk we would all have listened to with interest had it not descended into sarcasm directed at *Monsieur-Dame* le Président, informed us that now, as always, a grain of wheat requires eight months to become an ear. The olive bush and the almond tree produce annual harvests, and a calf still has a nine-month gestation period. In the era of supersonic aviation, how can we allow such sloth? Think for a moment, and you'll see that the cause of *disette* is not industrialization or chemistry, but the absence of efficient industrialization and chemistry applied to food production. Dr Nicola, tendentious and narrow-minded as ever, has it all the wrong way around. In his diatribe, in his appalling blasphemies against our most holy pillars, he cited authors who were well-known in their time. But he could have cited others: Fairfield Osborn, for example; Lester Walker, etc. Osborn's book *Our Plundered Planet* was controversial in its claims that man is squandering the resources of Nature and intensive farming is degrading and depleting the soil. Gunther Schwab and Aldous Huxley's sage Lord Tantamount believed the same. Tantamount was concerned that modern man is destroying organic nitrogen by incinerating corpses and constructing sewers. Yet he even seems to yearn for those old cesspits that bred so many epidemics. If Dr Nicola were familiar with such outmoded works, he would undoubtedly use them to reinforce his attacks against "modern" farming, because it is certainly the case, as Faulkner observed, that the heavy use of chemical fertilizers, mechanized practices, and the clearing of forests, caused significant damage to agriculture. But Nicola is so backward that he can only conceive of a return to the so-called Golden Age, and he would never be capable of understanding that if agriculture is destined for exhaustion, there are also limitless forces in the mineral world (any stone contains immeasurable quantities of atomic energy) and this is where we need to look for a solution. The progress made by nuclear disintegration technologies is undeniable. We have all just witnessed the parade of three thousand beautiful, intelligent robots, creations of the collective human spirit, of the brilliant Noosphere that Teilhard de Chardin prophesied. What are a few sporadic accidents in the context of such a magnificent spectacle? Alarmists who would place obstacles before such prodigies will be severely punished. They have sought to take advantage of the death of Lola, a prostitute from 1965 who was incapable of managing a modern machine–'

The tone, the choice of words such as 'narrow-minded', 'appalling blasphemies', and 'magnificent spectacle'. These weren't Andrea. Poor health and weeks of intensive study had forcibly altered her psyche. She could be hard when necessary, but she was habitually courteous, sensitive and kind. And, what's more, logical. ('In many ways I'm as much a prostitute as Lola,' she had once said.) She hated introits.

And her dialectics, while skilful, still amounted to sophistry. To claim that machine civilization taken to its ultimate extremes was as 'human' as using the wheel and lever, was simply unacceptable. Of course, man has always tried to derive maximum profit from the forces of Nature, and this gives rise to the odd imbalance, but while he worked with his muscles and his senses, including his common sense, imbalance did not become catastrophe: it was merely a passing biological disturbance occasioned by grazing sheep. The evil was unleashed by Galileo's telescope and given impetus by Louis de Broglie's ultra-microscope. The rifles at Fontenoy ('Gentlemen of the English Guards, do fire first!') were terrible, but the only thing they won or lost were battles. With nuclear fission, however, it would be possible to annihilate the whole of known and intuited civilization, of history and perhaps even prehistory.

My mind had wandered off, and when I turned my attention back to the present, Andrea had disappeared from the screen. The Senior Waiter was announcing that the second lecture would take place the following day at the same time. The crowd, cold and silent, headed away from Pleasure.

I didn't sleep that night. While I thought that Andrea was pursuing a wholly erroneous cause, some of her affirmations disturbed me. It was undoubtedly sophistry to equate the human progress of the *ancien régime* – the wheel and the lever are easily controllable – with atomic discoveries whose raw power could destroy the world in moments, just as we had witnessed in Russian and North America. Tossing and turning in bed, I repeated to myself that it was absurd to want to make comparisons, because we were talking about fundamentally different phenomena. Perhaps it all started going wrong with the telescope. Natural man had no doubts: the Sun rises and sets, and the Earth is immobile. So what if that's false according to experimental science? It may not be for much longer! The Sun isn't fixed as you believed, Galileo. It moves faster and further than your much scorned Ptolemy suspected. Everything turns, everything revolves, and at the present hour of the galaxies, it is impossible to determine objectively what revolves around what. Imagine two dogs chasing each other around a bullring concourse. There'll come a moment when we can't tell which dog is chasing which. It isn't a case of not looking for an 'absolute truth' which no-one is interested in and does not exist but rather a human, sense-based truth. Galileo had no philosophical inclination; he simply wanted to observe the Universe through the combined lenses of a monstrous eye and derive absolute or invariable consequences from this, without giving a thought to the fact that the consequences will fatally and radically change as the exploratory instruments themselves are refined. He deserved to be burnt.

And this is where the figure of Andrea came in, leaning over me, wise and ingenuous.

'So hun,' she said, 'does this mean we should give up the

lever? And the magnifying glass?'

No, of course not. Progress in human measure was beneficial. But whose responsibility was it to draw the dividing line between classical humanist science in the Greek tradition, tailored to man, and today's monstrous science? We would need to go back to key historical texts, J.J. Rousseau's *Discours sur les sciences et les arts*, for example. Andrea's graceful shadow came close again and looked into my eyes, asking me, 'At what point exactly did the apple in Paradise become sinful?'

Even before I underwent the cryo-cure, Gunther Schwab, the great Austrian pessimist, had already recognized that progress, as thousands of billboards and loudspeakers in Turclub echoed, could not be stopped. The man who created the machine cannot simply stop it at will, and this enslaves us. It's hardly an inducement to love it. Zischka, an optimist (unlike Gunther Schwab), nevertheless thought similarly: progress must be given its wings. If we bear in mind the world's current population density and the tendency of people to group together in urban centres, doing without technology would mean the annihilation through hunger of ninety per cent of Humanity. Zischka was right. Surviving on tinned food might be unhealthy, but cities like London and Paris couldn't feed themselves in any other way. The air in the big cities was poisonous, but it was the price we paid for other advantages. So what if we couldn't have automobiles or robots without a higher incidence of lung cancer? My cryo-cure colleague from 1965 was planning to return to the seventeenth century, to the divine right of kings, and to the order of classical precepts not yet out of control. But by what means? Einstein died appalled at the consequences of his discoveries. He had set out to deliberate on the structure of the atom, not to invent artefacts. But the inventors had come along and applied his deliberations to their technology. Einstein's horror at the Hiroshima bomb served no purpose, but guilty or not, it was all that he was left with. Progress is irreversible.

'No brakes, no reverse: Andrea's right,' I told myself mid-delirium. 'It can't be stopped, but it can explode, and it will explode. Hiroshima was a very modest test in comparison.'

Wakeful and on edge, I could see only the negative in this era. We were living in the realm of the fake. Man was subjected to the continuous pressure of advertising which dictated what he could do and what he should think. With every day that went by, we found it more difficult to form an opinion of our own. The possibility of freedom could be glimpsed only occasionally when advertising campaigns contradicted each other, but this also raised the spectre of a descent into chaos. We were being poisoned by words and there was no way back. The clandestine radio stations talked about a crash, prophesying the new Era of Simplification. Nicola had understood this, and so was waiting to die in his cell, hypocritically atheist, surrounded by plastic flowers and attractive-looking, vile-tasting synthetic fruit.

Through the closed window came insistent voices extolling the virtues of a new electric whisk called the Mixmaster deluxe: MIXES, BEATS, KNEADS, STIRS, EMULSIFIES, GRINDS, SLICES, GRATES, JUICES, SHREDS... MIXES, BEATS, KNEADS, STIRS, EMULSIFIES... It grated on me and shredded my nerves. When I telephoned the shop promoting this marvel, the nightwatchman replied saying that he had no authority to turn off the speakers, and that the manager wasn't due in until 9am in the morning. It was 1am. The speakers would repeat that mind-numbing psalm without pause for another eight hours.

As the days went by, more and more people began to dissent from the Regime's tyranny, though they were still outnumbered by those brutalized by custom and propaganda. In spite of police vigilance, pirate radio stations proclaimed that 'high living standards' were making life impossible (which was perfectly obvious), and that the cell-apartments in Paris, Genoa and Tur-club were suffocating their inhabitants. Compared with those torture chambers, poorer houses that still survived in forgotten villages of the Iberian peninsula, with their thick walls, yards and silence, seemed veritable palaces. Everyone had a motor car in which to flee the delights of the city at the weekend, but the urban exodus to the tranquillity of the countryside populated by transistor radios, bars and bellowing speakers was more of a blow to people's spirits than had they remained in their cages of steel and reinforced concrete. Economic wellbeing meant working to the point of animalization simply to acquire atomic appliances and emancipating automobiles which would allow owners to escape from those same appliances, creeping inexorably now across beaches and up mountains. Moreover, it was difficult to reach the most popular locations on busy days, and instead one had to follow the directions of the traffic helicopters. A friend of mine who had a house in Alcúdia was forced to spend three consecutive weekends in the forests at Lluc where the raucous parties at the monastery made sleep impossible.

The radio stations' words had come to pass, and the dictats of the authorities attempted to rein in the chaos, but there was nothing to be done. The atomic discoveries were too potent. On my bedside table I still had the Italian dagger, half weapon, half jewelled masterpiece, which Andrea had given to me one day. I could kill a man with the dagger, I could kill half a dozen, but what couldn't I unleash with a few grams of nuclear matter? How was it possible to compare a single murder to cosmic catastrophe? The more powerful and more effective the technology, the more tyrannical the system of control required. Progress depended on slavery. What had happened to liberty? The lack of freedom was already apparent as my friend in the rowdy hostel at Lluc discovered, suffering affronts to his religiosity and unable to access his perfectly habitable house in Alcúdia. Before I entered the cryo chamber, a relative of mine used to argue that farm tractors, harvesters and threshing machines were perfect instruments, and that in order to function, they needed level ground with wide borders, free of rocks and scrub that might cause obstruction. It was also important that the whole grain harvest ripened at the same time, because the harvester is most efficient when the grain is slightly soft, and much less so when oats in particular have ripened completely, because the grains become detached and a large part of the harvest is lost. 'If that's the case,' I said to him, 'it would make more sense to adapt the land to the needs of the machine.' 'Exactly,' he replied, 'and if not, we abandon the land.' A magnificent solution: just when famine was the most pressing danger, we preached growing only what could be harvested by machine. In the context of Mallorca specifically, this meant giving up on a third of the island. In more rocky and mountainous areas, for example, olives could not be harvested mechanically. 'Other oils are available, even if not of the same quality,' objected my interlocutor. I don't doubt it, but that it should be a machine that decided my diet was hard to stomach and it mortified my human dignity.

There was no doubt that the freedom I had known decades earlier was gone. And as for democracy... A baron and a sixteenth-century monarch might receive a peasant in audience, but the directors of a modern atomic lab forbade their subordinates from speaking to the engineers. Their justification was logical as they no longer even spoke the same language and wouldn't be able to understand one another. Those who endorsed such inequalities in the name of technology had no idea that they were sowing the seeds of a Middle Ages more feudal in nature than any that had come before.

I finally fell asleep in the early morning and dreamt that I was in a taxi on the Passeig Marítim seafront, stuck in a traffic jam of thousands of cars. It was summer, and stifling hot. Tower blocks now stood like a wall of concrete where the Bellver forest had been, the sun bouncing off them and turning the passeig into an oven. There were shouts of 'Fire!', flames advanced from Porto Pi, and people couldn't budge or open their doors because the cars were bumper to bumper. I was so frightened that

I woke up, or carried on dreaming, half-awake. I had foreseen this happening so many times in Turclub and it had already happened in Paris, where a backlog on the Rue Royale had caused thousands of deaths in just a few minutes. The heat was so intense that vehicles were combusting like grenades or fireworks. The air quickly became toxic and many people were asphyxiated before the flames reached them. On the Passeig Marítim, the lucky ones were those who could drive into the sea and drown themselves, and I witnessed an imaginative English lady in her eighties, laden with diamonds and not very able, who got out of her convertible and climbed onto the cars that separated her from the sea, seven deep, and before plunging herself into the sea with a hideous blasphemy against *Hola-Hola*. The sea around the port had started to boil, and the hotels on the seafront were burning as if a prelude to apocalypse. I got up, cleared my head, and left the building.

It was daybreak and, wondering what to do, I made my way to the bathhouse that advertised itself as *ouverte la nuit* where I'd witnessed the masochistic scene shortly after emerging from the cryo chamber. I thought a vigorous massage might calm my nerves but my subconscious was in fight mode. When the attendant asked me if I wanted to be kissed or beaten up, I punched him square in the face and knocked him out. Scared at what I'd just done, I made a hasty exit and walked the streets until a sensible hour when I could call the Palazzo Víctrix. I needed to speak to Andrea. They told me again that she was seeing no-one until the reception event in the park after the third lecture. I insisted, giving them my name, but they hung up on me.

The second lecture began at half past seven and I positioned myself in the same spot as the day before on Pleasure, overlooked by the huge screen at the Triumphal Arch. As well as hearing what Andrea had to say, I wanted to people-watch and see how the crowd reacted. Andrea appeared exactly on schedule.

'Just as the Vamp offered specific data, so shall I,' announced Andrea, laconically. 'In forty years' time and at current rates of increase, there will not be physical space in the world for humanity if the State...'

She launched into a series of dry statistics before returning to her subject.

'Of course, that won't happen because we will prevent it through the scientific control of natality, although I do not expect us to find favour with those mentally deficient obscurantists who have no idea what they want, demanding as *senyoreta* Mercier said at her trite best, "the right to have children and love them", even if this means dying of hunger. Dr Nicola cited the progressive Teilhard de Chardin to confirm his fears over the shortage of basic foodstuffs, and forgot that even though Teilhard was notionally Catholic, he favoured limiting the birth rate rather than imposing restrictions on sacrosanct Industry. In *Les Directions et les conditions de l'avenir*, Teilhard observed that in the seventeenth century the population of the world was around forty million, but began to increase rapidly until in 1940 it reached more than two thousand million. Such a demographic explosion was inextricably linked to the progress and wellbeing facilitated by industry, but it occasioned new necessities and difficulties. Teilhard de Chardin asked, "How can we guarantee that population density across the surface of our planet does not exceed an optimum beyond which any growth would mean famine and privation?". Bear in mind that the root of this curse we call *disette* is age-old and mentioned in the Bible: Original Sin, the sin of being born of parents and eating not just forbidden fruit, but also steak and lobster. It causes men to strive and kill each other from their very beginnings. We can redeem ourselves from this millennia-old sin by ensuring that no-one comes into this world without the consent of *Monsieur-Dame* le Président.'

My blood froze before that new interpretation of the Bible, which has been the subject of so many readings over the course of History, and for a moment I panicked that Andrea had become deranged. But at the same time, she seemed to be echoing Dr Orlando's belief that if high rates of natality weren't addressed, we'd be reduced to cannibalism. Dr Nicola, in the guise of the Vamp, had said similar things. Did this mean that the viviparous and oviparous were actually in agreement?

A heckler interrupted saying that hunger had begun to increase when Humanity had ceased to be viviparous in 1985, and this time Andrea took up the gauntlet. Her voice, however, was strange and I didn't recognise it as hers.

'*Disette* has spread because the enemies of the Regime insist on trying to resolve the problem by recourse to agriculture, which has long been impotent. The earth, "Mother Earth", as pornographic poets used to call it, and please forgive my re-sorting to such a shameful expression, obeys a rhythm that is incompatible with our civilization, as I indicated yesterday.'

An indignant voice shouted out, 'Death to our civilization!'

'Dr Nicola himself has recognised that this is the case,' continued Andrea, ignoring it. 'In his demented state he see-med willing to blaspheme against our most sacred pillars, es-tablishing the choice between Industry, man's rational sense, and what he calls "Nature" as a dilemma. Very well. If we have to choose, and in light of Nature's lack of ability – it takes eight months for a head of corn to grow and nine for a calf to be born – we will choose Industry. Machine civilization must not die.'

Listening to this riposte, I again didn't recognize Andrea's voice to the point that I'm convinced it wasn't Andrea speaking. Without warning, and presumably in an attempt to underline what she was saying and distract from the banality, the goddess hoisted her tunic to the top of her legs and flashed a thigh. This was a mistake, because although as a whole her body was still beautiful and harmonious , close-up it was sickly and haggard. The public were unmoved, and there was no reaction to this gesture of deference from the speaker.

'The mineral world isn't inert to us, as it was to the primitives,' she went on. 'Any matter may be transformed into energy. Or rather, all matter today is energy. Nor is there any essential difference between mineral existence and live matter. Long ago it was said that movement was what characterised life, and today we know that the atom is formed of incredibly fast particles–'

The speaker set out the basics of atomic physics clearly and with a certain agility. However, the more she entered into the detail of experimental data, ever more precise, more numerous, illustrating more and more remote causes which were tanta-mount to magic, her words filled me with a growing sense of unease. It was undeniable that those, let's call them mystical, theories had given rise to the atomic bomb and the robot, and the darkness of the ironic and malevolent causes that had casually and in a matter of minutes destroyed the two most powerful empires on earth was there for all to see. According to Andrea, it wasn't the case that we needed animal proteins and fats with a calorific value of eight per gram. On the contrary, there was a surfeit of calories and those who knew how to extract them from so-called 'inert' matter were capable of provoking a new inferno of devastation.

The crowd listened, at once horrified and ecstatic with pride as they realised they were capable of destroying the world. The example of Russia and North America was still fresh. Many people were trying to joke about it and laughed as they drank *Hola-Hola*, but others couldn't hide their panic. Like a miracle worker in the Middle Ages navigating magic and reality, Andrea led us into the darkest depths of possibility and uncertainty. While her lecture followed a certain logic, it reminded me of the Einstein anthem, which Lola had always said would herald nothing good. The Wagnerian trumpets were the strength and victory of human discoveries, the biceps of the warrior or the wand of the necromancer who splits mountains asunder and reveals treasure; but that hymn to glory never drowned out the liquid notes, the muted irony of a theme heavy with threat. Our strength was a fact, we possessed it, it was real. But where was it leading us? 'Wherever you want, it's down to you,' proclaimed the moralists. During the *belle époque*, Bergson had said 'the world will be what you, humans of free will, want it to be,' and the existentialists had said the same later in the twentieth century, as though it had never been said before. What we want it to be? Chaos, therefore. How can so many humans exercising their free will want anything other than diversity? In *The Re-discovery of America*, published at the end of the roaring twenties, Waldo Frank presented activity and action as symptoms of Western decadence: to consider action as intrinsically valuable was an exclusively modern phenomenon, chaotic and stupid.

'The machine, in a world in which machine is an expression of individual will, cannot signify anything but the progress of chaos,' he wrote.

Was he trying to demonstrate that we were being dragged back to dictatorships and tyrannies? Evidently. In religious epochs, there was only one truth. Now, in the era of experimental science, the senses were shockingly amplified by instruments and discovered ever more contradictory truths, because Creation contains everything. There would cease to be one truth as if for man facts are infinite, he could choose to build a subjective, provisional and variable truth with the facts that suited. Sooner or later the principle of authority, an infallible Pontifex, would be required to remedy such a state of affairs. The old religious dogmas would pale into insignificance alongside the prohibitions necessary to sustain a machine-dependent civilization. A free man armed with a powerful machine would be too dangerous, to say nothing of free will, heavens above. In the street the police would say 'walk' when we wanted to be still and 'keep right' when we yearned for the shade on the left. Now that everyone had a car, we'd seen cases of citizens being forbidden to use them in cities, but on this matter *Monsieur-Dame* wasn't keen to invite confrontation, at least with the conglomerates, because few cared what the public thought.

The manufacturers driving material progress were becoming ultra conservative while the ever watchful State made its atomic research available almost uniquely for military purposes. This was why in the year 2050 we still had combustion engines and private motor vehicles.

Without tyranny to keep it on the straight and narrow, technological progress would signify dissolution. Compared with a Catholic world in which Creation fits within the totality of God, there was nothing more savage or antagonistic than this combination of matter and force powerful beyond imagination and wholly at the mercy of whoever managed it. And Waldo Frank had reached the conclusion that machine would be a monster while man was ever an anarchic atom, morally disconnected from his peers. Frank was obviously hoping that one day man would achieve some kind of mutual fusion. Such optimism!

'And why not?' Andrea had said on one occasion. 'The human species tends towards engagement, towards concordance. The atomic bomb was a danger, but common sense prevailed and after the destruction of Russia and North America there have been no more wars.'

'That was the last one,' I'd said. 'The next one's still to come.'

'You're a pessimist,' she chastised me, as though I were under some kind of obligation to believe that the world was a bed of roses. 'There probably won't be another one. The last was a mistake. A mosquito, as you know.'

'And then you destroyed China very deliberately.'

'We got our retaliation in first,' she replied.

'That's why all wars are waged. How can you be so innocent, Andrea?'

That was months ago. Andrea continued her lecture, a concoction of science and witchcraft, scrawling figures on a blackboard and working out cabbalistic formulae that no-one could decipher. She quickly ran out of space and they had to bring her two more boards. Surrounded by numbers, she became more and more indistinct, and I attributed it to a fault with the television. But I didn't recognise her in this tedious, pedantic guise. Her movements, usually so harmonious, were at times unpleasantly rigid. I wondered whether I was watching a double's grotesque interpretation. She was always so bright, so socially aware, so why hadn't she realised that the public had stopped listening?

'What's Andrea talking about now?' one particularly brave individual called out. 'She's surely not going to convince us that we can eat stones?'

But the goddess was now so stupidly entangled in scientific

specialisation that she did precisely that, cooking up polynomials to demonstrate that because a stone doesn't just split apart and burst into flames, it contains more latent energy than a beef roast. When she had filled all of her blackboards with figures, she turned to face the public. She was horrific, like a jerky, artless puppet and in full, boorish suffragette mode, she addressed the heckler who had declared that he didn't want to eat stones.

'This is what it's about everyone. Feeding ourselves on rocks.'

The boos and whistles were deafening. This was blatant mockery before a whole country of starving citizens. But *Monsieur-Dame*'s Regime had kept its most craven statements until last, proposing that the Party worms should eat the soil itself. Andrea gestured obscenely and I knew for certain it wasn't her. She vanished from the screen.

The audience went their different ways talking animatedly among themselves. Some were indignant and many agreed that the lecture marked the end of the Regime, wondering what would come next. The way Andrea had mimicked a strident wo-men's libber, hands on her hips and chin thrust out in defiance, had wounded the sensibilities of the elite classes. The waiters were aghast and doubtless would never forgive her. And the proles could not forgive her blackboards full of equations and for advising them to eat rocks in answer to an imposing famine. But was it really Andrea Víctrix, the same goddess of love who won people over with her slender stature and charming smile, whom we had just seen on the screen? It couldn't possibly be.

I was feeling pretty hopeless, so I went into a café to try to make contact with the Palazzo, asking to speak urgently to the Excellency on behalf of the Party.

'On behalf of who?' asked a dispirited voice.

'The Party, and it's urgent. Special mandate of *Monsieur-Dame* le Président,' I improvised, desperately.

They hung up and I walked out onto the street. The night was dark and there were power cuts in some sectors. It wasn't yet ten o'clock and though I was in the centre of the city, there were few pedestrians about. Every so often a car sped by laden with suitcases. The sky was black, starless. I walked aimlessly and the silence was haunting. As I turned a corner, a loudspeaker yelling horrendous insults at *Monsieur-Dame* and Andrea stopped me in my tracks and my heart raced. The voice said that Andrea was a young criminal, a queer, son of a prostitute whose disgus-ting assignations with the President were well-known. I looked around. There wasn't a soul in sight until I saw some security guards emerge from a nearby building. I drew their attention to the scandalous broadcast, but they ignored me and continued on their way, talking in whispers. Further on, an old guy came up to me, begging. He explained that he had a 'jobless' card, but that his usual restaurant was refusing to accept his meal vouchers.

'The government's in crisis,' he said. 'No-one trusts anything or anyone. Lots of restaurants are closing and the revolutionaries have even been murdering waiters.'

I expressed my surprise at how quiet and empty the city seemed.

'If you go out to the suburbs,' replied the old man, 'you'll see the roads are completely congested, almost paralysed with cars trying to flee goodness knows where. They say the airports are closed.'

'Is there talk of insurrection?' I asked.

'No-one knows anything for sure, but some are saying that there's already rioting in Paris.'

I made my way to *Le Gaulois* hoping it would be open and that I'd be able to dine on biscuits and synthetic orangeade. Thankfully, it was. It was very busy, a hubbub of conversation, and the general opinion was that Andrea was dead and had been cremated in secret.

'You, sir, should know,' said the *maître d'hôtel*, rather rudely.

I decided not to dignify his insolence with a response. In an attempt to raise spirits, a group of twenty-five-year-old Ibizan waiters initiated a war dance which was entertaining but unsuccessful in its aim. The lady at front of house tried to keep a serene countenance, but she was clearly distressed.

'Do you think Andrea's dead?' I asked. 'Is there any news of *Monsieur-Dame*?'

'Things are getting serious,' she said, bowing her head and wiping away a tear.

She was elegant all in black, and with her cultured pearls she looked like a slightly down on her luck marchioness. A fine, respectable French woman of conservative tastes. She couldn't possibly enjoy the Regime's vulgarity and must have held up the example of the Classical University to justify powdering her hair like her eighteenth-century forebears while observing the old courtly manners without risk to herself. But it was difficult to find out anything about her except, so they said, that she came from the Paris Procreation Centre. The tear she had wiped from her face had been shed in deference to *Monsieur-Dame*, whom she might very well have detested but the possibility of his downfall terrified her. Yes, underneath it all I was sure she was a sensitive woman, somewhat altered from that awkward comptroller in whose guise she had appeared when we met. Weak, perhaps, but who could say?

People were apprehensive. They exchanged opinions under their breath and the optimism or at least violence that usually accompanies popular revolts was absent. It was as though a mysterious collective consciousness was making everyone realise that war and civil struggle could not, in the Atomic Age, engender the same passion, excitement and sense of sport that they had in more human times. There was an understanding that if Revolution broke out it wouldn't be like some kind of jousting tournament, but the end of a whole era. Those serious faces and half-whispers reminded me of sombre vigils from my youth.

The clocks struck twelve and the luminous silence indicators began to flash. *Monsieur-Dame* le Président was readying himself to speak against a backdrop of black clouds and silver lightning bolts. His moon-shaped face, the well-fed mask of a eunuch who has more to his diet than stones, illuminated the walls of Turclub as it did every night. His repugnant voice spoke.

'After Andrea's magnificent lecture this afternoon, I hope, *mes enfants*, that calm is once again in all our hearts. Our scientists are working on mineral nutrition. Tomorrow at the same time, we'll be able to hear the third and final lecture, followed by a reception at the Palazzo Víctrix, where Andrea will rise from the waters of the lake in a scallop shell. A night of pleasure and dreams... Poetry, flowers and fruit for everyone... A night of folly... *Oh, là, là... Quelle nuit et quelle reception... Ah, mes enfants!*'

In an age of licentiousness and dissipation, in which the body and its flesh caused revulsion (unless served roasted, on a platter), *Monsieur-Dame*, like an old bawd, embellished his words with mischievous gestures, winks and a freshly painted pout. He took his leave following etiquette.

'*Bonne nuit, mes enfants, Le Président vous envoie un tout petit baiser...*'

Afterwards, insults flew, as always.

'What a moron!'

'Imbecile.'

'Look at him laughing!'

In the Élysée, *Monsieur-Dame* must have been aware of the comments, but in his desperation not to be ousted from his role he had lost all sense of shame.

'*Bonne nuit, mes enfants, je vous envoie un tout petit baiser...*'

These words were always spoken in falsetto. This time, in a lower, bull-like snort, he added gruffly,

'Cameraman, six metres. I want them to see my whole body.'

The camera zoomed out to six metres and from a pedestal covered in red, *Monsieur-Dame*, fat and irrelevant, treated the U.S. of Europe to a few ballet poses and then disappeared. We never saw him again. The Einstein anthem played him out like a funeral march.

Everyone was wide-eyed. Just as in some of Shakespeare's plays, any sense of the ridiculous was washed away by the horror of tragedy. *Monsieur-Dame*'s ballet poses, previously the subject of mirth, now provoked tears. The death of Andrea – as there was no doubt she was dead – signified many things. In reality the Regime had fallen when Andrea left the Bureau of Pleasure to take on her economy and food brief and we were now crashing back to the Stone Age. Hunger was far more pressing than luxury goods and leisure activities and Andrea, or rather the double who had taken her place, had just told us to trust in nuclear physics because it was capable of deriving fire from rocks. Of course, we all need calories, but not flames. Yet this thought was illustrated when one notably eminent diner declared:

'The new Era to come will be known as the Great Flood of Flames.'

He was dressed like a patriarch, and I kissed the fringe of his toga because he seemed in need of reassurance. Shakespeare is ridiculous: my gesture of respect moved him, and he ruffled my hair, but in the end he turned out to be merely a purveyor of parsley-chopping tools.

'Young man,' he said, adopting a biblical tone, 'young cryo survivor, why did you ever come out of stasis? The Earth is a vale of tears and you have suffered it twice over.'

How had he known who I was? The front of house lady burst into hysterical weeping. Everyone looked at me, because calling me 'young cryo survivor' practically marked me out as an enemy of the Regime. A lady, at least I think she was a lady, offered me an almond.

'It's real,' she said quietly.

Two youngsters came up to me, curious.

'Is it true that people used to have bread rolls with real butter for breakfast?'

'Did you know your parents?' asked a possible girl, timidly. 'Is it true that you had an intimate connection with them?'

'Intimate, yes,' I replied. 'But in the broad sense, not carnal.' She opened her eager eyes wide.

'I don't understand,' she said. 'Did they love you or not?'

'Very much, but not as lovers.'

'So?' she asked.

'Disinterestedly.' I replied.

'They weren't interested? But you said they loved you...'

People were crowding around us, attracted by such grisly talk about a forbidden subject. The imminence of catastrophe made people less reticent and more likely to suppress their inhibitions.

'Excuse me,' a middle-aged man or woman said. 'Were you at Rufo's tavern when they showed the porno? Two people get married and have a child? I was behind you. Hard-core...'

'In my time,' I replied, 'they'd have called it a romance.'

'And... did everything happen like in the film?'

'More or less...'

'But if I haven't misunderstood, you said that parents loved their children and that they didn't love them, that they were disinterested; or perhaps that they loved them without receiving anything in exchange.'

'Yes, that's right, what you just said.'

'But love can't be disinterested. It's the most interested sentiment in existence.'

A scared voice called out.

'Everyone, we're getting into the pornography of meta-physics...'

No-one bothered. The grisly subject matter had a hold.

'They loved in exchange for love,' I said.

'But... without cohabiting?'

'Of course!'

'So without pleasure?'

'A pleasure that no-one here has ever experienced.'

A few people protested.

'You may be mistaken. Don't think that you're the only one born of a mother and father.'

This didn't come as a surprise. The failure of the Regime had encouraged a number of other viviparous souls to crawl out of the woodwork. They were beginning to show up everywhere. Everyday there were more and more mid-twentieth-century style Gilda dresses and denim jeans among the more or less hybrid Roman uniforms, with the difference that now only the men wore jeans and only women wore skirts. A single fashion establishment had sold more than seven-hundred latex breasts in just a few hours. At the beginning, the police detained men who were too manly and women who were too womanly, especially if they were wearing the yellow canary emblem, but then they stopped doing this without explanation.

Everyone's attention was on me, and I was flattered by my new-found popularity. A journalist approached, pen in hand, and began to ask questions.

'Sir, you are an opponent of the Industrial Era. Don't you think, though, that without machines the human race would shrink to a tenth of its size, as Zischka maintained?'

'It's possible,' I replied.

'Do you acknowledge that the economically disadvantaged enjoy a better standard of living today than they did previously?'

'Previously' was a very vague term. I decided the journalist was a bit stupid and was tempted to walk away.

'I do acknowledge that, yes, if we measure living standards by metres of ducting and litres of *Hola-Hola*.'

My words were met with a mixed reception, some applause, some whistles. The sacrilegious mention of *Hola-Hola* still scandalized many people. Some repeated Einstein's formula $E=mc^2$ under their breath to cushion the offence. Others atavistically crossed themselves. The journalist went on.

'They're about to issue a decree imposing special taxes on manufacturers in order to make subsidies available to agricultural producers because, as we know, food is becoming scarce. In such circumstances, would you still see yourself as an enemy of public limited corporations and atomic appliances, as Dr Orlando proposed? *Monsieur-Dame* le Président–'

'*Monsieur-Dame* is absurd,' I interrupted. 'The current Regime drove the workers and the capitalists from the land. It indulged them by creating a life that turned its back on Nature. The subsidies you mention will be mere sticking plasters because the problem is too generalized, too deep-seated.'

The interview degenerated into disagreement. The journalist needed his story, and he trotted out the old argument that the weaker classes live off the luxury of the wealthy.

'But Tonet,' the wife of Bearn had said during the *belle époque*, 'how does asking for a drink you don't like benefit the poor?'

Founding a whole economic system on the manufacture of huge stocks of unnecessary goods when we didn't have access to necessary supplies was never going to have a happy ending, and proved that our basic life instincts had been perverted.

My interlocutor looked at me with hostile curiosity.

'Do you think it's possible to slow down industrial progress in our Era?' he asked.

'They say it can't be done,' I replied. 'The slogan appears on every façade and at every street junction.'

'How do you think the populace would view a government that attempted to deprive it of atomic appliances?'

'They shouldn't have replaced the Catholic faith with the religion of domestic appliances.'

'You haven't answered my question,' he insisted.

'Well, it's no secret: they'd view it very negatively.'

And anyway, no government would attempt such a thing today because it would be brought down immediately by the big corporations.

'So do you recognize that our present system is the only system possible?'

'I recognize that this system cannot evolve any further. You thought you were progressives but you've become trapped in immobilism. In spite of everything, the world is about to undergo a mutation.'

I felt ridiculous uttering words of such transcendence, but all the attention fed my vanity and they seemed to like my performance. They were referring to me as the 'handsome cryo survivor.' One individual came up to me to kiss me, and whispered in my ear, 'It's true, we're asphyxiating. The great simplification is nigh.'

When I was about to leave the restaurant, a hunched old lady approached.

'The avenue is dark,' she said.

There'd been another power cut.

'I'm a little unsteady on my feet. Would you be so kind as to accompany me? I live very close by.'

I offered her my arm. We'd only walked a few steps when the old lady straightened up in the shadows and I saw that it was Dr Nicola.

'I escaped from prison,' he explained, 'but they're watching me. Tomorrow evening I need to see you after Andrea's lecture.'

'Is Andrea alive?' I asked, without much hope.

'She's just died,' Nicola said. 'Everything you've seen is tele-visual illusion. They're preparing a big clampdown. We have to go our separate ways now. Tomorrow, at midnight. Parmentier avenue, at the monument... Make sure you're there. Goodbye.'

He slipped off into the darkness.

I walked back towards my lodgings. It was almost two in the morning. The city was still blacked out and deserted, but behind many windows and with their radios on low, people were keeping vigil and anxiety was mounting. From time to time a shadowy figure went by carrying a torch. Near the Einstein Arch I almost tripped over something. Looking down, I saw it was a small child with their throat cut. I little further on I saw their white clothing, stained red. In my time we'd have seen this as some kind of monstrous violation, but now everything was permitted while sexual matters were actually protected. There could be no doubt that the crime had been committed by one of us cryo survivors, to whom any action carried out against the enemy would seem justified, as it would appear in turn to our enemies. Crimes and sabotage were becoming common and it had not taken long for me to realise that the situation was much more serious than I had imagined. Some said that in Paris there'd been an attempt to blow up the Élysée Palace. Others reported that in the forests of Vincennes, two-hundred and eighty people, most of them cryo survivors, had been gassed for having blasphemed publicly against *Hola-Hola*. Everything was confused, uncertain, but the paralysis of services, of water and electricity was a reality. So was the innocent child with their regulation smile lying dead at my feet, stopped obscenely in their tracks. It reminded me of Andrea.

Garbage was beginning to pile up outside houses with heaps of bottles, tin cans, and sticky plastic wrappers fluttering about like souls in torment. Amongst these objects I came across vilely soiled scraps of material that were embroidered with the formula $E=mc^2$. There had been no bread now for twenty-four hours, nor was there ham in the delis, and mobs were breaking into pharmacies to steal vitamins and liver extract. I witnessed one such attack when rioters drained bottles of viscous syrups as though they were wine. I later learnt that hoteliers were sending youngsters into the sewers to find dead rats to feed to the tourists.

I lived quite a distance from the city centre, but the metro wasn't running and there was no chance of a taxi. Fortunately, the sky had cleared and I could make my way by starlight though even then I became disorientated in those interminable streets. Little by little my eyes got used to the half-light and I realised that without the hubbub and pedestrians the city was beautiful, almost monumental. Even the plastic trees and pastiches dreamt up by the Classical University made sense in that setting. The skyscrapers possessed a tragic grandeur. In those nests, those cells, the cause of so much neurosis, people were working to the point of exhaustion, drinking *Hola-Hola* from their fridges and giving up all hope. But it wasn't the lack of commotion or the welcome absence of light that rendered the condemned city beautiful, but rather the pressing sensation that we were destined to die. Anguish had triumphed in spite of tranquillisers. Hunger had won despite wealth being calculated in numbers of white goods and metres of duct.

Wealth? But what was wealth? There's has never been a more equivocal term, even though it had already been diabolically twisted to deceive the masses, especially after the Great Machine Revolution. I remember that when my city was still Palma, before it became Turclub, it was considered a luxury to have a bedroom per person or have hot food to eat every day. And around 1950 it was a poor city. At that time, Germany was incredibly rich and people lived in steel cages (workers slept in dormitories of four or six) and survived on sandwiches. In Ourense or Cuenca province, by contrast, the houses were large and foodstuffs such as meat and corn were of high quality. Rousseau was right when in *Émile* he dreamt of living in a far-off country where 'abundance and poverty' ruled. One had to travel to hotels in more advanced, more industrialised, 'richer' provinces to eat sickly farmed chicken and butter substitutes. So what was wealth? Apparently, gold that supports strong currencies, like the Deutschmark under Adenauer. Yes, for an industrial nation, that was wealth. King Midas, the mythological figure who could transmute anything at all into gold, must have been an industrial financier... turning even the food on his plate into gold, he died of starvation, the covetous wretch.

My mind was absorbed with such thoughts as I walked past a cluster of working-class skyscrapers like gigantic dice, monotonous and inhuman. This infamous functional housing was the pride of Turclub. Steel cages you couldn't even stand upright in, squalid cacophonous soundboxes. I was on the edge of a district they called Bidonville, where the homeless whose 'jobless' cards had expired found refuge in a slum of car parts and tin shacks partly swathed in pieces of plastic sheeting in attempt to keep out the cold and rain. It was a vision of misery, but every dwelling had a TV aerial and this, according to the authorities, made the shacks habitable.

I heard a muffled voice from one of the seemingly abandoned shacks and stopped.

'I know for certain,' said the voice, full of youth and optimism, 'that a universal disaster is needed which will completely annihilate a civilization built on organizations and economies that have committed to mutually incompatible objectives we know are impossible to resolve. In the twentieth century, North America was only able to salvage its machine-led economy by investing in its war industries, and these in turn were what wrecked it. The only possible wars now are totalitarian, which is to say that they destroy the economy as well as the economy's victims.'

At this point the gentle voice became brighter and more cheerful, like the trill of a small girl holding out a bag of sweets:

'Dear listeners, my solution is very similar to Wagner's

Götterdämerung; I'm not a pessimist. Is this aesthetically displeasing to you? The drawback is that we won't get to see the spectacle and its flaming ruins because we are the combustible material of the drama.'

I was rattled. Maybe it was some madman, an anarchist talking to himself. Pushing the door open, I saw a radio. At the table was an elderly dead woman with her head in her hands. I carried on walking. Grey factories lined narrow roads that disappeared far into the gloom. Having always travelled through these places by metro, I was struck by how threatening they felt. Every so often I saw the ritualistic slogan PROGRESS CANNOT BE STOPPED emblazoned on the façade of a building. It reminded me of the Babylonian *Mene Mene Tekel Parsin* and there was a sudden low rumbling and the ground seemed to shake under my feet. Fearing that it was an earthquake, I started running and without realising quite how, found myself back at my lodgings. I was told that saboteurs had set off explosives in some of the metro tunnels, and the clandestine radio stations said that eighty percent of operators would not be at work the following day.

I lay down, physically and emotionally exhausted. As I dozed, the hideous figure of Andrea appeared to me, covering a blackboard with cabbalistic symbols and advising her public to eat stones before making an ugly gesture and disappearing. I closed my eyes so I couldn't see her, saying, 'Go away, you're not Andrea!' It was an energetic assertion, the expression of my desire, rather than of reality. 'You're not Andrea, you're a Regime puppet.' It had actually been Andrea. I don't know how long I lay awake before I finally dropped off. When I asked for breakfast it turned out to be five in the afternoon already. The landlady herself brought me what passed for a white coffee and informed me that the 'staff' hadn't turned up for work. At the same time, however, a government channel said that the insurrection had been quashed and announced with some confidence that supplies of potatoes would soon be distributed.

While the landlady gave me her news, the radio station repeated its stream of claptrap, and out of respect she paused to listen, wary but hopeful.

'The whole of the French Midi is overflowing with this wonderful tuber,' assured the radio announcer. 'It's not true that there's a shortage of wheat, or of course wheat substitutes, which are easily able to meet market demand. The transport strike organized by enemies of the Regime is responsible for the supply problems which have caused *disette* in some areas, and these are now receiving air drops of food. In the last hours, the police have uncovered a significant plot that the government was well prepared for. It has known for some time that neanderthal elements are seeking to crush machine civilization and send us back to the Agrarian Era and to the horrors of viviparous procreation. Such criminal intentions would clearly mean the ruin of the U.S. of Europe, undermine our moral foundations, and signify the triumph of the foulest misery and the most appalling demagogy. The government of *Monsieur-Dame* considers it our duty to save the country from such a terrifying conflict, and will proceed energetically...'

How many times had we heard similar speeches? Over the last two centuries every squawking parliamentarian had trotted out the same lines to the needy, credulous masses. The radio presenter continued.

'At the same time, we recognize the need for reassurance following the revolutionaries' abuse of the death of Pitusso the canary last March 7. We are therefore announcing a Day of National Mourning on that date, and a sumptuous mausoleum will be built for the interment of the ashes of this illustrious bird, eminent concert performer and pride of Mediterranean music. On many occasions *Monsieur-Dame* has demonstrated his love of birds and Nature, whenever this does not present a risk to the sacrosanct interests of human industry which is destined to elevate us to the Noosphere of Teilhard de Chardin. *Monsieur-Dame* therefore requests that on every anniversary of this sombre date, we hold a three-minute silence.'

'This is too much!' I cried, switching off the radio and picking up my drink, which tasted only vaguely of coffee. I then showered and, feeling calm and restored, got dressed and went out into the street. There was still an hour before the third lecture, and I walked towards Pleasure.

Even though many people had fled Turclub in the last twenty-four hours, a substantial crowd had gathered and was, for the most part, hostile, as could be judged from the women in Gilda dresses and the men in jeans. *Monsieur-Dame*'s decree on Roman clothing was openly flouted. The traffic police dared not intervene and the yobs baited them scornfully on immoral and forbidden subjects.

'Does your mother know you're here?' said one.

'You look old enough to be my grandad...!' said another.

'Hey sexy, if you come any closer you might end up pregnant...'

A few appreciated their wit, but most weren't in the mood for tomfoolery. The event was a disaster. Gossip about Andrea's death was rampant and once the TV farce was finally over and people had congregated for the reception in the Palazzo's park, the expectation was that we'd be shown from a safe distance a double of the goddess rising from the waters, illuminated by a subtle play of lights. Secular propaganda is less scrupulous than its religious equivalent, and this is aggravated by the fact that those behind it know that they have no absolute truths to draw on. Such knowledge ought to make them question everything like Socrates, but instead it makes them as stubborn and disingenuous as Xanthippe. This is what we have come to know as practical sense and cunning.

The cynicism and disorientation of Power was reaching a climax. Just as everyone was saying that the goddess had been cremated and her ashes scattered beneath a rose bush, a smiling, golden Andrea appeared on the screens. It was the Andrea of a year earlier, slender, graceful, and toned, promoting health and optimism.

'It's a report from Monte Carlo last summer,' said someone. 'You can see one of the turrets of the Casino through the window.'

They hadn't even bothered to edit out that detail and the words spoken by the lecturer, clichés lauding the Regime, weren't even synced to her joyful, charming image. During the second lecture it had still been possible amid the crude additions to discern something of Andrea's courteous style in tune with her amiable expression, punctuated now and again by incisive observations that were surprising in such a young, ingenuous individual. But this lecture was all scripted praise, ineptly thrown together for *Monsieur-Dame* or possibly written by him, making the most of the fact that Andrea was dust. It is said that King Jaume I won a battle after his death: Andrea lost hers spectacularly. Spectators whistled and insulted her image, hurling disgraceful abuse at *Monsieur-Dame*, and a company of robots fired into the crowd causing deaths and injuries. The reception at the Palazzo Víctrix was cancelled.

I headed to Parmentier Avenue before midnight, following Nicola's instructions. As on previous nights, there was a power cut. Thefts and assaults were on the rise and since I didn't possess a gun, I was carrying the jewelled dagger Andrea had given me in my belt. I covered almost the whole length of the avenue without seeing anyone. As I approached Pomme de Terre Square (it was curious that as foodstuffs became rarer, they were commemorated on marble plaques) a tall lad weaved his way towards me with a bottle in his hand. It would never have crossed my mind to think that this was the thirty-something year-old Dr Nicola. But his adolescent demeanour notwithstanding, it was indeed him.

'In these times we either learn to disguise ourselves, or die,' he said.

I suggested we go into a tavern nearby where there seemed to be light of some sort, but he refused.

'All the bars are wired with transmitters. We'd be better off sitting on the steps at the statue of Parmentier. If we're seen, we'll look like drug addicts.

He laid his head on my knees and asked me quietly, as though he were making an amorous proposition, where Andrea kept the detonators of the world's four atomic devices.

'Why do you want to know?' I asked.

'Because it's vital we destroy them before government agents get hold of them,' he replied. 'Things are starting to happen.'

In truth, I was reluctant to tell him. It felt like a betrayal of Andrea.

'You must be aware,' said Nicola. 'I know she confided in you about everything.'

There was a certain melancholy in his voice that I found

hard to explain.

'Why do you suppose she confided more in me than in you, if she did? I wasn't part of her cult.'

'She had limitless belief in you, as you well know,' he replied.

'That she did,' I said, mournfully.

'We're wasting time,' said Nicola. 'The fate of the world cannot end up in the hands of the freaks who rule us.'

Almost without realising, I relented, swayed by his words.

'They're in the bronze horse in the Roman salon. You have to turn the eyes and kiss the mouth at the same time.'

Nicola took the top off the bottle and I saw it was a transmitter. He spoke to the Palazzo in code.

'Our friends have taken over the telephones at the Víctrix,' he said. 'The Revolution is beginning. Do you know General Boum-Boum, a cryo survivor from some time back?'

'Sounds like Offenbach, nineteenth century... Resuscitated on demand,' I said.

Nicola was all-action at that moment, and the irony washed over him.

'Yes,' he said, 'these days he's very visible: tall, moustache. He's our leader.'

I gazed up at the night sky, ink-black against the shivering stars. So a General Boum-Boum was to be our saviour?

'We've re-engineered the volition circuits of the robot guards and they'll join us against *Monsieur-Dame*,' he continued.

'But what are you planning?' I asked.

'Be quiet now,' came the doctor's response.

A muffled bell rang inside the bottle and Nicola listened attentively and told them to await orders.

'They've found the four detonators. *Monsieur-Dame* has ordered that they be brought to him.'

'I trust you'll do no such thing.'

'Of course not,' Nicola said. 'You and I are going to take a supersonic flight. We'll be at the Élysée in minutes. Andrea's detonators are part of a set, and the president has another four in his own protection. The atomic matter in the core is inactive without the detonating explosives. This, of course, is about our securing *Monsieur-Dame*'s detonators, not handing over the ones in our possession. We need you because as Andrea's first consort, he'll trust you. He's already asked for you twice.'

'If we're going to de-escalate the situation quickly,' I suggested, 'surely it would be simpler not to give him our detonators, making it look as if–'

'And tomorrow we'd all be in the cremation furnace,' Nicola cut in. 'This is life or death.'

'So what are you proposing?'

'We hit reset. Take control of the atomic armoury and put an end to the Machine Age, the Inhuman Era. Can you think of any other way?'

'No,' I said, 'but the transfer of power requires tact–'

'On the contrary, it requires decisiveness! Or do you think we've got this won already? Mechanization and cybernetics are the religion of all *éclairés* who don't believe in God!'

There'd been times when I had said something similar to Andrea, and she'd reply saying that progress and evolution hadn't yet reached the point at which our happiness was assured, the Omega Point identified by Teilhard de Chardin as the pinnacle of the Noosphere that would fuse us with divinity. A divinity made to the measure of human intelligence and forces, a god who is fruit of evolutionism rather the origin of creation, who does not constitute the Absolute but rather searches for it in the sphere of relativity where experimental science belongs. According to Andrea, physical being wasted away to death. Man dies as an organism, but remains in his thought in books, objects, and technologies.

'Science is your god,' I'd said to her. 'Don't you realise that you won't get anywhere following this fitful, fluctuating god that promises everything and never says anything definitive?'

Things had become heated and Andrea had been on the point of tears. Nicola was now also animated and took a pill, his eyes shining.

'There's only one way!' he exclaimed. 'The materialists have failed and become immobilists! When they deny the individual soul and its immortality, the very essence of the future, they deny the hereafter. You ask what we're proposing? The destruction of Europe, the ultimate simplification. We're going to re-mould the Earth with a flood of fire!'

Another apocalypse. After a million years of existence, man had certainly known more than one, and it wouldn't go amiss to ask why this was so.

'Explain yourself,' I demanded.

'In Oceania and Indochina, we have hundreds of islands won over to our holy cause. Our missionaries have been ope-rating there for a long time. And as I said, we have General Boum-Boum...'

I listened with a heavy heart. Indochina, Coromandel screens, comic opera, Parisian boulevards, two centuries ago... Everything was so old! And above us the ink-dark heavens were set off by little golden dots that, while we call them stars, might perhaps be nothing more than matches.

'In the Pacific ocean, you say?'

'Yes,' replied Nicola. 'While the Industrial Regime contro-lled natality here, while we created a race of old people and invalids with false teeth weened on *Hola-Hola*, out there, among the unchecked archipelagos, lost in the Pacific, men proliferate freely. They are now more numerous than the Europeans. We contribute the technology, they provide the physical workforce with their muscles and teeth.'

'But I thought we'd opted for "simplification"?'

Like all men of action, Nicola didn't have time to argue.

'Of course,' he said. 'And then we'll destroy these technologies. We need to act criminally in order to save the world, but just once.'

Back in my time I'd heard similar arguments deployed to justify Hiroshima, but Nicola wasn't entertaining a reply. The man before me was not the man I'd known. He had meditated in silence for years and now he was swept along by a desire for action.

'And then,' he said, his mind almost absent, 'with barely a fight, we'll build a new world. We have to rid ourselves of everything old.'

'Barely a fight... after destroying Europe,' I insisted.

'They destroyed Asia.'

'And how are we different from them?'

'Perhaps we aren't,' he said, gripping my arm tightly. 'Or do you think we can achieve all this with a Socratic dialogue?'

'No, I don't. Let go of my arm and remember that you were once a civilized, university man.'

'Forgive me,' he said, releasing my arm, 'but I'm desperate. So are you.'

'True.'

'They killed Andrea, a goddess whom neither of us dared go near.'

He caught me by surprise. Had Nicola, once a linchpin of the Regime and now a dissident, felt all this time just as I did towards Andrea?

'They turned her into a fanatic when she was seventeen and at nineteen she was surplus to requirements. And she loved you.'

I broke out into tears and embraced my friend, my brother.

'You were in love with her too,' I said to him.

'But she wasn't with me,' he replied.

I was still in tears. Yes, they had radicalised her, prostituted her, and disposed of her before she was twenty. But was prostituted the right word? Andrea always acted in good faith for a cause she considered just. I don't know whether more recently she had lost all belief as the Regime fell apart. The only thing we could be sure of is that she died without having betrayed her sworn cause. Wouldn't that be enough to justify what she did, justifying in turn the whole mechanism that her civilization bought into? The minds behind Hertzian waves or the structure of the atom – veritable mystics – must have approached their work with the same pure intentions as Andrea.

'If we destroyed the machines,' she told me once, 'we'd just invent them again. Machines aren't evil…'

She was right, they were beasts. The good or evil was in the people who controlled the machines, unless, of course, they'd also become machines. Whose fault was it that everything had been debased so that we could talk only of metres of ducting, plastic carnations, and garbage bins?

The plastic flowers weren't in fact ugly, and even I had occasionally mistaken them for real flowers. It was their ubiquity, the ease with which they could be obtained, that I found unbearable. I'd experienced the same with affairs of the flesh. It was the easiness of the Collective Orgies that had made us bored, not the fire and brimstone of a mediaeval monk. Now that she had disappeared from the land of the living, Andrea's legacy would be determined by the struggle between the Viviparous Era and the Industrial Era: if the latter system survived and was able to consolidate, Andrea would have been a hero. Though if it succumbed and the old regime triumphed, she would be remembered as a shameless street whore, worse even than Lola. The subject gnawed at me, and one night when I had raised it tentatively in conversation, she had replied sprightly in her own language.

'*Bisogna che facciamo sempre il nostro dovere sia che siamo stimati o sprezzati.*'

Her health was irretrievable, but not so her emotional integrity.

'She was a martyr,' I said.

Nicola nodded, still holding me. He seemed like a child. I took a chance and asked him very quietly,

'Am I right that she was female?'

He shook his head.

I could barely get the words out.

'A man?'

Nicola smiled, 'Oh no, not at all.'

Neither of us spoke until Nicola broke the silence.

'I can see you don't understand, my poor friend. You've been in this world for less than a year. If you'd been around for as long as I have, then the shades and nuances wouldn't make you so uneasy.'

We were immersed in the greatest conundrum known to man. I recalled the rumours circulating about Andrea's viviparous origin, and others that suggested she was neuter, perhaps surgically mutilated, like the two little acrobats who broke their necks in my bedroom. These hypotheses couldn't explain the enigma of her morality as she had without doubt been led astray and assimilated by the Regime. Her soul was no less complicated than her sex, and I imagined her for a moment, candid and fastidious, in the figure of Herod, another fanatic, another tortured soul, ordering the massacre of the Innocents. Truth and lies meet full-circle, and the absurd is inches from the truth. Everything pure, special, chosen, is easily defiled: *corruptio optimi pessima*, as the ancients said.

In some ways Andrea was more of a misfit than we were. But I wasn't about to give up hope. Who can tell whether the offspring of incubators, the children of the Collective Being preached by the Marxist state, would end up adapting to this inhuman, machine mentality, to sexual promiscuity and eating stones? Perhaps we found ourselves on the verge of a historic mutation that would lead us in another guise to a surprising, new world…

Again, neither of us spoke.

'At least,' whispered Nicola, 'you were happy…'

'And you weren't?'

'No,' he said. 'She believed I was loyal to her credo, so I

wasn't interesting to her. She too was looking for something she couldn't find.'

The stars flickered in the darkness and were incomprehensible.

'But I need to know,' I insisted.

'Me too, my friend, but knowledge is a luxury. Andrea was a goddess, just like Einstein was a god.'

'What was her purpose in this world?'

'That's like wondering what those stars are doing in the sky,' replied Nicola.

'The ancients thought they were ornaments. Ornaments that people today don't appreciate because we have electric light.'

'Perhaps the primitives weren't wrong.'

He'd put his arm around my shoulder and was looking at me and in that moment I felt a closeness to him that... Andrea united us, gave us a sense of solidarity through complex sentiments. Although we were enemies of the Regime she symbolized, we couldn't detach ourselves from the allure of what we wanted to destroy, transcending time, turning this world into a new El Dorado, a Paradise Lost. Nicola was a noble soul, and for the first time I was struck by the beauty of his masculine features. He was taller than me too, more audacious and more generous. Capricious destiny hadn't made a rival of him, but a brother who searched my eyes for a torturous secret. What I say now will seem like madness, but I think I would have surrendered Andrea to him, so completely did I feel his tragedy. I was at the point of comprehending both existentialism and the doctrines of Teilhard de Chardin. I knelt down and kissed his hand, but in spite of his moral grandeur, he seemed oblivious. A helicopter hovered above us. The moment of rapture past, my friend was suddenly transformed, energized.

'They've come to take us to the supersonic plane. We'll be at the Élysée in no time. *Monsieur-Dame*, who murdered your Andrea' – or glorified her, I thought – 'will embrace you sobbing. You will do the same and give him four fake detonators. He'll check to see if they're real and you tell him that there are suspicious individuals at the Palazzo Víctrix and that it's important to guard against any possible deception. Lavish him with hugs, tears, and affection. He's like an old cat and he likes to be stroked, especially by strong, young men like you. He'll compare his detonators with yours, and while you distract him, I'll have a Parquidine injection ready... Remember,' he said, seeing me hesitate, 'that you're risking your life. Perhaps before dawn the whole of Europe will be in flames. Do you accept?'

Nicola had been clear: destroy the world and start again. Oust a lipstick-wearing *Monsieur-Dame* from the Élysée in order to install a general with an exquisite moustache... I recalled Chesterton's amusing line when they talked to him about the end of the world – 'that's already happened a few times' – but I stayed quiet. I imagined Andrea's corpse in the cremation furnace; Andrea, dead at nineteen. It was absurd! Dead like that Roman soldier whose skeleton they found in front of a door in Pompeii, and who had died when the volcano erupted because no-one remembered to relieve him. What a beautiful, heroic poem! What nonsense! And who knows how many millions of kilometres above it all, the stars twinkling in the darkness.

'Do you accept?' he repeated.

Roused from my reverie and forced to consider the magnitude of the crimes Nicola was proposing, I was suddenly inspired: I would kill Nicola. *Primus motus* as the scholastics would say, irrational and impulsive. I had the Italian dagger at my waist and it wouldn't be difficult. I gripped the handle and embraced him, readying myself to deliver the Judas kiss, but the weapon dropped to the ground. The Revolution was happening, progress could not be stopped, and that murder would simply increase the number of deaths I was trying to prevent.

The helicopter was beside us and Nicola, interpreting my silence as acceptance, guided me towards the craft. I reacted sharply and slipped from his grasp.

'I'm not going!' I shouted.

He looked at me, shocked.

'Have you gone mad?' he said.

'I'm not going,' I repeated, gazing at those useless, luxurious, inevitable stars in the baroque night. 'I'm not going. I'm wondering,' I said, bursting into laughter, 'whether perhaps *Monsieur-Dame* is also an ornament.'

EPILOGUE
LLORENÇ VILLALONGA

Those who recall Flaubert's phrase 'Madame Bovary is me' will not be surprised that Andrea Víctrix, a deity of eighteen years old, is in some way a representation of Einstein; nor will they be surprised that I have tried to symbolize the twilight of an age long past its expiry in a being who is both alluring and monstrous. Like Einstein, my character triumphed and died anguished by the consequences of being seduced by progress, devastated by the fact that the human body, if it did not possess so many empty spaces (according to F. Joliot), would only be visible through the lens of a microscope: it's not the ascetics but the nuclear researchers who remind us today of our insignificance.

The present novel, the action of which takes place in a very proximate future, is a satire on the world of 'today' and derives fundamentally from *Brave New World*, since in this work set in the year 632 After Ford, Aldous Huxley had severed all connections between his magisterial fantasy and human existence.

I haven't attempted to fly so high. The society I depict is so close to our world that some of the protagonists have experienced it first-hand. The tragedy is that we're living through a revolution that distorts classical morality and sensibility. A mutation is probably on the way. I have to acknowledge the influence that Teilhard de Chardin and other philo-marxists have had on my novel, but I also distance myself from them in respect of the consequences and the meaning of the process underway. According to Teilhard de Chardin's evolutionism, all mutations at every point have signified 'progress': in *illo tempore*, initial matter was simple, supergasified, ionized and spread across infinite immensities. Every mutation has caused this matter to become concentrated into smaller spaces and structured in more complex and potent forms. A cultural evolution continues 'natural' evolution: from individual reflective consciousnesses (isolated on Earth like the first particles of matter in space), we move to a collective super-consciousness that Teilhard calls 'Noosphere', that is, the advent of a single human Being: the Omega Point-God.

Not all of us would deduce such flattering consequences from this socialist mysticism. Teilhard does, however. Neither the nuclear arms race, nor the law formulated by Einstein on the degradation of energy, which condemns the universe to a descending evolution, diminish his optimism: '*Tout est pour le mieux dans le meilleur des mondes possibles*'. Heaven forfend I confuse Teilhard de Chardin with Dr Pangloss, but our existence is ephemeral and spattered with woes apportioned unjustly and unequally. Mechanized civilization, like so many others (the world is millions of years old), seems headed for decadence and death. There remains, of course, the compensation of a pure, eternal life in another world, inducing us to have faith in the other life, but not in this, and which instead of leading us towards Marxism, might turn us back to religion.

From which it should not be inferred quite that I have attempted to write a tale of despair. The narrator of my novel is certainly ill-tempered, but existence didn't treat him so badly, since although he may not have achieved plenitude with Andrea, he had fun with Lola, and in the end everything comes down to whether we conform or rebel.

Andrea Víctrix is a conformist work, and in this respect, yes, it coincides, up to a point and necessarily, with the optimists: it admits earthly existence just as it appears, and strives to see the smile in tragedy. Perhaps in death, Andrea recited a line from Valéry on the inevitable resurgence of life, and the narrator, when under the mystery of a starry, superfluous, baroque night sky, finally has the chance to exterminate *Monsieur-Dame* de Pompignac la Fleur, he refuses, to the great surprise of Dr Nicola:

'I'm just thinking,' he says, gesturing to the stars, 'that perhaps *Monsieur-Dame* is also an ornament.'

PROGRESS CANNOT BE STOPPED

With thanks to RL for the 'Minerva' couplet
—PLJ